HONEY CHILD

HONEY CHILD

a novel

by Raina Bell
illustrations by George LaRoche

ISBN 978-0-9777978-0-6

Printed in the United States of America

To order additional copies of this book, visit
www.rainabell.com

THE INTRO

I stay to myself a lot nowadays cuz most erybody I ever gave a fat rat's ass about is either gone or on they way out. I ain't one for puttin my business out there or talkin to strangers so consider yourself lucky that I'm lettin you inside my head for a lil while. This is goin against a lotta shit I done made a habit of not doin, but right now I just feel like talkin and I really don't care who hear me.

I'on exactly know where to start so I'll take it from the top. The name on my birth certificate say Rashaiyah Deshay Williams but don't nobody call me that 'cept teachers and people who don't know me too good. My mother be tryna sice* my head up and tell me she named me after my great grandma on her daddy side who was full blood Trinidad Indian, but far as I know that woman was Black as Whoopi and the only Trinidad my family's affiliated with is in Northeast, D.C. Most erybody call me Shai (yeah, like the early '90s singin group) or Suga Baby, Honey Child, or Honey if they know me like that. I'm a Gemini with a Scorpio moon so I got a tendency to be moody and what some may consider crazy, but the older I get the more I control it. People useta tell me I could pass for Da Brat's lil sister cuz I'm redbone with red hair and I got a baby face, but I always kinda shrugged it off cuz I ain't tryna look like or *be* like nobody but me…even though I wouldn't mind having money like Brat do. See, I'on come from no riches; my folks been strugglin since the first black-ass nigga in chains stepped off the auction block. My mother's people, the Thompsons, got roots in North Carolina but most of them live out Maryland in Mo County. I'on know a whole lot about my father 'cept he left my mother for some other broad in '88, and he been actin like the invisible man ery since. I still talk to his mama, my Grandma Rose, whenever I feel like I need some secondhand

---

* Slang terms are explained in the glossary that begins on page 345.

grandmotherly love. She live offa Kennedy Street where all them rowdy-ass Uptown niggas be at, in the same white and gray rowhouse her peoples been in since Frederick Douglass was out Anacostia. The majority of my father family live in the city but I'on know most them people to speak, and I'on think they'd have much to say to me even if I did. I guess I could whine about not gettin enough love and support from the other half of my family, but why bother? As the sayin go, you can't miss something you never had in the first place.

My mother wasn't never crazy bout kids so don't nobody understand why she went and had a tribe of us. Growin up, we was five deep in all: me, my brother Cerrone, my bratty-ass sisters Treasure and Sparkle, and the baby of the family, my lil sister Staria. I was raised in a two bedroom apartment with a racka kids and grown folks runnin in and out, so naturally I'm useta people but I'on particularly care for em. I useta have this plan to grow up and move to the mountains in Western Maryland so I could finally get some peace and quiet, but I kinda gave up on that idea after I had my first son in '96.

Me and my fiancée Twon put our money together and got this aight lil j'on out Forestville so we could raise our kids without anybody lookin over our shoulder tellin us erything we doin wrong. My mother seem to think we livin in sin (even though she ain't no stranger to shacking up) but who don't live together before they get married these days? You sure do find out a lot about a nigga once y'all in eachother face day in and day out. Like how Twon act like he allergic to laundry and will wear the same funky-ass basketball shorts to bed for a month straight, or the way he take a good hour hockin and spittin to clear his lungs in the morning. Not to say that I'm perfect, but damn. If I'da known all that…Sike, for real, Twon is my heart and it ain't nobody else out there who can get me like he got me. He's the realest nigga I ever known, next to my brother Cerrone, and he ain't never fail to be there ery time I really needed him…Youngin eat a mean coochie too, but that's a different story.

Anyways, I'm on a private mission this summer to help my lil cousin Karrysta (that's Krys for short) get her head on straight. Supposedly, she out there cuttin up and gettin into trouble despite the fact that she was raised right and should know better. As somebody who practically raised theyself and been through enough bullshit to fill a book, I can see why

Aunt Josie (Krys' mom) wanted me to be the one to sit youngin down and let her know some things before she get herself caught up. I done been there and done that with just about erything, so at this point in my life, I should be passing down what I know to the next generation coming up. It's a good way to make up for all the stuff I put my mother through. If I had the time, I'd probly go into teaching or something, but schooling my lil cousin is about all I can do right now. Krys was the last one I ever thought would turn fifteen and lose her damn mind, but the way Aunt Josie make it sound, Krys is doin just that and can't nobody say nothing to her about it. Which makes me wonder, despite my good intentions, who says she'll listen to me?

I ain't even seen Krys for real in about five years, since that time Mommy and Aunt Josie, got into this big fight at my Aunt Roz house over what to do about me when erybody found out I was pregnant the first time. Aunt Josie thought Mommy should handle it one way, and Mommy thought Aunt Josie should mind her business cuz what happent with me wasn't nobody's problem but minez. Next thing you know Aunt Josie's callin Mommy a bad mother and Mommy's callin Aunt Josie self-righteous, and since they always been bitter enemies in sibling rivalry, a lotta heated words was exchanged, then a couple punches and…let's just say shit ain't been the same since.

Anyhow, Aunt Josie and Uncle Travis is sendin Krys to stay with me for a lil while so I could possibly talk some sense into her hot ass, cuz they at the end of they rope and bout two seconds from puttin her out on the street. Krys be chillin with some knucklehead youngins who think it's cute to be bad so she be fuckin up in school, fightin, and doin stupid shit like gettin caught stealing and smokin weed. And if that ain't bad enough, the way they say she out there superfreakin, it's a miracle she ain't get herself pregnant or burned by some disease (knock on wood) cuz these niggas out here today think they gotta fuck erything they see, and girls like Krys is too scared or stupid to make em wrap it up.

I done been fifteen and headstrong so I know what she goin through. Believe me, it took a while to get my shit together but I'm still here and I think I'm doin aight. I mean, I'm only nineteen and I got my own place, a car, and a full time job with benefits so I must be doin something right, hunh? I know if I wasn't so unfocused I coulda done a lot more with my

iv

life, especially if I ain't start poppin out babies all young. I had my first son Kebian (we call him Man-Man) when I was fourteen and Keyjuan (we call him Tink) not too long after I turned sixteen. Believe me, this shit ain't been no slice of sweet potato pie, either. Sometimes I regret givin it up before I knew what the hell I was gettin in to, but I always been grown for my age and at the time I thought havin sex was what I was *supposed* to be doin. With Mommy as a example and me bein the oldest of five got-damn kids it's a wonder I ain't start having babies at ten. And even though Krys is a only child who live in a decent neighborhood, been spoiled her whole life, and got parents that actually got the time and patience to deal with her ass, she headed down the same path I went. It don't make sense to go backwards in life when most of us is strugglin to go forwards, but I see a lotta youngins who done had it too good doin that these days.

I was knocked out—snoring, slobbering and all—till the phone rang. That j'on scared me so bad I thought I'd peed the bed. I glanced at the caller ID, expecting it to be my mother warning me to come pick up my kids before she shipped em off to Kalamazoo, but it was a 240 number and I know Mommy ain't got no cell phone.

"Hello?"

"Ay, Shai. You sleep?" an unfamiliar female voice asked from the other end of the cordless.

"Who dis?" I demanded. I'on take too kind to strange broads callin my got-damn phone like they know me. Twon's other baby mother Rayel useta do that shit when we first moved in together this year and it drove me crazy.

"It's Krys."

"Krys? My cousin Krys?" I asked. She sounded a lot older without the squeaky, whiny voice I remembered her having.

"The one and only," Krys said.

"Oh, hey. Wsup, dog nuts?"

"Wsup witchu? Damn, what time is it?"

V

"Way past time for you d' get up, dat's what."

"And just when was that poseda be?" I asked, squinting from the sunlight pouring in through the mini-blinds.

"Well you said you was comin to get me at nine," Krys answered, then added with a laugh, "But I guess dat ain't gon happen now, hunh?"

"Not if I'm just fuckin wakin up," I snapped, gettin aggravated with her sarcastic comments already. I glanced at the clock radio on my nightstand and saw it was goin on eleven. Damn, I hate startin my day off schedule.

"I see you ain't change a bit. I'll just tell my muhva you comin later, dat's all."

"Gimme like a hour and I be—" I started, takin Twon's arm from around me so I could get outta bed.

"Whateva," Krys said, cuttin me off. "See you when you get hea'."

The phone clicked and I was left holdin dead air in my hand. No that heffa did not just hang up on me. I started to call back and straighten that shit out, but I decided to let it slide and headed for the shower instead.

I peeled outta my pajamas and pulled a plastic cap on, then stood under the showerhead for a while tryna get my bearings straight. The hot water beatin on my face snatched me outta sleep harder than Mommy used to when I ain't wanna get up for school. I got to thinkin about Krys and what I could possibly do to get through to her, *if* I could get through to her. I know if she anything like I was at fifteen, she ain't listenin to a got-damn-body, and whatever I say will most likely go in one ear and float right on out the other. Besides, I ain't seen Krys since she was ten, and back then we wasn't even cool. I useta couldn't stand her ass. Krys was such a goody-two-shoes, always tattle-tellin on somebody and cryin like a baby when anybody played with her too rough. And erybody was always sayin how she was such a perfect angel, then talk about me and my brother like a dog cuz we wasn't. On the low, Mommy would try to make us feel bad cuz we ain't bust all A's in school like Krys did, and would tell us we was hooligans cuz we was always gettin into shit insteada sittin down quiet like Krys was. Me and my brother got so sicka bein compared to that nerd, we ain't have no choice but to take it out on Krys. We ruffed her up, locked her in closets, made fun of her—I mean, we gave that girl the blues. And now I gotta be the one to try and talk to her, be her friend and guide her ass? How crazy is that? Not in a million years would I have seen this comin. Krys off the hook now? Lil Krys from Maryland? Not the same youngin who bust out in tears when we wouldn't let her play freeze tag with us. Not the same one who got on us for sayin cuss words when the grown-ups wasn't around. It's ironic how the wild ones like me turn out aight and the ones you least suspect be doin the most dirt later on.

I washed up and quickly slid into the first clean shirt and stretch jeans I could find and reminded Twon about pickin the boys up from my mother's house. I'on think he half heard me cuz he'll agree to anything when he sleep, but I was runnin late as it was and I couldn't stick around to make sure. I was jive pressed for time so I headed for the Beltway, popped in a UCB tape that was hiding in my car cushions, and leaned my seat back for the ride to Greenbelt. I'm tellin you, it ain't nothin like some go-go to get you started in the mornin. A lotta people who ain't from around here don't like it cuz they say it sound like pot and pan music with a buncha yellin in between. But that's fine with me cuz like them shirts we useta wear back in the day say— *"It's a D.C. thang...you wouldn't understand!"*

Aunt Josie and Uncle Travis got this nice-ass house by Eleanor Roosevelt High School, not too far from where that singer Myá useta live. Their neighborhood ain't as high class as Collington Station or them other new developments that come a dime a dozen in P.G. County, but it's nice and it's quiet and fulla Black folks who work hard for a livin. All you see is shiny new Caddies and Benzes parked in the driveways, tennis courts for the next Venus and Serena Williams, and enough trees and clean streets to make you really appreciate the suburbs if you never did before.

Uncle Travis was out front meticulously washin his big ol' Suburban truck. Other than a bit of gray hair and some extra weight, he looked like the same ol' Uncle Travis, all tall and new-penny copper brown with these wise old owl eyes that make you think he knew erything there was to know about erything. I fucks with Uncle Travis real tough, mainly cuz he from D.C. like me and I always felt a special kinda bond to them old heads who came up in the city during the late sixties and seventies. Uncle Travis don't talk a lot, but he cool as shit and got a real laidback way to him that make you wanna crack open a beer and play game after game of Tonk while he talk bout the old Summer in the Park parties and how D.C. useta be before they started building it up.

"Wsup, shawdy," Uncle Travis said, and threw his wet rag in the soap bucket. He took off his eyeglasses and wiped his face with a folded hand towel he wore like a collar around his neck.

"Wsup witchu," I answered. "Hi you been?"

"I'm still alive; can't complain."

"Hunh, man," I chuckled. "Keepin the 'Burban so fresh and clean I see. When you gon lemme get 'dis up off you?" I asked, and walked around to admire his ride.

"When you buy me a Escalade to replace it," Uncle Travis winked, leadin the way inside the house. "Ay, you hungry? Josie made scrapple and cheese grits if you want some."

"Mmm, that sound good. I'm starvin like Marvin."

Aunt Josie was in the livin room with her houseclothes on and a cup of coffee up to her face. She looked like she was mad about something till she seen me come in behind Uncle Travis; then her whole face brightened up with a syrupy sweet smile that surprised me so much I forgot all about my appetite. Aunt Josie look just like my mama, only she's a lot smaller and a lot nicer. Mommy swear Aunt Josie stuck up cuz she live in a nice house and she stay to herself, but I think she just jealous cuz erybody who know Aunt Josie always got something good to say about her. My aunt was a quiet, sensible woman who lived a quiet, sensible life that was so steady and comfortable it was almost *too* normal. At least, that's how it seemed. If Aunt Josie had any problems over the years, she managed to keep em covered up pretty good. I guess that's why when she called me three months ago with the idea to have Krys spend the summer at my house, I couldn't think of a single solitary reason to say no. It ain't like I got the extra money or the patience to be babysittin a fifteen year-old knucklehead I barely got along with, but Aunt Josie ain't never asked me for jack—especially nothin like bailing her out a troublesome situation. For her to come at me the way she did for help with Krys, I knew for damn sure she wasn't doin it to get some alone time with my uncle.

I could hear someone bumpin around and draggin shit across the floors upstairs, making more noise than necessary. Judgin by the looks on they faces, my aunt and uncle was waitin anxiously for Krys to hurry up and get her shit together so she could leave.

"So how's Brenda doin?" Aunt Josie asked about Mommy. Making viii

small talk I guess, cuz erybody know since the fight they ain't said much more than hi to eachother.

"She aight."

"How all the kids?" she asked.

I shrugged.

"They cool, I guess. Far as I know erybody stayin outta trouble."

"And your boys and Antwon?"

"Drivin me outta my damn mind," I sighed with a smile that she had to chuckle at.

The thumping from upstairs stopped. Then some ol' Trina-thick girl who look about my age came rumblin down the steps draggin a set of green suitcases behind her. She had on a too-short Sergio Valente jeanskirt and a tube top that showed off her belly ring and flat red sandals that strapped up to her calves like criss-crossin snakes. Babygirl looked like she was bout to go to the club or be in a video, especially with that face fulla make-up and them fire engine red cornrows goin down her back. I looked up at the top of the steps expectin to see Krys followin behind her, thinkin that this glamour girl was one of Uncle Travis' nieces or one of my lil cousin's friends or something. But when no one came, I looked at the girl's face again and almost fell off the fuckin couch.

Well I'll be got-damned. That *is* Krys.

Aunt Josie was right. This broad parading down the steps like she was that bitch ain't look *nothin* like the Karrysta I remembered. The old Krys was cock-eyed with fuzzy ponytails and feet too big for her skinny legs. Time sure did change that ugly duckling into a swan cuz Krys got her eyes fixed and she filled out real nice into an hourglass shape that rivaled minez. And even though my cousin's face was all chubby and young, she looked and carried herself like somebody much older. By the way Krys switched across the livin room floor with her nose all up in the air, I could see why Aunt Josie and Uncle Travis was havin so much trouble.

"Hey, Shai," Krys said, the both of us sizing eachother up in a couple short glances. This definitely wasn't the same Krys me and my brother useta tease cuz she wore big-ass Coke bottle glasses and stuttered when she got nervous. Not the same Krys at all. Something bout her made me uneasy as shit, but I couldn't figure out if it was the way she stood there analyzing me or the way her sneaky, almond-shaped eyes boldly locked into mine like she was tryna prove that she was on my level now.

"Dang, I look that diff'rent?" Krys asked finally, and switched her Polo suitcase from one hand to the other.

"Yeah," I told her. "You do."

Uncle Travis sighed like he was tired and went to take some of the bags out to my car with Krys draggin her suitcase right behind him. Aunt Josie stood up and went to the picture window, watchin her husband and daughter avoid eachother's paths back and forth along the walkway. She stood in silence for a while, sippin her coffee and watchin her baby girl strut around outside like she was puttin on a show for the neighbors. Sittin there seein the sick and tired expression on my aunt's face made me realize just how stressed out her and my uncle musta been.

"See what I'm talkin bout?" Aunt Josie asked. "I'on know what's got into her lately, but she ain't being herself and it's startin to scare me. At first, I just thought it was a phase, but…You know I found a pregnancy test in her trash a couple weeks ago?"

"Damn, f'real?"

"Yeah. It was negative, but still. I'on like the fact she even took one. That typa stuff worries a mother. So does the way she be hoppin in the car wit ery Tom, Dick, and Harry she meet on the street. Or her comin up in here smellin like reefer when she get home from school. I'on even think she be goin to school half the time no more. And don't get me started about her grades. She went from all A's and B's to D's and E's. She was well on her way to gettin a scholarship for college to anywhere she wanted to go, but now...who knows. I guess she think she's gonna make a living hangin out with them so-called friends of hers."

"Damn," was all I could reply. It was really strange to hear Krys acting out so. She was pulling a lotta the same moves I was pulling at fifteen, and that definitely wasn't a good thing.

"I'on know what to do no more, Shai," Aunt Josie continued with a desperate sigh. "Beatin her ass don't do nothin. She damn-near bigger than me now. And puttin her on punishment is a joke. She'll just sneak out and do what she wanna do anyhow. That girl is outta control. She out here runnin the streets like nothing can happen to her. Hate for her to find out the hard way that anything can."

I gave a grim, knowing nod as she continued,

"Look, I ain't expectin no overnight transformation or nothin. Just do what you can. Try to talk some sense into her. God knows I done already tried, but she don't listen to me. I figure she'll listen to you since y'all closer in age."

"I sure hope so," was all I could say as I followed Aunt Josie outside.

"I hope so, too, cuz I'm not about to put up with this any longer. If she keep it up, I'ma put her ass out. I've had enough."

Well if that ain't pressure, I'on know what is. My aunt was depending on me. Time to tie on my Captain Save-A-Ho cape and put in some serious work. I was sacrificing my time, my house, and my nerves (the three good ones I had left) to help my lil cousin. In the end I knew I wouldn't be gaining a damn thing for myself, but erything in life ain't all about gettin what you can from people. I learned a long time ago that sometimes you gotta give, especially if it's concerning your own blood. If family don't take care of family, then who else will?

Krys and Uncle Travis went back in a couple times to get the rest of her stuff. I was still feelin kinda doubtful and hesitant about the whole thing. What if Krys don't listen to me either? What if instead of takin my advice she do the opposite of what I say? What if she try to carry it and brush me off the same way she been doin her parents? This was gonna be a lot to deal with on top of my own problems. I wanted so bad to tell

Aunt Josie that I needed more time to get myself together, cuz I just mighta agreed to some shit before I gave it enough thought. But fuck it, I already promised, and one thing I hate more than seein bamma-ass dudes in muscle shirts, is a broken promise.

"Well, I guess dat's about it," Uncle Travis said when the last bag got tossed on the backseat. He brushed his hands off and went to go stand by Aunt Josie's side. They both gazed at Krys with eyes that was tired and fulla longing and hope that she would come back and be the sweet girl they raised. Lookin at them made me wish I was really the miracle worker they needed me to be.

"See y'all in September," Krys sighed and started to get in the front seat.

"Excuse you, " Aunt Josie fussed. "You ain't gon give nobody a hug b'fore you go?"

"I guess y'all gon be all pressed if I don't."

Krys stomped back to the front steps to show her parents some love and jumped back in my car just as fast. She looked irritated and ready to go.

"'Tween you and me," Aunt Josie whispered. "That lil hussy get on your nerves, feel free to go upside her head."

"I'll try not to hurt her too bad," I promised. I gave my aunt a hug.

"Take care of my baby," she pleaded, and pressed a roll of twenty dollar bills into the palm of my hand. "And call if you need anything else."

Uncle Travis gave me daps and a wink.

"Aight, shawdy," he said, watchin me go down the walk to my car. My stomach was overwhelmed by anxious butterflies for a second, but I took a deep breath and put all my doubts at the back of my mind. *Well, here we go.* I got behind the wheel and we was on our merry way.

CHAPTER ONE

"You hongry?" I asked Krys.

We was back on the road with a silence sitting between us that was heavier than that comedian broad Mo'Nique. For the first time in a long time, I really was at a loss for words. Five minutes seemed like forever with both of us just sitting there pretending that whatever we was thinkin was more important than conversation. The fact that me and her never talked much as kids, added to the fact that I had no idea what to say to her ass now, made the situation that much more awkward. The more Krys sat over there poppin her gum and staring out the window like she was bored, the less I could think to talk about. So I kept my mouth shut and so did she. I guess Krys was tryna see how I was comin at her, and I was tryna figure out exactly how to start.

"I already ate but it's a Denny's right up the street if you want some'n," she told me, and looked at me with her dark cat eyes.

"I got a taste for some pancakes," I said. "You mind?"

"I'on care."

I got on BW Parkway and headed for the IHOP by Forest Village Park Mall, my mind racing the whole time. Maybe neither one of us was ready for this. I mean, I know I ain't perfect and I damn sure ain't the type to be influencing nobody's teenage daughter. Shit, I drink on occasion. I like to smoke down. I like to party, and if I wasn't with Twon, I'd be out there goin at niggas like I useta before I got bunned up. Besides, I'm too easygoin to be pressin some youngin out like they one of my kids. Dealing with Krys ain't gonna be the same as raising my boys, or helpin my mother with my lil sisters. Krys a grown-ass child, almost a woman. Why would she listen to me?

"Mind if I hit 'dis?" Krys asked, rummaging through the red Guess bookbag purse in her lap. She pulled out a lighter and a black-n-mild, then raised a eyebrow at me. I just looked at her cuz I ain't figure my lil cousin for the type to smoke anything—not with the way she useta get on erybody for hittin jacks back in the day. She took my silence as a okay and sparked it up before I could answer.

"I'on believe I said 'yes'," I snapped, kinda irritated.

"Well do you mind or what?"

I gave her a look and decided to be easy about it even though I ain't appreciate her tone at all.

"I'on care. Just don't get no ashes in my car...Did you freak that j'on at least?"

"Freak it?"

"Yeah. You poseda take out the brown paper on the inside. It give you cancer."

"So? All them brown roll-ups give you cancer but *you* still smoke weed," Krys snickered matter-of-factly.

"Hi you know what I do?"

She pointed to the roach in my ashtray and smiled knowingly. It was from the j'on I hit after I got off work last night and went to take my sons up to Mommy's. Yeah, I know—I'm poseda be setting a example. But my kids was drivin me crazy (which is why I took em to Mommy's house in the first place) and I had to calm my nerves somehow.

"You ain't poseda see dat," I said and paused to throw the roach out the window into the mid-June air.

"But I did," Krys said. "So wsup wit a J right now?"

"'Scuse me?"

"*I said*, wsup wit a J right now?" Krys repeated all bold.

"I'on think dat's a option, slim."

"Why not?"

"It just ain't," I snapped, and left it at that. Even though Aunt Josie warned me, the idea of Krys smokin bud was absurd. I kept remembering her as a nerdy lil schoolgirl. Seeing her do anything remotely otherwise was really throwin me off.

"I kh see now you gon be doin a whole lotta fakin," Krys complained with a disappointed sigh. "You ain't gotta put up no fronts wit me, Shai.. I already know how you go. I do the same shit."

"What?...Look, nevermind me and you puttin up a J. What is *you* of all people doin smokin anyways? Wasn't you the one who wore them *DARE* shirts erywhere we went? Talkin all dat 'there's no hope in dope' shit?" I asked.

"Yeah, well dat was a long time ago," Krys sneered again. "People change."

Krys caught a attitude and turned to face the window like she was through with me. We was really starting out on the wrong foot. The tension in my car got so thick you could break off a piece and bounce it down the sidewalk. Thank God it ain't take long to get to IHOP.

The pancake house was packed wall–to–wall as it usually was on a Saturday morning, but somehow we managed to get the last available table. I think it had a lot to do with Krys's outfit and youngin who was seatin erybody bein pressed to get us in cuz he was tryna get her number. Either way, we got us a booth by one of the big windows across from this young couple arguing loud enough to put *all* they business out in the street. Their arguing got even worse when Krys switched by and cuz stared after her with this dumb, distracted look on his face. I had to jump in and tell his girl to chill when she tried to break bad cuz her nigga couldn't keep his eyes to hisself. Talk about a warning sign of things to come. Here, it ain't even been a hour yet and Krys was already bringin drama my way.

"You want anything?" I asked my cousin, flippin through the menu after erything settled down.

"Just some coffee."

"Coffee? Ugh, you drink dat?" I asked. It seemed like such a odd habit for a fifteen year-old to have.

"Yeah. It keep me calm," Krys told me like I came at her with a dumb question. "Believe me, I ain't nuffin nice when some'my start pluckin my nerves," she continued, and shot me what I supposed was a warning look. Like I was gon be scared. Hell, just a second ago, I was the one bout to punish a broad on her behalf while she just sat there lookin flustered. I smirked and decided not to pull her card about that one, though.

"Whatchu doin wit nerves, girl? You too young d' have nerves," I joked instead.

"Young? Please. Age ain't nuffin but a number," Krys told me with a unblinking seriousness and a sassy lil smile.

I had to sit on my hands cuz I got the urge to reach over and smack the shit outta her ass, just for the principalities of it all. All this smart-mouth, lip-smackin, and switchin around was really startin to get old with me. I could already tell the two of us was gon bump heads before the summer was over. Hell, we'd be lucky to make it through the resta the day without beefin.

"So where you live at anyway?" Krys asked after a long, awkward silence. She blew a kiss at the waiter after he took our order and almost caused him to bump into the waitress with a tray fulla food behind him.

"Right hea' in Forestville," I snapped, even more irked. Krys was too busy checkin her reflection in the window to notice.

"Like where, 'doe? I got a boyfriend who live down Walker Mill," she continued.

"I'm up the street in Forest Creek. Who you know from Walker Mill?"

"It ain't your man, so don't worry about it," Krys sassed, turnin back to me.

"So he's your boyfriend for real or just a nigga you fuckin wit?" I asked, deciding to let her slide for the last time.

Krys pretended to be offended and put her hands on her hips.

"C'mon now, Shai, I'm a good girl," she said, then bust out laughin when I gave her my *nigga please* look. "Sike, he just my booty call for real. Dat's my youngin wit d' big...well, I'll tell you bout dat later."

"So you got more'n one boyfriend?" I asked, even though I already knew through Aunt Josie that she had a rack of em. I just wanted to know all about Krys in her own words to get a better idea where her head was at.

"Yeah," my cousin shrugged. "I got me a nigga in Palmer Park and one in Seat Pleasant, too."

"When you start messin' wit 'hood niggas?" I wondered aloud. All the places she mentioned were the opposite of the environment where she grew up.

"When I seen how 'hood niggas get dat money."

"Is that right?...What, you some typa playa or some'n now?"

"Girl, please. I'm a pimp," Krys replied.

"A pimp, hunh?" I chuckled. What that girl think she know bout pimpin somebody? "Havin a racka niggas don't make you a pimp, shawdy. Sound like you rollin to me."

"What? Rollin? I ain't no rolla," Krys snapped, gettin all in her feelings. "If I was rollin, niggas wouldn't be buyin me cell phones and renta cars and outfits, or payin for me d' get my hair done and my nails done and passes to the spa. Rollas don't get shit but dick and McDonald's. I gets whateva the fuck I want," she continued with a huff.

"So you be hittin the spa, hunh? Dat's how y'all do it 'deez days?"

"You damn skippy. I'm pimpin 'deez niggas, young. Milkin em dry, just like they do us. Shit ain't easy but some'my gotta do it."

And with that, Krys pulled a compact out her lil red bag and started touchin up her make-up.

Damn. Ain't that bout a bitch? My lil cousin was tryna school me on a game I done had sewn up since I was thirteen. She was serious, too. I was tempted to keep her talkin so I could get in her business for real, but my food came and it was a long while before I could stop stuffing my face long enough to say anything.

"So, pimp..." I began, talkin through a mouthfulla syrup-drenched pancakes.

"Ugh, I'ma need you not d' be broadcastin my business like dat," Krys frowned before I could finish my sentence. "You fuckin up my game plan, mo. I'm still recruiting for my all-star team."

"Your all-star team? Girl, get a grip. You ain't gon meet no'by up in hea'."

"Says who? You seen our waiter? He cute as shit. And he got on the fresh GBX's so he probly got some bread, too."

Krys fixed her gaze on our waiter as he busied hisself at another table and I rolled my eyes for the millionth time that day. I had to hurry up and change the subject before she really did make me slap her.

"So when you getcha belly button pierced?" I asked.

"New Years. I'm bout d' get my tongue pierced, too."

"Why?" I asked, thinkin Krys, a tongue ring, and all them many niggas she had was a recipe for that special sauce—and I ain't talkin bout the kind they put on Big Mac's.

"Cuz it'll match my belly ring. Plus I think it's cute."

"Yeah, aight," I chuckled, knowin that was only one of the reasons. That's the same excuse I used when Mommy asked me why I got one. "You'on need to do dat. Besides, it's gon mess up your teeth."

"Hi you know? You got yours done?"

I stuck out my tongue and showed her the silver barbell goin through it. I guess that gave me big cool points cuz Krys all brightened up like I told her them twins from Jagged Edge was joining us for breakfast.

"Ooh, I ain't even see dat. Did it hurt real bad when you got it?" she asked excitedly.

"It hurt enough," I winced, rememberin how my poor tongue was swollen and sore for more than a week.

"You got any tattoos? I'm tryna get one before the summer's over."

I pointed to the one for my brother on my right arm and stood up so I could show her the one on the small of my back, then pulled down a corner of my shirt to show her the one over my right tiddie.

"Damn, you must love dat nigga," Krys said after she saw Twon's name tattooed above my heart.

"You fuckin right I do," I beamed. "Dat's my boo."

"Mnh. I wouldna did dat. I ain't neh' puttin no nigga name on me, joe. Dat's just a set-up to break up."

"Depend on hi you look at it," I told her. "I useta say the same thing. But me and Twon gettin married."

"Married?"

Krys looked at me all crazy-like.

"Yeah, you know, when two people fuck wit eachother real tough and they make it official. *Married*."

"Damn, who'da thought Honey Child would ever get married?" Krys smirked.

"The fuck dat mean?" I demanded, feeling myself gettin upset.

"I just ain't picture you gettin married no time soon, dat's all," Krys squeaked, gettin back on the defense. "Damn, you ack like I'm tryna carry you or some'n."

"Dat's what it sound like to me," I snapped.

"Well if I was tryna carry you, you wouldn't be aksin me—you'd know."

Man, youngin was really pushin me to the limit. If Krys were anybody else, I'da *been* went across her chin for gettin me wrong this many times in a row. But seeing as we family and all, I figured I at least owed Aunt Josie a warning before I brought her only child back home all beat up.

"Look, we need d' get some'n straight off the break," I started, punchin the palm of my left hand with my fist like I do when I'm bout to make a point. "I suggest you calm dat attitude the fuck down, slim. Don't think it's sweet cuz I ain't seent you in a while. Family or not, you keep comin out y' mowf wrong and I'll split y' muhfuckin shit. You got me?"

"Oh, so now you threatenin me?" Krys asked, rollin her eyes and actin all unimpressed.

"Take it hi you wanna take it. I'm just lettin you know wsup."

Krys crossed her arms over her chest and muttered something under her breath.

"You got some'na say?" I demanded.

"*I said* if you gon do some'n, then do it. I ain't scared uh' you."

She glared across the table like she wanted to fight me for real. I ain't know quite how to react cuz Krys never jumped out there with me like that. Her reaction was actually kinda funny cuz I knew I'd punish her if we ever went to blows.

"Lemme find out Krys tryna get buck," I smirked. "What, you think you hard now?"

"Nigga, I *been* hard," Krys siced it. I sized her up with one quick glance and saw the softness in erything from her face to the way her shoulders seemed to quiver even though she was tryna look tough. Hard, my ass. Krys barked a good bark, but that girl was bout hard as fresh Play-Doh.

"Oh yeah?" I asked, still smirkin. "Babygirl, this the real world, not a rap song. You kh make it sound tough all you want to, but don't let your mowf write a check yo' ass cain't cash."

"Whateva," Krys snapped, rollin her eyes. "I'm ready d' go now."

"So-fuckin-what? We ain't goin nowhere till *I* say so," I snapped, rollin my eyes right back at her. I took my time eatin the resta my breakfast, bein all extra slow about it on purpose just to piss Krys off. It musta worked cuz when we got back in the car, she lit up another black and started mumbling under her breath all mad.

"I hope you got cable at your house," Krys said when I pulled out the parkin lot and started down the road towards home.

"Why? So you kh sit around and watch videos all day?"

"Basically."

"Well I got news f' you, Babygirl. I got cable but you won't be havin a whole lotta time to watch it. Startin Tuesday, you comin to work wit me," I told Krys with an overly excited smile to make her even madder.

"What?!"

Krys looked at me like I had to be bullshittin her but I was serious as a heart attack. I already talked to my boss last week and told her the situation, and asked if it would be okay if Krys came to work as a shampoo girl at my job. Figured that way, I could keep an eye on her and make sure she stayed outta trouble. Havin some work ethic was a start at turnin her juvenile delinquent ass around, and besides, I ain't want Krys to discover none of them ruffians around my way and pick up any more bad habits than she already had.

"You deaf? I said you comin to work wit me. You know where P.G. Plaza is, right?"

Krys nodded.

"Well, I work at dat hair salon next to the bookstore in there. And now, so do you."

"I cain't do no hair, joe," Krys argued.

"You ain't got to. You gon be a shampoo girl."

"Shampoo girl? I cain't wash no hair. Why I gotta work witchu anyway? I thought I was comin to your house to get a vacation."

"Vacation? Whatchu think 'dis is? If I gotta get up and work, so do you."

Krys crossed her arms and turned toward the window like she was too through with me. I just smiled at the miserable look on her face and pulled into my assigned space in fronta my building.

Twon musta just got back from pickin up the boys cuz he was still out front lockin up his car. His chrome rims was sparkling like new money and the wax he buffed on the jet black paint yesterday was shiny enough to see your reflection in. Twon love the shit outta his car. He got a '96 Impala SS with limo tints, navigation, leather seats, and the whole nine. That car is so official they ain't even made a word for it yet. A week barely passed after Twon bought it with the money he got from sellin his old car when somebody broke in the j'on tryna steal it. My man kirked out and went around muggin and makin indirect threats at the people in our complex for days. If it wasn't for that loud-ass alarm and the engine freeze he had installed two days after he got it, that car woulda *been* gone. Niggas be gettin they shit split for bubbles out here in 2001.

"Come meet my cousin, Twon!" I hollered.

Twon was in his usual Saturday clothes—a white tee, jean shorts, fresh Hyperflights, and a All Dāz headband. As he came our direction, I looked him over like it was the first time I was seein him and couldn't help but smile. Twon is the kinda nigga that's sexy as shit but he act like he don't know it, so it makes him even more so. Other than the fact that he got cornrows and is bowlegged as they come with juicy D'Angelo lips, he got that Tyrese/Tyson Beckford look to him. You know, chocolate brown with chinky eyes, high cheekbones, and a hard body that make you wanna wrap your legs around him and never let go. When I met him at this club called the Black Hole three years ago, he was lookin good as a Checker's milkshake on a hot summer day. At first I was bullshittin on hollin at him cuz a nigga that look good enough to slurp through a straw be the type to make you fall in love with his ass then fuck it all up cuz he can't handle it, just like my first baby father Dartanyan did. But my girls convinced me that I should take a chance for the simple fact that he bowlegged—and you know what they say bout bowlegged niggas. I thought it was a dumb reason to holla at anybody, especially since all them *you-know-he-got-a-big-dick-if* assumptions wasn't always true with the niggas I met. But I said what the hell and went at him anyway, and we been pretty much inseparable ever since. I mean, over the years we done had our problems—serious problems—but no relationship is perfect. There been times when I wanted to kill Twon in his sleep. Then there was times when all I wanted to do was be up underneath him all day. We might not have always got along or treated eachother right, but we been down for eachother since day one and ain't nothin we been through changed that yet.

"Dat's your fiancee?" Krys asked, staring all extra hard.

"Yup. All dat right 'dare is minez," I bragged. "Ay, Pooh Bear, you gon come help me wit 'deez bags or what?!" I yelled in his direction.

"Mnh. Take your time," Krys mumbled, shamelessly gawking at him with me standing right there.

See now, she lucky I ain't the same as I was when I first met Twon. If this was three years ago, I woulda took offense and got all up in her face ready to throw down about that shit. I useta get into a lotta fights and arguments with other girls (and a couple bold-ass gay niggas) over Twon since we hooked up, but I had to mellow that shit out, otherwise I'll be wreckin muhfuckas the resta my life. Besides, the way I got Twon stuck in my honey, there ain't no need to worry bout him goin *nowhere*.

"Ain't gon be too much more uh' you rushin me, lovah." Twon

warned in a voice smooth and sexy as silk, and smacked me on the ass all possessive like he usually do.

"You betta stop!" I halfway warned with a giggle and a kiss that was just as possessive. Then I remembered Krys. "Oh, yeah. Krys, 'dis Twon. Pooh Bear, dis my cousin," I introduced em.

"Hi you doin?" they both greeted at the same time.

"So you the fiancee, hunh?" Krys said, givin Twon a flirtatious smile and the once-over.

"And you the bad-ass lil cousin."

"Yeah, and I gotta pee," I said, interrupting what coulda turned into a very sexually tense moment. "Kh we hurry up and get dis shit upstairs 'fore I have a accident?"

Twon reached in the backseat to grab some bags. Krys watched him bend over and flex his muscles when he pulled out two armfuls of her junk, her cat eyes fixed on him so hard I thought she could see the change in his pockets. I ain't like that shit at all. When Krys saw me peepin her peepin my bun, she straightened up.

"I hope your air condition work," she told me quickly, fanning herself and lookin away before I could say anything.

"Yeah, it work. Just don't fuck wit it."

We carried all Krys's stuff in two trips from my car upstairs to the apartment. Man-Man and Tink was sittin in fronta the TV in the livin room watchin the cartoon channel. They was already outta they shoes and in they zone, eatin a mountain of Captain Crunch out one of my good Tupperware bowls and spillin milk all over the got-damn-place.

"Y'all gon clean that up, too," I fussed, taking Krys's stuff to the den. My boys kept on eatin and ignored me. I came back out so I could introduce them to Krys, but the phone rang before I could so I had to hurry to the kitchen to answer it. I shoulda looked at the caller ID first. I sucked my teeth and cussed out my own damn self as the operator went through the whole you-have-a-collect-call-from bullshit. When I heard Dartanyan's voice, I felt the hair on the back of my neck stand up. What did his monkey ass want this time?

"Hello?" Dartanyan asked in a slow city drawl that reminded me of home.

"Wsup," I sighed.

"Wsup witchu, young? You busy?"

"Jye-like," I answered, hoping he'd get the hint and not run up my damn phone bill with his fussin and carryin on. "Whatchu want?" I demanded, cuttin to the bullshit.

"Damn. *Dat nigga* ain't givin you no dick or some'n, young? Why you ackin all mean and shit?"

"Don't start wit me, Dartanyan."

Two or three times a week Man-Man's father called from prison to pluck my nerves under the disguise of askin about his son. He never really wanted nothin. It ain't like he could offer to send some money or take his boy to see a Wizards game or nothin like that. He'd get all up in my business bout me and Twon, ask me bout Mommy and the resta the tribe, then talk to Man-Man for a while before sayin something smart to me and finally hangin up. The sound of his voice irritate the mess out me now, but I can remember a time when my day would be fucked up if I ain't hear from Dartanyan. He got locked up a lil while after I met Twon. I felt jive responsible for the whole situation cuz Dartanyan got hemmed up doin what he had to do to take care of me and Man-Man, and ended up gettin time for some bullshit-ass drug and gun charges. I made up for it by visitin him ery chance I got and lettin him call me ery day even though I got in trouble for runnin up the phone bill. I useta go way out D.C. Jail ery week before they transferred him, and I made sure he had erything he could ever need or want in his commissary. I barely had enough money to put Pampers on my baby's ass, but if Dartanyan wanted the new Jordans, I hustled any way I could to get em. It was that serious.

All *typesa* hell broke loose one day when I went up there to see him and found out he already had a visitor. Turns out, Dartanyan was puttin the wood to one of my so-called best friends before he got locked up, and she was goin up there seeing him on the days I wasn't. Somewhere along the line he got the dates fucked up and the truth came out. You know I had to act a ass after that. I ran up on homegirl and introduced her to my fists and the buckle of my heaviest Kenneth Cole belt. Then I wrote Dartanyan a letter tellin him he wouldn't be seein me again till Jesus came back or over my dead body—whichever came first. If it wasn't for Man-Man, I'd cut him off completely. But I got to thinkin bout how not havin a father affected me and my brother and sisters and decided that even if me and

Dartanyan ain't cool, he need to have some kinda contact with his son. It don't make sense to deprive a kid of they father just cuz the parents is beefin. Besides, I needed Dartanyan in the picture to show Man-Man what kinda man *not* to grow up and be.

Dartanyan know I'm with Twon but he steady be tryna act like I'm still on dicks cuz we got a history together. I guess he think I'ma come to my senses one day and he gon sweet talk me into givin up some pussy when he come home. I done already told his ass he got more of a chance sleigh ridin in hell with Santa's reindeer than hittin this again. Ain't my fault if he can't accept the truth.

"Hi my boy doin?" Dartanyan asked.

"He aight. You wanna talk to him?"

"In a minute. I'm talkin'na you right now."

"I told you I was busy—" I started, my bladder feelin like it was bout to explode. All that orange juice from breakfast was starting to do a number on me.

"I know...So hi you doin?"

"Fine, Dartanyan, fine."

"Good. I miss you, Honey."

"I'm sure you do," I smirked.

"Damn, why you cain't never say you miss me, too? Dat nigga around you or some'n? You be actin like you scared to talk to me sometimes," Dartanyan complained, oblivious to the fact that I wasn't scared—I just ain't wanna talk to him.

"Look, Cruddy, I ain't got time to be sittin here churchin it up wit yo' ass. I got shit to do and..."

"And what? Why you keep puttin me off, Honey? Tell dat nigga to back off, young. He got a problem wit me talkin to my baby muhva or some shit?"

I sighed. Dartanyan always been one of them typa niggas who don't appreciate what he got till it's gone. So when I started fuckin with Twon and let Dartanyan know for serious that I wasn't takin him back, he all tried to talk me into waitin for him to get outta jail and straighten up. Talkin bout he was gon go back to school for me and marry me so we could raise our son together, and he was gon buy us one of them old fashioned houses out Fairfax Village, and stop hustlin and stressin me out and fuckin my friends. But I knew he was fulla shit, and with all the stuff I was goin through then, shit was what I couldn't take no more of. Besides, I wasn't gon wait five years for him to come out and disappoint me again. So I told Dartanyan where to go and the fastest way to get there. That's around the time when all the *dat nigga* shit started.

"See, that's the shit that's gon get you hung up on, Cruddy. I ain't got time to be arguin witchu. And anyway, Man-Man is eating his breakfast, so you just gon hafta call back later."

"Call back? Dat's hi you goin? Fuck you, 'den!" Dartanyan snapped, then hung up on me like *I* was the one gettin on *his* nerves. God, he makes me sick. Times like these make me wonder what the hell I even saw in Dartanyan in the first place. More importantly, why did I let his simple ass get me pregnant? Just young and dumb, I guess.

I came out to introduce Krys to my sons real quick before I really did have a accident. They was taking peeks and sideways glances at her tryna figure out who she was without missing too much of their cartoons at the same time. But as soon as I came out and the commercials came on, their full attention went from the TV to the beautiful stranger standing in the middle of the livin room.

"Who the hell is you?" Man-Man asked, shoveling a handfulla cereal in his mouth. He had a bold, direct manner a lot like Dartanyan's and had the nerve to look just like the bamma with his same bright eyes and reddish brown complexion.

"Dat ain't how you say hi d' nobody," I pecked at my oldest son. "And don't be cussin in my got-damn house. You'on pay no bills, boy."

"Wsup," Tink said to Krys. He always was the more friendly one of the two. He could be sweet as a corn pudding on a good day and then be mean as a pregnant cat on a moody day—just like me. Erybody say he look like Twon cuz he came out with them chinky eyes and that same cute lil mouth, but he my color and got nappy hair red enough to keep me from ever denying him as my own.

Krys stood there lookin halfway amused.

"Krys, dat's Kebian and the lil one's Keyjuan. We call em Man-Man and Tink."

"Who is she?" Man-Man demanded again.

"Dat's y'all cousin Karrysta," I told my sons, their eyes glued to her.

They was actin like they never seen a creature of her sort. "She stayin wit us this summer," I continued.

"Hi," Krys said.

"She cute," Tink giggled, lookin her up and down with his lil fresh three year-old self. He reached up to touch her belly ring but I swatted at him.

"Keep your hands to y'self," I warned.

"I just wanna see what it is," he pouted, and continued to stare.

"You got kicked out y' house?" Man-Man asked Krys, and pushed his brother out the way so he could get another handfulla cereal.

"Get out grown folks business, boy," I told him before she could answer. "She stayin wit us and dat's all you need d' know."

Tink shoved Man-Man back and reached in the bowl.

"You wanna see my toys?" he asked, scooping cereal in his mouth and spittin all over erything in a five foot radius.

"No, you gotta see my toys first," Man-Man argued.

"She kh see y'all toys later. Let the girl get unpacked first, y'all, damn. And use a spoon! Why y'all eatin witchall hands?" I fussed.

"My toys is better," Man-Man snickered, ignoring me completely.

"No, minez!" Tink disagreed.

"Minez!"

"Minez!"

"Minez!"

"Mommy, he spit in my eye!" Tink whined.

"Both uh' y'all shut up! And go get some spoons!" I snapped.

"Ay, is you payin rent?" Man-Man asked Krys suddenly and very seriously as he stuffed another handfulla cereal in his mouth. "Cuz if you ain't, you kh at least get me a birfday present. It's August fifteenth. Don't forget."

"I know you ain't propositionin people. Boy, if you'on leave dat girl alone…" I threatened. "Don't pay him no mind," I told my cousin.

"My birfday on Christmas!" Tink piped up.

"No, it ain't. It's before Christmas," Man-Man corrected.

"Nuh-unh!"

"Yeah it is!"

"Y'all stop showin off! And get some damn spoons!" I shouted over they lil voices.

"It's Christmas!" Tink cried, ignoring me again.

"Before!"

"Christmas!"

"Before!"

Tink mushed Man-Man and Man-Man mushed him back, and before I could say anything, they was rollin around on the floor wrestlin and poundin on eachother like crazy. I started to break em up but decided against it cuz nature was givin me its last call and I had to answer *now*. Long as they ain't put one another in the hospital, I really ain't care who hit who how hard or with what. As a mother of two boys, I knew them fools was gonna fight and compete and fight some more, no matter what I did to stop em. So I threw up my hands and stepped over my sons like I useta step over cracks in the sidewalk and headed for the bathroom. Krys just stood there with this funny look on her face like she ain't know what to do next.

"I'ma go pee," I told her. "Make y'self at home."

She was still standin there when I shut the door.

CHAPTER TWO

Krys ain't take no time gettin comfortable. By the end of that first night she was already puttin her feet on my coffee table and diggin through the fridge like she bought the groceries herself. She got real familiar with the apartment and was attempting to get real familiar with Twon, but I shut that shit down quick with a couple evil looks. In between all that, her cell phone was ringin off the hook, so she spent most her time talkin on the j'on, which was more than cool with me. Long as her happy ass was outta Twon's face and outta my way, I ain't care what she did.

Anyways, Mommy called me bright and early the next mornin talkin bout she need me to come up to the house cuz she got something for me. Of course she wouldn't say what it was, but I was wishing like a mug it was that $150 she suckered me out of two weeks ago. Knowin Mommy, though, she probly tryna get me to do her hair or something like that. I asked Twon to watch the boys for a while and told Krys to come on.

To get to Mommy's house was a hike. More like a hike and a half cuz we lived on almost complete opposite ends of the Beltway. Mommy stays offa Bel Pre Road in this townhouse development called Georgian Colonies. Hers was the first neighborhood I ever lived in that had something other than Black people in it. In the city, the only white, Asian, and Spanish people I knew was passerby, social workers, maintenance men, and the people behind the counters at the carry out. In Wheaton, them same kinds of people was my neighbors, and being around em in the suburbs allowed me to realize there was more to the world than what I saw growin up.

My sisters Treasure and Sparkle was out on the playground near the house with some of they lil friends. Sparkle was sittin on toppa the monkey bars swingin her legs and her burgundy-colored ponytail like she was the cutest thing since the Care Bears. It was beyond me why a ten year-old needed weave like that (cuz I know good and damn well that hair ain't a bit more hers than it's minez), but Mommy always did let us come out the house any way we wanted. I made a mental note on toppa the ones I already had to keep a eye on her, cuz thinkin I was cute at that age got me a baby four years later.

Treasure was inside a fake horse carriage facing my direction. When she saw me, she said something to Sparkle, who jumped down and followed Treasure over to where I was parking.

"That's y' sistas?" Krys asked, almost like she was shocked.

"Yeah. They got tall, right?"

My sisters looked like they was on their way to the WNBA. Treasure was already two inches taller than me at five-foot-five and Sparkle wasn't too far behind, both of em with spidery long, skinny arms and legs. We got different fathers, and it was obvious they took after theirs, who was just as tall and bony as a picked-over Thanksgiving turkey. I'on know what Mommy was thinkin when she got with dude cuz he had to be one of the most anti-cute niggas I ever seen in my life, and he wasn't good for nothin but sittin on his narrow ass drinkin like a fish all day. With that kinda bum in they bloodlines, it's a wonder my lil sisters turned out aight.

"Whatchu doin hea', Donkey Butt?" Treasure asked when I got out. At eleven, she was the older of the two, even though most people got em mixed up. Treasure still be dressin like a tomboy the way some girls do before they discover they curves. She tugged at the HOBO headband she had tied Rambo-style around her plaits and squinted her eyes from the sun shinin in her face.

"'Least I got a butt, Skinny Bones," I retorted. "Where Mommy at?"

"In her skin," Sparkle answered, and flipped her ponytail. She had on some too-short jean shorts and a halter top, lookin like a tall mini-Mommy with her almond eyes and flawless cocoa brown complexion.

"She in'na house or what?"

"Do you see her out hea'?" Sparkle quipped.

"Don't get stole in fronta your friends, slim."

She waved a dismissing hand at me and stood with her knees double jointed back and her hands on her narrow hips, givin Krys the once-over. Treasure fiddled with her headband again and did the same.

"I remember you," she told Krys. "Ain't chu our cousin?"

"Yeah." Krys answered like she'd be havin more fun talkin to a rock.

"Stupid ass, dat's Karrysta," Sparkle said, and flipped her ponytail again. I had a mind to snatch that thing off her head before she got too beside herself, but I had a feelin it was already too late. "Where you been at?" she asked, continuing to look Krys over.

Krys shrugged. "Around," she answered simply.

"Ay, what happent to them big-ass glasses you useta wear?"

"Yeah, them big Coke-bottle j'ons wit the x-ray vision?" Treasure clowned.

"Why you all up in her business, joe?" I said, comin to Krys' defense. I shooed my sisters away. "Go play witchall friends or some'n."

"Whycome you chillin wit Shai now?" Treasure asked suddenly, all up in the sauce. I tried to push her back in the direction of the playground but her strong ass wasn't havin it.

"She stayin wit me for the summer, nosy," I snapped.

Sparkle's mouth dropped open.

"Shai, she moved in witchu?!" she cried. "Whycome you won't let me and Treasure move in witchu? We your sistas!"

"So?"

"Man, it be a lotta buns out 'dare where you live. And you right by the Hot Shop. You know Mommy don't be tryna take us 'dare since it's so far away," Sparkle complained, flippin that damn weave again.

"Hot Shop? Dat's where I be goin," Krys said, obviously amazed that my sisters knew anything about the same youngin go-go spot she frequented.

"No, they don't go and they don't need to go. Matter fact..." I looked at my sisters again. "Y'all better take y'all grown asses back to that playground and ack like you know," I ordered, pushing past them towards the front door.

"Hater!" Sparkled called at my back. I stuck out my tongue at her and went in the house.

Mommy was in the livin room braiding my baby sister Staria's hair into cornrows. I could tell she was in her zone by the way she smiled at us when we came in. With the almost empty pitcher of strawberry daiquiri by her foot and the Minnie Ripperton record bout as old as me playin, I could see why. Mommy was twisted. It was a wonder she had enough wits about her to make a straight part in Staria's hair.

"Damn, Ma, you drunk?" I asked, throwin my purse down in a empty chair.

"Shut up, girl. I been drinkin but I ain't drunk. I'on see how it's your business any-damn-way. I ain't gotta work till Tuesday."

I sat down on the loveseat next to her and plucked my lil sister in the forehead. Staria swatted at me and stuck the middle and ring fingers of one hand back in her mouth, then looked at Krys real hard like she was tryna figure out who she was. Mommy lit up a Virginia Slim and narrowed her eyes like she was doin the same.

"Well, I'll be damned," she said when she realized who was with me. "Look at Lil Josie! I forgot you was stayin wit Shai. Hi you doin, baby?"

"I'm fine."

"Good d' hear. You havin a good summer so far?" Mommy asked Krys, and pushed Staria's head forward all rough to make another part. My lil sister frowned.

"Yeah."

"So whatchu been doin? Just chillin?"

"Yeah."

Mommy took another look at her.

"Damn, you done got big, ain't chu? How old are you now?" she asked Krys.

"Fih'teen."

"Lord, y'all kids gettin old. Seem like just yesterday you was runnin round hea' in pigtails and corduroy jumpsuits."

"Dat's cuz it was yesterday," I joked.

Mommy waved a hand at me and began scrutinizing Krys from head to toe. She looked at the tight, red capris Krys wore with the white, see-through hoodie and matchin bra underneath. She examined the red polish on her toes and long acrylic nails, raised a eyebrow at the blood red lipstick and dramatic eye make-up, and peeped the "JUICY" nameplate hangin on the chain around her neck.

"Mnh. Bet Josie and Travis havin a time witchu," Mommy grunted, then went back to braidin. Krys seemed to blush a little and no one said anything for a while.

"Hi my sista doin anyways?" Mommy asked in the same flat tone that Aunt Josie asked about her.

"She fine," Krys answered.

"Y' daddy?"

"He fine."

"Bet they up there gettin on your nerves, hunh? I know how protective them two is."

"Definitely are," Krys answered.

"Dat's what happen when you the only child."

"Wish I was a only child," I said in my lil sister's direction.

"So y'all still live in Greenbelt?" Mommy asked.

"Unh-hunh."

"Hi you do in school this year? I heard you had a lil slump."

Krys shrugged, obviously embarrassed that Mommy pulled her card. Thanks to Aunt Roz, Mommy knew erything Krys been up to since she started actin up last year. In a way, I knew she was more disappointed with my cousin than she'd ever been with me. Krys was one of her last hopes that a child in our family could stay outta trouble.

"Y'know, it's okay to mess up, long as you learn something—"

"Yeah, I know," Krys cut in before Mommy could finish and started playin with her nails like she was done with the interrogation. Mommy raised a eyebrow at the brush-off and opened her mouth to say something. I thought for sure she was gon cuss Krys out the same way she woulda cussed me if I'da interrupted her all rude, but Mommy just shook her head.

"You betta stick to them school books and stay out them streets," she told Krys instead, and left it at that.

"Where Tone at?" I asked, changing the subject to my stepfather.

"He went out Largo to see how the house comin along. He be back soon."

"Oh, excuse me. I forgot y'all rich people was buildin a house," I huffed, still kinda salty that they decided to move to a bigger, single family home after I was already long gone. If erything went according to schedule, Mommy and them was gon be livin in they grand, six bedroom palace by the end of the summer.

"House already done but they still finishin up the basement and the walls and stuff," Mommy told me. "I cain't wait till they finish, too. I need d' get the hell out this house *now*," Mommy said, her eyes suddenly distant. I decided to change the subject again.

"So whatchu got for me, Ma?" I asked.

"Whatchu mean, 'what I got for you'?"

"Ain't dat's why you told me d' come down hea'? Cuz you got some'n for me?"

Mommy took a sip of her daiquiri and smiled.

"Dang, dat's the only reason you came to see me?" she teased. "Well, since you'on care how I'm doin, yeah, I got some'n for you. But I ain't givin it to you till later."

"Then what was the point of—"

"Shut up, Rashaiyah. Dat's only part uh' the reason I called you down hea'."

"Then what's the uh' part?" I sighed.

"Guess who showed up in'na ER at Holy Cross last week? Came in right on my shift wit a sprained wrist."

"I'on know, Ma, damn. Tell me already."

"No. You gotta guess."

"Who, man?" I asked.

"Guess!"

"Ma!"

"Fine, then, impatient ass. I seen your father. Now! You happy?" Mommy grumbled all upset cuz I ain't wanna play along with her.

"My father?" I choked.

"You heard me. I seen your father. David 'Redz' Williams hisself."

I started crackin my knuckles. Just mentioning my father got my blood boiling. I ain't seen him since last year, and even then it had been six years since the time before that. What was he still doin around? Last I heard from my Grandma Rose, his ho ass left his last girlfriend and moved to VA to live with his new flavor of the month.

"Oh, yeah? What he say?" I asked, kinda curious, kinda bitter that he waited so long to contact me.

"Same ol'-same ol'. He ain't really changed none as far as looks go. Still a handsome devil if I ever seen one. You know he work his bruh va garage in Northwest now? He still fixin cars and whatnot."

"Oh, f'real?"

"Yeah, he doin real good for hisself."

"Dat's nice. So wsup wit some back child support?" I asked.

"Yeah, he aksed about you, though," Mommy continued as if she ain't hear me.

"Oh, so *now* he aks about me."

"He wanna see you," Mommy continued, still ignorin me.

"F'get dat nigga, joe. I'on give a fat fuckin rat's ass what he wanna see," I spat, and crossed my arms over my chest.

Mommy's mouth dropped open with surprise but I'on know why. Was I poseda be siced that my father was finally showing me some attention? Was I poseda forget about them times I was lil girl sittin in fronta the window cryin for him to come home? Or them father's days I spent gettin high cuz I ain't have no father to spend the day with? What I look like being flattered that he cared enough to ask about me now?

"Look, I know you mad at Redz for not bein around, but like it or not, the man is your daddy and you should at least go see him to find out what he gotta say," Mommy sternly advised with another sip of her drink.

"How can you of all people say dat, Ma?" I frowned. If I recall correctly, Mommy shed more tears over my damn father than I did. For the longest time after he left, she ain't talk, smile, or eat. Even after she got over him, she was moody and evil for years, especially to me. I know it's cuz lookin at me, a carbon copy of my father, was a constant reminder of a love she useta have. It affected our relationship, caused me and Mommy to constantly be at odds with eachother from the time he left till way after I turnt eighteen. Imagine growin up knowin your own mother couldn't stand you cuz you looked like your father, and your father not bein around to do anything about it. See why I'on like that nigga? He been the source of all my troubles for as long as I can remember.

"First of all, Ma, Redz is my father—not my daddy. I'm on formal terms wit dat man. Second of all, I'on wanna see him. I'on need to see him. Whateva he gotta say to me shoulda been said a long time ago—when it mattered. He's doin too little, too late."

"Well, I still think you need to talk—"

"F'get it, Ma," I whined. "Why was you talkin to his bamma-ass anyways? Couldn't you got somebody else to fix his damn wrist? I know you wasn't the only nurse on duty up in the entire hospital."

"Will you just shut up and listen to me, Rashaiyah!" Mommy yelled, finally losin her composure. "I'on care what he did or didn't do before, dat's still your daddy and you gotta face him at some point or another!"

I rolled my eyes and got up off the couch. What-the-fuck-ever. Redz ain't deserve shit from me. He wasn't good for nothin but runnin all over the damn place and makin a buncha lil redhead kids like me, then leavin em behind for mama to raise. That nigga ain't give me shit but his last name and his good looks, and I *ain't* ask for that, so what was there to say to him? Gee, thanks for leavin without sayin good-bye, Pops. Thanks for decidin to stop sendin money and comin by to see how we was doin, Pops. Thanks for not givin a shit when we was sittin up in a dark apartment with no heat in the winter cuz Mommy couldn't pay the bill. Thanks for erything you wasn't man enough to do, and then some.

"So dat's whatchu called me all the way up hea' for?" I asked Mommy. "You coulda told me dat on'na phone."

"No, dat ain't what I…Ooh, Jesus, I'm sicka your mouth already, child. You just get out my face, cuz you makin my pressure go up," Mommy scowled, downing her last bit of frozen drink.

"So when you gon show me whatchu gotta show me?" I asked again anyhow.

"Just get out my face, Rashaiyah, damn!"

Well, if there's one thing I know, it ain't no use tryna get anything outta Mommy when she all drunk and worked up talkin bout her pressure. It's like tryna climb a glass mountain in socks.

"Yeah, aight, Ma," I sighed, and headed for the basement to kill some time on my sisters' Playstation 2. After that long-ass drive, I wasn't ready to leave. Especially since I ain't get that $150 back yet.

"Ay, Krys, I play you in *Knockout Kings*!" I called over my shoulder. Krys hopped up off the couch like she was more than glad to go and followed me downstairs.

The fan in the basement was blowin around some kinda heavy incense smell to cover up the weed smoke that's always lingering in the air. It struck me as kinda odd that the j'on still smelled lived-in like that, even though ain't nobody lived in the basement for goin on a year now. My brother's bedroom furniture was long gone and replaced with a big screen and a couch, but for some reason, it still felt like he was down there. It musta been cuzza the pictures.

Krys went in the direction of the couch to get comfy and stopped short to look at the "Rest In Peace" wall right beside it. Krys was stuck, I guess cuz she never seen so many funeral programs with teenagers on the front. I still get a sinking sadness in my stomach whenever I look at them j'ons, even though where I come from you learn to deal with death at a early age. The same youngins I useta slapbox with and play chase with, girls I useta party with and holla at buns with, drink and smoke and sit on the steps sharing food with, was some of the same faces staring back at me—all gone over some bullshit. Car accidents, police brutality, stray bullets, paybacks, lookin at somebody wrong…I mean, damn, I know we all gon die some day, but to go out over shit like that make me wonder how tough it's gonna be for my sons to survive.

"Dat's your bruhva?" Krys asked, motioning towards the far side of the wall. I pretended like I was too busy hookin up the Playstation to look up and nodded silently. I couldn't bear to lay eyes on that wall just yet. Lookin at it still stung like salt on a open wound.

As my cousin studied the photos behind glass frames, I started to think about how losin a friend is one thing, but losin family is another. I promised myself I wasn't gonna act all soft cuz my brother wasn't no soft-actin nigga, but it was like, as soon as I turned to face that wall, the tears clouded up my eyes anyhow. I'on see how Mommy can keep them damn pictures up. How can she come down here and sit comfortably with Cerrone staring back at her like that? I guess she keep em up cuz they make it seem like he still here, but that kinda shit would just creep me out and make me more depressed than I already am about him bein gone. Lookin at my brother stirred up something in me I'on normally let out unless I'm by myself. It took ery fiber of my being to keep them tears from falling.

Despite wanting to turn the other way, I went and stood beside Krys. Longingly, I traced the band of freckles that dotted Cerrone's cheeks and the bridge of his nose in a school picture from third grade. I looked deep into his mischievous cat eyes in a picture of all of us at Kings Dominion and remembered how he almost slipped out a couple rides that day cuz he was so skinny. Then I smiled at a picture of me and him when we was little, standin in the sprinklers outside our old apartment in D.C.

R.I.P.
Cerrone Devaughn Williams
May 8, 1983 – August 12, 2000
Son, Brother, Friend
See You on the Other Side

The words at the bottom of the T-shirt pinned up on the wall next to his pictures was the same as the tattoo I had on my right arm. It was taken a couple weeks before Cerrone died. He was in fronta this club called Deno's, squatted down in a pose with a smile that showed how confident, hopeful, and happy he was at the time. Just lookin at it ripped me up inside.

My brother was only seventeen years old, barely a man. Last year around this time Cerrone was here talkin bout how torn he was between workin and playin in his go-go band, or goin back to school so he could graduate and take some business classes in college. Now he can't do neither.

Krys was speechless, I guess cuz she was rememberin back when all of us as kids. My brother useta give her a hard time but he was always the first one to have her back when somebody other than family tried to mess with her. They might not have been friends, but Cerrone still looked out for Krys the same way he looked out for me. He was just that typa person. I'on remember seein Krys at the funeral, but Mommy told me she stood there and stared at him for the longest time before they closed the casket. She musta been shocked as the resta us to see that he was really gone. It was something we was all gon have a hard time gettin used to.

"You okay?" Krys asked awkwardly, and fidgeted like she was tryna decide to hug me or pat me on the back. Silent tears started pouring out my eyes and I was havin the damndest time tryna stop em.

"I'm aight," I lied, and ran back upstairs. I'm tough as teflon most times, but thinkin bout my brother and hearin bout my father was too much emotional baggage for me to carry in one day.

"Didn't I tell you to get out my face, girl? Why you come back up here so fast? What the hell's your problem?" Mommy asked after I sat back down beside her and gave a heavy sigh.

I shook my head as if to say nothing was wrong, but I was really tryna clear my mind. Mommy ain't ask me what was bothering me again.

She knew.

"Staria, baby, go upstairs and get dat yellow envelope on Mommy's bed for her," Mommy directed my lil sister after a while. Staria was gone and back in a flash. She dropped the envelope in Mommy's lap and obediently plopped back on her pile of pillows on the floor.

"This is what I had d' give you," Mommy said, handing me the envelope. It seemed to pulsate in my hands as if whatever hid inside it was alive and waiting to come out. That shit jive freaked me out for a second, so I stuffed it in my purse before anyone noticed me actin weird.

"What is it?" I asked coolly.

"Some'n from Redz. He gave em to me the day after I seen him. We both think you should have em since you the oldest."

"Is it pictures?" I asked.

"You'll see. I suggest you don't open it till you get home and you got some time to y'self, 'doe. Hea' me, Honey Child?"

"Yeah, I hea' you."

"Good...Now do me a favor."

"What?" I asked warily, forgetting about my brother and the envelope for the time being.

"I need some help wet-settin my hair. I need you to grab up them back pieces for me. You know I cain't do em too good myself."

"Ma, c'mon now! I'on feel like doin no hair today. I ain't at work," I griped.

"Stop your whinin. You can look out f' me this one time, Honey Child. Ain't like I be askin you for stuff all the time."

"*Sheeeiiit*, the hell you don't. Where dat hunned-fifty dollas you got me for last week?" I demanded.

"Got you for? I used that money to fix the DVD player you gave me for Mother's Day. Your damn kids the one who messed it up anyhow," Mommy fussed.

"Why you ain't just get Tone to get you a new one? Dag, Ma! You know I'on feel like doin no hair."

"So? I ain't *feel* like goin through eighteen hours of labor witcha ol' waterhead ass, but I did it, didn't I?"

"See, dat's exactly why your shit gon be all crooked inna back. I *really* ain't helpin you now since you tryna joan," I huffed.

"Fine then, Honey Child. I ain't trippin offa you. I really wanted you d' come hea' and get that stuff Redz left for you."

"Well, I got it now. So if dat's all, Ma, I'm bout d' dip," I said.

"Gone 'den, witcha dusty ass. I see you later."

"Bye, Ma." I was already halfway out the door, anxious to see what was in that envelope. It was burnin a hole in my purse.

"Kiss my grandbabies for me!" Mommy called from behind me.

"Whatchu say? Drop em off t'night?"

"Betta drop off a fifth uh' Bacardi for my daiquiris if you do!"

"You got y'self a deal, lady! See you later!"

I was sittin cross-legged on my bed in my draws, staring at the manila envelope in fronta me. After shakin, weighin, and peekin inside I could tell it was fulla old pictures. And now that I knew what they was, I was too afraid to open it for real. I knew I'd see Cerrone from times when he was alive and happy, and to tell the truth, I wasn't ready to face him yet. It'll be a year to that day in August and I still can't look at anything that remind me of him without gettin upset. I'on really like talkin to folks about it, especially if they ain't never lost a brother cuz they be quick to tell me that erything gon be aight and I should hurry up and get over what happened. But healin from grief ain't that easy. Not when you spent your whole life with somebody, been through erything with them, and then hafta go on ery day knowin they died before they time over some shit that coulda been avoided.

It was way past midnight now. The boys was at my mother's house, Krys was out in the den with the phone up to her ear as usual, and Twon was knocked out beside me, snoring like no tomorrow. So basically I was alone. And considerin this would probly be one of the last peaceful moments I'd have all week, now was the best time to do some alone shit.

My hand was shakin and my heart liked to beat out my chest when I tore open the flap and eased the pictures out the envelope. I had to take a deep breath when my eyes finally focused on what was in fronta me.

The first picture was of me in kindergarten. I had a zillion pigtails in my hair, ery row sporting a different color of barrettes. I useta love when Mommy did my hair like that cuz I would walk around thinkin my hair was long since the barrettes weighed it down. Damn, I'on even look the same. I was cheesin all hard with one of my front teeth missin, lookin innocent as a mug even though I can't remember a time when I actually was.

The next one was me and my brother down at the Tidal Basin 'round Easter time, standing under the soft, pink bloom of the cherry blossom trees. There was a racka baby pictures of both of us, a couple leftover wallet size pictures of us in a champagne glass (you know them j'ons from K-Mart's fake-me-out picture studio), and another picture of us pretendin to drive my father's old Coupe DeVille.

I laughed out loud when I found the blackmail shot of a two year-old me in the bathtub eatin a bar of soap. Felt a warmth in my stomach when I saw Cerrone at Christmas holdin up one of them remote control monster trucks he useta love so much. Found myself fightin tears when I saw the other one of me and him dressed up like Raggedy Ann & Andy for Halloween. Got an unsettling feeling in my chest when I saw the picture of me burying my father in the sand at Ocean City.

Before I could force myself to shake it off, the floodgates came bustin open and I was cryin. I went through the pictures over and over again, thinkin bout back when my father useta live with us and erything was cool. All them pictures, them living, memory-evoking pictures made me ache for the days when it was only me and my parents and my lil brother, and we always had enough. I desperately missed the days when Mommy fed us Star Crunch and peanut butter sandwiches on crackers and let me sleep in her bed whenever I had a Freddy Kruger dream. I missed piggyback rides and gettin tucked in at night and smellin my father's aftershave. I missed my childhood. I missed bein a lil girl and I missed the shit outta Cerrone.

Sensing something wasn't right despite being asleep, Twon woke up and looked at me all confused. I tried to wipe my face and stop cryin cuz I'on like actin all sensitive and shit in fronta nobody, but the tears just wouldn't stop comin.

"You aight?" he asked cautiously.

I nodded even though my eyes was still watering like crazy. Twon glanced at the pictures I had laid out like a patchwork quilt in fronta me and immediately put two and two together.

"C'mere," he told me, and patted the space where I usually laid beside him.

"I'm aight, Twon, damn," I argued tryna be tough again.

"If you aight den why you cryin?"

"Allergies," I lied.

He offered his open arms, but I wasn't in the mood for bein held. I sucked my teeth and scooped all the pictures back into the envelope. I was drippin snot and tears all over the place, steady cryin and in denial.

"Rashaiyah, come hea'," Twon sighed.

"I'm aight, young. Just leave me alone, aight."

I hopped up outta bed and headed for the bathroom to wash my face. I really hate cryin in fronta people. It be makin me feel weak as shit. The last time Twon saw me cry was at my brother's funeral and for a couple months after that, but for the most part I cry when I'm in the shower so the water hides my tears. I gotta be the strong one. Can't let nobody see me crumble. That's the way I always been, and that's the way I'll always be.

I turned on the faucet and bent over the sink to splash some water on my face. When I came back up, Twon was behind me twistin the ends of his plaits like he do when he sleepy.

"I ain't mean d' wake you up," I sniffed and tried to brush past him.

He grabbed me by my waist and pulled me into him. I tried to resist the warmth of his body against my back, tried to get away from that comfortable, safe feeling he gave me cuz I was sad and tired of holdin it in. The lump in my throat felt big as a orange. I wanted to cry some more so I could get it out my system but I needed to be alone.

"I ain't goin'na sleep till you aight," Twon said, and moved my hair out the way so he could kiss the warm spot between my neck and my shoulder. He wrapped his arms around me and held me close the way only someone who loves you could. I wanted to move away, go curl up in a corner and be miserable by myself, but Twon had this habit of always bein there when I needed him most, sometimes even when I ain't want him to be.

"Shai, ain't no'by hea' but me and you," Twon whispered. "Stop tryna hold it in."

"I'm aight," I insisted and attempted to crack a smile to prove it. But remembering Mommy weeping at the funeral and how pale and waxy my brother looked lyin cold and still in his stiff black suit stalked my memory like a presence in the fog. Then I thought about my father and all the unanswered questions I had for him, like how was it so easy for him to leave us, and why he ain't at least come around once in a while to see how we was doin. It wouldna killed him to spend a lil time and let us know that he cared. It wouldna fuckin killed him at all.

After a while I couldn't take no more. I turned to bury my face in Twon's chest and cried hard. Harder than I expected. Twon rubbed my back and kissed me, held me when I wailed so hard my entire body shook.

"Let it out," he whispered in my ear and gave me a squeeze. "Let it out."

So I did. And piece by piece, the memories came flooding back.

CHAPTER THREE

My parents met on the green line train Downtown back in 1981. To make a long story short, they hooked up, and two months later I went from bein a twinkle in my father's eye to the bun in my mama's oven. When my granny started noticing Mommy puttin on weight and craving potato chips and ice cream, she added it all up and told Mommy if she planned on keepin me she better find another place to live. It wasn't that hard of a decision since my parents was in love. Mommy packed up all her shit and followed my father from her childhood house in Takoma Park to his lil corner of the world in Northwest. I was born not too long after at D.C. General Hospital. Mommy had just turned seventeen and my father was barely eighteen.

For a while they stayed with Grandma Rose and them on 9th and Kennedy. But with three more brothers and a sister still livin there, that lil house got even smaller with Mommy and me. When Mommy found out she was pregnant with Cerrone less than a year later, my parents decided it was time to go. We moved to Northeast into these apartments on Holbrook Street, right in the middle of a small Black neighborhood called Trinidad. The old timers say it was pretty cool before crack came through in the eighties and destroyed the very fabric of community there, but those days was long gone by the time we moved in. Police tape, shootings, and blood-stained concrete became as common to me and my peers as the brick buildings that lined ery street. It wasn't unusual to see somebody get killed in broad daylight, or beat down by police for any number of small infractions of the law—or sometimes for no reason at all. Trinidad wasn't the best place to grow up, but it was home. Me and my brother was exposed to a lot at a early age, but Mommy and Redz did the best they could to keep us outta harm's way. And for a while, erything was great.

I remember growin up and watchin the big girls make up cheers in they drill team lines, and chasin down the ice cream truck, and watchin the big boys bang on old buckets and trash cans tryna be the next Junkyard Band or EU. I loved picnics in Rock Creek Park and goin to Haines Point to watch the planes take off. I loved huddlin in fronta the oven with Cerrone on cold winter days while Mommy told us made up stories and gave us Star Crunch for snack time. We never had much but with Mommy and Redz so lovey-dovey nobody noticed how hard shit really was.

Then, I guess the stress of being so young and tryna support a family off a mechanic's income while Mommy was in nursing school took its toll. It started out with loud-ass arguments over nothin and my parents not speakin to eachother for days. They would try to play it off and act like shit was all gravy for our sake, but me and Cerrone was old enough to see what was goin on. After a while, Pops stopped playin cool and started yellin at us for little shit like gettin crumbs on the counter or playin too loud. That would usually get Mommy yellin at him for being so mean, and him yellin at her for bein in his face, and the next thing you knew it was on again. Pretty soon, my father stopped sayin anything at all and went outside the house to find peace of mind. And Mommy gave up on tryna make him stay. After Redz started gettin in the habit of runnin the streets for days at a time, it was pretty much over. He would come home to shower, shit, and change his clothes and then be out again. Mommy put up with his disappearing acts for a while before she finally kirked one night and took a cast iron skillet to his ass. The two of them got to wreckin and cussin so loud, the whole block woke up and the police had to come pull em apart. Me and my brother saw the whole thing.

Needless to say, Redz ain't stay around long after that. Bout two weeks before Christmas, he got up one morning claimin he needed some jacks, kissed me and my brother good-bye, and was gone. Just like that. Left us without looking back. He useta come by the house when no one was home and slip money under the door to help Mommy out once and a while, and occasionally I'd spot him from the playground at school watchin me play. But for the most part he ain't deal with us, and pretty soon his money and infrequent visits stopped altogether.

What can I say? Papa was a rollin stone. That man ran from commitment like he owed it money. He was the true definition of a playa, you know—good lookin and smooth-talkin with a nice car and enough money in his pockets to entertain whatever pretty, young thing he could rap up tight for the night. And usually, that was any chocolate brown goddess with a bold attitude and enough curves to make a figure 8 jealous. Mommy was all that, plus smart and hardworkin, but it just wasn't enough for Redz. He wanted more than enough. A part of him wanted to bun up and be a family man, but he also wanted to go out and have fun and charm ery woman that caught his eye. Greedy, selfish, and restless—that's what Grandma Rose called him. Cuz even after Mommy, he'd hook up with a chick and treat her like a queen, then be out again once she started pressin him to settle down. Usually, this was after the kids started comin. I guess kids cramped his style. That, or he just plain ain't like children, which is the way me and Cerrone took it. We actually grew up thinkin our folks' splittin up was our fault, cuz the older we got and the more we needed, the more they relationship seemed to fall apart. Talk about making a youngin feel unwanted. Grandma Rose be tryna make it better by pointin out me and my brother was just two of nine children Redz left behind with a pretty girl and a house fulla empty promises. But knowin that shit don't make being deserted hurt any less, and the fact that it's more youngins out there feeling the same way cuz of my triflin-ass father don't help a damn thing. It just makes it that much easier for me to hate his ass.

Anyways, despite all the bullshit and memories, we stayed in our lil Trinidad apartment. Mommy finished nursing school just in time to pick up where my father left off, and got a job at Washington Hospital Center where she was on-call seven days a week. It woulda been easier for her to do like a lotta women in our neighborhood and sign up for welfare, but my mama wasn't goin out like that. She ain't like the idea of begging or taking nobody's handouts. Besides, my Grandmother raised Mommy and three other kids on welfare, and died in '85 with nothin to show for herself but a stack of overdue bills. My mother refused to continue the dead-end cycle of dependency. Of course Mommy's *I'll-get-it-on-my-own* attitude meant a lotta nights where we ain't had shit to eat but Spam and crackers, but I'm glad she held it down like that cuz she taught all of us the value of doin for ourselves.

Ironically, Mommy's closest friend was a regular welfare abuser. Her name was Miz Darlene and she lived upstairs in the apartment directly above us. When she wasn't busy watchin the stories or huntin down the mailman for her check, she kept a eye on me and Cerrone while Mommy was at work. Miz Darlene had a set of twins named Markis and Dhonica, or Pookie and Dhonni as we called em. They was jive-like extended family to us. Pookie and my brother Cerrone been tight from the jump, ever since our *He-Man*, *Thundercats*, and *Transformers* watching days. Them two went together like potato salad and fried chicken. They did erything together from collectin bottles and cans for money, to schemin on girls, and doin just about anything else two rowdy-ass boys do when they young and lookin for something to get into. They was like brothers for real, in ery sense of the word. Probly woulda been like that well into they old age had Cerrone not...

Anyways, me and Dhonni was a different story, at least in the beginning. We was both cute and liked being the center of attention so of course we couldn't get along for shit. We ain't even play with eachother when our mothers put us all together. There was a unsaid rivalry between us, the kind between two females when they see eachother as competition. I ain't like Dhonni and Dhonni ain't like me, so we just stayed outta eachother's way to avoid any drama. All that changed after the day of my seventh birthday party when we got into a fistfight.

See, ery year for my birthday back in the day, Mommy useta rent out the kiddie rink and throw me a party at this rollerskate spot called Crystal Skate Palace in Temple Hills, Maryland. Even if my aunts and uncles had to help her pay for it, my mama made sure her Honey Child had a party with ice cream, cake, balloons, and all the trimmings. Anyhow, Mommy bought me this cute lil striped-and-polka-dot Orphan Annie set from this discount store called Morton's to wear to the j'on, which just happened to be the same outfit Miz Darlene bought for Dhonni when they went shopping together. So you know I was beefin hard as shit when I seen Dhonni roll up to my party wearin the same thing as me. I start talkin shit to my girls Lakisha and Biggums, sayin I should go over there and beat Dhonni's ass for ridin offa me. And Lakisha, bein Lakisha, gon go over there and run her mouth, then come back to me hollin bout, Dhonni said I need to take off her outfit cuz *I'm* the one ridin offa *her.* I send Lakisha with a message that "At least I look better in it", and we goin at it back and forth till Lakisha tell me Dhonni started talkin bout my mother. Oh, that was it. I ain't never play that "ya mama" shit. Before Dhonni could even ask what was goin on, I skated right over to her ass and plucked the space above her right shoulder. For those of y'all who ain't from D.C., I knocked her mother off her shoulder, which was a definite way to start a fight back in the day. Anyways, I was expectin Dhonni to cry and run away, but she surprised the shit outta me when she balled up her fist and stole me slam in the eye. After the shock wore off, I came back twice as hard, and the next thing you know we was punchin, scratchin, and slidin all over the place tryna mop the hardwood floors with eachother.

Miz Darlene broke it up and beat the snot outta both of us for showin out in public, then sat us down and told us not to move till we thought about what we did. I was pissed at Dhonni cuz it was her fault I was missin my own damn party, but I couldn't help but to respect the hell outta the shit she did. See, I always been kind of a bully, so for Dhonni to get buck with me like that, it showed she had heart. Having heart was important where we was from. Dhonni mighta dotted my eye that day, but I fucked with youngin. It wasn't till then that I noticed she had the same boldness and confidence I did, and since she had on my same outfit, she obviously had some taste, too. Maybe slim wasn't so bad after all. I started talkin to Dhonni bout all the cake and cute boys we was missin out on by bein on punishment, all tryna break the ice and shit. After muggin me and ignoring my ass for a while, she let go of her attitude, and pretty soon we was plottin on ways to escape time-out and sneak over to the big rink where we could peek at all the big boys. It was on from there. At seven years old, me and Dhonni recognized the real in eachother and finally saw that being friends was more fun than being enemies. Youngin been my main apple scrapple ever since.

Anyways, while our brothers raced remote control cars and rode around on rusty ten-speed bikes terrorizin all the girls, me and Dhonni spent our days and nights exploring the ins-and-outs of ery street and alley in our neighborhood. We hung out with the big girls whenever they felt like having us around, and our minds soaked up erything they said and did like hungry sponges. When they got tired of us lil girls crampin they style, we got lost in our imaginations and played ery game you could think of to pass the time. If we wasn't jumpin rope, we was runnin 'round with the boys playin cops-n-robbers and hide-and-go-seek. We wrestled to see who was the strongest and rollerskated up and down the bumpy streets, watchin the boys play ball and dodge cars. If it wasn't handclap games like Rockin Robin, Slide, Miss Lucy, and ABC keepin us busy, we was learning how to dance playin Shake It Señorita, Fly Girl, and Jig-a-lo. And, we played freeze tag, TV tag, football, dodgeball, Mercy, and House. We would play Chase and Butt on the Pole for hours, sometimes well into the night. We jumped outta swings on the playground to see who could go the farthest and had chicken fights on the monkey bars till our bodies was bruised and our hands was a mess of blisters. When it was too cold to go outside we sat in fronta the TV and played Nintendo till we went cross-eyed or fell out from running on that stupid-ass Power Pad that went slow no matter how fast you was goin. We was the masters of "I Declare War", paper football, and pencil fightin. We wove gimp like there was no tomorrow and played cat's cradle with any piece of string we could get our hands on. Childhood, when I was allowed to be a child, was content for me. And like any other lil kid with a head fulla daydreams and all the time in the world, I thought it would be that way forever.

But it didn't, and shit changed, and I started growin up too fast for my own good. Not too long after I turned nine I was "fillin out" as Mommy called it, by ten I was bleedin ery month, and by the time I was eleven, I was passin for thirteen or fourteen and couldn't nobody tell me shit. All the old head broads around the way called me "fast" and "fresh" so much I thought it was a part of my name. They stayed makin assumptions bout me, sayin shit like I'd probly get pregnant by the time I turned sixteen, and that I'd turn out just like my mama with a racka kids by a racka different niggas. After a while I startin believin em, too. I mean, if it wasn't true, then why would they say it so much? Wasn't no denying that I was grown. Good genes and all that steroid-injected beef America fed my generation had me lookin grown. And, comin up in the neighborhood where I was at, thinking like an adult, meant I had a better chance of dodging all the bullshit and bullets around me. Besides, as the oldest, it was up to me to take care of my brother and sisters whenever Mommy couldn't, so insteada being free as any child should be, I was burdened with shit like fixin dinner, changin diapers, and showin my brother and sisters the difference between right and wrong as best I knew. All that responsibility made me feel like a grown woman, so that's how I carried it. I was a product of my environment. I grew up seein, hearin, and doin a lotta shit that lil kids shouldn't know nothin bout, which is the main reason I ain't turn out quite right (for real, nobody I grew up with did). And I ain't sayin none of this to make y'all feel sorry for me. I just want you to know where I'm comin from cuz it's a racka lil girls like I was still out here goin through the same shit.

It was the kinda Botswana hot where all you wanted to do was bust open the fire hydrant and splash around in the water till your street clothes got soakin wet. Mommy always had a fit when we came in the house trackin up her clear plastic runner with water, but we ain't care. If we wasn't allowed to go to the pool at Ruth K. Webb without her takin us, we figured the least we could do was make our own pool in the street.

"I wish you come on and stop starin at dat boy," Dhonni fussed, biting off a big chunk of her red Flavor Ice.

We was takin the long way home from the corner store when I seen Tut and some of his friends tossin around a screamin Nerf football in the street. If this had been any other summer, I woulda kept walkin my happy ass right on home cuz Tut was the farthest thing from interesting to me. I mean, youngin was cute and all, in a *he-got-Indian-in-his-family* kinda way. He was a smooth, Georgia brown color more flawless than chocolate pudding, and he had these alluring, deep-set eyes that seemed to smile even when his thick eyebrows joined together in a frown. His hair was jet black and silky, and just as soft and curly as a baby's, and he had a smile that was twice as sexy as it was charming. Erybody swore he musta been kin to that girl Chilli from TLC with his rare handsomeness, and cuzza that, a racka broads (both young and old) was on him. But I wasn't. Tut just wasn't my type and besides, he was annoying as shit. Tut was two years older than me but he was immature as any boy my age. He was forever tryna play and joan on me, even when I ain't feel like being bothered. He got on my nerves so bad we useta get into all-out fights...that is, until recently. Now that he go with this girl named Tiffani from H Street, Tut act like I'on exist no more. And for some reason I ain't understand, I found myself feenin for his attention.

"Dat's Shai boyfriend," Treasure giggled through a mouth fulla half-chewed Starburst. I cut my eyes at her and Sparkle circling 'round me and Dhonni on they Playskool skates, and wished for the tenth time in a row that *All My Children* would hurry up and go off so I could send em inside with Miz Darlene.

"Ain't no'by aks you," I snapped at Treasure, biting off a chunk of my purple Flavor Ice through its plastic wrapper. I stood in a fake bowlegged stance and watched Tut run up the street with the front of his T-shirt pulled behind his head to show off his skinny, brown chest.

"Ugh, Shai, he a bamma like shit. Nigga still wearin dat played out fade wit the S-curl on top. Ol' Special Ed lookin muhfuh. He need plait dat shit up and ack like he know it's nineteen-ninety-muhfuckin-three out hea'," Dhonni snickered.

Usually I wouldna minded her cattiness, but now that I was starting to like Tut a lil bit, I got in my feelings whenever someone said anything about him. I ain't like broads sayin he was cute cuz it made me jealous, and I ain't like anybody tryna clown him cuz it made me mad. It was weird and silly to me, but I couldn't control it.

"Tut do not have a S-curl, for your information. Dat's all natural. He got dat good hair," I said, quickly comin to his defense.

"Well, he need d' do some'n wit it. And he need d' put the bird back in'na cage," Dhonni said, shaking her fingerwaved head. "Ol' skinny bone, bird-chested self."

"He ain't *dat* skinny," I objected with a frown.

"*He ain't dat skinny?* Girl, you musta tripped and bumped y' head. I know you see dat nigga ribs, young! Ol' lunchtime special, hang off the plate, baby back rib-chested muhfucka! You *know* you see them j'ons!" Dhonni laughed, showin a babyfaced smile and a set of dimples that made most people think she was innocent.

Tut looked back at me one last time before he dashed up the street, and I gave him a wink on the sly.

"C'mon, witcha lil hot-ass self," Dhonni prodded, kickin the back of one of my locked knees.

"Stop 'fore I jap-slap you!"

"'Den bring yo' butt on," my best friend ordered. "I'on wanna stand hea' all day lookin like a retard."

I motioned for my lil sisters to follow and strolled down the sidewalk beside Dhonni towards home. It was the end of a sunflower seed and Rock Creek soda kinda summer day; the type where big girls braided hair on the front steps; grown men stood around drinkin one cold beer after another, and the younger ones played ball or ducked in and outta alleys to serve junkies they daily dose of poison, when they wasn't absently watchin girls go by. The same buncha old men hung around in those same alleys and worked on busted-down cars that needed to be in a junkyard somewhere, as old women with achy bones reclined on porches, and mothers stood behind screen doors or leaned over windowsills watchin they kids play outside.

I was in a pissy mood earlier cuz Cerrone thought it would be funny to splash a cup fulla cold water on my head and wet up my Shirley Temple curls while I was sleep. Mommy woke up just as I was bout to hang my foot up his ass, and jumped all on my case for yellin. Then she had the nerve to threaten to punch me in the mouth when I tried to explain what happened. I really shouldna been surprised cuz Mommy ain't never take my side for nothin whenever me and Cerrone bickered, but I couldn't rest without tellin her how fucked up she was being for lettin my brother get away with that shit. That's when Mommy took a belt to my legs and told me to get out her face before she do something so horrible to me that it'd be on the news. I locked myself in the bathroom and sat there mad as a wet cat till Dhonni came downstairs and dragged me outside with her.

Our girls Lakisha, Trayonna, and Biggums was sittin out fronta our apartment buildin in the dirt yard passin around a bowl of something so strong you could smell it way up the street. The three of them, added with me and Dhonni made up our crew, the Suga Sweet Huneyz. Where we was from, erybody that hung real tight was a crew, and ery crew had a name. Youngins would name theyselves after they street, they block number, they 'hood, or they apartment complex. We named ourselves like a lotta girl crews did, after things that was sweet or a reputation we had. See, we was Suga Sweet Huneyz cuz we could make your teeth fall out, either by being so sweet you get a mouthfulla cavities, or being so mean we leave you with a mouth fulla loose teeth. And we all had nicknames that followed it up. I was Suga Baby, Dhonni was Kiss (as in Hershey Kiss), our girl Lakisha was Lollipop, Trayonna was Skittles, and we called our girl Biggums the Jawbreaka cuz she was the biggest tooth-looser of us all. The five of us was tighter than the narrowest rowhouse hallways, and in my honest opinion, it wasn't no girl crews our age that could fuck with us.

"Ugh, young. What is dat?" Dhonni complained, screwin up her face as soon as we got close enough to sit down. "Some'n smell like feet."

"It's y' upper lip," Biggums told her, fanning herself with the black Redskin's cap she always wore. Biggums was the biggest one in our crew at a buck fifty, just a few inches shy of six feet, and without a doubt, the most overgrown twelve year-old I ever seen in my life. She was jive kinda Polynesian-lookin, all big-boned with slanty eyes and thick, fleecy hair she wore in one long-ass braid that reached the middle of her back. Biggums was a bully to most erybody else, but when it came to us, she was sweet as apple pie. Youngin been down with me since hi-top fades and patent leather police shoes was the shit, so I basically considered her family. Besides, having Biggums as a friend was a sure way to meet some cute-ass boys. She was a tomboy if I ever seen one, and she stayed mobbin with a racka niggas when she wasn't chillin with us.

"Y' muhva."

"Y' fahva."

"Y' muhva, y' fahva, y' whole entire generation," Dhonni retorted, and Zorro-snapped her fingers in Biggums' face for emphasis.

"Don't dat include you, too?" I asked, floppin down in a old kitchen chair where I could keep a eye on my lil sisters. I peered in the bowl and made a face at the vinegar-soaked sunflower seeds.

"Damn, them j'ons *is* hummin, 'doe," I agreed.

"So is y' breaf, nigga. But do you hea' me sayin anything?" Biggums joked.

"Aww, dat's cold. She said y' breaf kickin like Jean Claude Van *DAMN!*" Lakisha laughed, unwrapping a root beer Dum-Dum lollipop. She was the instigator of the bunch, been that way since she got me and Dhonni in the fight that sealed our friendship. Lakisha was forever sicin shit and runnin her mouth bout other people's business to see what kinda drama she could cause. I done seen her make best friends wreck over some bullshit, just cuz she talked it up so much. Dhonni seem to think Lakisha don't know no better and that's why she always runnin her mouth, but I know youngin be doin that shit for attention. As the least interesting and least attractive out the crew, she had to do something to get all eyes on her. Lakisha got on our nerves cuz she was the only one out the bunch quick to start some shit and leave us to finish it, but no matter how many times we tried to carry her, she just wouldn't go away. We jive-like got useta her after a while. You might even say we started to like her cuz it was kinda funny to see the way people acted after she stirred up some trouble.

"Shut up, Lakisha," I said.

"Shut don't go up."

"It will if I drop-kick yo' ass in'na chin," I warned, smoothin out the wrinkles in my plaid body suit. Dhonni plopped down beside me on an overturned bucket and bit off another piece of her Flavor Ice.

"Ay, y'all bring me one?" Biggums asked, pointin at Dhonni's frozen treat. Me and Dhonni shook our heads no and slurped on ours like they was the last and the best ones on earth.

"Lemme get a piece, young," Biggums begged.

"Say 'please'," Dhonni told her.

"Bitch, whateva. You ain't like dat."

Trayonna giggled at their bickering.

"I'on know whatchu laughin at," Dhonni snapped. "Sittin ova' 'dare lookin like a Treasure Troll Teenie witcha hair all stickin up."

"Awww, dat's cold!" Lakisha instigated.

Trayonna rolled her green eyes to the sky and smoothed down her short, sandy brown spike of a ponytail. Next to Dhonni and my play mother Kia, Trayonna was my ace, which only made sense cuz the three of us was Kia's play daughters anyway. Me and Trayonna got to be related back when she moved here two years ago and erybody kept askin me if we was sisters cuz we was both lightskinded with light eyes and shit. After hearin that question one too many times, I went up to her house on Staples Street and asked her bout who her father was, thinkin she coulda been a part of my father's rainbow coalition. Turns out her daddy was a white boy from Jersey, but we started claimin to be play sisters anyway. Naturally, Kia and Dhonni claimed her, too. Trayonna always been quiet in a sneaky-secretive sorta way like she had something to hide, but I fucked with her just the same cuz she was pretty and as much fun as Dhonni when we all got together.

"I'on know why you talkin. Dat's why y' fingerwaves flickded. Witcha ol' dusty head ass," Trayonna retorted.

Before Dhonni could say anything back, the front window to her apartment came swingin open and a rain of colorful water balloons splattered down all over us from the second floor. The five of us jumped up and ran out in the street to see what the hell was goin on, only to find Pookie and Cerrone hangin out Pookie's bedroom window laughin they asses off.

"You stupid freckle-face self!" I hollered at my brother. "You play too much! I'ma tell Mommy when she get home t'night, too!"

"She gotta work till t'mar mornin, so OOOOOHHHH!" Cerrone laughed. "See how much you know; see how much you don't!"

"Keep playin, hea'! Both y'all gon catch one!" Biggums threatened the boys, cradling the bowl of sunflower seeds.

"Man, shut yol' Sasquatch-lookin ass up!" Pookie teased, and hurled another water balloon down in her direction. It missed and splattered on the ground in fronta Dhonni instead.

"Pookie, I'ma straight beat chu in y' face!" Dhonni screamed, pickin up a hand fulla pebbles to throw up at him. Her and Pookie looked nothing alike for em to be twins. Where Pookie was tall, red, and bony as Tut with a lazy eye and ears like open car doors, Dhonni was chubby, cocoa brown, and cuter than a baby doll with her smiling eyes and deep dimples.

"Do it 'den!" Pookie dared her.

"C'mere, 'den!"

"I'on come to dogs; dogs come to me!"

"F'get chu, Pookie!"

"F'get chu, too!"

"F'get chu, f'got chu, don't even know you!" Dhonni declared, and started wringing out her T-shirt.

Our brothers threw the last of they balloons and disappeared back inside, cackling like hyenas. It never fails in the summer with them two fools and they water balloons. If they ain't hittin us up with them j'ons, they ridin round on bikes sprayin erybody with water guns. Pookie always got me extra cuz he been havin a crush on me since back in the day but I ain't never pay him no mind. I thought Pookie was goofy-lookin with them big-ass ears and that eye of his goin ery-whicha-way but straight. Besides, he was my best friend's brother and my brother's best friend.

Gettin with him woulda made shit really awkward.

"I cain't stand them," I grumbled, smoothing down my water-soaked hair for the second time that day.

"Tell me about it. Wait till 'day come outside. I'ma punch both of em out—"

Biggums stopped mid-sentence cuz somebody was laughin and it wasn't none of us or the lil girls playin with they Skip-Its a few doors down.

"Some'n funny d' you?" I snapped at the two faces peering at us from across the street. Miz Cunningham's granddaughters Baby and Precious stopped gigglin and stared between the heavy, black iron bars that surrounded they house. Theirs was the only house on the block that had a gate around the porch. It looked like a cage, and to me, Baby and Precious looked like some miserable-ass creatures you'd see on exhibit at the National Zoo.

"Eye problem?" Dhonni asked, jumpin all up in it. Precious, the older of the two sisters, crept back in the shadows. Baby, who was our age, stood her ground and put her hands on her hips.

"Nah, but keep it up and you gon have one," she said, swiveling her neck around like she been waitin all day to tell somebody off. Dhonni looked like she was bout to light Baby up but decided against it at the last minute. Ain't nobody mess with Baby and Precious. They was too quiet and stayed to theyself too much for anybody to know what to make of em. That was all they grandmama's doin, though. Miz Cunningham ain't never let em come out and play with the resta us, and any time she caught Baby or Precious off the porch, or one of us too close to it, she'd have a fit and make em go inside. She protected them girls too much, but I guess she figured she had to since they came up so rough. See, Baby and Precious ain't have no mama. She got that sauce and died two years ago. Before they moved in with Miz Cunningham, Baby and Precious lived in a rooming house off North Capitol where they mama would sometimes come home with food, sometimes with money, and sometimes with a seedy hustler lookin to work out a deal for her to repay all the yak she smoked up. Unfortunately, that left Baby and Precious to act as currency from time to time, which explained why Precious was so unusually quiet and scared of erything, and Baby was hotter and fresher than a batch of baked bread from Subway.

"Ooh, she bust you out! Don't chu feel like a doggy biscuit?!" Lakisha exclaimed, sicin it as usual.

"'Dis a A and B conversation so why'onchu C your way out, Lollipop!"

"Ay, don't be gettin mad at me cuz you got carried."

"I ain't *get* carried, joe," Dhonni argued, then made a face. "And you need d' be quiet 'fore I smack you wit 'dis popsicle!"

"Dat's whatcha mowf say," Lakisha egged her.

"Dat's what my mowf know."

See what I mean about that broad Lakisha? She don't rest till she get a reaction outta you.

"Who tryna play double dutch?" I asked, changin the subject before Dhonni really did smack her with her popsicle.

"Me!"

"Dat's my cue to be out," Biggums announced, and pulled on the brim of her Redskin's hat. "Y'all know I'on do dat jump rope shit."

"'Den get d' steppin," Dhonni told her.

"Why'onchu stay and turn one time?" I asked. "You know Lollipop double handed and Skittles don't like to turn."

"I'm ain't double handed!" Lakisha objected.

"Yes, you is. C'mon, young, just do it till my go is over, at least."

"Nah, joe, it's too hot," Biggums declined.

"I'on know why you aksin her. Boys cain't turn no double dutch nohow," Dhonni snickered. She stayed gettin on Biggums for walkin, talkin, and dressin like a boy, especially if she ditched us to go hang with the boys when we was all poseda be chillin together.

"Oh, so I'm a boy, now? Dat ain't whatcha bruhva said last night," Biggums retorted.

"Ooh! Busted! She gettin on you, young! I say you steal her!" Lakisha instigated again.

"Lollipop, shut the fuck up," Biggums frowned, then handed the bowl of sunflower seeds to me. "Ay, if anybody come by lookin f' me, tell em I went 'round Syco j'on."

And with that, Biggums strolled off towards Queen Street where her boy Syco lived.

"Aight, nigga," I nudged Dhonni. "Where the rope at?"

"Up your butt and around the corner."

"F'getchu. Go get it."

"Only if I go first."

"Second!" me and Trayonna called at the same time. "Jinx!" we shouted, and pointed at eachother. Dhonni said my name so I could speak and I called second again.

"Ugh, y'all cheatin like shit," Lakisha complained. "We need d' do One-Potato, Two-Potato."

"But I'm second," I argued.

"Suga Baby, just put cha hands in."

I folded my hands into one big fist and waited impatiently for Lakisha to tap me out first. Unlucky for me, I ended up bein fourth, and it seemed like forever till I got my chance to go from corner to corner tryna decide what side to jump in on. Then it seemed like forever for Trayonna and Dhonni to get the two old clothes line we was usin for ropes to turn right.

"Wouldju hurry up and go, Suga Baby?" Trayonna sighed after I went around all four corners twice. "We ain't got all day."

"Don't be rushin me," I fussed, finally jumpin in. "And don't Skin me, neiva," I warned, hoppin from foot to foot like a duck.

"Shai tryna do Skin, y'all!" Lakisha cheered.

"I said *don't* Skin me!" I argued.

Trayonna and Dhonni started turning faster anyway.

"S-K-I-N! SKIN!" they yelled, and started flippin the ropes as fast as they possibly could. I was keepin up for a while, until the door to the buildin next to mine squeaked open and my play mother Kia and her girl Niki came outside. I turned to look and my foot got caught. The ropes smacked me in the legs then collapsed right on toppa my head.

"Ooh, y'all playin double dutch! Lemme get a go right quick," Kia asked, playfully pleading with her fox-like eyes. If it had been anybody else I woulda said hell no and told em to gone about they business. But Kia was a big girl and my play mother on toppa that. It was a respect thing.

"I'on care," I shrugged nonchalantly, and got out the way. Dhonni and Trayonna automatically started turning.

Kia been my play mother since my first day of kindergarten at Phyllis Wheatley Elementary when she was in third grade. She the only one next to Mommy that I allowed to call me Honey Child as a nickname. She was a slim but shapely, creamy butterscotch girl who *stayed* with the fresh hair and nails and always had the latest erything from shoes to clothes to purses to whatever. Erybody in Trinidad knew who Kia was, either cuz they liked her or was jealous and wanted to break ery bone in her pretty face. My girl was a lil on the feisty side and had a rep for fightin, stealin, and breakin hearts, and she was the first teacher I had who showed me how to manipulate niggas into givin me anything I wanted. Mommy said Kia reminded her of them wild-ass teens they always be havin on talk shows and ain't like me hangin around her, but I looked up to Kia for the same reasons Mommy wanted me to stay away from her. She wasn't exactly the brightest Christmas light on the string, but she taught me a lot of what I know bout how to get minez no matter what. The way Kia knew something about erything, and the way she carried it kept me in constant awe. She was badder than youngin who played Laura on that old show *Family Matters*, went harder than Pam Grier in all them *Foxy Brown* movies, and had more game than Milton-Bradley and Parker Brothers put together. I thought Kia was cooler than them T-shirts that changed color with the temperature. She represented erything I wanted to be by the time I turned fourteen.

"C'mon, Kia, we gotta roll," Niki fussed, and lit the cigarette she had been rolling around between her fingers.

"Damn, joe , why you bein pressed? Cain't you see I'm tryna talk d' my daughters?" Kia snapped. She stopped jumpin and held out her hand to get deuce on Niki's jack, then stood fake bowlegged and blew out a cloud of thin gray smoke. Kia was dressed for a party in her tight Guess jeans, hot pink quilted vest, and matchin belt and sandals. Even her sunglasses was pink. Her short hair was slicked down flat to her head except for the squiggly pieces gelled around her face. Her neck, wrists, ears, and fingers was draped with gold and fake pink diamonds we called pink ice. My girl Kia was so fly, I felt like I was in the presence of En Vogue's fifth funky diva.

"Where you goin at, Kia?" I asked. She smoothed down the nappy edges of my damp, bandana-wrapped bun and traced my curly-Q sideburns all in one sweep.

"Downtown on a mission," she answered, pointin to the empty shoppin bags her and Niki was carryin. They was bout to hit the stores and go on a five-finger-discount shoppin spree. "I gotta get 'dis girl a leather coat and do a lil birthday shoppin for me. You wanna come?"

"Hell yeah!" I beamed. I was all set to pick up a decoy bag and roll with em, but I caught a glimpse of my lil sisters skating up and down the sidewalk.

"Damn, I gotta babysit," I sighed helplessly.

"Too bad. I's gon show you how d' break them chains they be havin on'na racks wit the leather coats. I just show you next time, 'doe."

"Yeah, next time," I said, watchin her and Niki make they way up the street towards the bus stop.

"Y'all be careful wit these cars out hea'. And Dhonni, come d' my house around ten so I kh wash them fingerwaves out. Them j'ons bout dusty now."

"Aight, Mommy. Bye!"

"See ya!" I piped up.

"See ya! Wouldn't wanna be ya!" Kia called over her shoulder.

I waved at her retreating figure, my eyes all wide and smilin cuz Kia, the coolest youngin in the neighborhood, who just happened to be my play mother, took a minute to holla at us. What a boost. Kia showed me more love and attention than my own mother did sometimes. And she was always willin to teach me something, or show me something, not tell me get out her face cuz she was too tired after workin all day to deal with me. Yeah, I fucked with Kia tough. That was my bitch for real.

"Toldju your fingerwaves was dusty," Trayonna teased Dhonni, startin to turn the ropes again.

"Shut up, Treasure Troll Teenie."

"Damn, Skittles, you gon let her keep callin you dat? I say you steal her, young," Lakisha siced it. Dhonni and Trayonna started fussin back and forth and Lakisha stood on the sidelines laughin. I just shook my head at all of em and started jumpin again.

CHAPTER FOUR

I turned twelve the summer of 1994 and found myself walkin the thin line between stayin a young girl and becomin a young lady. In a lotta ways, I was the same ol' Shai, just as sassy and headstrong as ever. But a lotta things about me was changing, and I'm not just talkin bout the way I looked. Hormones ricocheted through my body like pinballs back in them days, and they controlled erything I did from being unruly with my mother to sneakin my first kisses under starlit skies at the playground. I still played double dutch and hung out with my crew in fronta my buildin talkin shit and startin trouble, but something in me wanted to be like Kia and the other big girls I knew who wore they hair in French rolls and went to parties and had boyfriends.

I had a growin curiosity about erything I ain't experience, and things that normally made me shrug with indifference sent tingles of excitement up and down my spine. All of a sudden, I was interested in clothes and make-up and comin across as a lady insteada the rugged-ass lil girl I always been. I was done with my baggy jean shorts and them T-shirts I wore that had cartoon characters dressed like Kriss Kross on the front of em. I wanted to wear smoky black eyeliner and roll my jeans over at the waist like Kia did, and cut my hair in a bob so I could finally be done with my *Let's Jam* and bandana days. Smokin weed started to appeal to me cuz all the coolest big kids we knew was gettin into it, and goin with Kia on them missions of hers went from bein a sometime thing to a part-time occupation. Boys became more than people I could play around with, and I was lettin go of the fear of rejection my father's absence caused to be more than friends with em. Of course, Mommy found out about me havin boyfriends and threatened me to stay away from em. I chalked it up as her bein jealous cuz she couldn't keep no man, and kept on doin what I wanted to anyways. I broke my in-by-dark curfew and practiced smokin cigarettes with Dhonni and Trayonna behind my buildin. I went from long shorts to short skirts and crept out my bedroom window ery Friday to hit the all ages go-go with my crew. I hung out at the basketball courts and went to house parties where I got my tiddies sucked for the first time in dark basement corners. I was goin hard. And for what? I'on know. I guess cuz them first experiences of my adolescent life was too sweet to stop chasin once I started. Besides, I liked the thrill of it all. Sneakin around to do shit I knew I'd get in trouble for gave me a rush and made me feel like I was bein cool. Muhfuckas around the way called me and my brother and sisters "Brenda's Kids" (like *Bebe's Kids*), so I figured I was just livin up to my name. Besides, I was only goin through what ery kid go through when they get to a age where they tryna figure out who they is. I mighta did it a lil earlier than most, but hey, that's the story of my life.

"Ay, who you think would win in a fight? Boyz II Men or Tony Toni Toné?" Cerrone asked from the back spokes of the squeaky old bike him and Pookie was ridin.

The four of us was makin our getaway from the corner store where we ruffed handfuls of snacks and ran out before the owner could catch us. It was near the end of August, after the dog days of summer, and the third day in a row I been tryna cope with stifling humidity and no air conditioning at home. I was dyin to sit down somewhere and dig into my Ninja Turtle ice cream so I could finally cool off, but first we had to make it to Trayonna's house where the resta the crew was waitin, and second, I had to get ridda my lil brother before he made me snap.

"You hea' me, Shai? Who you think would win, Shai, hunh?" Cerrone repeated. He hopped off the back of the bike and tried to sweep the backa my feet with one of his so I'd trip.

"Stop it, boy, damn!" I yelled, swatting at him all irritated.

"Answer my question, 'den."

"I'on know. Don't none of em look like 'day kh fight," I shrugged, rollin my eyes.

"Ooh, I got a good one. Whatabout Queen Latifah and Lady of Rage?" Pookie asked.

"Mmm! catfight!" my brother exclaimed.

"Rage remind me uh' Biggums a lil bit. If she anything like my girl

Jawbreaka, I got Rage winnin dat one," Dhonni commented, takin a bite of the big, juicy hot pickle she snatched from the store.

"Aight, whatabout Mariah Carey and Mary J. Blige?"

"Yeah, I wanna see dat!" Cerrone chimed excitedly.

"I'on know why boys always wanna see girls fight. Be swearin 'day gon see some tiddies," Dhonni frowned.

"So what? I'm tryna see tiddies whenever I can."

"Me too," Pookie added, and gave me a look.

"Ugh man, why'onchall go home?" I grumbled, mushin Pookie away from me.

"Why'onchu make us?" Cerrone challenged.

"You ain't gon be satisfied till I knock yo' yellow ass into next week, is you?" I threatened. Erybody was always calling Cerrone yellow on account of his baked cornbread color. It was odd how he came out lighter than me with freckles, but looked exactly like Mommy as much as I looked like our father.

"I dare you, young," my lil brother instigated. I swung at his head again, but he ducked out the way.

"Miss me! Miss me! Now you gotta kiss me!" Cerrone taunted. He tapped me on one side of my face, then the other, and kept doin it and runnin away before I had a chance to get his lil ass back. Ooh, that boy was drivin me crazy!

"See, dat's why I'on like you comin nowhere wit me. You'on know how d' ack," I fussed, rollin my eyes at my brother again.

"So? Dat's why I'ma tell Mommy you was stealin."

"You was too! You the one got a pocket fulla Nah-Laters!" I accused.

"What Nah-Laters?"

Cerrone threw a handfulla purple Now-or-Laters at me and laughed when one hit me in the face.

"I ain't got no Nah-Laters," he whooped.

"Sho' don't. I'm bout d' get all them j'ons," Dhonni said, scoopin em up from the ground. Cerrone took one of the candy Fireballs he had in his pockets and threw that at me, too.

"Aaagggghhhh! Go away, nigga, damn! Whatchu still followin me for?" I growled.

"Cuz I love you," my lil brother gushed, and jumped on my back to gimme a bear hug. We told eachother we loved one another all the time, but he was being extra dramatic and it was makin me mad.

"Get off me, boy!" I yelled.

"Why you tryna get ridda me, Shai?"

"Cuz I'on like you!"

"Well, I'on like you neiva!" Cerrone declared, then karate chopped me in the backa my neck as hard as he could. He hopped off my back and took off down the block after Pookie before I had a chance to go to his body.

"Wait till I catch you, young! See what happen!" I yelled at his back.

"You cain't catch me! Nanny nanny boo-boo! Stick y' head in doo-doo!" he sang, before disappearin around the corner.

"Damn, he get on my nerves! You want a lil bruhva?" I asked Dhonni. She just gave me a dummy look and kept on walkin.

We ducked into the next alley goin towards Trayonna's house, right along the street where Tut's friend Bernard lived. Suddenly, I was overcome with butterflies at the possibility of crossin Tut's path. I'on know why he be makin me feel that way. Usually, I'm pretty cool around boys; I just kinda boss em around like I be doin Cerrone and Pookie. But Tut, man, he had a way of makin all that cool shit go right out the window. I still tried to convince myself I ain't like him, but even I couldn't lie that good. After a whole year of watchin him from afar, my attraction to Tut was undeniable. He occupied all my daydreams. He was the reason I walked with a switch and talked extra loud with my friends whenever he was around so hopefully he'd notice me.

"Ooh. 'Dare go your boy," Dhonni whispered, lookin ahead and spottin Tut and Bernard about to go into Bernard's back door. "I'ma go say hi f' you."

"No you not, eiva," I objected.

"Why?" Dhonni asked as if I ain't tell her a million times already how jittery that boy made me. She gave a dimpled smile as if to say she was gettin a kick outta messin with me and asked all oblivious, "What's wrong wit sayin hi?"

"Dhonni, stop playin. 'Day bout to go inside anyways."

"Nuh-unh. Watch 'dis."

"Dhonni!"

"Aight, man, dag!" she skulked like she was givin up. Then, "*Sike!*...

Ay, Tut! Shai wanna talk d' you!" my best friend called out when we got closer. I shot Dhonni a look that gave new meanin to the term "evil eye" and nervously followed her to where the boys had stopped to wait for us.

"Whatchu doin on my block?" Bernard asked with a frown, comin our way like he had a problem. Dhonni put her hands on her hips and grit on him till she couldn't hold back her smile no more.

"Nigga, don't get stole. 'Dis my block. Suga Sweet run all this. Ain't dat right, Suga Baby?"

"Mmm-hmm." I was too busy tryna avoid eye contact with Tut and open my ice cream without sayin or doin anything too stupid.

"Yeah, aight. Ay, y'all went to the store?" Bernard asked, openin his rusty, chain link gate to come meet us. Tut was right behind him. "Whatchu get me? Lemme get a bite uh' dat."

"I letchu get a bite uh' 'dis knuckle sandwich," Dhonni sassed, holdin up her fist.

"What?"

Bernard grabbed Dhonni up and tried to wrestle her pickle out her hand. I swear, if I ain't know them two like I did, I wouldn't know all that tough talk and rough-housing was just they way of flirting.

"Ay, Shai, come handle my light work," Dhonni called, holdin Bernard off with a chubby elbow.

"My name is Bennett and I ain't in it," I said, and bit off a piece of my ice cream. I had to do something to keep me from talkin cuz Tut was comin towards me and I ain't want him to know how bothered I really was.

"You don't speak?" Tut asked as he approached, his squinty eyes fixated on the short, white jean skort I was wearin.

"No," I snapped.

"'Den why your girl say you wanna talk d' me?"

Tut was suddenly standin so close I could smell the outside and sweat on his skin, and for some strange reason, his fragrant, musky heat was makin me feel light-headed and warm all over. Good God Almighty. Tut was so fine I was havin a hard time breathin. Bein next to him was like bein next to a celebrity, like somebody I dreamed of meetin, but once I finally did, I couldn't think of nothin to say.

"I'on know. She be lyin…Damn, why you gotta be all up on me, 'doe?" I asked like I was annoyed, moving away a lil bit.

"I ain't all up on you. *'Dis* is all up on you.*"

Tut backed me into the fence with his arms on either side of me and pressed us so close together I could feel the knotted drawstring of the extra pair of shorts he wore under his jeans. I went from lightheaded and warm to tingly and burnin hot in two seconds flat. I shoulda been useta his boldness by now cuz Tut been lookin at me and sayin a lotta slick shit to me lately. But like I said, for all the things I did to get his attention, I ain't know quite what to do with it when I finally got it.

"You betta stop, 'fore you getcha self in trouble," I warned, lookin around to see who else was in the alley. Other than us and Dhonni and Bernard over there actin all simple, we was all alone.

"Whatchu mean 'fore I get in trouble?"

"Don'tchu still go wit dat girl Keena?" I asked.

Tut's latest girlfriend, this ol' wide-mouth, big-faceded heffa named Keena, defined the word pressed. Erywhere Tut went, she went. Erything he did, she did. Ery time she heard about him and another girl, her and her crew, the 1-3 Hunniez, jumped the broad without askin questions. Creepin with Tut was like playin with fire cuz Keena was a big girl and her crew was even deeper than minez. If she seen me and Tut together, I knew there'd be drama. The two of us already wasn't cool. Keena been beefin with me ever since I beat up her lil sister Chanel at school last year cuz she called me a bitch for cuttin in fronta her at the lunch line. I wasn't scared of Keena or anybody she rolled with, but I wasn't tryna get my ass kicked by a buncha fourteen year-olds, neither.

"I'on see her out hea'," Tut said, still leaning on me.

"So? You still betta back up," I warned, grabbin the burnt end of one of my Patra braids to have something to do with my free hand.

"Or what?"

"'Fore you start some'n you cain't finish," I said. I heard Kia say that to a youngin before and now just seemed like the right time to bust out with it. Tut raised his eyebrows and looked at me like he couldn't believe his ears. F'real-f'real, I couldn't believe I said it. There I was, talkin like a pro who could turn him out, when the truth was, I was still a virgin. I ain't really mean to jump myself out there like I wasn't. It was just the most smart-mouthded thing I could think to say at the time.

"It's like dat?" Tut asked.

"Yeah, it's like dat," I frowned, holdin my ground anyways. I sure as hell couldn't take it back now. I ain't want him thinkin I was scared, or worse yet, a tease.

"Why'onchu come to my house 'den," Tut suggested, and looked over his shoulder like he was tryna make sure nobody overheard us.

"Hunh? F-for what?" I stuttered. My heart was poundin so hard I could feel it in my ears. Tut looked around again and leaned towards my face for a whisper.

"So I kh finish what I started," he said. That's when Dhonni came runnin over and bumped him out the way.

"Damn, joe, why you got my girl all pinned up like dat? C'mon, Suga Baby. Skittles 'nem probly think we done got lost or some'n."

"Hunh? Oh, yeah," I nodded, and pushed past Tut to go four doors down to Trayonna's house.

"You heard what I said right?" Tut asked, grabbin my hand before I could get too far away.

"Yeah."

"So you gon do it?"

I had to think about it for a second. Was ready to go there with him? Was I gon forgive myself if I didn't? Was gettin with Tut worth catchin a beat down?

"Yeah," I answered with a bashful smile.

"Aight, 'den. Don't fake."

Days went by before I decided to take Tut up on his open-ended offer. I was still too scared to be alone with him, especially under them circumstances. The thought of being naked and vulnerable, and probly havin to fight Keena, Chanel, and both they crews once they found out about us was enough to make me say forget the whole thing. But them hormones racing through my blood and my friends' constant urging wouldn't let me pass it up. The way Kia and Trayonna made it seem, my virginity was something I had to hurry up and get rid of anyhow. Yeah, it was gon hurt, and yeah, we'd probly never talk again, but havin a bun like Tut as my first was something I had to jump on before he lost interest. Lookin at it like that made me come around quick. All I really wanted was Tut's interest in the first place. Havin no relationship with my father left me starving for male attention and affection, so Tut's sporadic attention and affection was just what I thought I needed. If the only way to keep him interested was to have sex with him, then I guess I was just gon hafta knock boots with the boy. I know, I know—I couldna been more wrong. But at twelve years old, it made perfectly good sense to me.

"Ain't no'by home, is it?" I asked, followin Tut up the steps to his house on Oates Street. It was the Friday before the first day of school, perfect timing for me to start seventh grade in junior high the next Tuesday as a bona fide big girl.

"Nah. My muhva don't come home till five," he replied, and swung open the front door. I ain't even get a chance to admire the fluffy black and white furniture in his livin room before Tut was grabbin me by the waist and movin me towards his room upstairs.

"Damn, why you rushin me?" I asked, stumbling up the dark stairwell in fronta him.

"Cuz I gotta get my lil sista from daycare at two-thirty and it's two o'clock now," he told me. I ain't like the idea of bein hurried through one of the biggest moments of my life, but one more glance at the puddin-brown boy with the silky black hair and the eager look in his squinty eyes and I decided to let it go.

Tut took me in his room and turned on the TV while he neatened it up a lil bit. I kicked off my shoes and got comfortable at the edge of his bed, pretendin to be absorbed in the rerun of *My So-Called Life* playin on MTV. I ain't know what to say but I felt like talkin, so I started to ask him all the things about him I always wanted to know. Like when was his birthday; if his parents was from another country, and if that had anything to do with him and his sister Nefertiti bein named after Egyptian royalty. But before I could say a word, Tut was on the bed beside me with one hand on my thigh and the other one goin up the backa my shirt tryna unhook my bra. I froze like a block of ice.

"What? What's wrong?" Tut asked, feeling me tense up.

"Nuffin," I lied.

"You ain't scared is you?"

"Nah."

"'Den why you got y' legs closed so tight?" he asked, and tried to pry my knees apart. "You ain't neh' did it before or some'n?"

I started to lie and say I did but I couldn't think of a story to back it up quick enough.

"Damn, you ain't neh' did it before?" Tut asked, amazed.

"No," I mumbled. I couldn't figure out why he, like Kia and Trayonna, came off like being a virgin was such a bad thing. But I knew one thing for sure — I wasn't tryna have the same answer to that question anymore. It made me feel like such a lil girl.

"Damn, I got me a virgin," Tut said after a short pause with this look on his face I couldn't read. Then he surprised me by smiling and adding, "Dat's aight. At least I ain't gotta strap up."

He started pullin off his T-shirt like erything was poseda be cool after that, but I frowned at him like he lost his damn mind. I mighta been inexperienced, but I hung out with enough teenagers to know that skippin on protection was askin for trouble.

"Fuck dat. You betta put on two rubbers, joe. I ain't tryna get pregnant," I told him.

"I ain't gon getchu pregnant. I know what I'm doin."

I gave him a doubtful look.

"F'real, young. I'ma be careful," Tut told me.

"You promise?"

"Promise. Cross my heart and hope to die; stick a needle in my eye," he vowed.

Well...I guess I could trust him this one time...I ain't make no more objections when Tut started kissin on my neck and undoin my clothes. I awkwardly slid outta my shirt, then my jean shorts, and erything else till I was down to nothin but my yellow Friday underwear.

"You sure you aight?" Tut asked one last time, standin up briefly to kick off his pants and shoes.

I nodded and took a deep breath. Well, here we go. Tut gave me a sloppy kiss and laid me down across his mattress. I closed my eyes and imagined us takin it slow, relaxin a lil bit when I felt his fingers pry me open and probe in and outta me like he was lookin for something. It was a tickly, arousing feeling and I couldn't help but squirm while he kept doin it, adding fingers and taking fingers out. I guess that was enough for him to think I was ready, so Tut pulled his boxers down and started to force hisself inside.

"Ow, got-damnit!" I fussed, when I felt a piercing pain shoot through my belly. He was tryna push it all in at once.

"What now?" Tut asked all exasperated.

"It hurt."

"It only hurt for a minute," he assured me.

"But—"

Tut moved my long braids out the way and started kissin and fingering me again, and for a minute, I was really feelin it. That is, until he started poking me all hard with that ramrod of his and the pain spread like fire through my whole entire lower body.

"Ow, man!" I exclaimed, scooting back.

"Damn! Why you keep movin away?"

"Cuz it hurt!"

"Stop movin, 'den."

"I can't," I snapped. "Feel like I'm bout d' die!"

"Just keep still," Tut ordered, tryna hold me in place by my hips. He started pushin against my resistance again, but this time, insteada scooting back, I closed my eyes, clenched my teeth, and he slid right in. Bein all filled up for the first time hurt like a mug and it felt too weird for me to like just yet. I ain't start to enjoy the feelin till I got useta the spreading pain, and then it was only for a few seconds. Seem like soon as Tut started gettin into it, cuz was all pushin and grindin into me like he was tryna see how far up in me he could go. I was hurtin so bad I couldn't even complain. I wanted to slide back again and end it all or better yet, hold him still, but Tut had a kung-fu grip on my hips and was not tryna let go *or* stop movin. So I grabbed my ankles and grit my teeth, and forced myself to take it like a big girl. I thought the madness would never end. I tried to concentrate on anything other than the pain—the TV, the SWV poster pinned up on the wall ahead of me, the water spots on the ceiling. Just when I thought I couldn't take no more, Tut gave me three of his hardest strokes, then collapsed on toppa me all outta breath. Then just like that, it was over.

Tut rolled to the other side of me and put his hands behind his head like he just finished the greatest show on earth. I looked down at the milky white mess seeping outta me onto the comforter between my legs, then back at him.

"Damn, girl! I couldn't even hold dat j'on," Tut told me all outta breath, leaning over briefly to wipe up the nut with the corner of his T-shirt.

"So what dat mean?" I asked.

"Nuffin. You be aight."

Disappointed, I pulled my braids over my shoulders to cover up my breasts and tried to sit all the way up. I *know* that wasn't all there was. Didn't we forget to do something? That shit ain't even last from one commercial break to the next. I ain't even feel the heat in my body or the flutters in my stomach like Kia said I would if I got some good ding-ding. All that pain for nothing? Something had to be missin. I turned over on my side and looked at Tut.

"So dat's it?" I asked. Tut looked at me all crazy like I just told him I was really a man or some shit.

"Yeah, dat's it," Tut answered, wiping his sweaty forehead with the back of his hand.

I looked at him like he couldn't be serious. The worst part was knowin that he was. Tut fixed hisself back in his boxers, leaned up to grab the remote, and started flippin through the channels. I sighed.

"What's wrong witchu? It ain't feel good?" he asked, lookin at me all concerned.

"No," I pouted. "It hurt."

"Dat's cuz it's your first time. Next time it won't hurt so bad."

I started to ask if that meant we was gon definitely see eachother again, but I ain't want him thinkin I was pressed.

"So dat's it, hunh?" I asked again.

"Yeah, boo, dat's it. Why you keep aksin?"

"Cuz," I started, and stuck the tip of my thumb in my mouth. "I thought it was gonna be more to it 'den dat. Ain't it poseda last longer or some'n?"

Tut shook his head no.

"Nah," he told me in his most assuring tone. "Two, three minutes is bout right."

"You sure?"

"Yeah, I'm sure. I'm the one who did it before, remember."

I sighed again and attempted to get comfortable on his narrow bed. I was *up-set.* I mean, I guess Tut did aight and all, but this sex shit ain't impress me like I thought it would. I was expectin fireworks like the Fourth of July, but all I got was a sparkler at best. Maybe he was right. If we did it again, maybe I'd like it better. I started to ask him what was up with round two, but Tut was already outta bed and pullin on his pants.

"It's almost two-thirty. I gotta jet," he said frantically, lookin at the clock on his VCR.

Before I could object, he was tossin my clothes at me and smackin me on the feet to get up and get moving. Embarrassed and blown, I hurried into them. It took erything in me not to punch that nigga in the backa his head. Took even more not to cry. I'on know why I felt used, but I did. Used and unappreciated. I wanted to ask who he thought he was for dismissing me like that, but it would have been foolish. I wasn't his girl. He ain't hafta treat me like no princess. Instead, I slid into my shoes and sulked behind him as Tut led the way downstairs and outta his house.

"Aight, 'den," Tut said, already jogging in the direction of his sister's day care.

"Aight."

"I'll holla atchu later," he promised.

"Whateva."

I gave Tut one last look and rolled out, walkin stiffer than a sore cowboy. I thought about how much Dhonni and Trayonna would flip when I told em what happened, and how Dhonni would probly laugh and tell me I shoulda just stayed a virgin with her. Walkin down the street with wobbly legs, feelin like I just got cheated outta something special, I kinda wish I did.

"Ay, Shai! Look what I got!"

Krys slammed the front door shut and scurried to the kitchen all excited with her arms fulla something red and tan. I was too busy fryin pork chops to see what it was till I noticed some lightskinded broad come trailing in my house behind her. My full attention on both of em now, I looked from the girl to Krys to the stuff she was holdin, then over at the clock showin me it'd been almost three hours since Krys left for the gas station store up the street. Wonder what took her so long. Before I could ask, Krys and the girl was in the kitchen jabbering at me.

"Look! Ain't 'dis cute?" Krys asked, holdin up a red Christian Dior purse, visor, and sandal set. It wasn't real—probly something from the Chinese store or a street vendor. But it was cute and exactly like the set I been wanting to buy from Nordstrom's for months.

"Yeah, dat's nice. Where you get it?" I asked.

"Some'my got it for me."

"Got it for you?"

"Shai, please. I toldju I was a pimp," Krys answered all cocky with a pop of her collar.

"Well, some'my need to get you a watch, *pimp*, cuz you'on know how to keep track uh' time," I snapped, seriously contemplating poppin her in the damn forehead. "Whatchu been doin all this time? Why it take you three hours to go somewhere two minutes up the street?"

"Cuz...I got sidetracked."

"Sidetracked?" I frowned. "How the fuck you gon—"

"Damn, Shai, you bein all rude and shit. Don't you see my friend standin hea'?" Krys interrupted before I could finish bombing her out. My attention immediately went back to the lightskinded girl.

"You the one bein rude. Introduce her," I said.

Krys did some dramatic Kiki Shepherd thing like she was presenting an artist at the Apollo and introduced the girl as Iyania from the next building over. With that said, I nodded a hello and went back to Krys.

"So back to my question. What took you so long?" I asked.

"Damn, man, it's Sunday. Cain't I go outside and chill once in a while?" Krys complained.

I guess the girl did deserve some free time, seein how she worked five days a week alongside me in the shop. I had her up there puttin in long hours like that was her real job or some shit, but I figured the longer I kept her in my sight, the better off she'd be.

Just like I anticipated, Krys ain't take no time gettin friendly with the youngins in my neighborhood. It's only been two weeks since the girl got here and she already had a damn entourage. A lotta nights after we got home from work, she'd go sit on the front steps with one of them black-n-milds and be out there shootin the shit for hours. Krys wasn't bold enough to ask if she could go wandering off with none of her new friends yet, but I knew it was only a matter of time before she did. I done seen that girl Iyania hangin around a racka boys on more than one occasion, and the way I kept catchin her and Krys lookin up at the balcony to see if I was watchin, I could tell they was cookin up some kinda scheme.

"Y'all hongry?" I asked, settin up a plate covered with paper towels to drain the grease off the pork chops that was done.

"Nah, we bout d' go eat," Krys told me, tryna walk out the kitchen all fast.

"Eat where? Did I say you kh go somewhere?"

"Dang, man, we just goin to Friday's."

"Dat still don't sound like you aksin me," I said, rollin my eyes.

"Aight, fine. *Can I go to Friday's?*" Krys asked, rollin hers back.

"Wit who?" I quizzed.

"Iyania."

I stopped cookin to look her in the face and see if she was lyin. That lil heffa had the nerve to look me in the eye like she wasn't, but I could tell she was leavin out something. She was too anxious to go and too reluctant to gimme all the details.

"Well, I kh see you bout d' start swellin, so—"

"Dag, man," my cousin laughed. "Why you always think I'm lyin? I *am* goin wit Iyania."

And probly some of them boys, too. Probly someplace nowhere near a Friday's. Krys musta forgot it ain't been that long ago since I was fifteen and gettin into erything. She was obviously gonna bullshit around the bush till I agreed to let her go, so fuck it. I ain't tryna run no prison here. The last thing I need is for Krys to feel like she still at home with a racka rules and regulations she was just gon find creative ways to lie her way around anyhow. Then again, I ain't want Krys thinkin she could run wild the whole summer. I mean, she was here for a reason and I was poseda be stoppin her delinquency—not addin to it.

I decided to be cool about it, though. Maybe if I eased up, she'd see me more as a friend—you know, somebody she could talk with and listen to.

"You kh go," I said. "Just call me if you gon do anything else."

"Oh, well, we goin to the movies too," Iyania volunteered.

"Yeah, so we gon be out real late," my cousin added.

"How late?"

"Real late. Why? I got a curfew or some'n?"

I thought about comin off as a warden again.

"Nah. Long as you hea' before the sun come up, you good."

"Aww, boosted!" Krys exclaimed.

She hurried off to the den to change, and came back minutes later in all red and tan to match her new Christian Dior set, the most noticeable thing on her bein a red V-neck shirt of minez. The j'on was already low-cut, but Krys had fixed her boobs in it so they was practically fallin out.

"Hope you'on mind me borrowin your shirt," Krys started before I could say anything. "It was in that basket uh' clean clothes you put in my room yesterday."

"Exactly. I just washed it and now you got your body in it. You just gon ruff my shit like dat?"

"I ain't gon stink it up, man. Chill," Krys sneered. She flipped her braids over her shoulders and adjusted her tiddies again. "What?" she asked when she saw me glaring at her.

I coulda got on her for takin my clothes or leavin out the house lookin like she bout to end up on a *Girls Gone Wild* tape, but I ain't wanna embarrass her in fronta her friend. Besides, I had to get back to my pork chops.

"Don't take my fuckin clothes no more," I warned, goin back towards the kitchen.

"Fine. I won't. Bye," Krys said, turnin to leave.

"Bye. Be safe. And I mean dat in ery way."

"Oh, you ain't gotta worry bout me, champ. I got rubbers."

"Yeah, you gon need a lotta those in Friday's," I remarked sarcastically.

"Sure will," Krys winked.

And with that, my lil cousin tossed her braids over her shoulder one last time and was out the door. I watched after her, my fingers crossed that she wouldn't do anything too out-the-way. Then again, it looked like she was bout to do just that and then some.

Man, oh, man. What did I get myself into?

CHAPTER FIVE

I always thought turnin thirteen would make me an adult cuz more than a few teenagers I knew held down jobs, had kids, and struggled to support they families like they parents did. Where I was from, not too many of us had both parents in the house, so becomin a teenager meant it was time to grow up and be responsible—especially if you had lil brothers and sisters to help look after.

I turned thirteen the summer of '95 but I considered myself a adult way before that. Between hangin out with Kia, raising up the lil ones when Mommy wasn't home, and havin a whoever, whatever, maybe this time will be better attitude when it came to sex, I did more before I officially became a teenager than some big girls I knew. I was barely old enough to be into boys before I found myself jaded towards em. I mean, I was still fulla adolescent heat and the want for male attention and affection. But insteada gettin all silly over a nigga I liked, I nursed my wants and needs with a steady stream of boyfriends that I chumped and dumped before they could dump me. Gettin with Tut made me realize just how easy it was to get all worked up and disappointed when my feelings was involved. The beef I got into with Keena and Chanel because of him changed me, too. After they ran up on me and Dhonni nine deep with baseball bats and broken bottles tryna crack our heads open, I decided it was time to stop sleepin. I started carryin a blade on me to slice a bitch up in case I ever got caught in a jam without my crew. My blade was my protection. It was also my main work tool. Kia taught me how to pop security sensors offa whatever I stole when we went on missions. My knife became as close to me as the girls I grew up with. Many a time I used it to scare off haters and steal something we needed at home cuz Mommy's checks ain't stretch far enough.

Turnin thirteen only made me officially grown in ery way that I wasn't already. I took care of our house, I stole for a livin, and I had just as many man problems as my mother. Far as I was concerned, I was a adult. And with me lookin the way I looked, and knowin the shit I knew, couldn't nobody tell me otherwise.

My birthday fell on a Friday that year, and I wanted to have a house party like Trayonna did for her big thirteen. Mommy wouldn't let me cuz we ain't have the room or the extra money for no party, but I pouted about it so much that my Aunt Roz felt bad and decided to throw me a cookout. Gettin together at my aunt's house with family wouldn't be the same as freak-a-deekin in a dark basement with my peers, but a cookout was a cookout, and I always liked seein my crazy uncles and hangin out with my cousins Sweet Nika and Irshad around they way in Southwest. Since it was a family affair, Mommy ain't think it woulda mixed well to bring none of my friends along, but it was all good. It still ended up being a tight-ass day.

"So whatchu wanna do? Play Truth or Dare?" I asked my cousin Sweet Nika. As usual, we crept off from the resta the family to girl talk and fill eachother in on what we been up to since the last time we was together at Christmas. Now we needed something to do other than sit around the house watchin videos on The Box.

"We gotta get more people. Where Cerrone and Irshad go at?" Sweet Nika wondered about our brothers.

"Who knows? 'Day outside somewhere. Wanna go look for em?"

"Aight, but I'm tryna get anuh' plate first."

We was on our way through the kitchen to the back door, where the sound of several yelling voices comin from the alley outside got louder and louder. The first thing I thought about was all that beer and gin my Uncle Ray-Ray brought in his giant styrofoam cooler. I knew from experience that any time there's *that* much alcohol and *that* many Black folks in one place, you can bet there's gonna be some kinda drama goin down before the night's over—especially if my family's involved. I was definitely not tryna see another scene like last summer when Uncle Ray-Ray got drunk and was tryna cut his Spades partner with a four-inch pocket knife for reneging on a book. Me and Sweet Nika hurried to go look out the screen door and see what in the world was goin on.

"Don't tell me they done got d' fightin," Sweet Nika said, squeezin out the back door with me.

My Uncle Ray-Ray, Uncle Travis, and my great Uncles Willie and Boo was sittin around the same raggedy card table they always migrated to whenever we all got together, playin a serious game of Spades. Judgin by the nearly drained bottle of Seagrams at the center of the table and the empty beer cans on the ground around em, I knew they was good and to' up. They was slappin cards down and talkin shit loud enough to wake the dead. A couple of my younger boy cousins was gathered around em tryna hang with the big dogs, sneakin sips of Colt 45 and commenting on the game. They quieted down for a second after Uncle Travis dealt the cards and erybody was tryna see how many books they had. But when *Holy Ghost* by the Bar-Kays came on the radio and Uncle Ray-Ray started singin all wrong and off-key, the racket started up again.

"Look. All of em drunk as a skunk," I observed.

"F'real," Sweet Nika agreed, leadin the way into her backyard alley.

It was a nice day outside, just the right kinda cookout weather that only early summer along the mid-atlantic coast could bring. It was warm enough for shorts, but too cool for the pool. A slight breeze blew and the smell of hot dogs, hamburgers, and BBQ chicken and ribs floated on the air from where Cousin Peanut was gettin down on the grill. It started to make me hungry all over again, but after three plates of all that and Mommy's potato salad, I was so full I was ready to pop. Any more food and they'd hafta clean me up off the side of the house.

Sweet Nika fixed herself another plate and looked around for somewhere to sit. Of course she had to go over to the end of the long table where Mommy and them was busy grubbin on two bushels of Maryland blue crabs. Soon as we sat down, the conversation stopped and all eyes was on us.

"Well, well, well. Look what the wind blew in," Aunt Roz teased, dippin a cracked crab leg into a bowl of mustardy sauce.

"Nice for y'all to finally join us," Mommy said, pluckin a pinch of crabmeat out the pile that her new boyfriend Tone had made for her. "Baby, save me the dead man fingers," Mommy told Tone when she saw him pry the gills off a just-opened crab and toss em in the trash pile.

"You ain't poseda eat them," he said, retrieving em anyway.

"I know, but I like em cuz 'day salty."

Tone wiped the sweat from his brow with the back of his hand and went back to cleanin Mommy's crabs. For those of y'all who ain't familiar with crab-eatin culture, cleanin somebody's crabs for em is a big sign of affection. Them j'ons take so long to dig out enough meat worth eatin that most people quit tryin before they even get full. The fact that Tone was sittin there doin all the hard work for Mommy let erybody know he was really into her. My mother had Tone so sprung he was basically hand-feedin her, which surprised the hell outta me cuz mosta Mommy's boyfriends was so stuck on theyself that doin something for her was a stretch. And I thought Kia knew how to keep a man wrapped around her lil finger. Lemme find out Mommy had a lil some'n up her sleeve, too.

Ery since the two of them hooked up this past October, Tone been addicted to Mommy like she was made of fine wine and shots of exstacy. A fifty-two year-old widower from Norfolk, Tone owned a auto collision repair shop not too far from American University. It was a fledgling business on a rich side of town with a lotta potential to make a lotta money. Anyways, Mommy was on her way to see about gettin a job at Sibley Memorial Hospital when her '77 Nova quit on her and she had to trot down Wisconsin Avenue in four-inch heels to find help. She ended up at Tone's shop and enticed him so much that he offered to get her car fixed and take her out to dinner that night. It's been on ever since. Tone was far from Mommy's type cuz he had a career, a self-made business, and more on his mind than where he was gettin his next bag of weed from. He was jive kinda old and he wasn't all that cute neither, but he was dedicated to keepin her happy, paid some of our bills like they was his, and was more cordial than mosta Mommy's niggas to me and my brother and sisters. I could do without all his corny jokes and that loud, rambling way of talkin he had, but for the most part Tone was aight. And for once, Mommy had a better attitude and she was actually being nice to me for a change. But because of Tone she wasn't her old chain-smokin, mean-ass self no more, and I couldn't figure out if that was a good thing or a bad one.

"So whatchall girls been up to?" Aunt Roz asked, and slurped the beer broth out the crab shell she just cracked open.

"Nuffin," me and Sweet Nika answered at the same time.

I wished my cousin would hurry the hell up, or at least take her plate around front so we could get away from all they probing eyes. Whenever Mommy and her two sisters get together, there's always a million questions.

"Hot dog, look atchu. Dat's a sharp lil outfit you got on, Shai," Aunt Josie commented. I had on a turquoise China doll dress with my new high heel Mary Janes and knee-high socks that Mommy got for my birthday. Cerrone tried to joan and tell me I looked like a busted-ass version of Stacy Dash from *Clueless*, but who cares what he think? My outfit was straight outta *Seventeen* magazine. That boy don't know style when he see it.

"Girl, I got that from Marshalls," Mommy told her. "Honey Child, stand up and let Aunt Josie see you."

I started to get self-conscious cuz I knew as soon as I got up, they'd start makin a big deal bout how much I grew since last year. And I wasn't in the mood to have that conversation in fronta my cousin and the resta the hens at the table. I stood and did a quick spin and sat back down just as fast.

"Lord, that girl get bigger ery time I see her. You see the caboose on that child?" Aunt Josie squeaked. I rolled my eyes to the sky like *here we go again.*

"I'm tellin you, it's in the water," Mommy announced to erybody at the table.

"Gotta be. Damn, Honey Child, how tall is you now? Five-two? Five-three?" Aunt Roz asked me.

"I'on know."

"Shai useta be a lil ol' thang," Aunt Roz said. "Useta walk around lookin like a stick wit toothpicks for arms and legs."

"Toothpicks, my foot. Look at them legs now, Roz. Look like she walkin around on hams."

I turned to Sweet Nika and pleaded with my eyes for her to hurry up but she ain't catch the message. She was too busy stuffin her face and laughin at me.

"Mmm-hmm. You know what dat mean. Hey, Shai, you got a boyfriend yet?" Aunt Josie asked me suddenly.

"Yeah," I mumbled.

"Get outta town! Brenda, you let her have a boyfriend already?! What is wrong witchu?"

"Whatchu mean what's wrong wit me? Whatchu so damn uptight for, Josie?" Mommy snapped. "Ain't nothin wrong wit the girl havin a boyfriend. It's perfectly natural."

"Perfectly natural?". You lettin her run buck wild, Brenda."

"Buck wild? Excuse me, but I'on believe I asked for any advice on how to raise my damn kids. I think I know what I'm doin since I got more than one, thank you very much."

"What the hell do havin a housefulla damn kids mean if you ain't there watchin em? Got four kids and don't know what to do wit none of em —"

"Hey, hey, hey got-damnit! Stop dat shit!" my Aunt Roz exclaimed, raising her hands to quiet they arguing. Lord knows if she ain't say something, Mommy and Aunt Josie probly woulda got into it like they did at almost ery other family gathering.

"I'm just sayin, Brenda. You let Shai have a boyfriend and you know what's gon happen next," Aunt Josie warned. "Your *baby* gon come home wit a *grandbaby* for you one uh' these days."

"She betta not," Mommy said, and gave me a look. "Shai know better."

"Well, whatchu think gon happen, Brenda? You let the girl have a boyfriend and she bound d' get pregnant. Whatchu think they be doin when you ain't home?"

"I'on know. But Shai know I'll tear into her ass some'n terrible if she even *think* about havin sex in my damn house."

"So she'll just end up doin it somewhere else," my aunt tried to make her realize. My lips twitched to tell her shut up cuz that's exactly what I was doin when Mommy was at work. I think a part of Mommy knew it, too, but what could she do to stop me? Havin a new boyfriend herself and workin twelve hour shifts four, sometimes five, days a week kept her out the house too much to be on my case. She ain't have time to keep up with my hot ass *and* worry bout my brother and sisters. She ain't have time to focus on any one of us, for real.

"I know Nika call herself havin a lil boyfriend," Aunt Roz said, understandin Mommy's predicament and tryna get her out the hot seat. "Even though she know I'on play dat. What's his name, Nika?"

My cousin started lookin around like she heard something faraway that got her attention.

"Ay, I be right back. I hear some'my callin me," Sweet Nika said, and started to get up.

"Sit 'cha ass down, girl," Aunt Roz ordered. "See how she be doin? Won't admit it to me but I know what's up. I be seein em walkin 'round together. I see erything. This neighborhood ain't but so big."

"'Day at dat age, Roz. Bein all secretive and whatnot. You remember how we was wit Mama," Aunt Josie said.

"Oh, Lord," Mommy sighed, and the three of them started gigglin at the memory of how they was as teenagers. I found it hard to imagine em that young.

"Damn, y'all remember when Josie was goin wit dat boy Eddie from up Langley Park?" Aunt Roz asked. Aunt Josie tried to shush her.

"I remember Eddie!" Mommy exclaimed. "The yellow boy wit dat big-ass afro. He useta cut the grass in fronta our house sometimes."

"Yeah, he useta cut Josie, too."

"Hush now, Roz," Aunt Josie laughed.

Me and Sweet Nika made faces and looked at eachother cuz we couldn't imagine our mothers, let alone Aunt Josie the angelic one, doin the wild thing. Not even the one time it took to make each of us.

"God, I hope minez don't never get like dat," Aunt Josie said, shakin her head.

"Krys is such a sweetie pie, I doubt she gon do some of the shit we did," Aunt Roz assured her.

"*Sheeiiit*, you never know," Mommy warned. "Girls get to actin all stank and secretive like dat, no matter how sweet 'day was when 'day was younger. Once 'day start bleedin, you betta watch out, boy. Believe you me, dat attitude ain't gon be nuffin nice."

"My baby ain't gon be like dat," Aunt Josie argued. "She gon be a good girl as long as I got anything to do wit it. Cuz if she don't, I'ma lay her ass out."

"More power to you," Mommy told her, and gave me an accusatory look. "I said the same thing, but you see what I'm dealin wit."

"What?" I snapped and made a face at her. I had about enough of they asses talkin bout me like I wasn't even sittin there. "Nika, is you ready? I thought we was gon find Cerrone and Irshad."

"Aight, c'mon. Let's be out," my cousin said, pickin up her last couple BBQ ribs and leadin the way down the alley. Krys came bouncin after us, twirling a pink and silver baton in her hand.

"Whatchu want?" I demanded.

"It's a free country. I kh go where I please," she said in that annoying-ass, squeaky voice of hers. I wasn't in the mood to hear her or have her tryna follow me and Sweet Nika around like she always did before we ruffed her up and sent her away.

"Aunt Josie, come get this girl 'fore I hurt her!" I called back at the table.

"Shai, leave her alone!" Mommy cut in. "You need d' be nice to her. Matter fact, take her witchu. And y' sistas, too!"

I rolled my eyes and watched in dismay as the three tag-alongs tagged along with us. Sweet Nika saw the look on my face and laughed.

"I'm sicka gettin stuck wit 'deez kids," I complained, followin her out the alley into the street.

"F'real 'doe. Fuck all 'dis babysittin shit."

"Ooh, I'ma tell you said the f-word!" Krys exclaimed, pointin a finger at Sweet Nika. My lil sisters started sicin it, all pointin and *ooh*-in, too.

"No you not. Cuz if you do, I'ma smack you so hard your eyes gon uncross," Sweet Nika threatened. "Dat goes for you, too," she threatened my sisters even though they eyes was already straight.

Bet all three of em shut they asses up, though. We started walkin across Delaware Ave in the direction of the park by Friendship Baptist Church. Our brothers usually went there to play ball and hang out after they ate. Soon as we set foot on the mulch, Sweet Nika started sniffin and lookin around.

"Hmm, you smell dat?" she asked, flaring her nostrils so she could take a deep breath. I started sniffing, too.

"Smell like bud," I said, catchin the scent of burnin herbs in the breeze.

"You mean some'my smokin weed?!" Krys exclaimed.

It was comin from the direction of a clump of boys across the field from us. Telltale clouds of thick white smoke hung in the air around em.

"So dat's where 'day went," Sweet Nika said, squintin hard to get a better look, then nodded when she recognized her older brother. "Yup, 'dare go Irshad."

"And Cerrone, too," I said when I saw my brother's tall, skinny frame. "Who them uh' two niggas, 'doe?"

"Dat's just Cruddy and Fat Chris," Sweet Nika told me, going towards em. Krys paused and started makin noises like she was tryna talk, all nervous like she usually get when we bout to do something she scared of.

"W-w-why we goin where 'day at?" Krys asked, lagging back a lil bit. "W-w-we gon get in t-t-t-trouble."

"No we ain't, you big scaredy-cat. Why cain't you just shut up and c'mon like Treasure and Sparkle? 'Day lil babies and you'on see them cryin," I snapped, grabbin my lil sisters by the backa they necks and pushin em in the direction of the boys.

"Is you comin or what?" Sweet Nika asked Krys. "I'm tryna hit dat bob and you slowin me up, joe."

"I'm t-t-tellin you, we g-g-g-gon get in trouble," Krys repeated, still hesitatin.

"Damn, Stutterin John. You'on neh' wanna have no fun," I sneered.

"F'real 'doe," Sweet Nika agreed, leadin the way over to the boys. Krys followed reluctantly.

Cerrone was the first one to notice us when we got close enough. He nudged my cousin Irshad, who tried to hide the J behind his back while the chunky darkskin boy beside him stood there lookin caught. The cute boy in the white shirt tried to fan the smoke away like we ain't see it already, but there was no denying that shit. It was too late to play it off.

"Whatchall want, comin ova hea' lookin like a broke-ass Xscape?" Cerrone demanded.

"Boy, shut up," Sweet Nika snickered. "Whatchall doin anyway? Smokin?"

"Yeah, and 'day got the nerve d' be doin it behind the church, too. Y'all goin to hell on a skateboard," I said, leanin against the stone wall they was all posted up on.

"You must be imaginin things," Irshad told me.

"'Den explain the smoke." Sweet Nika crossed her arms over her chest and tapped her foot, waitin for a answer.

"It's 'dis j'on, man," the chunky boy said, holdin up a unlit cigarette. Me and my cousin looked at eachother.

"You's a lie. You ain't even light dat j'on, Fat Chris," Sweet Nika pointed out. Youngin made a face like he ain't know what to say. That's when the cute boy coughed out a chest fulla smoke and the four of them bust out laughin.

"Fuck it," Irshad said, and brought the J to his lips.

"Y'all betta not tell, eiva," Cerrone warned. "'Specially you, Krys the Cross-eyed Lion."

"W-w-why you lookin at me?" Krys whined. "I ain't gonna ssssay nuffin."

"Yeah, aight. If we get in trouble, you the first one I'm comin after."

Krys pushed her glasses up on her nose and crossed her arms.

"T-t-t-toldju I ain't gon say nnnnuffin," she stuttered.

Irshad passed the J to my brother.

"The fuck do y'all want man, damn?" Cerrone demanded when he realized we wasn't goin away.

"What it look like? We tryna hit dat bob witchall."

"*Sheeeiiit*," Irshad said, and gave us a look like we had to be playin. My brother held the J out to Sweet Nika, then snatched it back when the resta the boys started complainin bout us fuckin up the rotation.

"Sike-a-boo-boo," he said, and blew smoke in her face. "Like the song say, 'if you ain't put five on it, you cain't get high on it'. Y'all betta go down K Street and getchall own."

"Dat's messed up," I complained. My brother shrugged and blew another tower of smoke in Sweet Nika's face. Some of it drifted down to Krys, and of course she had to have a fit.

"S-S-Stop, C-C-C-Cerrone! D-D-Don'tchu know w-w-weed burns brain cells?!" she screeched. "Haven't you ever heard the sayin 'there's nnnnno hope in d-d-d-dope'?!"

"N-n-n-no, I hhhhhhaven't," Cerrone teased.

"L-l-l-leave me alone! D-D-D-Dat's why I-I-I-I'ma tell!"

Krys stuck out her tongue and ran across the grass towards Sweet Nika's house.

"You betta not, Krys!" Irshad yelled.

"S-S-S-S-Stupid!" she called over her shoulder.

"Damn, I cain't stand her ass," I grumbled. I went over to the other side of the cute boy in the white shirt and leaned against the wall. Up until then, I ain't really pay him no mind. I mean, I had a boyfriend and a couple youngins back home that I was messin with on the side, so it ain't like I was lookin. But when I noticed him cuttin his eyes at me and the strange sensation it sent through me, I started singin a whole different tune. That was the first time I ever really looked at Dartanyan and I'll never forget it.

Back then, he was the same rugged-ass, babyface boy I fell in love with. Even if I knew then how he was gonna turn out to be the complete asshole he grew up to be, I still woulda got with him. Something bout Dartanyan was magnetic. Irresistible. *Sinfully* irresistible. He was short and kinda stocky but cut, with a reddish brown complexion like he was mixed with something and a soft, funny texture to his bushy hair that couldn't decide if it wanted to be kinky or straight, so it did both. I knew he was cute when we first walked up, but being that close to him gave me butterflies, hot flashes, and tingles from head to toe all at once. Fuck bein cute. That boy was *fine*. Dartanyan looked like a young Allen Iverson with his bright, seemingly innocent eyes, and thick, sexy lips that kissin was meant for. He had a thin mustache and a line in one of his eyebrows where the hair ain't grow. Something bout that and the way he was leanin against the wall made him appealing in the same way youngin in my third grade class who always got sent to the principal's office was appealing. He looked like he wasn't no stranger to trouble. There was a carelessness about him, a fearlessness like couldn't nothin in this world scare him or make him back down. I liked that shit. Somebody like that could handle me and all my badassdedness. The way Dartanyan stood there smokin and watchin me but pretendin not to sparked my curiosity. That's when it all started.

"Now dat Miss Goody-Two-Shoes is gone," Sweet Nika began. "Wsup wit passin dat bob?"

"Maybe y'all ain't hea' me the first time, so I'll say it again. *Hell* no."

"Ugh, Cerrone, you a egg. You see how he goin, Shai?"

I tried to tear my eyes away from his. Dartanyan looked up just a few seconds before and caught me lookin at him, and I was havin the hardest time breakin the stare.

"Hunh?" I asked, finally lookin away.

"Neh'mind. You missed it. C'mon, young. Don't no'by want dat bush 'day smokin no how. Shit smellin like burnt cat hair," Sweet Nika sneered.

I grabbed my lil sisters by the arms and told em to come on. As we went back in the direction of the park, I glanced over my shoulder to see if youngin in the white shirt was still watchin me. Sure enough he was.

"Ay, Nika," I whispered, leanin in close so no one could overhear.

"Who y' bruhva friend?"

"Fat Chris? Ugh, Shai, don't tell me you think Fat Chris is cute."

"No, dummy. I'm talkin bout cuz in'na white shirt."

"Oh, Cruddy?" Sweet Nika asked. "I wouldn't trip offa him. He got a girlfriend."

"So? I got a boyfriend. I just wanted d' know his name," I told my cousin, somewhat disappointed.

I glanced back again. I knew I could get Dartanyan, girlfriend or no girlfriend. The question was, did I really wanna put myself in that kinda situation again? I wasn't tryna get jumped or be outside with my crew scrappin over some nigga no more. Besides, I had to share enough shit at home. Why would I wanna share a boyfriend, too?

"Well, now you know," my cousin concluded. "Shai, you'on wanna mess with him. He cute as shit, but dat boy is terrible. His muhva kicked him out his house back where he useta live."

"F'real?" I asked, interested. "Where he from?"

"I'on know. Don't care, neiva."

"Well, I do."

I looked back one more time. I knew Sweet Nika was only tryna protect me, but something about Dartanyan wouldn't let me go. I had to go talk to that boy if it was the last thing I did.

"Don't say I ain't warn you," my cousin said, readin the expression on my face. "Cruddy ain't nuffin but trouble."

"Yeah, yeah. Watch them," I said, noddin at my lil sisters. Girlfriend or not, I at least had to go talk to youngin. It was rare for me to let a cutie like that pass by. I turned back around to face the direction the boys was standin and to my surprise, Dartanyan was motioning for me to come to him.

"You come here!" I called.

"Halfway!" he called back.

So we met halfway with erybody watchin us to see what was gon happen next. Before I could think of something clever to say, I was eye-to-eye with Dartanyan and my knees had turned to jelly.

"Wsup?" Dartanyan asked, lookin me over with that intense stare of his. His eyes was kinda low and glossy cuzza the weed, but they still made me feel like he saw erything about me, inside and out.

"Wsup."

There was a pause as the two of us checked eachother out.

"I ain't think you was gon talk d' me," Dartanyan started, with a smile in his big eyes that made me wanna smile, too. "I thoughtchu was gon carry me. You look mean as shit."

"I do?" I asked, touchin my face as if I could feel my expression. Dartanyan's powerful presence made me do stupid shit like that. He made me lose my cool in a goofy kinda way. Automatically, I was even more drawn to him for making me act outta character.

"Yeah. Whatchu poseda be anyways, Red? Pippi Longstocking?" he teased, flickin one of the long, auburn ponytails Kia had pinned in my hair Pocahontas-style.

"Fuck you mean?" I demanded, a lil irritated cuz he was joanin. I ain't like the way he was callin me Red, either. That shit got under my skin cuz it reminded me how much I looked like my father, but bein redbone with red hair, I heard it a lot.

"Damn, you feisty, ain't chu? I like dat shit. I like y' lil dress, too. Showin off them big, pretty legs," Dartanyan said boldly with another one of them smiles in his eyes. I felt my neck gettin all hot like it do when I'm blushing.

"Where you from? I ain't neh' seent you around hea' before," I said, feelin a lil friendlier. I was a sucker for blunt compliments.

"Southside," he told me.

"We is on 'na Southside," I pointed out. Sweet Nika and them lived in Greenleaf Gardens in Southwest, not too far from the Waterfront.

"Nah, young, I'm from the *real* Southside. 'Round 14th and Congress."

"Oh, Sowfeass? Anacostia?"

"Yeah," Dartanyan answered, and smiled for real this time. "Whatchu know bout my side, Red?"

"I know enough," I told him, even though I rarely ever went into Southeast. It wasn't my territory.

"Oh, yeah?" he nodded, then asked, "Where you stay at, sweetheart? I know you from 'na city. You'on look like no Mar'land girl."

"Norfeass," I told him proudly. "Trinidad."

"Trinidad, hunh?"

"Yup."

"Oh, so you think you bad now?" he asked with an amused half-grin. My neighborhood was one of the most infamous in Northeast.

"Nigga, I ain't gotta think it; I know it," I boasted, knowin me and erybody I ran with was worthy of the rep.

"Yeah, you talk a good a good one. So what's y' name, Red?"

"Is you gon stop fuckin callin me Red if I tell you?" I snapped.

"Maybe."

I made a face. This nigga was a asshole for real, but I gotta admit, I was kinda amused by it. Most youngins was intimidated by me and went outta they way *not* to press my buttons, but Dartanyan was the opposite. He went against the grain for the hell of it, just like me.

"Well, what's y' name?" Dartanyan repeated.

"My friends call me Suga Baby, but my real name Shai."

"Shai like the singin group?"

I nodded.

"Shai like…*And if I ehhhhver fall in looooove agaiiiiiin…*"

"Yeah, like dat," I snapped. I had to go through the same shit ery time I introduced myself. "It's short f' Rashaiyah, but don't no'by call me dat. 'Day cain't neh' say it right."

"Yeah? Don't feel bad. Eryby be fuckin up my name, too."

"What *is* your name?" I asked, even more attracted to him by the way he talked. Youngin had that funny Southeast twang and the kinda semideep voice I ain't see myself gettin tired of hearing no time soon.

"Oh, my bad. Dartanyan. My folks call me Cruddy, 'doe."

"Cruddy? Why 'day call you dat?"

"Cuz I'm a cruddy muhfucka," Dartanyan explained simply with a shrug.

We stood there for a while, absorbing eachother and lookin eachother over. Sweet Nika was right. Dartanyan was trouble with a capital "T". I could see it in erything from the battle scar in his eyebrow to the way he stood there all confident like nobody in the world could fuck with him. He was probly more trouble than he was worth, but I ain't care. That lil nigga stirred up something in me that my thirteen year-old vocabulary couldn't find words to describe. I had to concentrate to play cool and act like he wasn't phasing me — even though he already had me got. Dartanyan gave me a burnin heat from head to toe that was my hormones' way of tellin me I wanted him. My fast heartbeat and the trickle of honey in my draws was my body's way of sayin the same thing.

"So how old is you, *Suga Baby*?" Dartanyan asked me, sicing up my nickname.

I was useta talkin to older boys and lyin about my age so they wouldn't start actin funny when they found out I was just a kid. Most niggas ain't care how young I was but some backed off quick claimin they ain't wanna rob the cradle. I started to tell Dartanyan my real age cuz I was jive siced bout being thirteen, but I wasn't tryna scare him away, either.

"How old I look?" I asked.

"I'on know. Sixteen? Sehnteen?"

"I'm fih'teen," I lied, just to play it safe. "How old are you?"

"Sixteen. Be sehnteen in December…Damn, you kinda young in'na face d' be fih'teen," Dartanyan observed, lookin me over again. "But the resta you—got-damn, girl! You musta been drinkin y' milk, hunh?"

"It does a body good," I bragged.

"Yeah, you ain't neva lied. You phat t' death, young. When you gon lemme call you?" he asked, and pinched one of my thighs. "I'm tryna do some'n wit all this."

"Don'tchu got a girlfriend?" I asked accusingly, and smacked his hand away. He was turnin me on with the way he talked, but damn if I was gon make it easy for the nigga. I was schooled by the best on playin hard to get so I could get what I wanted later on.

"Don't worry bout dat," Dartanyan told me.

"Well, *don't worry* bout callin me, 'den."

I started to walk away and leave his ass standin there wonderin where he went wrong, but Dartanyan had game, too. He took a couple steps after me and started rappin me up.

"Damn, young, who toldju dat shit anyway? Sweet Nika?" Dartanayn asked. "Man, I ain't got no girl. I got friends, but ain't none of em my girl. I'm tryna make *you* my girl."

"How I know dat?"

"Cuz I'm tellin you," Dartanyan answered like I was gettin on his nerves. "You gon let me getcha number or what, slim? Cuz I'll leave you alone right now if you gon ack all fucked up about it."

He had switched it on me so fast and so smooth I ain't even know what hit me. Dumbfounded, and suddenly desperate at the thought of

losing him, I said,

"Gimme some'na write wit, 'den."

Dartanyan flipped out a pen from one of the pockets in his baggy jean shorts and handed it to me. I heard Kia's voice in the back of my head warning me to stay away from niggas who carry pens and paper on em, 'specially if they ain't comin from school, cuz they be the type to book a lotta girls. I ignored the warning and wrote my name and number on the back of his hand anyway. Call me hardheaded or whateverthefuck, but I was curious about the boy called Cruddy, and I wasn't tryna let him go.

"What's the latest I kh call you?" Dartanyan asked, lookin at my bubbly handwriting.

"Wheneva. My muhva don't care."

"I'ma call you tonight, 'den."

"You betta," I said as our eyes met one more time.

Dartanyan watched me walk away in the direction Sweet Nika and my lil sisters was waitin. I knew he was probly lyin bout havin a girl, but I wanted to do it to him anyway so my curiosity would be satisfied and we could go our separate ways. I already knew how the game went. Dartanyan seemed cool but I ain't figure him to stick around. He was too fuckin sexy and I knew I wasn't the only girl that thought so.

Ery Saturday, it's the same. I drag myself outta bed, go to work, and stand on my feet from ten in the mornin till almost eight at night, fryin and dyeing hair. My motivation to get through it was knowin I ain't hafta work Sunday or Monday. The money I made was also a boost, but sometimes it's hard havin to work so hard. Especially since I can remember a time when work to me was stealin a Gucci bag to resell for 100% profit, or helpin some nigga side hustle his dope. I wasn't makin as much steady bread then as I be makin now, but at least I had time to spend with my kids and shit. That's just how it is these days, though. Either you work like a dog and try to have a life in between, or you hustle and constantly look over your shoulder while you tryna live your life.

"Ay, Shai, you got a rattail comb?" Betina asked, checkin the pockets of her smock to see of she had one. She worked at the station next to minez and was forever losin something, then tryna borrow it from me.

"Ain't you just have a box of em?" I asked.

"Somebody took it out my drawer."

"Ain't nobody stole nothin from you. You just absent-minded," Miz Pam interrupted from the other side of the room. She was a older woman bout Mommy's age who was always ear hustlin and addin her two cents into shit that ain't concern her.

"What do bein absentminded gotta do wit anything?" Betina asked.

"Don't you remember takin it back there to the shampoo bar?"

"Krys, you see my combs back 'dare?" Betina shouted across the room.

Krys sighed and stopped readin her *Vibe* magazine to look from where she sat in fronta one of the shampoo bowls for Betina's box of combs. I grit my teeth cuz she was sittin on her ass again insteada foldin towels and sweepin up hair like I told her to when she ain't have nobody to shampoo.

"I'on see nuffin," she shrugged, goin back to her magazine.

"I know you see them towels need to be folded," I said.

"What towels? I ain't see no towels."

"Krys, don't play wit me. Stop sittin around and do some'n."

She was makin me look bad being all lazy like that. I could see my boss, Fatima, smoldering with disapproval from the front of the salon. It was like this almost ery day lately. Krys just refused to work unless I put some fire under her ass. I guess she thought I'd say forget it and let her stay home so she could chill with her friends, but I wasn't bout to let her off the hook that easy. She had to earn her keep somehow if she planned on stayin with me the resta the summer.

"Man, is it break time yet?" Krys yawned. "I need a Coke or some coffee or some'n. I'm tired as a mug."

"Dat's whatchu get for tryna stay out all night," I said.

"So what? I kh do that."

I ain't know if she was tryna carry me on the sly or not, but it sure did sound like it. I guess that's what I get for lettin her come and go as she please. Krys dipped out almost ery day this past week to go chill with her lil friends and pretty much stayed out till the first birds of the morning started chirping. I tried not to concern myself with where she was goin and what she was doin. I figured she'd be more honest with me since I ain't lock her down with a whole buncha rules and whatnots. But it wasn't quite workin out that way. Krys kept her business to herself, and closed up like a clam whenever I tried to get into it. I had to think of another way to handle this situation, and fast. At the rate we was goin, the whole summer was gon fly by with her still cavorting the streets and avoiding me. I could already see the disappointed looks on Aunt Josie and Uncle Travis' faces when I brought her home worse than she was before.

"Ay, I be back," Krys announced, draggin her feet to my station. She opened up the bottom drawer to grab her purse and started goin towards the front like she was bout to leave.

"Where you goin?" I demanded.

"To get a soda, I told you. I'm sleepy as sh—*Damn*, who is dat?!"

I turned to see who she was talkin about and kinda chuckled to myself as all eyes were fixed on my client coming thru the door. I could almost hear the tingle of excitement that rippled thru the shop when Shon strolled in just as casual and nodded hello to erybody who was suddenly in his face. He got the same reaction whenever he stopped by. I guess cuz it ain't often you see nice-lookin Black dudes with startlingly blue eyes and a smile that could charm the stripes off a zebra.

"Wsup, Shon," I called. Erybody who ain't already know I was the whole reason he stopped by, looked at me like they was surprised I was talkin to him.

"Wsup, Shai. Ay, when can you tighten me up? I'm wolfin it right now," he said, liftin up his hat to show me his bushed out hair.

"You know him?" Krys asked me under her breath, all amazed.

"Yes, nosy. He work around the corner at the barber shop. I braid his hair ery two weeks."

"Ay, hook me up, young. I'm tryna put dat to sleep."

"Girl…Dat boy like twenty, Krys. He too old f' you," I told my cousin in a sharply dismissive tone. Then I walked away before she could say anything else and made my way up front to check the appointment book. Of course Krys came sashaying up front too, all up in Shon's grill like a police light.

"Hi you doin?" she purred, twirling one of her long braids around her finger and givin him the eye.

"Wsup witchu, young."

Shon gave her a quick glance, then a long stare as I reached around the receptionist for the appointment book.

"Come back at five and I gotchu," I told him, findin the only gap of time I had left. Shon blinked hard and looked away from Krys to me like he just snapped out a trance.

"Hunh? When?" he asked.

"At five, boy."

"You should let me shampoo you first," Krys suggested.

"Yeah, I'ma probly need all dat. I ain't got my j'on washed since the last time."

"I'ma make sure I take *real good* care uh' you, 'den."

"Aight," he smiled. Krys twirled another one of her braids around her finger and gave him a wink. God, that girl was sickening. Not to mention unprofessional. As my boss Fatima looked over at her again with another disapproving frown, my face burned with embarrassment.

"Bye, youngin wit the pretty blue eyes," Krys beamed.

"Bye, um...what's your name?" he asked her.

"Jailbait," I interrupted. "Dat's my lil cousin, Shon. *Jailbait Jones.*"

"Oh, aight. I gotchu," he chuckled. The two of us exchanged looks before he strolled off, still smiling.

Krys rolled her eyes at me and stomped off towards the food court, mumbling under her breath bout me always blowin up her spot. I snickered at her back and took a second to write Shon's name in the book. Just when I was bout to go back to hot combing the client in my chair, somebody else came up to the front desk. I coulda left it to the receptionist to see what they wanted, but I wasn't all that enthusiastic bout rushin back to straighten no more of my client's thick-ass, heat-resistant hair.

"Kh' I help you?" I asked the tall, chocolate Amazon that suddenly materialized in fronta me. She ran a hand over her elbow-length dredlocks and gave me a warm smile.

"Y'all do kids' hair hea'?" she asked.

"Sure do."

"Good, cuz..." she tugged on the arm of the lil girl at her side, who looked up at me with big, light brown eyes that for some reason made my heart skip a beat. "I'm tryna get my daughter hair done," the woman continued. "I'on know if she need a relaxer or a press or some plaits, but I need some'my to do some'n with it by July Fourth cuz we goin outta town. That's this Wednesday, right?"

I found myself staring at the lil girl, tryna place her face with a name. She looked familiar as shit, like one of my cousins or something. She was orangy-brown like a ripe peach with eyes like minez and a mess of kinky auburn hair her mama twisted into short pigtails all over her head. She reminded me a lot of a cousin I remember from my father's side, but I couldn't figure out exactly who for the life of me.

"Yeah, the Fourth's on Wednesday...Umm...how old is she?" I asked, both to be nosy and to see if the girl was old enough to get a relaxer.

"Seven."

"Dat's a lil young to be puttin chemicals in her hair. Lil kids sweat a lot from goin to the pool and playin outside all day and stuff. Her hair gon break off a lot cuz it's gon be hard to keep moisturized. I kh press it, 'doe. Or give her some cornrows," I offered. I reached over the desk to grab a pinch of the girl's coarse, red hair to stretch it out and see how long it was. It jive put me off to find it felt just like minez did before I relaxed it, all rough and tight as wool on a sheep's ass.

"You kh press and curl it?" the woman asked.

"Mmmm...She be better off gettin some cornrows," I said, still feelin the lil girl's pigtail. "She got good braidin hair."

"Aight, well, plait it up for me. Put some extensions in it, too. That'll probly last longer."

I nodded and started flippin through the appointment book, tryna shake the funny feeling bouncin around the walls of my stomach. Something about that lady and her daughter was odd to me, and I was havin the damndest time tryna figure out what. I could tell the woman sensed my wonderment cuz she started lookin at me funny after a while like she was tryna figure me out, too.

"When kh you bring her in?" I asked, gettin back to business. "I got time in'na mornin and afternoon on Tuesday."

"Lemme get dat mornin appointment. I'm tryna beat rush hour on my way out," she told me.

"I heard dat. Well, you kh bring her in when we open at ten. I'll have her all braided up and ready to go by twelve at the latest."

"Sounds good d' me. How much you chargin?"

"For her? Sixty-five."

The woman nodded as if to say okay, and I started to write down the appointment. Then I caught myself.

"I ain't get y'alls name," I said, lookin up from the desk.

"Oh. I'm Kim and this is Jasmine," the woman told me.

"Aight. I'ma see y'all then. My name's Shai, by the way."

"Aight, Shai. See you Tuesday."

I gave Kim an appointment card and watched as she walked off with her daughter, wonderin what it was about the pair that had me so got. It wasn't till after I started workin on my next client that I realized I was still thinkin bout that lil girl's woolly red hair.

CHAPTER SIX

"Whatchu say dat boy name was again?" Kia asked me, scratchin her bare, round stomach.

I was upstairs in Kia's closet-sized room on the single twin mattress she called a bed, sittin between Dhonni and Trayonna, and waitin for the flatiron to heat up. I was tryin not to count the minutes by cleanin the dirt lines from underneath my nails, but I kept catchin myself lookin at the clock on top of Kia's milk crate nightstand. It was almost six, exactly one hour before I was poseda go meet Dartanyan in Congress Heights. Me, Dhonni, and Trayonna was bout to hook up with him and two of his friends to go back to his mama's house and chill till she came home from work at eleven, or at least till one of us decided it was time to roll out. Next to goin to the movies or hangin around Union Station, goin to a nigga's house was dating at its finest for us. The three of us was forever on missions like that, so this one wasn't nothin special. That's what I kept tellin myself anyhow. I usually ain't get all nervous and anxious before goin to go see some boy, but then again I wasn't usually gon go see no boy like Dartanyan.

"I said, what's his name, Honey Child?" Kia asked again, parting off another box in Trayonna's hair.

"Dartanyan, but eryby call him Cruddy," I answered. I buffed the airbrushed palm trees on my acrylic nails along the edge of my shirt to make em glossy again.

"Dartanyan? Dat's cute. Why 'day call him Cruddy, 'doe?"

"He say cuz he a cruddy muhfucka," I shrugged.

"Damn, he lettin you know how he goin off the t-o-p, hunh? At least he honest. Is he cute, Honey Child?"

"Kia, please. Eryby I mess wit is cute."

"I'on know," Dhonni interrupted. "You be slippin up sometimes."

"She sure do," Trayonna added, screwin up her face as Kia roughly brushed her hair into a rubber band. "'Member dat boy she was goin wit not too long ago, Kiss?"

"Ugh, young," Dhonni groaned. "Dat nigga grill was on E. He all looked like Craig Mack and shit."

"More like Craig Mack and Dennis Rodman put t'geva."

"So what? He had a car," I shrugged.

"And don't f'get about slim who work at Sports Zone."

"Yeah, cuz wit the wide-ass *Alien Nation* head! I bet *all* the necks on his shirts be stretched out! What his name was, Suga Baby? Waterhead? Apple Dapple?" Dhonni teased.

"Y'all wasn't sayin dat when he was givin me the hook up on all them muhfuckin shoes," I snapped at my two best friends as they cracked up laughin. "Anyways, *Kia*, youngin is definitely a bun."

"He betta be," Kia said. "I'm tellin you, Honey Child, don't neh' mess wit no'by you'on think would make pretty babies. Cuz if you accidently get pregnant, you *do not* wanna be worrin if y' child gon come out lookin like Magilla Gorilla or some shit."

"C'mon now, Mommy. Your girl got good taste," I assured her.

"Aight. I still gotta see him f'myself, 'doe. And he betta have him some money in his pockets, too. *Always look for the niggas wit money,*" my play mother emphasized. "Ain't none uh' my daughters messin wit no ugly-ass, bamma-ass, broke-ass niggas. Y'all too cute d' be goin out like dat."

And she was right. Me and my play sisters was top notch bitches in training. Whatever Kia said was gospel as far as we was concerned.

"Damn, this child," Kia groaned suddenly, clutching her stretched out stomach. She messed around eight months ago and got pregnant by this boy she been chillin with since she broke up with her main bun. He was some fine-ass youngin named Tejuan from Riggs Park, who was broke as a joke but looked enough like DeVante from Jodeci to make Kia let his lack of funds slide. I was still trippin off the fact that play mother was becomin a real mother at sixteen years old. Now Mommy *really* ain't like me hangin around her. She carried on so bad sometimes you woulda thought pregnancy was a contagious disease and Kia was out to infect erybody.

"Hi the baby doin?" I asked, puttin a hand on Kia's stomach to feel for a kick. I was more amazed by her expectant belly than I ever was when

Mommy was pregnant with my sisters. I guess it jive lunched me out that a girl I knew since she was eight was actually havin a baby.

"Gettin on my last fuckin nerve kickin me to death. Cain't wait till this lil nuisance come out. Mama tryna party again."

"You know what it's gon be?" Trayonna asked, squintin her eyes shut while Kia coiled her hair into a Nubian knot.

"No," Kia griped. "Dat lil bastard won't sit still for no sonogram. I'on care what it is anyways. I just hope it get Tejuan gray eyes."

"Whatchu gon name it if it's a boy?" Dhonni asked.

"I already toldju. If I have a boy, I'ma name him Jodeci. If I have a girl, I'ma name her Zhané."

"Kia, you pressed. You actually gon name the boy Jodeci cuz Tejuan look like DeVante?"

"Yup. And if I have a girl, I'ma name her Zhané cuz them bald-head bitches kh sing! What's dat song 'day got: *Sendin my looooooove to yoooooouuuu...*"

"You bout d' set dat child up f' life," I said. I couldn't imagine naming no baby after a damn R&B group on purpose. Believe me, the poor kid will never hear the end of it once they start goin to school.

"Nah, you bout d' set *yourself* up if you keep dat on," Kia smiled, nodding at the Reebok tennis skirt set I fished outta her closet. I was only poseda be tryin it on, but it was too cute not to wear to Dartanyan's house.

"What's wrong wit it?" I asked, standin up to straighten out the pleats.

"Girl, is you blind? Wit dat big ol' booty you got, dat j'on gon be short as shit in'na back. You be lucky if it cover your whole ass. Watch, dat boy gon be all up on you, Honey Child."

"You say dat like it's a bad thing," I winked, and wiggled so the skirt hem danced.

"Ugh, don't be thinkin you cute, heffa," Dhonni said.

"Girl, please. I'on *think* I'm cute; I *know* I'm cute."

"I know dat's right," my play mother laughed. "C'mon, 'den Miss Thang. Lemme bump y' ends for y'all won't be late."

I sat back down on the springy mattress so Kia could curl the ends of the tracks she wrapped around my high ponytail.

"So where y'all goin at?" she asked after a lil while, parting off a section to fry and lay to the side.

"Dartanyan house."

"His house? Damn, whatchall plan on doin?"

"Dependin how his friends look, it's whateva," Dhonni said with a wicked dimpled smile. Me and Trayonna slapped her five in agreement.

"Lissen'na you," Kia chuckled. "I know y'all been hangin wit me too long. *All* y'all fast."

She was right about that, too. Me, Dhonni, and Trayonna had the sex lives of women in they twenties at the tender age of thirteen. We went through boys like Kleenexes. We was tryna experiment and learn as much as we could about passion and gettin them fluttery feelings in our stomachs that the big girls always talked about.

"Well, look, I know y'all think you know erything there is to know bout chillin wit niggas, but trust me—it don't hurt to know more. It's rules to 'dis shit. You gotta know how to play the game before you go actin like you big," Kia started, suddenly and very seriously.

The quizzical look that came over the three of our faces seemed to ask what she meant by that, so Kia continued,

"First of all, don't *ever* give up no ass on'na first date. Dat's just trashy and I ain't raise y'all to be trashy," Kia directed. "Second of all, make a muhfucka spend a lil money on you before you go jumpin in'na bed wit em. 'Day betta take you to the movies a couple times, out to eat, or buy you a pair of Princesses or some'n. Don't just *give up* the pussy. Make em work for it. Niggas like to chase, so the more you avoid givin em what 'day want, the more you kh get out of em. Usually works pretty good unless you get a stingy muhfucka always lookin for you to do some'n for them cuz 'day do some'n for you. I *hate* a nigga who's dat pressed."

"Well, what if you just tryna have fun?" I asked, not knowin whether or not I felt like playin mind games with Dartanyan. Personally, all I wanted from him was a reason to have achy thighs come tomorrow mornin.

"Yeah, why play games? Like R. Kelly say, '*I don't see nuffin wrong wit a lil bump and grind*'," Dhonni sang, and me and Trayonna slapped her another five in agreement.

"The hell it ain't. I'm tryna save y'all the trouble. You ain't guaranteed a nut, so you migh'as well get *something* out the deal. You betta get ery nigga for all he got, joe…Besides, I was *just havin fun* wit Tejuan, andju see where dat got me. You'on wanna end up pregnant and stuck in 'na house like me, do you?"

"Hell nah!" Dhonni exclaimed, and looked at me to agree with her again. I gave a confused shrug cuz as young as I was, my maternal instincts was already kickin in. It was due to a combination of all my responsibilities at home and what I heard and saw on TV and in the streets.

"Look, just don't do no dumb shit, aight. Please be careful. Know who you dealin wit. Niggas is gon try d' getchall twisted so y'all won't know what's goin on, and the next thing you know, you gon wake up on'na couch witcha draws missin and dat muhfucka talkin bout some *'I gotchu now'*. 'Den you gon be all pregnant and fat and stuck in'na house for no reason, waitin for 'dis bamma-ass nigga d' come through wit some money for you, but he ain't got no job and he too dumb d' hustle so he ain't got shit andju ain't got shit and it ain't even your fault cuz he the one pressed to have a baby, all tryna trap you and shit..." Kia griped, scratchin her stomach again and lettin her emotion-choked words trail off.

Me, Dhonni, and Trayonna looked at eachother and tried not to laugh at our play mother's awkward moment of fuming, but it was hard as shit to keep a straight face after that. Dhonni flipped open one of Kia's new *Black Beat* magazines to play it off and started tearing out a page to add to the wallpaper of Immature posters in her room.

"Well, alrighty then. I think you made your point, Mommy," I told Kia after a while.

"Sorry, y'all. Dat's just my hormones talkin," Kia apologized. "But f'real. Try d' be good."

"I ain't makin no promises," I said.

"Andju know I ain't," Dhonni co-signed with another one of her wicked, dimpled smiles.

A few minutes later, Kia curled my last lil piece of hair and told me I was good to go. After grabbin a couple Jolly Ranchers and some kiwi lip gloss from off her dresser, I checked my flattened bangs in the mirror one last time and led the way outside. Me, Dhonni, and Trayonna ran all the way to Montello Avenue and caught the bus to Union Station. From there, we got on the green line train to Congress Heights. I was kinda jumpy when we got to Southeast cuz it wasn't like us to be so far outta our element, but just when I was about to suggest we get the fuck back on the train and haul ass back home, I spotted Dartanyan out the corner of my eye. He was posted up where the busses was at with two of his boys—one slim and buttery yellow, the other tall and deliciously dark, all three of em lookin good as I expected.

"'Dare 'day go," I told my girls, pointing with my chin. "Dat's Cruddy in'na wife beater."

"He sexy as shit," Trayonna said, lookin Dartanyan up and down like she was ready to sop him up with a biscuit. I made a note to myself to watch her ass around him. Trayonna was a sneak and a freak. She was that bitch you ain't dare leave around your boo if you loved him. Granted, I played the man-stealer role from time to time, but her ass *stayed* fuckin wit a dude who already was already bunned up. She liked the drama.

"His friends is cute," I said, changin the subject and givin the other two boys the once-over. Dartanyan got cool points for bringin buns for my girls. Blind dates is awkward enough without havin to stare at a Biz Markie look-alike all night.

"I got the yellow boy," Dhonni told Trayonna. From where we was standin, he looked like Bizzy Bone, all lightskin with the long, curly hair and erything.

"I'on care. I'on like lightskinded boys no how."

"You'on need to, yellow as you is," Dhonni teased.

"Bitch, I ain't yellow. I'm french vanilla, thank you very much."

"Yeah, whateva. Trayonna so yellow, she look like youngin on'na Lemonheads box!" I joked, and me and Dhonni cracked up laughin.

Dartanyan looked even better than he did the first time in his sleeveless undershirt, jean shorts, drop socks and flip-flops with his confused hair parted in lil puffballs all over his head. Evidently, I looked good too cuz he took one look at me and the short tennis skirt swishin against my thighs and started cheesin hard as a mug.

"Suga Baby...," he said, lookin me up and down while he nonchalantly chewed on a clear plastic straw. "Got-damn, girl. Dat's hi you goin t'day?"

Dartanyan's eyes sent that same anxious quiver through my stomach I got when I first met him. He was makin me feel like I was the *Sexy Girl* the Huck-A-Bucks made a song about.

"Yeah, wsup," I smiled as sultry as I could. "'Deez my sistas I toldju I was bringin wit me. 'Dis Hershey Kiss and dat's Skittles."

"Damn, all y'all got them sweet-ass names," one of Dartanyan's friends observed.

"Dat's right," Dhonni said. "Suga Sweet Huneyz, nigga. You betta recognize."

"Lemme find out," Dartanyan chuckled, lookin over my friends before he introduced his. "'Deez my bruhvas right hea'. 'Dis Whiteboy and dat's Black," he told us even though I knew they was bout as related as me and my girls was.

"Y'all look kinda young d' be fih'teen," the lightskin youngin Whiteboy commented, eyeing babyfaceded Dhonni suspiciously.

"Ain't no'by say we fih'teen," my best friend told him. "Suga Baby the oldest. Me and Skittles only fourteen," she lied. Trayonna turned thirteen in January and Dhonni wouldn't be up there with me and her till November. It ain't matter, though. None of us acted our age.

"Nah, young, how old is y'all f'real?"

"Damn, is you the police or some shit?" Dhonni sneered. "Toldju, Suga Baby fih'teen and me an' Skittles fourteen."

"What year you was born, 'den?"

Dhonni was tryna calculate the math in her head, obviously strugglin for a answer. I jumped in it to play it off.

"What the fuck? We gotta go on a interview d' chill witchall?" I asked.

"Yeah, getcha friend, joe," Trayonna complained to Dartanyan, who was too busy staring at my assets to hear.

"Man, fuck all that," the darkskin boy Black said. "I'on care how old y'all is. I fucks wit a young broad, expecially youngin hea' wit the green eyes," he continued, and checked Trayonna out again.

"Dat's what I'm sayin," Dartanyan agreed. He patted me on the ass like I was already his.

"So what we gon do—stand hea' lookin stupid all day?" Dhonni sassed, drumming her acrylic nails on the railing we was all posted up on. She ain't seem all that enthusiastic about Whiteboy anymore.

"We kh do whateva y'all wanna do. It's hi you wanna carry," Dartanyan answered.

"It's whateva," I said with a shrug. "Who got the bud around hea'?"

"Yeah, where the green at?" Dhonni co-signed.

"Damn, lemme find out y'all be partyin," Black siced it. I was findin that niggas love to chill with girls who get down like them when it came to drinkin and smokin. I thought it was cuz keepin up with them made us look cool. Little did I know, niggas only asked so they could find the quickest way to get us fucked up and outta our lil panties, just like Kia warned.

"So who got dat?" I asked again.

"You ain't playin no games, hunh?" Dartanyan chuckled, fingering the thin, gold herringbone around my neck. "Damn, you gon hafta be my girl f'real."

I ignored his lil comment. Dartanyan probly gave ery broad willing to let him tap that *you-gon-be-my-girlfriend* shit. I started to tell him there wasn't no need to sice my head up, and that he could keep his girl if he wanted to cuz I had a boyfriend back home anyways. I was just tryna get my cuts, plain and simple as that.

"I'on know bout all dat," I said, rollin my eyes. "But I know I'm tryna blaze. So you got the bud or what?"

"Red, I always got the bud. I be pumpin dat shit 24/7/365."

"Dat's what I'm talkin bout. A nigga wit connections. Where we smokin at, joe?" Dhonni asked.

"My house," Dartanyan answered, and threw down his chewed-up straw. "It's right up the street."

Dartanyan put his arm around my shoulder like we went together and led the way down Alabama Ave. It took erything in me to stay cool and not melt into a pile of goo from bein that close to him. Dartanyan's body heat, the smell of outside, the CK One on his skin, and the way he swaggered down the sidewalk like he owned it sent me swingin. I thought he could feel my heart poundin outta my chest and sense the tingles that was tickling me giddy as shit on the inside.

So much for bein a good girl and makin him wait like Kia said. Dartanyan already had me open with his confidence and take-charge attitude. When we got to his house on 12th Street, Dartanyan led the way to his backyard where we all got situated on his mama's rusty, old patio set. We all sat around makin small talk while he rolled up a couple J's. Bout fifteen minutes and one J later, Dartanyan was leaned close with his hand on my thigh tellin me how good I looked in my tennis skirt. By the time we finished the second j'on and I was high as a runaway balloon, he was grabbin me by the hand and tellin me to come in the house with him.

Despite Dhonni's worried look and Trayonna's somewhat jealous glare, I jumped up more than ready for whatever he was tryna give me. No sooner than we got upstairs in his room to lock lips and do our thang, Dartanyan's pager went off all loud and fucked up the whole mood. He sucked his teeth and looked to see who it was, then started cussin like a sailor before he told me he had to call the number back.

"Man, dat's my bruhva," Dartanyan informed me when he got back from usin the phone. "He need me d' do some'n for him right quick. You tryna roll?"

I thought about my soakin wet draws and considered beggin Dartanyan to come finish what he started, but Honey Child ain't beg for nobody.

"Aight," I sighed instead.

We ended up leavin our friends at his house and runnin up the street to a park behind some elementary school where Dartanyan's brother, Tristan, was waitin for him. The two of em talked for a minute before Tristan handed Dartanyan a folded paper bag, stuffed full and wrapped closed with a rubber band; then we was on our way again. I tried to act uninterested but the curiosity was killin me. I knew Dartanyan sold bud and I could tell Tristan hustled by the simple fact that he was grown and chillin at a playground. I also knew that whatever was in that bag had something to do with drugs. And as much as I hated drugs and what they did to people, I knew where there was drugs and niggas who sold drugs, money wasn't too far behind. Kia's voice echoed in my head: *Always look for the niggas wit money...*

I changed my whole shit up after that. Dartanyan had more than good looks goin on for hisself afterall. Cute, sexy, *and* a hustler? In my book, that was bun material. Kia's advice ended up being right cuz I knew I could get a racka shit outta Dartanyan if I was his girl—more than I could if we was just part-time lovers. Yeah, I was gon hafta hop up on that for real. My play mother ain't school no fool. Good thing Tristan called before I gave the boy some.

"Damn, my stomach growlin like shit, young. You hongry?" Dartanyan asked as we headed back to his house with the package in tow.

"Yeah. Why, you got some'na eat at y' house?"

"Nah, I's bout d' hit the carry-out and get me a fish samwich. Them j'ons a beast when you off the munchies."

"It's a long walk?" I asked, lookin ahead down the sidewalk. The end of the street seemed miles away.

"Don't worry bout walkin. We gon take my bruhva car."

Damn, he drive, too? That boy was fulla more surprises than a magic show. We stopped back the house to get the keys, then climbed into Tristan's steel blue LTD. Dartanyan started up the car and fiddled around with the dash till *You're All I Need* by Method Man and Mary J. Blige came bangin out the radio speakers. Dartanyan leaned back in his seat and whipped the car's big, boxed body down the street with one hand, pimpin the shit out the j'on like he been drivin for years. He looked so smooth and confident and so adult-like for a bright-eyed, sixteen year-old, man-boy. I leaned on the elbow rest between us and started singin along wit the radio, wonderin if Dartanyan would ever be all I needed to get by. Youngin was fulla possibilities.

We ended up makin a stop someplace around Naylor Road. Dartanyan had me wait in the car while he took the bag his brother gave him and disappeared inside an apartment building for a few minutes. When he came back out, he drove the lil ways up to Eddie Leonard's and got us some food. We ate right there in fronta the j'on. All you heard above the music was us smackin food and slurping soda like that was our first meal in years. Between scarfing down bites of fried chicken wings smothered in mambo sauce and me smackin Dartanyan's hand away when he tried to steal my fries, I found myself liking him more and more. It wasn't just cuzza the money, either. I liked the way he carried it. The more time I spent around Dartanyan, the more I started to see how much we was alike. He was rough around the edges like me, smart, and a lil bit stuck on hisself. For some reason, that made me want him all the more. He was the top dog type, the sharpest, the most noticeable one that all the girls wanted. It was in erything from his walk to his talk to the way he so seriously handled his business. I always did have a thing for dudes like that. They seemed to be the only ones who could handle someone like me.

There was something else I liked about Dartanyan, too. Something that said we shared the same kinda void inside. There was a emptiness in all his bravado, a part of him that needed to be kissed and hugged tight with some genuine tenderness. I wanted to know why. So I cut the small talk and started askin him bout hisself. Dartanyan told me he was born and brought up in Southeast with his brother, and just like me, moms raised em all by herself. As Dartanyan spilled out stories bout his growin up, most of which was spent learnin the streets when his moms was at work, I started to understand why else I was so drawn to him. He was a black sheep, his mama's least favorite child, just like me. Dartanyan was the one who got in trouble first when something went wrong. He was the one who got overlooked or shortchanged with time, presents, and affection. I related to his pain, his starvation for something to fill up the part of him that felt alone and forgotten. The neediness in his eyes made me wanna pull him close and hug away all the hurt that made it so hard for him to smile. Dartanyan was broken and I wanted to fix him. I wanted to fix him as bad as I wanted him to fix me. I started to think maybe we could fix eachother.

He was an emotional wreck underneath it all, but he covered it up well with over-confidence and his ambition. The boy had a single lofty dream that kept him going. See, Dartanyan dropped outta high school a lil after he turned sixteen and moved in with his aunt out Southwest since him and his moms ain't never get along anyhow. He tried goin the honest route cuz auntie was hittin him up for half the rent, but once he realized workin mall jobs and fast food wasn't bringin in enough money to pay bills and stay fresh, he decided it was time to step his game up. Youngin been slangin ery since. Dartanyan had plans to start movin big weight and be the next DC kingpin, but he knew it was gon take time to get there. Right now he was just sellin weed and runnin packages back and forth for his brother. But one day, he assured me, he was gon be the man.

Dartanyan had a determination about him that made even the most impossible plans seem doable. Youngin definitely had a way with words. I knew damn well Dartanyan's plan was doomed from the start cuz anybody that even came close to being the HNIC of the drug trade since the 80's done got killt or locked the fuck up. But, shit, he convinced me. That boy could make me believe in anything he said. I thought he was the best thing since pink lemonade. Dartanyan's boldness, alluring eyes, pipe dreams, and unsoothable, deep-down hurt was just my flavor.

When he asked me about myself, I was surprisingly honest. I told him how it made me mad ery time he called me Red cuz it reminded me of the father I never saw. I told him bout Mommy and how she favored my brother over me. And my assumption that my mother was jealous of me because i was young and fine without the limitations she had, which had to be the reason she carried me the way she did. I even admitted to being thirteen. I just knew Dartanyan was gon change his mind bout talkin to me after that, but to my surprise, he shrugged off my confession like I told him the sky was blue or something.

"Fuck it," Dartanyan said all cool and nonchalant. "'Day just gon hafta call me *Chester, Chester Child Molester.* I still wanna mess witchu."

"F'real?"

"Hell yeah," he said, his eyes reflecting the attraction I felt towards him.

I shoulda had sense enough to run away from that fool like he had the booger touch, but by the time it got dark and Whiteboy had paged him lookin for us, I was already disappointed at the thought of goin home.

"When you gon come see me again?" Dartanyan asked as we pulled the LTD back into his driveway and got out.

"I'on remember tellin you that I was."

"Oh, you *gon* come see me again."

"F'real? Says who?" I teased.

"Says me. I'm tryna put some'n up in you, shawdy," Dartanyan said boldly, his hands sliding down to my butt for the millionth time that day.

"Boy, stop! We all in'na middle uh' the street and shit!" I fussed, fake mad even though he was gettin me hot and bothered again.

"So what? I'm lettin 'deez muhfuckas know you my girl. I toldju I was gon make you my girl," Dartanyan said.

"Yeah, right," I blushed, rollin my eyes to the sky. I liked the sound of it so much I wanted him to say it again.

"I'm dead serious, joe. You minez. You migh'as well kiss them uh' niggas good-bye."

"I'd rather kiss you," I smiled cleverly.

"Oh, yeah?"

"Yeah. Whatchu think uh' that?"

Dartanyan complied with a kiss that made my head swim. Nobody, I mean *nobody*, ever kissed me like Dartanyan did. Until then I wasn't much one for lettin somebody else put they tongue in my mouth or vice versa. I'd always end up with a youngin who was too rough, or too sloppy, or had breath like hot trash. Dartanyan's cola flavored kisses put me in the zone, that's for damn sure. He licked, teased, and damn near made love to my mouth like I tasted better than the first honeysuckles of the summer. He showed me what kissin was *really* poseda be like, and I was lovin ery single second of it. I thought I was gonna bust into flames when I felt his hand creep down to the cinch in my waist, then up the front of my shirt where he squeezed my breasts tenderly like he couldn't wait to kiss them the right way, too. I threw my head back and hiked my leg up on one side of his waist as a invitation to do more, but Dartanyan stopped. He looked at me through lust-lowered eyelids and smiled.

"Mnh. Suga Baby," he said, and gave my ass another squeeze. "You gon make me getchu pregnant, girl."

I pulled down my shirt and adjusted my skirt, tryna get myself together since we was out in the middle of the street and all. Me and Dartanyan's eyes met again and I knew then that we wasn't just gonna have some hit-it-and-quit-it type relationship. Even though erything about him screamed that he was doggish, controlling, and clingy, Dartanyan was definitely special. All the shit we had in common made me feel like I known him forever. And the way he was holdin me then made me feel…wanted. And needed. Plus, he had money, he could dress his ass off, and he would definitely make pretty babies. He was erything I wanted and erything Kia told me to look for in a man.

"C'mon, we betta get inside 'fore your girls start lunchin," Dartanyan told me. I nodded in silent agreement and followed after him.

It was Tuesday, the day before July 4th and I was all too ready for the holiday. I was busy thinkin bout who's cookout I was crashin and where I planned on takin my kids to see the fireworks, when my ten o'clock appointment came waltzing in. It wasn't till I saw the darkskinded lady with the elbow-length dreds and the lil redhead girl, that my mind switched back into work mode.

"Kim and Jasmine, right?" I asked, as the receptionist led them over to my station.

The lil girl answered with a shy nod of her head. I grabbed a booster seat to get her situated in my chair and gave Kim a couple magazines to kill time since she wanted to stick around till I was done. I started lookin around for Krys so I could get her to wash the lil girl's hair before I did anything to it, but she was nowhere to be found.

Now why don't that surprise me?

The receptionist told me Krys went to get some change from the bank across the mall parkin lot, so she should be back soon, but I already knew the seventeen-year cicadas had a better chance of making they triumphant return before my lil cousin did. The last time that heffa went for change, it took over a hour. Man, I'on know how much more of this I can take. Seemed like ery time I turned around, Krys was runnin out the house or sneakin off from work to go do whatever it is she be so pressed to do. I done already tried to be nice about it and let her know in so many words that I ain't have no problem sendin her home if she wasn't gon be serious bout work and the generous curfew I gave her. It was enough to make her chill out for a day or so, but apparently, that shit was only temporary. Youngin must think I'm a chump. I ain't wanna hafta show her that I wasn't.

Annoyed, I started washing Jasmine's hair myself and sat her back in my chair to blow it dry and grease her scalp. That's when my girl Betina came in from break and started cleanin up her station beside minez so it'd be ready for her next client.

"Damn, Shai, you gon bring your whole family up in hea'?" Betina asked after sayin hello to Jasmine and Kim. "Y'all be tryna joan when my sistas come up in hea', but you be the main one bringin half your cousins out 'dis j'on."

"Dat's cuz you got eight sistas and they all be tryna get the hook-up. Only family uh' minez you done seen is Krys, my muhva, and my two aunties."

"Oh, my bad. I thought babygirl was one uh' your peoples, too. Y'all all look alike and stuff."

"Who, me and lil Jasmine?" I chuckled. "She ain't my cousin."

"Well, y'all do favor eachother," Miz Pam interrupted, adding her two cents as usual.

"You think so?"

"Yeah," her and Betina agreed in unison. "Sure y'all ain't related?" Miz Pam asked.

"Hunh? Nah," I answered, and me and Kim smiled at the same time. "Far as I know, we ain't."

"Well you need to find out for sure, cuz dat girl look more like one uh' your kids than your own kids do."

"You sicin it now, Miz Pam."

"I'm just statin a fact. You don't think 'day look alike?" she asked Kim.

Kim started to shrug an answer, but after one more hard look at me and her daughter, she surprised me by nodding her head yes.

"You know, I guess they do."

Me and Kim locked eyes, all of a sudden searchin eachother's faces for answers to a question that's probly been at the backa both our minds since we met. At least, it's been at the backa minez. I ain't really have time to sit and think about it, but that musta been what struck me so odd about her that day. Jasmine did look a lot like me. Some of her features was different, but she had the same light eyes and bright, red hair that's been my trademark since I was little. Maybe she was a cousin of minez. Or maybe…maybe she was even closer kin to me. I mean, her moms sure did remind me of minez in a way. Pretty and darkskinded with some meat on her bones…I ain't know what typa person she was, but as far as looks go, she was definitely my father's type. If Jasmine wasn't my cousin, she coulda very well been one of them seven illegitimate kids my father had after me and my brother.

"Where y'all from?" I asked Kim.

"Lewisdale. Right offa University Boulevard. It's around the corner from hea'," she answered.

"What's y' last name?"

"Hill."

"Hill, hunh? You ain't got no family in'na city?"

"Nah." Then she motioned towards Jasmine. "Her father from D.C., though."

"Well, where he from?"

"Northwest."

"F'real?"

"Yeah."

"Ohhh. My fahva from Uptown, too."

"Well, if you say his name David, I'ma be too through," Kim joked, after studying my face again. She probly didn't think it was possible, but I knew anything was possible when it came to my father and his kids.

"Well, his name *is* David," I told her, then added seriously, "David Williams. But eryby call him Redz cuz he—"

"He got red hair?"

The two of us said the last part at the same time and stared in open-mouthed awe as the shock registered. Wait a minute. She knew my father. Did that mean?

"Redz is her fahva?" I asked, noddin at Jasmine. Kim nodded yes and sent us into another spell of shocked silence.

"I knew it! Y'all sisters?" Miz Pam asked, all up in the sauce as usual.

"Dat's what it sound like," Betina added. "Ain't dat some wild shit? How many times you ever meet some'my you ain't know you was related to?"

I could honestly say I never had the pleasure. My father probly had kids from here to the Carolinas, but I never actually met any that was my real half brothers or sisters. Then here, today, I finally do. Of all the things to find out, man. I had me a lil sister by Redz.

All at once, I wanted to know erything about Jasmine. When she was born, how Kim and my father hooked up, if Jasmine had brothers and sisters at home by him. I wanted to know if Redz still came around and saw her, if he gave her a nickname or ever took her around and showed her off like he useta do with me and Cerrone. Did Jasmine already feel that anger I carried towards Redz when I was her age? Did she ever get to know him? Did she remember him? Did she miss him?

I ain't end up finishin Jasmine's hair till way past three. I was so eager to talk to Kim and compare stories with her that I kept puttin Jasmine to the side and workin on somebody else so I could make em stay longer. I was amazed. Shocked. And part of me was a lil bit disturbed. Boy, I thought I was trippin offa dealin with Krys. This newfound family shit damn-near blew me out the water. It was like some kinda set up, y'know, like something you'd see in the movies and shit. Funny how fate and destiny make life work out. I mean, first, Redz just happens to show up in the emergency room at Mommy's job. Then he just happens to give her a racka old pictures and asks to see me. And now I meet a lil girl who ends up being my sister. All this shit pointin me in the direction of a man I swore I'd never speak to again.

Was God tryna tell me something or what?

CHAPTER SEVEN

"Rashaiyah, what the hell you in there doin?" Mommy hollered from the other side of the bathroom door. I was too busy callin Earl to answer. Erything that had been sittin in my stomach since the night before was comin back up through my mouth, through my nose, and it felt like through my eyes cuz they was watering so much. My head was spinnin a hundred miles a minute and my stomach was churning even faster. I could barely catch my damn breath to try and stop. I thought I would die for real.

"Rashaiyah!" Mommy barked again. I looked up at the bathroom sink, glad that I left the water runnin at full force to cover up the sounds of me throwin up. This was the second mornin in a row I found myself kneeling at the toilet, and I was gettin more and more worried bout what coulda been wrong with me. It was the dead of December (December 25th to be exact), so my first thought was maybe I was catchin a vicious-ass stomach flu. Then I thought it had something to do with the hot dog and ketchup spaghetti I been eatin for a week now, or that lil cup of Christmas Eve egg nog I had at dinner last night. My biggest fear was the possibility of being pregnant since me and Dartanyan been doin it like "it" was goin outta style nowadays, but I got my period two weeks ago so that couldna been the problem. I had no idea what was goin on.

"Rashaiyah, if I gotta come in'nere, you gon wish I didn't!" Mommy threatened. Her angry voice clashed with the mellow rhythm of Chuck Brown's *Merry Christmas, Baby* playin on the livin room radio.

I pulled myself up and went about washin my face and brushin my teeth. Then I opened the door all calm like nothin was wrong, and scooted past Mommy where she stood scowling at me in the tinsel-decorated hallway.

"You gon make me smack the black off you," she muttered before slamming the bathroom door behind her.

"Merry Christmas to you, too," I said, and flipped up my middle finger at her back.

I made my way out to the livin room where my brother and sisters was gathered around our plastic Christmas tree goin through they gifts. Mommy's boyfriend Tone was at the dining room table, re-hanging a length of fake pine bough around the edges of it. If nothin else, the decorations in our house had the Christmas spirit. Mommy always made sure of that. Ery year she took to hangin red velvet bows, candy canes, tacking up holly, and settin them electric candles all up in the windowsills and on the tables. She even used that frost-in-a-can stuff to write "Merry Christmas" and "Happy Holidays" all over the windows. And we always had that big, fake-ass tree decorated with them colorful, string-wrapped styrofoam balls, plastic ornaments, and homemade strings of Kix cereal that doubled as roach food at night. Even when we ain't had no presents to sit under it, a Christmas never went by without that got-damn tree.

"Look, it's Sleepin Ugly, y'all," Cerrone teased when he saw me shuffling over to the couch to sit down.

"Y' muhva," I retorted, drawing my knees to my chest. I winced cuz my boobies was tender like I was bout to come on my period again.

"See, dat's why you ugly now, makin all them faces," my brother teased from behind the TV.

"Why'onchu shut up!" I snapped, and threw one of Mommy's elf pillows at him.

Tone came over to where I was sittin, I guess to intervene before me and Cerrone got to fightin. He stood for a while lookin down on me with his dark stare, puffin on a black and vanilla cigar and not sayin anything. I braced myself cuz I was halfway expectin him to yell at me like Mommy would have even though my brother was the one who started it, but Tone surprised me by crackin a smile instead.

"Glad to see you made it out okay," Tone finally commented, blowin sweet-smellin smoke in the air above my head.

"Whatchu talkin bout?" I grumbled. I wasn't in the mood to talk to him or anyone else for that matter. I'da rather been in my bed sleep till this whole Christmas bullshit was over.

"Me and y' mama thought you fell in'na toilet," Tone chuckled, patting his round, Santa Claus-like belly. "Y' mama, she says, 'Tone, I believe that girl done fell in the toilet' and I says, I says, 'Brenda, that girl too damn big to be fallin in some toilet! You betta see if she done made a tunnel and 'scaped out the back way!'"

Tone tilted his head back and roared with laughter at his own corny joke. I just shook my head cuz I ain't get it.

"Well," Tone started, when he finally realized he was laughin alone. "You gon open y' present?"

I looked over at my brother and sisters by the tree. Cerrone was busy tryna hook up a brand new Sega Genesis to our old floor model TV, and my lil sisters was scootin a long pink Barbie limo with two new dolls inside across the floor on they hands and knees. There was a lone box wrapped in comic strip newspaper left under the tree but I figured that it belonged to one of them, too. I wasn't used to gettin Christmas presents. Like Cerrone, I was always in trouble for some kinda bullshit like fightin or gettin bad grades. But unlike him, I was the only one who ever got punished by not gettin no Christmas presents.

"I ain't know I got nuffin," I told Tone bitterly. The only thing I got for Christmas so far was the purple Raekwon tape Cerrone snuck to me this mornin after I gave him the floppy fatigue hat I ruffed outta Hecht's for him. Mommy ain't get me shit cuz she was still mad bout our next door neighbor catchin me and Dhonni in the alley smokin bud with these two dudes a couple weeks ago.

"Well, now y' do. Go open it b'fore it grow legs and walk away," Tone jested, and cracked up laughin at his own joke again. I shook my head once more and eased over to the tree.

"What is it? Clothes?" I asked, pickin up the arm-length rectangular box and shakin it. I slit the paper open with my thumbnail one piece of tape at a time, careful not to rip any, then pried open the box. Staring back at me was a fresh pair of Tommy Hilfiger blue jeans and a matchin T-shirt. My eyes almost fell outta my head.

"Daaaaaaaaaaaammmmnn! You got me some Tommy?!" I exclaimed, my surly attitude automatically turning sunny. "Aww, 'deez j'ons is like dat! Thanks, Tone!"

"You welcome, Babygirl. Merry Christmas," Tone smiled.

"Yeah, Merry Christmas!" I exclaimed, holdin up my new clothes. The way I was actin, you woulda thought I just got some Dolce & Gabbana.

I was already planning on wearing my new clothes the first day back to school in January so I could show off.

"Ha-ha, I got Tommy jeans!" I bragged, waving my clothes in fronta my brother.

"So? Tone got me a flight jacket," Cerrone said, and got up to show me his black nylon bomber with the gold zipper and orange lining on the inside. "You cain't borrow it, neiva."

"So? If I cain't borrow dat j'on, you betta not aks d' wear my shirt, nigga."

"I'ma tell Mommy you said the N-word," Treasure threatened from the other side of the livin room, all up in the Kool-Aid.

"Shut up, dat's why you got draws on y' head," I teased her about the underwear-turned-nightcap that Mommy made her wear over her dookie braids.

Sparkle whispered something to Treasure and they started laughin at me in them high-ass chipmunk voices of theirs. They was four and five years old now, and twice as irritating as before. I couldn't stand my lil sisters. Neither one of em was my favorite. And after years of being stuck with them as tag-alongs, and me blatantly resenting them for it, they learned to team up and terrorize me as a means of revenge. It was kinda like the way me and Cerrone terrorized them for being the youngest and having a father who at least came to see them some weekends.

"Move, Shai. I'm tryna see if 'dis j'on work. Your daddy ain't no glassmaker," Cerrone fussed, turning on the TV to test what was poseda be *all* of our Sega Genesis. I rolled my eyes and slung my new clothes over one shoulder.

"Dat's why you ain't got no Tommy jeans. Bamma," I retorted, and headed back to our room to try on my new outfit.

I stripped down to my underwear and jumped into my jeans, then stood sideways in fronta the long, broken mirror in the corner. They was a lil tighter than I'da liked, but that was cool cuz the T-shirt covered all that up. I sucked in my stomach but it ain't go down much. The bulge under my belly button was the problem, so I poked it to lay flat but that ain't do much either. It was too hard.

My body been goin through all typesa changes since Dartanyan made me his girl this summer. He made my hips spread, my butt fatter, and now my jeans was too tight and my stomach was hard. I'da been real mad, too, if I ain't have so much fun while he was makin them changes. Doin it with Dartanyan was like a Olympic event. He was always flippin me around and twistin me this way and that, pullin me, bouncin me, and grindin me from ery angle. I wasn't complainin, though. That lil nigga was wearing me out. Between the things he did to me and the way he made me feel, it was impossible to stick to my playa ways. Dartanyan was my fire and I was his candy rain. When he wasn't out gettin money, we was bunned up at his aunt's house, bunned up at the movies, or bunned up in the stands at Ballou senior high watchin his boys play ball. Dartanyan started sellin crack to put his hustlin plans in motion, and it made me feel closer to him when he included me in his dreams to get out the game after his first million, then buy one of them quaint rowhouses in Adams Morgan and open up a T-shirt shop so we could live happily ever after. It boosted me whenever we went to the malls out Maryland and ran into broads Dartanyan useta mess with and they looked at me all jealous cuz he was buyin me shit. It made me wanna smother him with hugs and kisses when he told me he never really felt loved till I came along. He told me I filled up all the holes in his life, and truthfully, he filled up minez. For a change, I had somebody takin care of me, spoilin me, goin outta his way for me cuz I was the most important person in his life. It was all the attention and affection I could ever want, and I needed it as much as Dartanyan needed someone to love him back.

"Shai, Mommy want chu," Sparkle said, interrupting my thoughts. She was suddenly in the doorway, watching me lost in a daydream with a puzzled look on her face.

"What for?" I asked. Thinkin bout Dartanyan had me uncontrollably giddy inside and I knew hearin Mommy's mouth would bring me crashing down off that natural high.

"She said gotta tell us some'n."

"Like what?" I wondered aloud, comin outta my new clothes and pullin a thin, yellow pajama shirt over my head. I stepped over all the junk on the floor and went out in the livin room after my sister.

Mommy had turned off the radio and erything, and was standin there with her hands on her hips and her feet spread apart like it was that serious. I rolled my eyes to the ceiling, thinkin that whatever it was she had to say probly wasn't even that damn important for all this show.

"Aight, y'all, lissen up. I'm pregnant," Mommy announced. I squinted to see if I could find a baby under all that belly of hers, but I ain't see nothin unusual. Mommy looked pregnant all the time.

"Again?" Cerrone whined. He sucked his teeth and glared at Mommy and Tone. I glared at em, too. All this meant was another body crowding our tiny-ass apartment, another kid for me to babysit, and another crumb-snatcher eatin the lil bit of food we did have. What did we possibly need with another kid? The way I saw it, I already had a brother and two sisters, so unless Mommy was gonna give birth to a doberman or something, this kid wasn't gonna be nothin special.

"Whatchu mean 'again'? I ain't had a baby since Sparkle," Mommy retorted. "Damn, I woulda thought y'all been happy to hear that."

"Not me," I grumbled. "Don't you think you got enough kids?"

"Yeah, man," Cerrone added with his own miserable groan.

"First of all, it ain't up to no'by but *me* to decide if I done had enough kids. What the hell kinda question is that?" Mommy snapped.

"Well, I hope you plan on movin to a bigger house cuz ain't no'by else gon fit in dat room wit us," I snapped back.

"Yeah. Bad enough I gotta sleep on'na couch so they kh get dressed," Cerrone complained. "And Shai dumb ass wanna be kickin people out when her stupid boyfriend come over."

I stuck up my middle finger at him and faked like I was scratchin my temple to play it off.

"Ma, I know you saw dat!" Cerrone cried.

"Saw what? What I do? You always tryna get some'my in trouble, boy, damn!" I fussed at my brother.

"Shut up, y'all two. I ain't done sayin what I gotta say yet."

"But, Ma, she givin me the finger!"

"No, I'm not! Shut up!"

"I wish both of y'all would shut the hell up!" Mommy shouted. "I ain't finished tellin y'all erything I gotta tell y'all yet!"

"C'mon, man. What more you gotta say? You havin anuh' brat. What else is new?" I sighed.

"Say some'n else smart, hea'? I will slap the teeth right out y' mouth, Rashaiyah Deshay Williams. Just try me."

I started to get buck with her, but Tone shot me a look that begged for me to let it go, so I did. For him, though. Not Mommy.

"So what's the resta the news?" I asked instead.

"I'm gettin married," Mommy announced, flashin the gold and diamond band on her left ring finger. "And we movin out to Wheaton with Tone. He bought us a house out 'dare."

Tone nodded for reassurance as we registered the shock.

"Married?"

"Tone?!"

"He bought us a house?"

"Wheaton?"

"Kh we get our own rooms?"

The four of us filled the air with questions and Mommy tried her best to answer em all. She was standin there tryna shush us and get us to talk one at a time but it wasn't workin. When Mommy got fed up and started yelling for us to shut the hell up before she lost her religion, I raised my hand like I was in school to speak. Fuck bein quiet—she had some explainin to do. First she pregnant, and now this gettin married and movin out to Maryland shit? I was *up-set*.

"What, Rashaiyah?"

"You marryin Tone?" I asked Mommy in disbelief. I'da been better off if she told me she was gonna sell us off into child slavery in the Philippines. Anything but marryin some damn Tone. I mean, cuz was a aight dude and all, but the last thing I wanted was a nigga up in my face tryna regulate like he was the man of the house. Tone wasn't my daddy and I wasn't gonna sit there and pretend like he was. I ain't have no daddy and I wasn't bout to accept a fake-me-out one, neither.

"Yes," her and Tone answered at the same time.

"Well, why we gotta move d' Wheaton? I'on like Mar'land, joe. Why y'all cain't just get a house around hea'?" Cerrone asked.

"Cuz I wanna get out this damn neighborhood already. The longer I stay here, the longer y'all criminal records gon get," Mommy answered, lookin pointedly at me.

"Why you all up in my face? I ain't the only one who get in trouble!" I objected.

Shit, I wasn't the only one smellin myself, as Mommy liked to say. Cerrone done been in worse trouble than me, out there hangin with

Pookie and the resta them fools, stealin bikes, breakin into peoples cars, and gettin brought home by the police and shit. He done been suspended from school way more times than me, too, but Mommy chose to ignore that part. When it came to Cerrone, he could do no wrong.

"Why you gotta be bringin my name into shit?" my brother snapped at me.

"Cuz I'm tired uh' her ackin like I'm the only one who do anything bad."

"You tired uh' me?" Mommy asked incredulously. "Well, if you so tired uh' me, you kh take your grown ass somewhere else, lil girl. You ain't gotta move wit us."

"'Den maybe I won't."

I wasn't too gung-ho bout movin to no bamma-ass Maryland anyhow. Anything that wasn't Trinidad wasn't home, and anything that wasn't D.C. wasn't shit as far as I was concerned.

"Do we gotta share rooms when we move?" Treasure asked.

"I like sharing rooms," Sparkle said.

"Dat's only cuz you scared uh' the dark," Cerrone teased.

"No I'm not!"

"Yes you is! You still sleep wit d' night light cuz you scared uh' the boogeyman."

"Nuh-unh!"

"Unh-hunh! Look, 'dare go the boogeyman now!"

Sparkle turned to look where Cerrone was pointing so fast that her underwear nightcap came flyin off. Of course it wasn't nothing there, though.

"Ah-ha! Gimme dat neck!" Cerrone exclaimed, and slid his fingers real hard across the backa her neck.

"Ow! Mommy!" Sparkle whined. "Mommy, he got my neck! It burns!"

"Shut up, crybaby!" I fussed, extra annoyed now.

"All y'all shut the fuck up!" Mommy exclaimed. "Enough is enough! Me and Tone is goin down to the courthouse in two weeks and we movin at the end of July. End of discussion!"

I wanted to say more on the matter, but the queasy feeling in my stomach came back twice as bad as it was before, so I slipped away to the bathroom. No sooner than I got the faucet on and leaned my head over the toilet, the lil bit of water I had in my stomach came rushing back up. I was terrified of my body now, and this news of Mommy's wasn't makin me feel no better. I had to talk to somebody. I rinsed out my mouth and hurried back in my room to throw on some sweats under my nightshirt, then went upstairs to see if Dhonni was home. Pookie answered the door in his boxers and a Santa Claus hat, boppin to Pleasure's *Go-Go Christmas* crankin out the stereo.

"Ugh, put some clothes on," I fussed, lookin over his slim, muscled body. With that hat leaned to the side and his cross-eyes all low and sexy, Pookie actually looked good for a minute. Not that I would ever go there with him, though. I still thought of him as a brother.

"Howboutchu take some clothes *off*?" Pookie said, obviously not on the same page as me.

"Move, boy. Where y' sista at?" I asked, pushin him to the side and lookin inside they apartment.

"She went to the store d' get a turkey wit my muhva. You wanna come in and wait f' her?"

"'Day gon be back soon?" I asked.

"Nah, but you kh chill wit me till she do. Ain't no'by hea' but me n' you, so *it's whateva*."

"Bye, Pookie," I said, already on the way to the buildin next door to find Kia.

"You betta stop sleepin, Shai! You know you want me!"

"Yeah, whateva, Pookie."

I got to Kia's and made it back to her room right as my stomach started up again. She was hunched over on her knees changin Zhané's diaper on her old, beat-up twin bed.

"Hey, Honey Child. How y' Christmas goin? Santy Claus bring you erything you want?"

"Nah, dat nigga still be tryna ack like he'on know nobody," I joked. "My muhva boyfriend got me some stuff, 'doe."

I sat down on the springy mattress beside them. Zhané looked over at me and her fat, butterscotch cheeks rounded into a blissful toothless smile. Kia smoothed her curly, baby soft hair and kissed one of her fat, dimpled hands. Except for her keen nose and pointy chin, Zhané was the spittin image of Kia. She'd probly grow up to walk and talk like Kia, too, or at least how Kia useta walk and talk. I wasn't the only one that noticed how much she calmed down after havin Zhané back in late July. I mean, Kia still ran around showin her ass and talkin loud as usual, but she eased up on all the drinkin and partyin and recruiting niggas to support her fashion habits. You might catch my play mother sneakin in the Ibex or hittin the Eastside for a go-go ery once in a while, or occasionally see her on the block hustlin off some stuff from one of her missions. But for the most part Kia laid low these days.

"I gotchu a Christmas present," Kia told me, pickin up Zhané and sittin her in her lap. "You want it now?"

"I'on know...We movin," I said abruptly.

"Damn, f'real?" Kia asked, her eyes mirroring the disappointment I felt in my heart.

"Yeah. In July."

"Where at?"

"Wheaton."

"Wheaton? By the mall? Dat's way out 'dare, ain't it?"

I shrugged.

"Damn, I wish you kh stay hea' wit me."

"I wish I could, too," I sulked. "Maybe Miz Darlene uh' lemme stay wit her," I said, thinkin of Dhonni's mom as my last hope.

"May-be. You know she cool bout shit like dat. Is y' muhva gon let chu, 'doe?"

"I'on know. Probly not. I tell you she gettin married, too?" I asked, droppin another bomb.

"F'real?"

"Yeah, dat's why we movin. She marryin dat nigga Tone. He the one who bought my muhva dat house out Wheaton."

"Damn, Miz Brenda! Break em like he owe you some'n!" Kia smiled. I wanted to return the enthusiasm for my mother's pimpishness, but I couldn't.

"Damn, you look bad," Kia said suddenly, staring all up in my face for the first time since I got there. "Why you so outta breaf? And why you got them bags under your eyes?"

"Bags under my eyes?" I asked in amazement. I got up to go look in the mirror hangin behind her door. She was right. Not only did I have bags under my eyes, but my eyelids was all puffy and droopy like I ain't get no sleep. With my hair tied up in a dirty silk scarf and the sickly shadow over my face, I was walkin around lookin like who-done-it-and-why.

"You catchin a cold?" Kia asked, feelin my forehead for a temperature.

"I'on even know no more," I confessed. "My stomach been all fucked up and I been earlin and shit. And I keep gettin dizzy spells."

Kia's face got serious. She started bouncin Zhané nervously on her thigh.

"Dat sound like trouble," Kia told me finally. "You get y' period 'dis month?"

I nodded.

"Yeah, bout two weeks ago."

"Was it normal?"

"I'on know. A period is a period d' me. I was all cramped up and bleedin, I know dat much," I answered jokingly.

"I'm serious, Honey Child."

I thought for a minute. Now that I think about it, my period went for four days insteada six and I ain't bleed all that heavy either. I ain't think nothin of it before cuz I was just glad to see the muhfucka, heavy or not. Me and Dartanyan wasn't too good with using condoms, so seein *any* blood was good enough for me.

"Nah, I guess it wasn't normal," I told my play mother.

She started checkin the whites of my eyes, then peering down my throat like she was a doctor and knew what the hell she was lookin for. I rolled my eyes.

"Khhhaaaa, khhhmnow," I fussed, my mouth all open.

"Shut up and lemme see."

"C'mon, now, Kia. What's dat gonna do?" I asked, pullin away.

"I'on know. Doctors always check y' throat."

"Dat's cuz 'day know what 'day lookin for. You ain't no doctor."

"I am too, Honey Child. I be watchin The Learnin Channel."

"You be lunchin, too," I laughed. Kia shrugged.

"You know what I think?" she asked, cocking her head to one side and lookin at me real hard again. I crossed my fingers and hoped it wasn't the same thing I was thinkin.

"You might be pregnant."

"Kia, don't say dat shit, man," I begged. The way I saw it, by her puttin it out there, it was gonna come true.

"Nah, f'real. You been sick and y' period ain't been normal? And as thick as you gettin, dat kh only mean one thing. Well, uhva 'den Dartanyan hittin it right."

"I *been* thick," I shrugged, lookin myself over. My sweats was a lil tighter than usual but I ain't think I put on no noticeable weight. Besides, I always been healthy lookin. I got it from my mama.

"Well, now you thick-*er*. And your tiddies grew, too."

"You sicin it," I said, lookin down at my breasts. "'Day the same."

"No 'day not. You bout d' have you some tig-o-biddies. I bet them j'ons been itchin, too, haven't they?"

"A lil bit," I admitted.

"Unh-hunh. Dat's cuz 'day growin."

"Don't look like it. You think 'day dat big f'real?"

"Nah, f' fake," Kia answered, lookin me over again with a motherly scrutiny. "I'm tellin you, Honey Child, you pregnant."

"Impossible. I still got my period. Ain't it's poseda stop when you pregnant?"

"Honey Child," Kia started, sittin Zhané on the bed between her legs. "I was pregnant wit 'dis one for three whole months and ain't even know it. Three months! I was bleedin and erything, wasn't gettin sick or showin or *nuffin*. I ain't even know f'sure I was pregnant till I finally did start showin, and by 'den it was too late to do anything about it."

By *doin anything about it*, I knew she meant havin an abortion. I wondered if it was too late for me to have one. *If* I was pregnant, cuz I wasn't ready to believe that I was just yet.

"I'm glad I kept her, 'doe," Kia said, and kissed Zhané on one of her fat cheeks. "'Dis lil girl is the love of my life."

"You so crazy. I thought Tejuan was the love of y' life."

"Tejuan aight," Kia said flatly with a shrug. "He gave me Zhané so I cain't be mad at him. 'Dis lil girl is one uh' the best things ever happent to me…Make me wonder what my uh' baby woulda been like if I'da kept it."

"Maybe dat one woulda got Tejuan gray eyes," I said.

Kia had an abortion not too long before she got pregnant with Zhané. My girl hardly ever mentioned it (she never even told me bout it till after she had Zhané), but when she did I could tell by the way her eyes got all distant and sad that she regretted gettin ridda her child. At the time, though, it was her only option. Tejuan was broke and Kia survived on her good looks, so havin a kid woulda definitely been a problem. The only reason she kept Zhané was cuz, like she said, she ain't know about her until it was too late.

"Kia," I asked. "Do it hurt?"

"Do what hurt? Havin abortion or havin a baby?"

"Both."

"Well," Kia started. "When you have abortion, 'day open you up wit 'dis metal thing and scrape your insides. Then 'day stick 'dis vacuum up in you to suck out the baby piece by piece. 'Day be givin you drugs for the pain, but that shit ain't work on me. I felt *erything*. It pinches real bad. Dat scrapin hurt like a muhfucka, too. Andju bleed and get cramps for a few days, but after dat...the only thing dat be hurtin is y' heart cuz you killt a baby."

I nodded, takin in erything she was tellin me. Until then, I never thought of abortion as killin another person. It was just something you did cuz you had to.

"And havin a baby, well...dat's the worst pain I ever felt in my life," Kia continued, stretchin her expressive eyes wide for emphasis. "'Day gave me drugs for dat, too, but it wore off by the time Zhané was ready to come out. I was hurtin, boy! I cain't even begin to explain the shit. It's like havin real bad cramps times ten and feelin like y' body gonna split right up d' middle. And don't let the baby head be all big like Zhané was, cuz then y' pussy gon start tearin and dat shit is a whole 'nother pain in itself."

"Damn, Kia," I cringed. She was makin it so I wished I ain't have to go through either ordeal. "Both of em sound bad."

"Oh, 'day are, believe me," Kia agreed. "But at least when you have a baby, you get some'n nice out of it," she added dreamily. "A baby is a blessin. A real blessin."

I thought about it for a while. I wasn't sure what I wanted to do. If I was pregnant and I decided to have the baby, I'd hafta worry bout gettin money to provide for it, raising it, and givin up all my free time to take care of it. Tellin Dartanyan was only part of the problem. That nigga been sayin since day one that he wanted to get me pregnant anyway, so he'd probly be the first one poppin bottles to celebrate. Tellin Mommy was gonna be the real issue. She'd have a fit cuz even though I may not act like it, the fact remained that I was only thirteen—barely a baby my-damn-self. Not only that, I'd be pregnant at the same time as her. How embarrassing. I can hear it now, all them gossipin-ass broads around the way shakin they heads at us, sayin they just knew I was gon get knocked up before I turnt sixteen. By havin a baby, I'd be erything they said I'd be since I started gettin all bootylicious at a early age. Havin a abortion sounded bad, but at least I wouldn't hafta worry bout none of that shit. And I wouldn't be pregnant and sick no more, either. Decisions, decisions.

All the thinkin was makin my brain go in a whirl. My head started spinnin and I felt the familiar slimy queasiness in my stomach again. I hopped up and bolted to the bathroom just in time, kneeling at the toilet and throwin up for the third time that mornin. I wanted to die for real now. Why was God doin this to me? I wasn't ready for no shit like this.

"You betta think of some'n," Kia advised, comin up behind me and standin in the doorway. She started bouncin Zhané on her hip. "You betta think of some'n real quick, Honey Child. You might not have dat much time to decide."

Mixed feelings. That was the best way to describe my mindstate after finding out Jasmine was my sister. I wanted to keep hatin my father and blaming his absence for erything that went wrong in my life. But at the same time, I was ready to let it go. I was curious about the real Redz. I wanted to find out what made him tick and why he left ery family he ever started. I really ain't know much about him 'cept his name, where he was from, and that I looked just like him, which was one of the main reasons Mommy treated me different growin up. Other than that, he was pretty much a stranger to me. Damn shame, hunh?

The mystery of my father had been plaguing me long enough. I called Mommy up the same night I found out Jasmine was my sister and asked for Redz' number, agreeing to make peace with him and start up the father-daughter relationship that's been missin between us since I was six years old. I knew damn well I wasn't gon call that man and try to be his friend, even though that's what I told Mommy cuz I knew it's what she wanted to hear. I ain't wanna be Redz' friend or hang out and do whatever else daughters and fathers did. I just wanted to talk to him, you know, get to the bottom of things. After thirteen years without the bamma around, it ain't like he could gimme guidance or advice bout shit I done already learned through experience. I wasn't lookin for him to drop no words of wisdom or promise to be there from now on or nothin like that, either. He could disappear again for all I gave a rat's ass. I just needed some typa closure.

So there I was, home from the food and fireworks of July 4th, sittin on my balcony with the cordless phone in one hand and a shred of paper in the other. My whole body was shaking with anticipation cuz I knew I was out there to clear my head and call Redz to find out when we could get together and talk. Only problem was I was I couldn't stop concentrating on my bitter feelings long enough to dial his number. I stared at my angry handwriting on the scrap of paper where I had his info written down and wondered just what in the world I could say to the man who abandoned me. Should I flip back to the old Shai and cuss him out fifty different ways before hangin up and never callin him again? Or should I be my calmer, more mature self and try to have a conversation with the man? For a whole day, I been conflicted bout the shit, both for me and my dead brother. Redz left a lotta loose ends with us, not to mention years of pent-up resentment. I mean, don't get me wrong, me and Cerrone did just fine without him around. We mighta ran wild and did a lotta shit we ain't have no business cuz Mommy ain't have nobody there helpin her with us till Tone came along. But I wouldn't call us traumatized. Then again, my taste in men and the reckless way I lived my life mighta been a direct result of havin no pops around to help keep me in check. I could say the same bout Cerrone's lifestyle and his attitude towards men with authority. Yeah, I at least owed it to my brother to talk to this bamma and get answers to the questions we had since he left. If nothin else, I'd finally have Redz' side of the story.

I unballed the scrap of paper in my hand and dialed the number before I could change my mind. Blood rushed to my head in a dizzy nervousness that threatened to make me pass out, but I took a deep breath and told

myself to chill. Ery ring of the phone made my heart flutter. *Brrrrinnnng.*
Brrrrinnnng. It seemed like forever till somebody picked up.

"Hello?"

"Yeah, um..." My mouth went dry and I suddenly forgot my whole reason for callin. "Uh...is Redz 'dare?"

"Who's this?" asked the suspicious man's voice on the other end.

"It's his daughter. Rashaiyah."

There was a silence.

"Shai?"

"Yeah," I answered, gettin butterflies at the thought that I just mighta been talkin to my father already. Who else could it be answering his phone after eleven o'clock at night? Why else would he pause in a awed silence like he couldn't believe it was me on the other line?

"Damn, I cain't believe you called me," Redz finally said. "Hi you been, shawdy?"

"Dat's you, Redz?" I asked.

"Yeah, it's me. 'Dis my cell phone number. Brenda ain't tell you dat when she gave it to you?"

"Nah."

Silence again. My brain went numb. As much as I wanted to say, I couldn't think of a thing to talk about. I guess cuz I couldn't believe I was actually talkin to Redz and he was being so cool about it. You'da thought the last time we said more than hi and bye to eachother was a day ago insteada several years.

"So hi you been?" Redz asked again. I listened to the distantly familiar baritone of his voice and was reminded of being a lil girl.

"I been good. You?"

"Can't complain," he said with a too-cool ease. "Damn, I'm really glad you called me, shawdy. I knew you'd get around to it sooner or later. You probly been waitin a long time d' cuss me out."

"What make you say dat?" I chuckled.

"Considerin dat's whatchu did the last time I seent you..."

"Oh, yeah. Well, dat was under some fucked up circumstances, if you don't mind my sayin," I told him. The last time we came in contact with eachother was at my brother's funeral and...I may have cussed him out in fronta the whole church for having the nerve to show up. But I was upset that my brother had to die before our father came to see him. You understand, right?

"So, I heard you got some kids," Redz said.

"I heard you got some, too."

"Yeah, I do. You my oldest, though. My Baby Redz."

I smiled, feelin a mixture of joy and sadness after hearin my father call me by the nickname he gave me when I was a baby. I remember when him and erybody else useta call me Baby Redz so much I thought it was my real name. They useta look at the two of us, all fiery red and unique, and say it wasn't no way Redz could deny me. I looked like he spit me right out. I useta be real proud to hear that, knowing if nothin else, I was my father's child.

"Um..." I cleared my throat to dissolve the lump tryna form in it. "Yeah, I met one uh' your daughters the uh' day. Jasmine," I said.

"Oh, yeah? Kim's baby, right? You met them?"

"Yeah. It's kind of a long story."

"I bet."

Redz paused as if he was remembering how he met Kim at Republic Gardens a lil over seven years ago and romanced her for a week before dippin in and outta her life till Jasmine was born and he completely disappeared. I wanted to ask what made him heartless enough to do such a thing, but I wasn't really tryna get into all that. We was poseda be talkin bout me. I closed my eyes as if to focus and took a deep breath to get my nerve back. There was a million things I wanted to ask Redz, but I had to do it face-to-face.

"Look, Redz. I really need d' sit down and talk to you bout some shit," I started. "We need d' get t'geva, so whenever you got time...It ain't gotta be no all day thing..."

"Whatchu doin t'mar?" he interrupted.

"Thursday? I gotta work..."

"Oh," came Redz' disappointed response.

"I kh go in late, 'doe. I'on have no appointments till three," I told him, quickly remembering my schedule.

"Aight, well I get off at twelve. We kh hook up and have lunch or some'n," Redz suggested.

"Aight, dat's a bet."

"Now, you ain't gon carry on like you did the last time we saw eachother, is you?"

"Nah, man," I chuckled. "I just got some things I wanna aks you."

"I betchu do," Redz said. "I know I got a lotta explainin to do. I probly shoulda done it sooner, but..."

"Shai, I'm bout d' go chill wit Iyania," Krys said suddenly from behind me. I looked back at her poking her head out the balcony door with a rushed expression on her face like she was tryna hurry up and leave. I wanted to ask where she was goin at this damn late on a Wednesday night, but I ain't wanna cut Redz off to find out. He sounded like he was bout to pour his heart out.

"...I ain't got no good reason for a lotta shit I did, or didn't do. You hea' me, shawdy?" Redz asked, his voice snatching me back to our lil heart-to-heart moment.

"Yeah, I hea' you," I answered, half payin attention. I gave Krys the one minute finger so she could wait till I got off the phone with my father, but she waved her hands frantically and shook her head.

"I gotta go *now*, young. 'Day bout to leave me," she whispered loudly. I frowned at her and motioned for her to wait again.

"I always wondered hi you was doin, 'doe. I might not came around, but I thought about you and y' bruhva a lot," Redz told me on the other end.

"F'real?"

Krys rolled her eyes and shut the balcony door like I dismissed her or something. I watched through the blinds as she gathered her purse and headed for the door, too distracted by Redz to stop her, and too distracted by her to keep talkin to Redz. Before I knew it, she slammed my door shut behind her, came out the front of the building, and hopped in the front seat of this white, Crown Vic bubble on chrome that glided up in the parkin lot like a ghost. Then, just like that, she was gone.

"Anyhow," Redz said. "I'ma take you out t'mar and we gon talk about all that. Like I said, I get off at twelve, so we kh meet any time after dat."

"Uh...Howbout one? I kh meet you at y' job if you want."

"Nah, just meet me at a restaurant or some'n. You like seafood? Soul food? Steak? What?"

"All of it. But I kh do some seafood."

"Aight, well meet me at Phillip's in Sowfwess. We kh hit the buffet."

"Aight," I agreed.

I left Redz with my cell phone number and both of us promised to call if anything came up between now and our date. As much as I doubted him over the years, I could tell Redz was gon make good on his promise to meet with me. Something in his voice told me he had a weight to get off his chest even bigger than the one pressing down on minez. I hung up the phone feelin a tornado of emotions all at once. Nervousness, anxiousness, anticipation. I was actually gon meet up with my father. What would he say? How would he act? Was I gon be able to get through the meal without bustin into tears? Could I handle talkin bout the past and Cerrone and erything in between? Unbelievable.

I couldn't believe I was really gon sit down with Redz, any more than I could believe the nerve of Krys rollin out on me like that. What the sam hell was that girl's issue, anyhow? Did she think I was gon let that go? I dialed her phone and tried to find out where she was goin and with who, but that lil heffa had the nerve to forward me. Man, between the apprehension I was feeling for tomorrow and the way Krys was workin my nerves, it's a wonder I ain't lose my damn mind already.

CHAPTER EIGHT

Kia was right. I didn't have that much time to decide. After I spent Christmas day sick as a dog, I figured the sooner I found out what was goin on, the better. Dhonni went with me that day I rolled up to the CVS behind Hechinger Mall and ruffed a pregnancy test. With her and Trayonna nervously by my side, the three of us went back to Kia's house where I squatted my ass over that stick and pissed out an answer to the most crucial question of my young life.

I was pregnant.

I was *thirteen* and pregnant.

I ain't know how far along or none of that shit, and I really ain't wanna know. All that mattered was that I was for real-for real pregnant. Just when I thought it couldna got no worse, after Mommy said she was gettin married and we was gonna move to Maryland and leave behind erything I ever known, shit got worse.

"Whatchu gon do?" Kia asked, standin over me in the same tiny-ass bathroom of her apartment where I got sick the week before.

I was on the floor with my knees drawn to my chest, my head buried in my arms, tryna think of an answer. But I couldn't. It was like my brain was stuck in neutral. My already unstable world had gone from being just a lil shaky to shook off the damn Richter scale in a matter of minutes. I couldn't have no baby, that's what I did know. The more I thought about it, the more it made sense to get ridda the child growin in my womb. Fuck if I was killin another person or not. I ain't have a pot to piss in or a window to throw it out of, and I ain't wanna raise no baby the way I was raised—on saltine crackers and pipe dreams. I was too young to get a job, and Dartanyan's dope money wasn't always steady, so how could the two of us really take care of a child? And damn! What would our folks say?

I knew Mommy was gon kirk when she found out. She already told me before if I ever came home pregnant she was gon send me to a convent, then send me to boarding school till I turned eighteen. Nah, young. As much as I wanted a baby, I wasn't tryna go out like that. So I made up my mind right then and there.

"I ain't keepin it," I told Kia, a single tear runnin down my cheek. Dhonni wiped her own watery eyes and came and sat on the floor beside me to wrap her arms around me in a supportive sisterly hug. Trayonna was sittin on the side of the tub lookin like she wanted to cry right along with us. The emotion was so thick in that bathroom you could see it collectin and drippin down the grimy, white walls.

"Aww, man Honey Child. You sure you wanna do dat?" Kia asked. Her face was twisted with anticipation, like she was debating whether to talk me outta it or not. But wasn't nothin changin my mind, not even Kia. I couldn't have no baby.

"I'm sure," I said. "I cain't keep 'dis j'on.'"

So two days later, Kia took me down to the clinic across town where she got her abortion done. She ain't say nothin the whole bus ride, just put her arm around me and pressed my head to her shoulder like Mommy useta do me when I got upset as a child. Up until that morning Kia had been tryna make me change my mind, and I guess once she realized I was gonna do what I thought I had to no matter what she said, she was at a loss for words. I knew she was mad at me but she ain't let on cuz she musta remembered how hard it was for her to be forced into the same decision. Dartanyan, on the other hand, was so pissed that after he gave me the money for the abortion, he looked at me like he was disgusted and walked away with his head hangin down. I think that's what bothered me the most.

The sky was overcast like it was gonna snow, and it put a dark gloom in my heart that matched the dreary, winter scenery outside. I felt numb inside. Dead like my baby was gon be. After I signed in and used Kia's cousin's ID to say I was eighteen, I sat in a cold room in a paper gown, lookin at the posters of mothers with they children and the female reproductive system all over the walls. A middle-aged nurse who acted like she ain't wanna be there no more than I did, took my vitals and drew some blood for testing. Come to find out, I was bout nine weeks along, just one week shy of what Mommy was at the time. That was two months and some change! Two whole months. I couldn't get that shit outta my mind. My baby was two whole months and there I was bout to kill it.

That shit got me thinkin. What if Mommy killed me when I was two months inside her? I wouldn't be here, just like the three babies she aborted between my sisters and the new baby comin now. I mean, my life wasn't great and I ain't know what I wanted outta it yet, but I was glad to be alive—that was for damn sure. As sure as the realization of what I was really bout to do. I was gon kill a baby. *My* baby. A baby that only came about cuz me and Dartanyan was so much in what we thought was love. Could I honestly kill something that was a result of that young, confused devotion? Was I really so fucked up and selfish that a innocent child had to suffer cuz I couldn't keep my damn legs closed? The more I thought about it, the more I saw images in my mind of babies: lil babies, big babies, beautiful, chubby, brown babies gettin tore apart piece by piece by a vacuum that sucked em into a dead, bloody nothingness. All cuzza me. It was downright disturbing.

Right before the nurse put the anesthesia mask over my face to send me into la-la land, I sat up, feet in the stirrups at the end of the table, coochie all out, feelin the lowest I ever felt in my life, and started cryin. Bawling cuz I couldn't go through with killin my baby, but I wasn't sure what else to do. The doctor just stared at me and shook her head like she seen the same shit happen a hundred times before, but I ain't care. I got dressed and Kia got my money back, and we got on the bus towards home. It was one of the smartest decisions I ever made in my life.

To make a long story short, life went on as normal from there. I still went to school, still took care of home, and still hung out with my friends. I even had Mommy thinkin I was still bleedin ery month cuz I made used sanitary napkins outta red food colorin and tuna fish juice, and left em in the trash where she could see. I took advantage of the winter and cool spring months when I started showin, hidin myself in hoodies and sweats, and made sure to stay outta the house as much as possible, away from Mommy's knowing eyes. I spent more time with Dartanyan whenever he wasn't busy with his new job at Safeway helpin folks with they bags, or out on the block with Tristan helpin folks chase they high. I went on missions to any place with bad security with Kia and them to get stuff I'd need for me and the baby, and sold whatever I ain't want so I could save money for later. I ain't go to no doctor the whole time I was pregnant (somebody woulda found out I was a minor and got Mommy involved) but I made sure I ate whatever foods and vitamins I read about in them baby books Dhonni and Trayonna got for me. Except for tryna get useta my body havin a mind of its own, and not being able to sleep flat on my back or my stomach, my pregnancy wasn't that bad. I wasn't too tired, I stopped gettin sick after a couple months, and I was able to hustle and save some money so me and Dartanyan could rent out this old lady's basement over on L Street. By the time August rolled around, we was gon be straight. Erything was goin along just as planned till springtime sprung and my spot got blowed up.

I was lookin through a book of baby names when I heard Mommy yellin at my lil sisters out in the livin room. It wasn't nothin unusual, so I ain't pay em no mind. But the next thing you know, here come Mommy bustin up in my room dragging Sparkle by the arm behind her, all mad bout something I was too caught off guard to understand. Before I could slip the book behind the mattress me and my sisters slept on, Mommy came over and yanked up my sweatshirt, exposing my bare, protruding belly. By this time it was May and I was over seven months along. I only gained fourteen pounds the whole time I was pregnant so my figure wasn't real noticeable, especially if I was in baggy clothes. Despite the fact that my nose was spread halfway across my face and I went from rockin short, tight shit to big-ass T-shirts and sweats, most people (includin Mommy) had no idea I was pregnant. Thanks to Sparkle, though, all that changed. I shoulda known better than to trust her lil ass with a secret, but I had no choice tellin my sisters what was up since we shared the same bed and changed clothes in the same room. Besides, I already told my brother months before and I thought my sisters would understand the importance of the situation when they saw how long Cerrone kept it on the hush. Yet no more than a month later Sparkle opens her big mouth and makes a comment bout how tight it would be if me and Mommy had our babies on the same day.

Mommy saw the truth with her own two eyes and I knew right away what I had to do. Between duckin blows and listenin to Mommy call me erything but a child of God, I packed all I owned in a garbage bag and dragged it upstairs to Dhonni's. Miz Darlene met me at the door and after I explained what happened, agreed to let me stay for as long as I needed. This, of course, prompted a big-ass shouting match between her and Mommy that ended with Miz Darlene slamming the door in my mother's face. They stopped being friends that same day. I felt bad for causing a rift between the two of em like that, but I ain't have nowhere to go and I ain't know what else to do. I was thirteen, pregnant, and confused.

Anyways, to make a short story even shorter, Mommy warned me to stay out her house and stopped speakin to me from that point on. She claimed I was a bad seed and a even badder example for my lil sisters to look up to, but I knew the real reason she was salty was cuz I had her fooled for so long. That, and the painful fact that erybody and they mama started talkin bout her, sayin she was a unfit mother for not havin a hold on me, "that fast-ass red gal of hers". It ain't like I was the first young girl in my neighborhood to get pregnant (and certainly not the last) but since it was me and erybody always assumed it would be, my pregnancy was definitely something to talk about. The gossip and all the pointing and snickering erybody did embarrassed me too, but nothin shamed me worse than my own mother actin like I ain't exist. Even when I turned fourteen two weeks later, Mommy ain't wish me happy birthday, send a card, or gimme a birthday shout-out on WPGC or nothin. I acted like I wasn't phased by her actin all petty, but that shit wounded me to my soul. If nothin else, my mother know how to hold a grudge. And she wrote the book on hurtin people without liftin a hand or sayin a word.

Mommy still wasn't speakin to me the night I went to the goin away party for Cerrone at his boy Foots' house, the same night before they was poseda be movin. It was pretty much a done deal that I wouldn't be movin wit em. Erybody swore Mommy would come to her senses, but the situation wasn't lookin very optimistic. I wasn't trippin, though. Just like I told Dhonni, if Mommy was plannin to leave me behind in D.C. that was just fine with me. I ain't wanna leave my old neighborhood no how.

"So y'all movin t'mar?" Biggums asked, runnin a hand over the neat trail braids I gave her earlier that day. I was still mad as shit at her for cuttin all that long, fluffy hair into a bush, but I had to admit, short hair fit her a lot better. She was sittin with my brother, Pookie, and her weird-ass friend

Syco on the steps below me, Dhonni, and Trayonna on the porch swing.

"Yeah, t'mar mornin at the ass-cracka dawn," Cerrone answered.

"Damn, y'all cain't even stay till the end uh' the summer?" Lakisha whined from her spot on the porch ledge. Her eyes was almost pleading, like my brother was the one she had to convince.

"Nah, we poseda be gettin useta our new neighborhood and shit before school start. I'on know why, young. I ain't tryna make no friends. Fuck I need to chill wit a racka Mar'land bammas for?"

Dhonni moved a few strands of my invisible braids out the way and put her head on my shoulder. Me, her, and Trayonna was dressed alike in Chocolate City T-shirts, New Balance 996s, and drop socks slouched to the rolled-up cuffs of our Bongo stretch jeans.

"I'ma miss my girl," Dhonni fake cried, and sniffled a couple times.

"What's 'dare to miss? I ain't goin nowhere," I said. "My muhva leavin me hea'."

"Girl, y' muhva ain't leavin you," Lakisha said, smackin her lips on her cherry Tootsie Pop.

"Sho' ain't," Trayonna agreed.

"You wanna bet?"

"Yeah," Biggums volunteered. "Bet five you gon move out d' Mar'land. I'on see y' moms leavin you hea'."

"Aight, bet," I said, holdin out my little finger. We locked pinkies and pressed our thumbs together till our fingers snapped apart.

"You gon owe me five dollas, too, nigga."

"Whateva. You gon see. I'm tellin you, y'all don't know my muhva," I said, rubbin my stomach and lookin around at the party.

For a last-minute house party with no drinks except tap water and a couple bags of ice from the corner store, the turnout was pretty good. Bammas was out that j'on deep as shit, all piled in the basement, spillin out into the back yard, the front yard, and the street in fronta Foots' house on Trinidad Ave. I wished I could go inside and put my *One Leg Up* to the Pure Elegance tape Cerrone popped in the stereo not too long ago, but it wasn't no way I could be in a crowded-ass house party all pregnant and whatnots. Just my luck, I'd get elbowed in the stomach or some shit.

"Damn, nigga. You gon keep slobbin dat j'on down or is you gon burn some'n?" Biggums fussed at her friend Syco. He finished licking shut a fresh-rolled J and passed it to my brother.

"Spark it 'den," Syco ordered, standin up to shake the sticks and seed crumbs off his black DDTP World shirt. For him to be so far from what I considered cute, Syco was attractive in a odd kinda way, like cuz who carried around the severed head in that movie *Dead Presidents*. With his dark, piercing eyes and a roughness to him that was both scary and sexy at the same time, Syco made you nervous yet curious of what it'd be like to go a couple rounds with him. Erybody who remembered the day he stabbed this boy in the face with a pencil for callin him a crackbaby called him Syco, and either sweated his nuts cuz he was a go-hard kinda nigga, or was scared as shit of him for the same reason. He definitely wasn't nobody you'd wanna cross, but I'on think Syco was hardly crazy as erybody made him out to be. He was just strange. It probly had something to do with the Ritalin his mama fed him all through elementary school for his so-called hyperactivity. I knew a racka niggas with loose screws from taking that shit.

Pookie pulled a lighter out the pocket of his green camouflage shorts and gave it to Cerrone.

"I do. Hea'. And don't be tryna cuff dat j'on eiva, nigga," he warned with a faintly sad smirk. Pookie was being unusually quiet and I knew it was cuz he was gonna miss my brother.

"I got deuce on dat j'on," Biggums said, noddin at the J.

"Nah, I got deuce," Pookie argued. "You ain't put up on 'dis."

"Dat's fuckt up, Pookie."

"So what, nigga. 'Dis my weed. Y'all smokin, too?" Pookie asked us. Lakisha and Trayonna nodded.

"You blazin?" Cerrone asked Dhonni, shining a big, black flashlight in her face for a second.

"And you know this, man," my best friend answered, swingin blindly at Cerrone till he got the light out her eyes. "Foots, you sure it's aight we smokin in fronta y' house?"

"Yeah," Foots shrugged. "My muhva don't care. Long as it ain't no fights out 'dis j'on, she ain't trippin."

The strong herbal scent of weed smoke mixed with the leafy smell of summer, filled the air around us. I leaned deeper into the swing and rubbed my stomach. I couldn't wait till the baby was born. I felt like I was missin out on erything.

"Don't trip, Suga Baby. I'ma have a fat-ass bob waitin f' you soon as you drop dat youngin," Biggums promised, brushing ashes off her crisp, burgundy Redskins jersey.

"Yeah, wheneva dat finally happen," I grumbled. I wasn't sure of my due date cuz I ain't been to the dotors since my lil abortion fiasco. I was too scared to go cuz I thought the authorities would get involved and try to take my baby cuz I was so young. From readin all them pregnancy books, though, I knew it took anywhere from 36 to 42 weeks for a baby to come. According to my calculations, I still had bout a month to go. Just the thought of being pregnant for four more weeks made me wanna scream. I was tempted to just jam a ruler up there and get the baby out myself.

"Know whatchu havin?" Foots asked. He was my brother's friend, and one of the only ones who wasn't into all that criminal shit the rest of us seemed to gravitate to. Foots was a goody-goody who read books and ran track. Youngin was pretty swift on his feet, too. Tha'ts why we called him Foots. Anyhow, the worst thing Foots did was smoke a lil weed once in a while, so I couldn't figure out how him and Cerrone got to be friends. I was glad they was cool, though. Cerrone needed somebody like Foots around to balance out all the mischief Pookie got him into.

"I'on know. I hope it's a boy," I told him. I ain't want no daughter cuz the way I saw it, a baby girl would take all Dartanyan's attention away from me. You know how niggas get all gooey over they daughters.

"She carryin low so it's probly a boy," Dhonni said, pattin my belly.

"What the fuck do carryin low mean?"

"It's how far down the baby is in my stomach. If it was high up, I'd be havin a girl," I explained.

"Man, hi you know dat?" Cerrone asked, shakin his head.

"Muhfucka, I *reads*, aight. Besides, dat's what 'dis lady at the Discount Mart told me."

"Well, since you havin a boy, you needs d' name dat lil nigga after me," Pookie said.

"How Pookie sound as a first name?" Trayonna joked.

"Not Pookie, man. I mean —"

"You need d' name him after me," Cerrone suggested. "I'ma be the most important nigga in his life anyhow."

"Ain't the fahva gon be most important?" Lakisha asked.

Cerrone shrugged and left it at that. I knew he was hinting that Dartanyan would leave me like most niggas left they kids, like our daddy left us. Cerrone been sayin since day one that Dartanyan was a Redz type but I just couldn't see it. Apparently, I was too far up Dartanyan's ass to notice how sneaky and selfish he really was. Don't get me wrong—Cerrone and Dartanyan was bout as cool as a overprotective brother and the bamma who knocked up his big sister could be. But Cerrone ain't think Dartanyan was right for me. Then again, according to my lil brother, wasn't *nobody* right for me.

"I'on know what I'ma name him. I—I wish you'd stop blowin dat shit in my face."

"Oh, my bad," my best friend giggled. Dhonni was purposely blowin smoke in my direction so I'd catch a contact.

"Keep messin 'round, hea'. Don't say nuffin when y' godbaby come out retarded."

"Shai, stop trippin. My muhva smoked bud when she was pregnant wit me and Pookie and we turnt out fine. Ain't we, Pookie?"

Pookie stuck out his tongue and moaned, then started beatin his arm against his chest like he had cerebral palsy. I tried not to bust out laughin but I couldn't help it. That boy was a lunchbox.

"You know you wrong," Trayonna chuckled.

"He stupid as shit. Stop playin like dat, Pookie. Dat shit ain't funny," Dhonni fussed at her brother, who was still beatin his chest and carryin on. He kept up his act even after two girls hesitantly walked up to the porch and stood in fronta the house like they wasn't sure if they was at the right place.

"Who dat?" Cerrone barked, shining the flashlight on they two figures. One was short and solid like she was built for wreckin cows, and the other was tall and thin with a graceful dancer's form.

"Who is *dat?*" the short, sassy one replied.

"Ay, muhfucka, we askin 'na questions," Biggums snarled.

My brother shined the light in the girls' faces and ery jaw on the porch dropped when we saw who they was.

"Is dat Baby and Precious?" I asked in amazement, gawking at the two café au lait colored girls like they just fell out the sky.

"Lemme find out Miz Cunningham let y'all off the porch," Dhonni teased in a mocking tone.

Baby twisted a watermelon Blow Pop around in her mouth before she popped it out and smacked her lips. She put a hand on one of her hips and stuck out a foot like she was showin off her chunky-heeled jellies.

"Heard y'all was movin t'mar," Baby said, lickin her lollipop at my brother. "So is you or ain't chu?"

"I'm is," Cerrone answered like he was in a trance, obviously taken by Baby's china doll cuteness and the erotic moves she was makin with her tongue. Me and Dhonni gave eachother a look and smirked. Lakisha started muggin cuz being seductive with a lollipop was her thing.

"So 'dis where d' party at?" Baby asked, pointing to the house with her lollipop.

"Don'tchu see all them muhfuckas in'na street out front?" Dhonni asked back, givin her a hard time.

"Ooh, she carried you, young!" Lakisha jeered, causing Precious to start nervously fingering the Absolüt Madness lanyard around her neck. Baby grit on both Lakisha and Dhonni and turned back to Foots.

"Is 'dis the right house or what?" she asked him, wrinkling up her forehead like she was gettin annoyed.

"Yeah, you at the right house, sweetheart," Foots answered.

"Go right through 'dare," Pookie directed, eyeballing the two sisters like he couldn't decide which one was fine enough to hold his attention. He pointed to the basement door under the porch. Baby, with one last glare at Dhonni, motioned towards her big sister and headed for the door. Dhonni bucked at they backs and grit on em as they went by Syco, Foots, Pookie, and Cerrone's ogling stares.

"Got-damn, youngin," my brother said as Baby wobbled past. He shined the flashlight on her behind. "Lemme find out Baby got a dunkey."

"Put the spotlight on'na buttcheeks!" Biggums sang, cuttin her eyes and staring after Baby and Precious right along with the boys.

"Y'all some hounds," I commented.

"F'real," Dhonni agreed.

Biggums and the boys started barking and howling like a yard fulla noisy dogs and I cracked up laughin again. Them fools ain't make no sense.

A lil while later, Dartanyan rolled up with Black and Whiteboy, lookin sexier than ever. He was dressed in all black from his Reeboks to his T-shirt, 'cept for the city scarf he wore over his shoulders and his favorite Madness hat with the triangle on the front, his neighborhood 14th & Congress on one side, and his nickname, Cruddy, on the other.

"'Dare go my bun-bun!" I beamed, hoisting myself up to go meet him halfway. Dartanyan saw me comin and upped his step to get to me. He bent down to kiss me and we hugged as tight as we could without squishing the baby between us. I felt complete for the first time all day. Dartanyan seemed a lot more distracted nowadays than he did before I got pregnant, but we was still on eachother pretty hard. It was almost to the point where neither one of us could seem to function right without the other. Dartanyan filled up the empty, loveless spaces in my world and I filled up his. That nigga was my heart!

"Hi you feel, boo?" Dartanyan asked, walkin me back over to the porch. He slapped Foots, Pookie, Syco, and my brother daps and said wsup to my girls. Whiteboy and Black followed suit.

"Better now dat you hea'," I gushed, and snuck him another kiss.

"Ugh, y'all two, get a room," Lakisha sneered.

"F'real. Ay, Crud, you got some bud, young?" Cerrone asked, breaking up our lil moment.

"C'mon, now. You aksin *me* if I got bud?" Dartanyan chuckled, pullin a fat-ass J from behind his ear. "*What is it dat get chall high, get dat smoke all up in yo' eyes...*"

"Dat's what I'm talkin bout, cuz. Pass the rocket," Syco said, holdin out the lighter for him to spark it up.

Dartanyan and his friends got situated with the resta the boys on the porch steps and started smokin down. Before the j'on even went around once, Dartanyan's pager started beepin all loud. He pulled it off his waistband to see what number came up, and a funny look crossed his face like he recognized the number but ain't wanna call whoever it was back. Then he clamped the j'on back on his Levi's like it never even went off.

"Who dat?" I asked, being all nosy.

"Pipehead nigga. Don't worry about it."

I started to ask Dartanyan why he was passin up money like that but I ain't wanna get into a argument like we did the last time I got on him for ignoring a page. I know it sounds like I'm being all up in the sauce, but you gotta understand—Dartanyan *never* useta ignore his pages. Even if we was way out Northwest and a youngin in Southeast call him lookin to cop a bag, he'll take the train all the way down there just to get that serve. And don't let em be lookin for the buttas cuz Dartanyan will drop erything, including me, to make a crack sale. Lately, though, he been gettin a racka pages and not answering em. I wanna believe that he doin it cuz he miss me and wanna spend some uninterrupted time together, but I be havin a hard time ignoring the ill feelin I get in my gut tellin me he's hidin something. I'm almost positive it's other girls, but the way I take up all Dartanyan's time when he ain't at work or on the grind, I can't imagine who he got time to be seeing on the side. Besides, my baby wouldn't go like that on me. He might be a lil crazy but he ain't stupid.

"How dat j'on lookin?" Black asked my brother and them about the party.

"Like d' Icebox on a Saturday," Syco told him.

"It's a lotta broads down 'nere?"

"A rack," Cerrone jumped in. "Bout three or four for ery nigga out dat j'on."

"You sicin it," Black accused my brother, lookin at him doubtfully.

"Aight, 'den. Go look f' yourself. It's *too* many broads."

"I gotta see 'dis shit, cuz," Whiteboy said.

"Yeah, no buh'shit," Black agreed, oblivious to the look Trayonna was givin him for ignoring her. My brother, still puffin on the J, led the way to the basement door under the porch with Pookie, Foots, Syco, Black, and Whiteboy behind him. As soon as they opened the door, steam and the sound of All-N-One puttin *Mandingo* in the pocket floated out and started to lure me in. I sighed another bored and desperate sigh cuz I knew I couldn't party, no matter how much I wanted to.

"Ay, I be back, Boo," Dartanyan said, springing up at the last minute to go in with em.

"Did I say you kh go?" I demanded.

"Did I aks for your permission?"

"Escuse me?"

"I ain't gon be gone dat long, man, damn," Dartanyan fussed.

"Fine 'den. Get out my face!" I spat jealously. "Andju betta not be freakin on no uh' broads eiva, Dartanyan!"

"Whateva, man," he scoffed, and disappeared into the darkness behind my brother and his friends. I rolled my eyes at his back, knowing damn well he was gonna be doin just that.

"Damn, 'day took the weed," Lakisha complained after the raggedy basement door slammed shut.

"Ol' stingy-ass nuckas," Biggums added.

"Fuck it, I'm smacked anyways," Dhonni said, leaning deeper into the porch swing with me.

"At least some'my is," I grumbled, and crossed my arms on toppa my stomach. I sat seething for a while thinkin bout the party I was missin and how Dartanyan was probly in there all up on some other girl's ass till Dhonni changed the subject.

"You really think Miz Brenda gon leave you hea'?" she asked, kickin her foot out to get the porch swing rockin again.

"She probly will. Dat bitch still ain't speakin to me," I answered.

"Well, if she do, you know you kh stay wit me. I'on care what no'by say—I ain't gon see you homeless and shit."

"Thanks. I appreciate dat."

"You ain't gotta thank me," Dhonni shrugged. "You my muhfuckin play sista. I got y' back no matter what. I mean dat shit," she told me with an exposed truth in her eyes.

"Yeah, and I gotchu if you need some extra money or some'n," Biggums offered.

"I be y' babysitter," Lakisha volunteered.

"I getchu some baby clothes," said Trayonna.

"Damn, y'all." I tried to fight the smile that pulled at the corners of my mouth. It was nice to know I could count on my girls. Ain't none of us have shit to give, but we shared whatever we had. That's how real it was with us.

"Dag, I hope you'on move," Dhonni said, putting her head on my shoulder again. "Shit ain't gon be the same witout chu."

"Yeah," I agreed with a sad smile of my own. It was unlikely my mother would take me to Maryland since she was so hell-bent on punishin me, but even if she did, I knew I could always come back and feel right at home. Trinidad would always be my 'hood, and them Suga Sweet— they'd always be my crew. I ain't see it being no other way.

Redz was late. It was exactly fifteen minutes past our one o'clock date and I was seriously considering gettin up and leaving. I already felt like a fool for letting my butterflies keep me up all night, and taking a hour to get dressed today cuz I couldn't decide if I should dress up or dress down for my date with my estranged father. After tryin on just about erything in my closet, I figured I couldn't go wrong with some jeans and a nice shirt, so I put em on and took that long, expectant drive to Southwest where I been waitin for the past half hour for his ass to join me. I knew I shouldna left the house so early. Better yet, I knew I shouldna thought Redz was actually gon come through for me. Knowin him, the nigga probly wasn't even gon show up. And there I was all dressed up with my good shoes on, waitin to see a man who's promises was flimsier than tissue paper.

I picked up my phone and stared to dial his number again so I could leave a message tellin him to go to hell, but a flash of light at the dining room entrance caught my eye. I purposely picked a table in the cut where I could see whoever came in the door without them seein me first. Good thing I did, too, cuz I probly looked all typsa dumbfounded when Redz strolled in like somebody would stroll up in they house, and stood in the doorway lookin around for me.

Redz had the same confident air of ery man I ever been attracted to, and a flirty smile that left the hostess who escorted him in, blushing redder than a fire hydrant. He was a poster boy of that old head coolness that Uncle Travis possessed, with a bop to his walk and a look in his eyes like he seen erything but he was still eager to see more. Dressed like a young bun in his black We R One shirt, baggy blue jeans, and fresh Nike boots to match, Redz coulda passed for a college boy even though the age in his face advertised his grown-ass manness. With them iced out studs in his ears and his red hair trimmed in a Caesar shaped up crisper than Steve Harvey's, Redz was out-doin most youngins I knew. The sunlight hit his earrings again and made the same flash that caught my attention the first time. Damn, Pops! I felt like I shoulda got up and brushed his shoulders off, he was so muhfuckin clean!

Redz stood there chewin a toothpick, tryna look nonchalant as he scanned the enormous lunch crowd for a familiar face. I could almost see his heart skip a beat when he turned to the right and our eyes met. I watched him register the shock of seeing me, a female version of hisself, studying his ery last detail for the first time in years. I was numb with nervousness, staring back at a face that looked so much like minez it sent a tingle through my scalp. It was him. My father. The same the same honey brown eyes, the same bright red hair, button nose, full lips. He was lighter than me, a lil more yellow than red, and had the same spotty, brown freckles all over his cheeks and the bridge of his nose like Cerrone had. As Redz walked over to my table tryna contain the excitement busting at the seams of his smile, I started to say hi and give him whatever kinda greeting a daughter would give her father. But I ain't know how. I wasn't sure if I should give him a hug or shake his hand like a stranger. I mean, Redz was my father and all, but I ain't exactly know him like that.

"It's like lookin in a mirror," was the first thing he said when he was right in fronta me. "Stand up, Baby Redz. Lemme see you."

So I stood, feelin all gangly and awkward like a lil girl being admired in her Easter Sunday clothes. Despite myself, I started smiling right along with him, and stepped into the stiff hug he offered me.

"Jeez Mo Christmas," Redz said, shakin his head at me. "You all grown up, Baby Redz. Guess I cain't call you dat no more, hunh?"

"I'on mind," I shrugged, even though it did feel kinda weird being called Baby. Hell, it felt weird being called *anything* by my father. We sat down across from eachother and stared in awe for a while, neither one of us really knowin what to say or do next.

"Well," he started.

"Well?"

"Sorry I'm late," Redz apologized. "I had d' wash dat grease off me and change my clothes. I ain't wanna come hea' all dirty and shit. I know you was probly blowin my phone up, but I left dat at home. I was in such a rush I forgot it. Dat's my bad, shawdy."

Redz leaned back in his seat and gave me a apologetic smile. I was too jittery to tell him I wasn't even mad no more. I was still tryna get over the fact that I was actually sittin there with his ass in the flesh. It was hard to know how to feel.

The waitress came by to take our drink order and I watched my father like I was seeing him for the first time. There was a lotta things about him I never noticed before, I guess cuz he never stuck around long enough for me to have the chance. Like how we both held our mouths the same way when we talked, and how his personality had a presence that demanded attention, even when he was tryna play it low key. I got a glimpse of his irresistible charm, too. No wonder women fell for his ass. Redz had a way of stimulating your eyes and ears so much that all you could do was hang onto his ery word. He made you feel special, like you was the only one in the room and shit. He was something rare and different and magnetic all at once.

"You still workin on cars?" I asked him after the waitress brought us our drinks. Redz flashed me his hands so I could see the ingrained dirt under his nails and nodded.

"I'ma be workin on cars till 'deez old hands give out," he told me. "My older bruhva, dat's your Uncle Michael, he manage 'dis garage off Missouri Avenue. Dat's where I be at ery day. So whatchu do? Y' muhva told me you got a job at the mall or some'n."

"Yeah, I do hair at 'dis salon in P.G. Plaza," I said.

"You like it?"

"Yeah, I like it. I'd like it even more if I ain't had d' stand up all day."

"Yeah, I feel you," Redz shrugged, then smiled at me. "Dat's good, 'doe. I'm glad d' hear you doin some'n worthwhile wit yourself."

My chest swelled with happiness at the thought that my father was proud of me, but I quickly played off my tickled smile by sipping on my glass of iced tea. Neither one of us said anything for a while. We just pretended to keep ourselves occupied with stuff on the table and observed eachother silently. It was jive kinda awkward cuz it really showed how much we ain't know eachother. I watched from behind my glass as Redz tore open a pack of sugar and stirred it into his iced tea in that sloppy, man-boy way my brother useta do things. I found myself fighting another smile as I realized yet another similarity between the two of them.

"So Brenda tell me you gave me some grandkids, hunh? Tryna make me a old man and shit," Redz joked after a nervous gulp of tea.

"Yeah. I got two boys," I told him. I dug in my purse and pulled out all the pictures of Man-Man and Tink I had in my wallet. Redz looked over each one carefully with a smile in his eyes that almost hinted he was sorry he ain't know em personally.

"Hi you pronounce they names?" he asked, squinting at my handwriting on the backs of they pictures.

"Kebian and Keyjuan. I call em Man-Man and Tink, 'doe."

"'Day look like a handful," he commented.

"Who you tellin? The lil one's the worst."

"He the one dat look like you, too."

"Yeah, wit all dat red hair," I smiled. "He got his fahva's eyes, 'doe."

"'Day both got the same fahva?" Redz asked off-handedly.

"Nah."

"Well, why not?"

I started to get offended that he of all people was gettin on me for havin two kids by two different dudes, but the expression on Redz face was innocent. He was just askin, not tryna condemn me like damn near erybody else did when they found out I was so young with so much baggage. I thought back to Dartanyan and all the circumstances that ripped us apart. The stress, the abuse, his trouble with the law...If shit ain't go down the way it did between us, I'da probly stayed with his ass. But, hey, erything happens for a reason, and me and Dartanyan not being together was *definitely* for the better.

"Well, Man-Man fahva and me, we useta fight a lot. *A lot*, a lot. It was a real bad situation, y'know? Better for us not to be together. We was lil youngins tryna play grown up and it just got to be too much after a while," I explained.

"Dat's usually how it happens," Redz said with a sober nod of his head. "Only two ways it kh go from there. Eiva you stay t'geva and end up killin eachuhva or one of y'all leave."

"Is dat why you left?" I asked suddenly, surprising myself. I ain't mean to get to the meat and potatoes of our meeting so soon, but Redz left his statement open for the one question that's been burning in my mind forever. I just couldn't resist.

"Damn. You gettin on me already," Redz chuckled with a smirk that exposed his reluctance to answer. I ain't back down, though. I stared right in his eyes and waited. He took a deep breath.

"All I kh say is, I ain't never been the marryin type," Redz began after a while, leaning on the table towards me. "I told y' muhva dat when we first got t'geva. Even though she knew dat, she still wanted to get at me and I wanted to get at her, so we made it happen. And lemme tell you, dat shit happent fast, too. One day we just hangin out, goin to the Classics and shit. Next day, she tellin me she pregnant and her moms is kickin her out."

Redz paused and his eyes got this faraway look like he was goin back in time.

"I wouldna been no typa man if I left her out to dry like dat. I'da just felt wrong leavin my girl and my baby wit nothin...Man, Brenda was so young. She couldna did it by herself, not at no seventeen years old. It was on me to be there, so I moved her in wit me and she had you and...I remember lookin at my baby girl, my Baby Redz, tellin myself you was worth settlin down for. As much as I wanted to go out 'dare and be in'na mix like I useta be, I looked at you and decided wasn't nothin out there worth more than my baby."

I blinked hard. The emotion in my fathers eyes was so real I could feel it, so real I had to bite my lips to keep from lettin the tears fall. I couldn't believe what I was hearing. There was actually a time in my life when Redz thought I was the most important thing in the world. To a girl who went through most of her life feeling rejected and unloved, here was my father tellin me he loved me so much I inspired him to change his entire lifestyle.

"Yeah," Redz smiled. "You was my world, Baby Redz. And when y' muhva told me she was pregnant wit my lil man, he was my world, too. It was only right to be a family. Me and Brenda moved out Norfeass and I made it my business to come home ery night after work to be witchall. All I did was work and play daddy. It felt like the right thing to do. I *knew* it was the right thing to do...But I got restless, shawdy. Nigga like me was useta comin and goin as he please. Being a family man started to feel like a jail sentence..."

Redz shook his head and his voice trailed off. I waited again.

"I worked all day but we was still broke. Y'all needed shit and it fucked me up when I couldn't pay the rent and all the bills and give you shit, too. I was gettin stressed, so I started goin back around my old neighborhood, chillin wit y' uncles and my friends from back home and shit. Hangin out all night, smokin reefer, chasin skirts. You know, just tryna escape. Y' muhva ain't like dat shit one bit. She'd call my folks house lookin for me, call my sister, erybody on my block — anybody she kh get a hold of to talk to me. Youngin was tryna keep up wit what I's doin like she was my P.O. or some'n…I just couldn't take it no more."

Redz leaned back and shook his head again. He had said enough. He cleared up a lotta things I already kinda knew cuz I been through it myself but there still was some things I couldn't figure out. Things that left me angry and confused for years.

"Why you ain't never come around again? Why you keep havin kids wit uh' broads and shit?" I asked.

Redz sighed.

"Look, I ain't wanna leave. I coulda kept runnin the streets and comin home to y'all forever. But y' muhva wasn't havin dat, shawdy. She told me I couldn't have it both ways. I had to choose between bein daddy or goin out 'dare and bein ol' Redz. And the way I saw it then, dat was like choosin between prison and freedom. Guess I liked my freedom more," Redz concluded.

"So why you keep havin more kids? Bad enough you did us like dat, but to keep doin it, Redz?…How many baby muhvas you got anyhow?"

"Hmm," he sighed, thinking. Then after a short pause, "Six, including y' mama," he informed me honestly. "Let's see…I had two wit Brenda, one wit Lynn, one wit Sharon, two wit Niecy, two wit Dana, and one wit Kim. Kim baby girl Jasmine is my youngest. Don't ask me how old the resta them is, 'doe. I'd *really* hafta think about dat."

I just looked at him in disbelief. My father was out there making babies like we was in the *Wild Kingdom* somewhere. It's a wonder he made it through the eighties without catching his death. Ain't too many folks out here these days who can say they had unprotected sex with six different people and only walked away with a kid.

"Got-damn, Redz! Six baby muhvas?!" I exclaimed. "Why? What was the point? Don't you think dat was a lil bit selfish to start a life wit six different women and leave em all hangin in the end?"

"Well…I really ain't mean for shit to happen the way it did, but that's just how nature works. Besides, I know for a fact that Lynn, Niecy, and Dana was lyin bout bein on birth control. I'on know why anybody'd wanna trap a nigga like me; I ain't got shit to my name. Guess they just wanted some red babies wit light eyes," Redz mulled aloud.

"So you gon blame it all on them?" I asked.

"Nah, I ain't gon be no bamma nigga and put my mistakes on some'my else —"

"Oh, so we all just a buncha mistakes to you?" I demanded, insulted.

"Nah, shawdy, not at all. You know what I mean. I was irresponsible. Young, dumb, and fulla *you-know-what*. I kept lettin myself get caught up the same way after I left y'all," my father continued to explain with a guilty shrug. "I meet somebody, we do what we do, then hea' come baby and…I get to feelin like I'm in a cage again. Sometimes I tried makin it work, I really did. Sometimes I'd try to stay my ass put and play daddy for a while. Other times, I ain't even stick around long enough for the results of the damn pregnancy test. You be surprised some uh' the shit them girls did to try and keep me, too, tryna make a playa like me settle down. But as you kh see, I ain't settled down yet," he halfway smiled with a wink. "It just ain't in me, shawdy. I ain't built for it. I cain't stay in one place too long."

Redz seemed to be real amused with hisself, but I wasn't smiling at all.

"So why you ain't come see us? What dat gotta do witchu bein a playa?" I asked with the sentiment of a hurt lil girl crackin my voice. Redz' face got serious again.

"I ain't had shit to offer y'all. Dat's why," he answered simply.

I frowned. He had plenty to offer. He was our father. If nothin else, he coulda gave us some advice. He coulda alleviated Mommy's role as the backbone of the family. He coulda helped her hold it together so me and Cerrone wouldn't hafta be out there stealing for survival. He coulda stuck around to put some fear in our hearts when we got too big to be scared of Mommy. He coulda did all that for us and it wouldna cost him nothin but a lil bit of time.

"Why you say you ain't have nuffin to offer?" My voice was thirsty now, beggin for a answer to satisfy the emptiness that's been aching inside me for long as I could remember.

"Cuz I didn't. I ain't have shit. Don't no man wanna be looked up to if he cain't stand on his own two feet."

"Whatchu mean?"

"Lissen, baby. Child support was kickin my ass so I ain't have no money. If it wasn't for my bruhva payin me under the table, I wouldn't have shit to my name. I was livin offa whoever would take me in, mostly women, and a lotta times dat just made my situation worse cuz I'd end up havin more kids. Half the time I was livin back home. Shit, I'm *still* livin back home. Don't got nuffin now, ain't have nuffin then. Nuffin to give y'all. No kinda example to be. I wasn't shit to be lookin up to, and definitely no'by to be lissenin to. I ain't see the point in comin back around. I made a real mess outta my life and I ain't wanna drag y'all into it. I figga'd y'all be better off witout me," Redz said.

"You still think dat?" I asked.

He jabbed around in his mouth with his toothpick for a while, then answered,

"Nah...Not after what happent to my lil man."

Then, we both was quiet for a while.

"Part uh' me feel like it was my fault," Redz started, gettin that faraway look again. "I know I wasn't 'dare and I know the shit happent so fast no'by kh stop it, but...I cain't sleep at night knowin my boy died like dat. What make it worse is dat I ain't even know him. Wouldna known him if he passed me in the street."

Silence again.

"Cerrone. Dat was my granddaddy name, on my muhva side. You know dat?" Redz asked me. I shook my head no.

"Yeah, my muhva come from Louisiana," my father began to explain. "Her peoples is Creole. Dat's how we came to have 'dis red hair and freckles. Dat ain't my point, 'doe. I named Cerrone after my granddaddy cuz he was a fighter. Really, he was. Granddaddy useta box small time, then he went off to fight in World War I. Came home and moved to D.C. with medals and shit. Had trophies for winnin boxin championships and shit. He was all the way live wit it. The way my lil man useta kick and carry on when y' muhva was pregnant wit him, I knew he was gon be a fighter, too, just like the old Cerrone. I ain't never gon forgive myself for not hangin around to find out, 'doe. 'Specially now dat he gone."

Tears escaped my eyes and splattered on the fronta my shirt bigger than thunderstorm raindrops. *Damn!* I thought to myself, *Didn't I say I wasn't gon cry?* The memory of my brother and the truthfulness in my father's words wouldn't let me control myself, no matter how hard I tried.

"Don't no parent think they gon outlive they child," Redz continued with a heavy sigh. "I ain't never think I'd see the day when one uh' my kids name was in the obituaries. But I opened the paper and there it was: Cerrone DeVaughn Williams, dead at seventeen. All this time I'm puttin off my kids, thinkin I'ma holla at y'all when I get my shit t'geva and let you know what's been up wit yol' pops all these years. Thinkin I got time to make it right witchall, or at least let you know why I ain't been around. Then I find out my lil man got shot. Shit threw a wrench in my plan. People live and die on they own time, not minez."

I dabbed my face with the napkin in my lap as he continued,

"He probly went through his whole life thinkin I ain't give a fuck about him. And me like a dumbass, waitin for the right time to tell him I did, I just wasn't man enough to show him. Now it's too late."

Redz eyes had the same wells of sorrow behind em that Mommy's did whenever somebody brought up Cerrone. He was really broke up about the whole situation. And it seemed to me he was lookin to me for forgiveness of some kind. But for what? Not being there? Not knowin my brother? What could I possibly say to relieve his tortured conscience?

"Look, shawdy. I still ain't got shit to offer you," Redz started, wiping his own wet eyes with the back of his hands. "I'm just a old muhfucka dat took too long d' grow up. Don't got no money. I live in my mama basement. Got a racka kids I'on know, who all probly hate my fuckin guts. I ain't got no magic wand to wave and make erything aight. I just felt like I owed you a explanation, shawdy. It's the least I kh do. I'm sorry for not bein there. I really am. I just wanted you to know dat before it's too late."

And with that, Redz leaned back with a *so-what-you-think-now* look and waited for my response. Only thing was, I ain't have one. To tell you the truth, I ain't know what the fuck to think.

CHAPTER NINE

Biggums gave up that five dollars the day after my brother's goin-away party. Just like I thought, Mommy ain't make no effort to take me with them to Maryland. She left my ass right there on Holbrook Street, ain't even bother to come upstairs where I was stayin and let me know she was leavin or nothin. If it wasn't for Cerrone and my lil sisters dragging behind him to say good-bye, I wouldna even known they was gone. It was all good, though. By then I was so used to Mommy's cold-ass attitude towards me that I wasn't even phased—at least, that's what I told myself. Deep down inside I was hurtin like shit, cuz now in addition to havin no father, I was a motherless child. And even though I got to stay in Trinidad with my friends and my play family, I couldn't ignore the emptiness I felt without my real family. My brother and sisters was the reasons I got up most mornings. Who was gon look after em way out there in Wheaton? Who was gon take care of em while Mommy was busy at work or smiling up in that nigga Tone's face? And what was I gon do without them? My world was upside-down. I mighta played it cool on the outside, but on the inside I was devastated.

I took it like a soldier, though. From that point on, I wrote off Mommy the same way I wrote off Redz. I ain't need they asses anyways. Shit, I wasn't no stranger to takin care of myself. And I damn sure ain't need em to help me raise my baby since I been takin care of babies bout long as I been alive. Not livin with my mother was just that—not livin with my mother. I wasn't abandoned or helpless or no shit like that, cuz at fourteen years old, I was a grown-ass woman in ery way but age-wise. I had a man, I had a baby, I had a hustle, and when me and Dartanyan moved into the basement apartment on L Street in Northeast, I had my own place, too. In my book, it ain't get no growner than that.

The basement apartment was small and had water bugs in ery corner, but the boost was that it had its own entrance, its own bathroom, and a refrigerator and stove already in the j'on. The space was less than half the size of the apartment I grew up in, but at least it was clean, and more importantly, it was minez. Couldn't nobody tell me what to do or when to be back from doin it—not even Ma Beth, the lil old lady who rented it out to us. And as long as me and Dartanyan helped her out around the house and came up with $200 for rent ery month, Ma Beth respected us like the real tenants we was.

Being on my own was the shit at first. I finally had the freedom to stay up all night watchin movies, talkin, and doin whatever the hell else I wanted to without being bothered by nosy parents or annoying siblings. I got to invite my friends over and have em stay long as I wanted—ain't even hafta ask permission if they wanted to spend the night. And for once, I had enough elbow room to move around. No more locking myself in the bathroom when I wanted some time alone, no more feeling crowded when Cerrone and his boys took over the livin room, no more gettin the shit kicked outta me by Treasure in her sleep, or waking up wet cuz Sparkle pissed all over the bed *and* me. It was just me and Dartanyan, and all the space the two of us could ever want.

It was like that until the day I woke up from an afternoon nap with what felt like the worst gas pains ever, and found myself in a puddle of something slimy, wet, and disgustingly warm. My water had broke in my sleep and no sooner than I realized what was goin on, the pains gripped my stomach again and I was officially in labor. I was scared as a *muhfucka*. Neither one of us really knew what to do but Dartanyan was there for me. He was the one who ran down the street to get Kia and called the ambulance for me later on that night when I was in so much pain I could barely speak. He was there in the delivery room with me through the whole shit, and when I gave that final push at two thirty-seven a.m. and birthed Kebian Dartanyan Calhoun into this world on August 15, 1996, Dartanyan was still there.

After the doctor laid our son (yes—a boy!!!) on my chest, I watched Dartanyan stare down in disbelief at what the two of us had created. I still to this day can't begin to explain the look on his face. I guess it was like a mixture of awe, pride, and excitement that turned Dartanyan's eryday mug into a tender smile. He studied the bright eyes, the serious expression, the reddish-brown coloring on the tips of Man-Man's ears and saw a reflection of hisself, somebody that would grow up to look just like him and call him Daddy. I smiled too, findin it hard to believe that I just passed another human being outta my body. After all the funky humping and stuffing balloons under my shirt when I was little, I was a Mommy for real at fourteen years old.

I was amazed at what I did, what we did together, and wondered where my son's life would take him. Would he grow up to be a leader like Malcolm X or Huey Newton, or a musician like Marvin Gaye or Duke Ellington? Would he be a warrior like Shaka or Hannibal? Would me and Dartanyan, with both our troubled childhoods, even be able to raise him right so he *could* be all those things? I vowed right then and there to out-do my mother and give my lil Man-Man erything I grew up without. Made Dartanyan promise to stay and help raise our son so he could have all the fatherly love and understanding that me, him, and countless other lil Black kids missed out on. As I lay there exhausted, watchin Dartanyan smiling and baby talking at Man-Man, I saw a conviction in his eyes that told me he would stay, that he would end the pattern of missin daddies and strained father-child relationships. And together, we would break the mold and do what our parents never did—we would stay a family and raise Man-Man in a loving home.

It was a nice thought, hunh?

Dartanyan was true to his word in the beginning. He was the perfect family man at first, goin outta his way to feed the baby when he woke up cryin, even changin diapers without being asked and walkin the floor with Man-Man till he fell asleep. He cooked and cleaned for me when I was too tired to do it myself, he worked hard at Safeway all day and went on the grind all night so we wouldn't want for nothin, and he even agreed to help me save the money to go to night school and summer school so I could graduate early (which he never did, now that I think about it). Dartanyan was a regular supernigga for a minute there. But after a while, givin so much of hisself and not gettin a whole lot in return started taking its toll. It ain't take long for that selfish, jealous, lil boy he always been on the inside to come out bit-by-bit.

I was so wore out tryna balance being a mother with all my other roles in life that I ain't notice the change at first. I was always busy with

Man-Man or hunched over my school books tryna get through ninth grade, or upstairs on Ma Beth's phone listening to Cerrone tell me how Tone and all his new house rules was gettin to him so bad he felt the need to hop the train back to Trinidad ery chance he got. I was so wore out from stressing over my baby, my falling grades, and my brother and sisters' welfare that I ain't have no energy left to deal with Dartanyan when he needed me. I was complaining at him to watch Man-Man or leave me alone so I could finish my homework and get some sleep more often than I said anything nice to him.

We started driftin apart. I found myself peepin out the windows at three in the mornin, wonderin why Dartanyan ain't call to tell me where he was, and prayin that the reason he wasn't answerin my pages was cuz he was laid up in a gutter somewhere. Found myself holdin grudges and not speakin to Dartanyan for days for makin me worry, thinkin that my icy silence would make him stop. But it didn't, and I ain't realize till way after the fact that Dartanyan was actin up cuz he needed *more* of my attention, not *less*. He needed my affection to make him feel important, needed me to fuss over him and be all up underneath him to let him know I cared. Dartanyan wasn't a mama's boy, but he was starved for that unconditional, attentive love that most people get from they mama—the mother-type love he was used to gettin from me cuz it was the only kind I knew how to give. I was the one who was givin him erything he ain't get emotionally as a child, and before he came across me, he lost hisself lookin for it in the streets. But with school, a new baby, and my brother and sisters constantly on my mind, I couldn't give Dartanyan what all he needed when he needed it. And before long, just like he looked to the streets when his mama paid him no mind, he went somewhere else to find what he needed from me.

Pretty soon them unanswered pages started rolling in the like waves at Virginia Beach. Me and Dartanyan hardly ever joked around anymore, and our contact was limited to arguing, cussin eachother out, and fuckin when we got tired of fightin. Shit was goin bad. Real bad. And neither one of us was mature enough to put the bullshit aside and talk it out. So the tension built up like soap scum on a shower wall, and before long I came to the startling realization that the tension between me and Dartanyan started to feel exactly like the tension between my parents before Redz rolled out on us.

"Whatchu doin home so early?" Dartanyan asked as I pushed and struggled through the door with a overstuffed bag fulla books.

"I always come home 'round 'dis time," I told him absentmindedly, and looked at the clock on the VCR. It was almost three.

"Oh," Dartanyan said. He shifted uneasily from his seat at the edge of the bed, right in fronta the TV. I got the feeling that something wasn't right and it had a lot to do with Dartanyan fakin like he was glued to the nature documentary about badgers on PBS. I studied the blank expression on his face, then looked him over from head to toe. His hair was all frizzy and wet around the edges and a damp towel was thrown over his shoulder like he just got out the shower and dried off. Dartanyan takin a shower at two-something in the afternoon when he already took one this morning was strange enough, but it was the way he was tapping his foot all fast that really caught my attention.

"Whatchu all jumpy for?" I asked suspiciously, lookin at his knee bouncing up and down. Dartanyan only tapped his foot like that when he was nervous bout something.

"Ain't no'by jumpy."

"Why you shakin y' knee like dat, 'den?" I asked, peeling off my patent leather jacket and matchin knee-high boots. Dartanyan acted like he ain't hear me and started playin with the baby. That's when I got mad. He was starting to do that bamma shit a lot nowadays — usin Man-Man as a excuse not to deal with me. Dartanyan had always been an attentive father, but now it seemed as if he was purposely overdoin it to justify ignoring me. He'd always try to get to Man-Man first when he started cryin, or be the one to do this or that for him. If I dared to interfere, Dartanyan would get mad because we'd have to temporaritly interact. He was such a asshole. Dartanyan seemed to resent the attention I gave Man-Man, I guess because it meant I had less for him, and I ended up resenting him for the same reason. I ain't know whether to be thankful that Dartanyan was being a father to his son, or jealous cuz he paid more attention to Man-Man's shitty diapers than he did me lately.

"I guess you hard uh' hearin now," I said, rollin my eyes at his back. I pulled on a pair of faded Calvin Klein jeans and the matchin black T-shirt I always wore with em. Dartanyan smirked.

"So you gon tell me what gotchu all noided up? I interrupt you or some'n?" I snapped, puttin my hands on my hips in exasperation.

"Fuck is you talkin bout, joe?" Dartanyan hissed. "Why you sweatin me? You all on my case soon as you step in'na muhfuckin door and shit."

"Whateva, Dartanyan. I ain't got time for 'dis."

I got on the floor and pawed through the shoes under our bed. I had to get the hell away from him, maybe go down the street and chill with my girls for a while. Anything but stayin in that stuffy, old basement with his bamma ass.

"Where my black Griffeys at?" I asked, rummaging through all the loose shoes.

"How I know where y' Griffeys at? What I look like, the shoe man or some shit?"

"You know what? Fuck you, Dartanyan. You always gettin smart."

I started pullin out shoes one by one from underneath the bed when something at the far end of the box spring by Dartanyan's foot caught my eye. It was hot pink and shimmery like that silver lamé shit they be sellin at Rave and all them cheap-ass $10 clothing stores. I stopped, tryna think of what I owned that was hot pink with silver lamé. An ill feeling instantly balled up and sat like heavy food in my stomach, and my woman's intuition started screamin that something was very, *very* wrong. I reached over with a shaky hand to grab the pink fabric and literally felt all the blood drain from my head when I realized what it was. A pair of pink bikini underwear.

"What is 'dis?!" I exclaimed, holdin the silvery pink draws up with two fingers like they was contaminated. Judgin by the shit stains in the back and the stench of month-old fish comin off the patch of moisture in the crotch, they probly was. I looked from the underwear to Dartanyan in disbelief.

"Look like underwears to me," Dartanyan finally said with a shrug. I watched his face for signs of guilt to prove he just got finished smashin off some broad (one who ain't know how to wash her ass at that) minutes before I came home, but Dartanyan's face was straight as a Indian chief's. He was gon play dumb.

"Well whose is 'day?" I demanded. I could feel my whole body shaking as the tears that clouded my eyes started rollin down my cheeks. I was so hurt I felt weak and I could barely breathe or talk over the lump that settled in my throat. I looked into Dartanyan's eyes, those same bright eyes that made me fall for him that day by the mural wall in Southwest, hoping to see the same boy who took care of me and loved me and thought enough of me to make me his baby mama on purpose. I desperately stared into the eyes that useta look right through me and undress me and make me feel wanted, the eyes of the Dartanyan I useta know, not the stranger who was breakin my heart now.

"Must be yours," Dartanyan said, lookin away. The gesture set off a crushing pain in my chest where my heart was, and unwillingly, the tears started comin down harder.

"Day ain't minez andju know it! You's a liar!" I yelled, smackin Dartanyan in the face with the pink panties. He backed away quick and grabbed my hand tryna wrestle em from me. I was almost strong as he was so it was one helluva struggle. I fought dirty and kicked and threw elbows until,

"I know you betta stop hittin me!" Dartanyan warned after I yanked free and smacked him in the face with the draws again.

"You lyin-ass, ho-ass bitch! Fuckin dirty bitches in my bed?! You probly burnin now, you nasty self!" I retorted, smackin him again and again until he pushed me away and I fell back cryin on the floor.

Dartanyan stood up and started picking through the pile of clothes on the couch till he found something quick to put on, then stepped into his navy blue Timbs and tied a Nautica windbreaker diagonally around his shoulders like he was gettin ready to leave.

"Where you goin?" I yelled at him. Dartanyan ain't answer, just stooped down to Man-Man where he sat in wide-eyed confusion on the middle of the bed, and kissed him on the forehead like he did ery afternoon before he went to work.

"Where you goin?!" I demanded again. Dartanyan ignored me and headed for the door. That's when I kirked out. We'd been through too much for him to just turn his back on me and roll out like I wasn't worth a good-bye. I lunged at Dartanyan from across the room and got all up on him like tight leather pants. I pounded him with my fists, cryin and callin him ery kinda muhfucka I could think of. I hated Dartanyan more than anything right then. I hated him for gettin me pregnant, for takin me away from my family, and for puttin me through more shit than re-usable toilet paper. And I especially hated him for breakin his promise to never hurt me or leave me like my father did.

Dartanyan warned me to get off him before he hit me back but I ain't care. I kept on stealin him as hard as I could in the face, the neck, and basically anywhere I could get one in. It was the only way I knew to make him feel the pain he was givin me. After I got him one good time in the mouth and split his lip, Dartanyan shoved me away and sent me flyin into the wall so hard that Man-Man's baby picture fell down and glass shattered all over the floor. Dartanyan turned to walk away again, but I grabbed him by the back of the shirt and rubbed the funky draws all over his face. That's when Dartanyan two-pieced me like he was in the ring with Mike Tyson, and I fell down into the broken glass in total shock.

"Toldju d' stop hittin me," he scolded somewhat apologetically. Dartanyan looked down at me in the shards of glass, face wet with tears, clothes bloody from the fresh cuts all on my hands and arms, then looked back up at Man-Man screamin at the top of his lungs in the middle of the bed. Guilt radiated offa him like them stink lines they be drawing on cartoon characters as he tried to help me up and I smacked his hands away.

"Don't touch me, Dartanyan! Just get the fuck away from me!" I yelled. Slowly, he backed away, and after one more conflicted look at Man-Man, Dartanyan went out the door without another word.

I was hurt to my soul. Not so much because he lied to me; I was useta Dartanyan makin up stories for his wherabouts that sounded like something he pieced together on his way back home. I was hurt cuz he hit me. Stole me like I was some nigga on the street insteada the mother of his child. Dartanyan mighta got up in my face pointin fingers and shook the shit outta me when I tried to swing on him, but not once did he ever put his hands on me. I ain't know how to feel. Did what just happened mean he ain't love me no more? Did he hate me? I couldn't believe the same youngin who useta rub lotion on my feet when I was too pregnant to do it myself would actually go like that on me. Dartanyan had changed. He was so unfeeling, so mean, so different. Cruddy.

I laid in bed with Man-Man cried myself to sleep that night. Dartanyan came home two days later fulla apologies, but nothing he could say was gon make shit between us any better. He wasn't the same. I wasn't the same, either. The youngin in the white T-shirt with the boyish smile and the captivating eyes was gone. The youngin who promised me the world and erything in it was gone. We was older, colder, and lost sight of loving and understanding eachother. Our icy silences and heated arguments was soon replaced with an unbridgeable distance, hostile words, and angry fists hurled back and forth like ping-pong balls. If Dartanyan caught a attitude with me, I caught a attitude with him. If he yelled at me or hit me, I yelled back and punched the shit outta him. We fought in ery way possible, turnin all that emotion, all that feeling, all that love we had for eachother into pure hate. Pretty soon, it got to the point where fightin was the only way we knew how to communicate.

I had a mind to leave Dartanyan but I stayed cuz I ain't have nowhere else to go. I was too proud to ask Dhonni or one of my aunts if I could stay with them till I got my shit together, and I was too scared to ask Mommy if I could move out to Wheaton with her cuz I knew she'd say no. Besides, I was determined to have my son to grow up with a father, no matter what—even if that meant putting up with Dartanyan's shit. So I did what I thought was the right thing at the time and stayed. For Man-Man's sake. And I coped with all Dartanyan's cheatin and carryin on by doin some of my own.

I got back on my pimpin with a vengeance. I bought me a pager and started hittin all the parties and hangin at the basketball courts again, prancing around the city in scandalous summer outfits with my girls tryna pull ery nigga I could. I wasn't lookin for love cuz love hurt like a bitch. Fucka love. It was a second-hand emotion just like Tina Turner said. Instead, I was lookin for material things to fill the void: money, clothes, shoes. My days of falling in love and givin it up to be some nigga's bun was over. The way I saw it, if a youngin wasn't comin out the pockets and takin me to get my hair done and my nails done and buyin me Versace jeans and DKNY, then there wasn't no point of us even talkin. Except for twerkin, what else was a nigga good for? Fuck being somebody's boo and being loved. I ain't need that. Money was all I needed. Shit, at least money ain't buy itself $200 Air Pippens before it got you anything for your birthday. At least money ain't leave another girl's nasty pink draws under your bed and beat your ass cuz you found out. At least money ain't lie to you and hurt you on purpose. At least money ain't break your heart.

My visit with my father hit me like a sudden impact. I mean, outta nowhere comes this nigga I swore I'd punch in the nose if I ever saw him again, offering answers to questions I done had for years. Redz gave me the truth, straight up and raw about erything, and even though he ain't ask for it, I knew in my heart he wanted forgiveness in return. I was puzzled, though. The part of me that spent all these years hating my father was suddenly being questioned by the part that begged me to understand where he was comin from. Redz was only human, and as confused and crazy as I was, I could see why he chose to do things the way he did. I had a habit of running from things, too, which was the main reason I was out on my balcony just one day after our lunch date, hittin a J and tryna quiet the voices in my head tellin me to let go of the past. Redz had finally manned up and gave me his side of the story. But was it on me to excuse him from never gettin to know his late son?

"Ay, I'm bout to walk to the store wit Iyania," came Krys' voice from behind me.

I snapped outta my weed-clouded daze and turned halfway around to see her stickin her head out the balcony door just like she did the other day. She tapped her nails impatiently on the glass, obviously itching to get a move on.

"C'mere, young," I barked, and pointed to the chair beside me. "Have a sit-down, lil cuz. We gotta talk."

I still ain't forget about the way she disappeared on Wednesday. Or how she ain't come back till bout six in the mornin the next day like that shit was okay. Dealing with my father kept me kinda distracted from askin her what all she did that night, but now I was ready to put Redz on the back burner and find out what was really goin on with her ass.

"What we gotta talk about?" Krys huffed, sliding the door shut behind her. She flopped down in the padded wicker chair and crossed her arms over her chest.

"Where you go at the uh' night?" I demanded.

"Out wit Iyania, like I told you."

"Dat ain't what I asked. Where the fuck y'all go at? Why you stay out so late?"

"I came home before the sun was up," Krys argued. "You said dat was aight, right?"

"*Sheeeiiit.* Six in'na mornin is *not* before the sun is up. Four or five, maybe—and even dat's a damn good curfew for a fih'teen year-old to have."

"Your point?"

Bitch! My point?

"My point, muhfucka, is it was light outside when you came home. Birds was all singin and shit…"

"So?"

"*So?* Whatchu mean so? Fuck you go at?"

"Damn! We went to see Rare Essence! Satisfied?!" Krys snapped.

I cocked my head back and looked at her like she was crazy. No this lil girl was not raising her voice at me.

"Who you gettin loud wit?" I demanded.

"Why you pressin me out? I came back when you said come back, ain't I?"

"First of all, Essence don't play till dawn. And second—"

"Man, f'get 'dis." Krys stood up all abrupt before I could finish scolding her. "I gotta go, young. Iyania waitin for me outside. You got anything else to say, you call my phone," she said dismissively over her shoulder.

I stopped and looked at my J to see if it had magically turned into a hand fulla 'shrooms cuz I musta been hallucinating. Did youngin really just carry the shit outta me? Boy, I was bout this close to smackin her upside the head with the wicker chair she almost overturned gettin up, but that wouldna done nothin 'cept start a fight Krys was sure to lose. So I decided to hit her harder where it hurt more instead. Afterall, I was the one in charge. Fuck all this tryna be cool and lettin her do her thing so we could be friends. It obviously wasn't workin. Time to lay the smack down.

"You ain't goin nowhere," I said in my most serious tone of voice. Krys' face got all balled up like clothes that's been sittin in a hamper for weeks, and she grit on me like she was tryna decide to steal me or call me crazy.

"Don't be lookin at me like dat. You heard what the fuck I said. Since you wanna get smart, you ain't goin no-muhfuckin-where."

Krys stood with her hand on the balcony door and stared at me in open-mouthed disbelief for a second before she realized I wasn't playin. "You cain't make me stay! You ain't my muhva!" Krys declared. She slid open the door indignantly and stomped across the livin room where she grabbed her purse and headed for the front door. I maneuvered across the floor in my bare feet and beat her to the punch. I blocked the door with my body in a stance that dared her to move me and repeated, "You ain't goin nowhere."

"What the fuck is you lunchin for?" Krys demanded.

"Who the fuck is you cussin at?"

"You cain't keep me locked up in hea'!"

"I know you betta lower your muhfuckin voice!"

"Lemme go, 'den! You cain't keep me locked up! You ain't my muhva!"

By now, both Twon and the boys came from where they been occupied in they respective rooms to see what all the commotion was about.

"Ooh, 'day bout to fight! Mommy's gonna win!" Man-Man exclaimed. Twon shooed him and Tink out the way and rushed to stand between me and Krys before we really did start throwin hands.

"Move, young! I gotta go!" Krys shouted, reaching around him like she was actually bold enough to move me herself. She was showin off now, and usin Twon separating us as a excuse to push up on him. That shit just made me even madder.

"Let her go, Twon. I wanna see if youngin got some wreck in her. C'mon, Krys. If you so bout it, 'den bring it," I taunted.

"Ain't no'by scared uh' you, Shai!"

"You need to be!"

"Ay, chill out," Twon ordered the both of us. "Whatchall mad about now anyhow?"

"She keep gettin smart," I said. "I'm sittin 'dare tryna have a civilized conversation wit the girl and she carried me for no reason!"

"Well, she won't lemme go wit my friends!"

"Fuck your friends! You bout d' not see them muhfuckas for the resta the summer, you keep it up!"

Krys started reaching around him again and I tried moving closer so she could grab me and see what happened next. Twon held us apart.

"Why you won't let her go?" Twon asked.

"Cuz I'm sicka her tryna walk all over me. I ain't been nuffin but nice to her ass —"

"Nice? You the one bein a asshole!"

A asshole? Oh, f'real? I got a asshole for her.

"Aight, you know what? Fuck it," I said with a fake calm, and started to undo the locks on the door. They both looked at me surprised, probly thinkin I was joking. But I wasn't playin at all.

"I take dat back, Krys. You kh go," I told my cousin seriously.

She twisted her lips in a self-righteous smirk and started to go around Twon. I held my finger up before she could get all the way to the door and stopped her dead in her tracks.

"If you do, 'doe, you betta take erything you brought up in hea' witchu," I continued, just as serious. "You walk out dat door, you don't come back. Fuck all this arguin shit. It's my way or the highway. Go home and see if mommy and daddy let you get away wit much as I do."

Krys stood there lookin stupid for a long time. I could tell she was wondering if stayin here was better than being at home. She musta been thinkin bout which one of her bamma friends' house she could crash at for the resta the summer, too. Then, I guess when she finally figured out she couldn't stay nowhere else as rent free and trouble free as she could with me, she stomped towards the den in defeat.

"You is one fucked up individual, young. You know dat?" Krys complained.

"Whateva. I'll be dat," I shrugged.

Krys slammed the door to the den shut and that was the end of that... For now, at least.

CHAPTER TEN

"Whatchu ova' 'dare cheesin about?" Dhonni asked me, sweeping the front of her long Senegalese twists into the scrunchie she took off her wrist.

I shook my head and tried to cover up my mischievous smile. It was the second of many uncomfortably hot Friday nights during the summer of 1997, and right before Dhonni and them came and got me, I was standin in fronta the closet plotting on bleaching and shredding Dartanyan's clothes. He squeezed a bruise on my arm when we was arguing earlier and that shit still hurt. I had the house all to myself since he took Man-Man to his niece's birthday party at his mama's house where he was probly gon dump him and run the streets till sometime tomorrow. I was all set to do a lil damage and enjoy the resta the night alone with me, myself, and I when my girls came over. They was gon party with Backyard, and I was comin with em—like it or not. I wasn't really in the mood to go to the go-go and get all sweaty from dancin or hafta throw hands cuz somebody got to fakin and had to be put in they place. Nor did I feel like being in a dark room gettin groped, grabbed, and smacked on the ass more times than I could count. But after thinkin bout how mad Dartanyan would be once he found out I went (he call hisself banning me from partyin cuz he know how I be dancin), shakin my ass against other niggas' pants zippers for a few hours ain't seem like such a bad idea afterall.

"Damn, Syco, slow down! You tryna kill us?!" Lakisha cried from the front seat, holdin onto Syco's younger brother Mo so she woudn't fly through the windshield. The four of us in the backseat lurched forward as Syco slammed on brakes to avoid hittin a shiny black Acura CL and swerved back into the lane to keep straight down Florida Ave. We was rushing to get to the Black Hole before the line got too long outside, but the way Syco was swerving and taking that Steel Reserve to the head insteda keepin his eyes on the road, our asses would be lucky to even make it there at all.

"You gon get us pulled over, you keep doin shit like dat," Dhonni warned, passin me what was left of a fat, cone-shaped bob. I took it and leaned back into the softness of the Delta 88's gray, velvet seats and closed my eyes so I wouldn't see the blur of streetlights streaking past my window.

"Ain't no'by stoppin me," Syco said, tilting his head back to take another gulp out the 40 oz. bottle in his lap. "We in'na city, joe. 'Day busy lookin for them niggas out 'dare bustin on cops, not me."

"Dat's besides the point. You know how dirty we is right now? And it ain't like you got a license—"

"Yeah, I know. We straight, 'doe. Like I said, ain't no'by stoppin me."

"But still—" Dhonni started to argue.

"Just squash it," Biggums ordered, and gave Dhonni one of them *you-know-how-he-is* looks from the other side of the back seat. She knew as well as I did that Syco wasn't the type to go for too much backtalk and criticizing about anything he did, especially his driving. Cuz mighta been reckless behind the wheel, flying over speed bumps, bouncing over potholes, and weaving in and outta traffic like the boogeyman was chasing after him, but damn anybody that called him on it. Syco took that shit to heart, like you was talkin bout his mama or something. He was famous for kickin bammas out his car in the middle of the night no matter what side of town they was on, just cuz they talked shit and he caught feelings.

"Cain't wait till I get my own car," Dhonni said low enough so only I could hear her over Scarface bumpin out the cassette tape deck in the dash. "Ridin in'nis bucket wit dat nut has got to go."

"Who you tellin?" I agreed, lookin down at the milk crate behind Mo and Lakisha to keep the seat from fallin back, then up at the ceiling where thumb tacks held the upholstery in place. Syco's car was a bucket fo' real, complete with a window that wouldn't roll up in the front, a back door that wouldn't open from the inside, and a hanger wrapped around the rusted muffler to keep it from dragging along the street and catching sparks. Shit, half the time you had to bargain with the muhfucka so it'd even start up, but Syco was the only one we chilled with who had a car and ridin with him was way better than taking the bus.

"You think Cruddy gon show up at d' Hole t'night?" Dhonni asked, pinching one of my thick, auburn, corkscrew braids.

"I'on give a fat fuckin rat's ass if he do. Dat's his business."

"Damn, you all hostile."

"Fuck dat nigga, joe," I spat. "Ain't no'by thinkin bout him. As many uh' niggas gon be up in'nat j'on t'night..."

"I know dat's right," Dhonni laughed, takin a gulp of 211 out the bottle Mo passed back. "Gone and do y' thing, Suga Baby. I ain't mad at cha."

Next to Kia, Dhonni was the only one I told bout the time I found the pink panties and all the cruddy shit Dartanyan been doin since, like threatening to take Man-Man away from me ery time I came home after being with another nigga, and all the punches and harsh words he been throwing in a backwards attempt to make me wanna be with him again. After knowin all that, Dhonni encouraged me to leave his ass ery chance she got. She swore I could do better, but I'on know—for some reason I just ain't think I could. I was dependant on Dartanyan, not only for the money, but cuz I knew I'd be lonely if I ain't have him around to fight with. All his attention to me was negative nowadays, but I still desperately needed it.

"Cruddy some trash, joe. I wish you leave him alone already. He ain't doin shit but drivin you crazy and puttin a racka bruises on yo' ass."

"He gimme money, 'doe," I pointed out like it would negate all the bullshit.

"Fuck his money! We know how to get dat. Don't no'by need dat chump change he comin wit," Dhonni sneered.

"I know, but...I'm aight, man. I'on let him get to me," I assured her, even though some days Dartanyan made me wanna slit my wrists so I wouldn't hafta hear his mouth no more.

"You fakin like shit, but whateva. Keep lettin dat nigga dog you out... Just lemme know when y'all break up so I kh whup his muhfuckin ass myself. Speakin uh' which, do y'all even still go t'geva cuz I ain't seen his ass at the house in bout a week?" Dhonni said with a pinched look on her face as she passed me the beer.

I took it to the head with a shrug. Me and Dartanyan still went together, but like I said, it was more outta dependence than love. When we wasn't arguing and finding new ways to make eachother miserable, we pretty much stayed outta eachother's way—ain't even have sex no more unless it was during them wee hours of the morning when Dartanyan rolled over half sleep and instinctively reached for me. Sometimes we got along good enough to put up a J or go to a movie together, but it ain't happen all that much. Only often enough to make me realize that deep down I still loved Dartanyan—I just ain't *like* his bitch ass.

"Some'n like dat," I answered. That's when Trayonna looked up from playin with her electronic Giga Pet kitty, being all nosy.

"Hold the sauce, young. You'on go wit Cruddy no more?" she asked, her eyes wide with concern. "Y'all finally broke up?"

"Look atchu, all up hea'," Dhonni fussed, waving her hand between the two of us.

"Well, you shouldna been talkin so loud."

"Andju shouldna been ear hustlin."

"F'getchu, Kiss. Is it true, Shai?"

"Girl, please. Me and dat nigga don't even talk no more," I admitted to Trayonna with a sigh. "I'on care, 'doe. Long as he still payin the bills and takin care uh' his son, dat black fool kh do whateva and *whoeva* he want. I'on see no rings on 'deez fingers."

"Basically," Dhonni huffed, taking the roach from me and desperately tryna get one more pull off it. "He doin his thing so you damn sure betta do yours, Suga Baby."

"F'real, young? You cool wit him fuckin uh' girls now?" Trayonna pressed. I coulda sworn I saw a spark of interest flicker behind her sneaky, sea green eyes but I quickly dismissed it as more concern. Trayonna couldna been thinkin what I thought she was thinkin. She mighta did a lotta foul shit when nobody was lookin, but she wasn't dumb enough to try and pull a stunt like that.

"I wouldn't say all dat," I answered cautiously. I was bout to ask why was she so worried bout me and Dartanyan's relationship, when Syco made a sharp turn onto 7th Street that sent us all flyin to one side of the car. The tires squealed so loud that erybody at the Popeye's on the corner looked in our direction to see if there had just been a accident. Dhonni made the sign of the cross over herself and bowed her head. Evidently her lil prayer did something cuz less than five minutes later, Syco was parallel parking into a tight spot bout a block and a half down from the club. Before he could even cut the engine off, the six of us was jumping out the car like rats abandoning a sinking ship.

"Ay, young, I'm takin'na bus home," Biggums announced to no one in particular, smoothing out the wrinkles in her black Polo jeans. She was the only one in our crew dressed like one of the fellas in baggy pants, red and black Mitch Richman Nikes, and a oversized T-shirt underneath the Da*Link*Went shirt she shredded, braided, and beaded along the bottom and the sleeves. With her tomboy look and her hair always in plaits of some kind, Biggums was starting to look more and more like a nigga ery day.

"I'm rollin witchu 'den," Trayonna said.

"And I'm rollin wit boo-boo right 'dare." I nodded at a handsome brownskinded youngin bout our age walkin towards the club with four of his friends. He had on black sweats, the black Total Max Uptempos, and one of them purple, blue, and green tie-dyed Madness shirts with silver lettering that read "Nasty Boy 69" on the back.

"He probly don't know *nathan* bout no sixty-nine," Dhonni snickered. "I'on know why niggas be puttin dat shit on they shirts like 'day really eat pussy. Lyin asses."

"I'on know, young—cuz do got them lips, 'doe," I giggled. Youngin turned around when he heard me talkin bout him and licked his top lip all freaky-like at me.

"Mnh. Nasty ass. I know why he wearin them sweatpants, too," I said, and blew a kiss back at him.

"You need d' stop."

"Don't she, 'doe?" Trayonna chuckled.

"Stop? Girl, please, I'm just gettin started." I bent over to fold down the tongues of my red hi-top Chucks and felt that mischievous smile curl around my lips again. I was feeling too good and lookin too luscious to be on anything *but* freak status that night. I had on my just-below-the-cheeks cut-offs with the slits up the sides and a halter top that was red as it was tight, showing off ery curve where messing with Dartanyan made a woman outta me.

"Where y' shirt at?" Lakisha asked suddenly, eyeing me jealously. "Ain't we poseda wear our shirts t'night?"

"I got it right hea'," I snapped, holdin up my Madness T-shirt like the ones her, Trayonna, and Dhonni was wearing. It was black with red and white letters that read Suga Sweet Huneyz on the front, my nickname on the back, and a big-ass 12 for our block number 1200 right under it.

"Well ain't chu gon put it on?" Lakisha demanded, crossing her skinny arms over her chest. She was muggin on me like I just yanked the cherry and cream lollipop out her mouth, and I knew it was cuz that nigga Mo couldn't take his eyes off the round honey-brown peeking out the bottom of my shorts. Ery since Lakisha gave that nigga some pussy the last time we all went out, she been actin like they go together, all ready to fight and shit ery time another female got in the way. Which really wouldn't have a damn thing to do with me if Mo wasn't always up in my grill talkin bout how bad he wanted to fuck the dog shit outta me. I ain't pay him no mind cuz Mo wasn't cute enough or paid enough to get my honey drippin, but unfortunately, Lakisha had it fucked up like *I* was the one tryna get with *him*. Picture that! Me with a broke-ass nigga who look like J.J. Evans from *Good Times*? Lakisha must be off the yak if she think I'm goin like that!

"Why you bein pressed?" Dhonni asked, jumping to my defense.

"F'real," Mo added, adjusting his black coofie over his cornrows. "Dat lil shirt she got on now is fittin propa."

Lakisha cut her eyes at him and it took erything in me not to bust out laughin. Dhonni wasn't helping matters, knowingly elbowing me in the ribs and shit.

"Aww, face!" Biggums teased. "Tight face, young! You poseda keep y' nigga in check, Lollipop. Why he all ova' hea' in Shai business, 'doe?"

"Shut the fuck up, Biggums."

"You want me to shut the what up?" Biggums snarled, her smile growing sinister. I could tell she was itching for a reason to steal Lakisha's annoying ass.

"I said shut the fu—"

"Ay, look," I jumped in before shit got too outta hand. I could see Lakisha gettin all reckless and defensive and Biggums puffing up to put an end to all her tough talk. "I'ma put my shirt on dis-play when we get inside. Is dat aight witchu, Lollipop?" I asked sarcastically, dodging Dhonni's nudges.

"Whateva, man," Lakisha scoffed, and rolled her eyes. She smacked her lollipop at me and followed after Syco, Mo, and Biggums in the stream of people walking towards the club.

We mobbed down the street to the entrance, then stood back to check out the line snaking down the sidewalk in fronta the Black Hole. Friday was all ages night so erywhere you looked was junior and senior high school youngins posted up outside tryna look grown. Dressed up in they best street clothes with fresh hairdo's that was bound to get sweated out by the end of the night, we represented ery corner of D.C., Maryland, and North VA that you could get to from the Beltway. Girls stood around hittin casual poses to be cute, mostly talkin and people-watchin to see what erybody had on, and hatin like shit when they seen somebody better-lookin than theyselves pass by. Boys, holdin R.I.P. shirts and towels scribbled with the names of they crews to put on dis-play, pretty much played the background and watched all the girls, scheming on who they was gon get behind when they got inside. I could hear a ear fulla comments and feel dozens of eyes lookin us over as me, Dhonni, and Trayonna made our way to the front of the line behind Syco and them to get in with some youngins we knew from Saratoga.

"Ay, didju see Baby back 'dare?" Dhonni asked as we stood off to the side waiting for Trayonna to go through the metal detector.

"Baby? From around our way? Lemme find out Miz Cunningham let her off the porch."

"I know, right? She hea' wit them twins from 18th Street. Shakara and Shakira," Dhonni told me, peering over my shoulder to look at the crowd comin in. "Matter fact, 'dare she go now."

I turned around just in time to see Baby parading our way in a stretch denim one-shoulder catsuit that drew more attention to her thick frame than I did minutes before in my shorts. Me and Dhonni watched in awe as she strutted right past like she ain't know us from two holes in the wall, and disappeared into the dark room up ahead. Next to Syco's driving, spotting Baby at the Black Hole (in a fuckin catsuit, no less) was bout the craziest shit I seen all night.

"You see her walk by and ain't even speak?" Dhonni squawked, her wide eyes narrowed to disgusted slits. "Dat bitch must think she rock. She still a bamma, 'doe."

"F'real," I agreed, even though from the looks of it, Baby was starting to come up in the world.

Trayonna finally joined us after the guard checked her hi-top Princesses, and we made our way into the steamy, black room that earned the club its name. The atmosphere was real dark, real sexual, and harder than pit bulls and pistols—just the way we liked shit in Chocolate City. Flashes from dim colored lights guided us through the sea of sweaty, gyrating bodies towards the front where we bogarded our way to the stage. All typesa cigarette, cigar, and weed smoke polluted the air and mixed with that heavy layer of steam that tends to build up when Black folks get together. Hot body niggas was comin out they shirts left and right and girls who ain't do the same was rolling up theirs and tucking em into they bras, showin off bare, sweaty skin that looked glossy under the lights. Between the people fog and ice-cold blasts of Super Soaker water that the groupie broads was spraying into the crowd from the stage, erything from the ceiling to the floor was wet. Youngins was cuttin through the crowd in lines we called trains, holdin up towels and T-shirts to rep they crews and pushing back other youngins who was busy reaching over they heads to snatch em down so theirs could be seen. That alone caused a couple fights and sumo wrestler-sized bouncers dragging niggas out in the street to finish whatever they started. Youngins who ain't come with banners threw up signs and yelled out where they was from whenever there was a pause, and even in all the noise somebody on stage would hear em and put em on. The whole Trinidad, that Lincoln Heights crew, Good Hope Stars, 640, 35-Double-0, Simple City, C.T.U., 7 Woods, them Sursum Corda niggas, 5-Triple-0, and just about ery other crew, mob, and neighborhood in the house was gettin a shout out. Erybody got love, whether they was gettin they names dropped in a song, bantering back and forth with the band on stage during the show, or gettin on the mic when it got close enough to they face—erybody who made theyselves known got put on.

It was like that in the go-go. Along with the pulsing congos, roto-toms, drums, and the soulful plucking of bass guitars, cowbells, and keyboards, the shout-outs is what made me love comin out to them j'ons. Wasn't nothin like hearing your name booming out the amplifiers or shouting out your crew and having the whole crowd partyin with you. Wasn't nothin like losing yourself in that raw-ass rhythm that throbbed through ery cell in your body till all you could do was ruff it off or plaster yourself against a stranger and freak em like your mama ain't raise you right. It got you like that. I'd later see how ery city had its own sound and its own way of gettin down. But the energy at the go-go back in them days was like nothin else I seen before in my life.

When Back started hittin that *Thug Passion* j'on, muhfuckas liked to lost they minds up in there. All the rowdy-ass niggas started pushin and elbowing eachother around mosh pit style or squared off to beat they feet. Freak niggas scrambled to get behind girls like me with junk in the trunk, pushin eachother out the way and sharing with they boys the one chance to live out wet dreams by grinding into stretch jean-clad asses that shook like Jell-O against anything in they path. Others stood around just to watch girls work the walls and work niggas in ways that would make Luke blush, pointing em out and egging em on with smacks on the ass, flashlight spotlights, and comments like *"Damn, girl, y' mama know you dance like dat?!"* For somebody who wasn't from here, it musta looked like erybody was doin it with they clothes on, but to the resta us it was just proof that the band was definitely crankin.

At intermission, me and the crew went to go take a mob picture in fronta some airbrushed backdrop, then stood around mingling and gettin numbers till we heard the band start playin again. They was warming up with a slow pocket to pull erybody back in before hittin a song that would send us all into a frenzy. Glad for the break, I mopped my forehead with my T-shirt and rocked side to side, all in my own lil zone till some sweaty, bare-chested nigga rubbed up against my back. In D.C., askin somebody to dance was a unnecessary formality, so by that time, I was pretty much useta niggas just comin up behind me and gettin into my groove. But after a hour and some change of gettin freaked by strangers, I wasn't in the mood no more. I started to get mad and push youngin's horny ass the fuck up off me cuz I was tired of gettin breathed on and felt up, but something bout him kept me in place. I felt like I knew him. The way he slid his arms around my waist and interlocked his fingers with minez, I coulda sworn he was Dartanyan. But whoever it was seemed taller and darker than Dartanyan with a lot more meat on his bones, and I thought I noticed a tattoo on his forearm where Dartanyan ain't have one. Besides, it'd been ages since Dartanyan held me the way cuz was holdin me, like he needed me and wanted me more than anything else in the world. I smiled to myself, figuring the mystery man behind me was probly one of my youngins I been creepin with on the side, or maybe even "Nasty Boy 69" from the parking lot. I leaned back against his chest and rested my head on his shoulder as our bodies swayed a familiar sway like we did it a million times before.

I closed my eyes and sighed, feeling more at ease with this stranger than I ever did with anybody else. Usually, I ain't get all bunned up with niggas at the go-go cuz it seemed like ery time I did, I'd turn around expecting a cutie and come face-to-face with full-fledged ugly instead. But judging by what I saw outside, and the way Trayonna was cheesin and givin me the thumbs-up, it was safe to assume that "Nasty Boy 69" or whoever was just as fine up close. So I let myself sink into his hardbodied comfort and snuggled a lil closer when he intuitively squeezed me back. I giggled at the tingle that rushed through me when his nose gently brushed over the sensitive spot on my neck, and moved my braids out the way so he could kiss me for real. But instead of following my lead, cuz changed sides and started teasing my earlobe with the softness of his lips. That shit was drivin me crazy. I tried to fight the desire and tell myself I ain't really wanna feel him all up in my guts, but the ooze of honey slickin up my draws was proof that main man had me goin. I wanted more. I got a lil too carried away and tried to guide his hand down to unbutton my jean shorts, but once again he did just the opposite and ran his fingertips over my sweat-slicked thighs. I could almost hear him smiling. That nigga knew exactly what he was doin.

He was making me want him bad as shit.

I started to pull away and stop him from playin his lil game with me but I couldn't pry myself offa him. I reached up to caress the back of youngin's neck and grabbed a hand fulla teeny, sweat-soaked plaits, my mind racing to figure out who I knew with hair like that. But when he blew cool air along the sweaty curve of my neck and grazed his thumbs lightly over my nipples, it ain't even matter if I knew him or not. Youngin had me ready to do *whateva*. I coulda went extra hard like the triflin-ass girls I seen in my day wearin short skirts and takin it from the back in dark corners, but with AIDS and all that other shit floatin around, gettin some anonymous action in the club wasn't hardly worth losin my life over. I wasn't that dumb or that horny. Besides, I'on think cuz woulda went that far. He wasn't tuggin on my clothes or tryna get his fingers up in my honeycomb like any other nigga woulda done. He seemed to be enjoying making me squirm.

"Damn, sweetheart. You givin it to em in'nem shorts," youngin whispered in a unfamiliar, seductively deep voice that sent a quiver down the trail of nerves from my ear to my tail bone.

"I know," I answered, slow grinding my hips to show him just how much more I was willin to give. Next thing you know, faster than you could say *Southernplayalisticadillacmuzik*, I felt a swell rising through his jeans like the mercury was rising in my body's thermostat. *Oh, no he didn't!*, I thought to myself, even though I was jive turned on that he did.

"Damn, Redbone," youngin teased with a hint of a laugh. "You done woke up my man and shit..."

"Lemme put him back d' sleep, 'den," I offered in a lust-husky voice I never knew I had. I could hear that smile again and suddenly I wanted to see who in the hell was really behind me. I tried to pull away and find out for myself but cuz was still holding me in place with his arms wrapped around my waist.

"Don't move," he ordered, teasing my spot with his lips again and pressing us back together. My body flushed and my knees went weak as warm water, and all I could do was nod in surrender. As big as that lump in youngin's pants was starting to feel, I ain't plan on movin for shit. Not even if Big G stopped the show and announced that Jesus was outside with Tupac signing autographs and givin away $100 bills. *Sheeeeiiit.* Wasn't nothing taking me away from this nigga.

Nothing except the music of course. Soon as Back started hittin the *Unibomber*, the same electricity that had erybody all siced up before rippled through the room again. I pulled away to tell youngin to meet me by the door so I could give him my pager number, but a train of niggas reppin Brightseat Road cut between the two of us and we got separated before I could say anything. I jumped up to look over em and tried to push my way through em but it was no use. Just like that, youngin was gone.

Someone started pullin on my arm and I whirled around expecting to see him there, but instead, Dhonni stood in fronta me hopping from foot to foot like she was tappin with a frantic urgency in her face.

"Come wit me, joe. I gotta piss," she half-asked, half-told me before linking her arm with minez and draggin me through the throngs of people towards the bathroom. I kept tossing hopeful glances over my shoulder expecting to see my mystery man pushing through the crowd tryna catch up with me, but all I saw instead was dozens of hungry eyes glued to me and Dhonni's behinds as we passed by, none of em belonging to the passionate stranger who left me more hot and bothered than I been in ages.

I went back to partyin like ain't shit happen, but for real, cuz was on my mind the whole resta the night. I felt like I knew him, but I knew I didn't. Weird, hunh? Who was dude? How could he make my insides quiver and my heart feel all fluttery when I ain't even see his face to be trippin like I was? What was *that* all about? I tried to find him through the darkness and all the people, but then I remembered I ain't even know who he was for sure and I had no idea what he looked like. So I gave up. I told myself that whoever he was, "Nasty Boy 69" or whoeverthefuck was probly a crudball like Dartanyan or another broke-ass nigga like Mo, and he probly wasn't worth my time anyhow. Tried to convince myself that it was just a dance, and I was probly overreacting. A dance ain't nothin special. Ain't nothin to get all siced about. So why was I so disappointed when the show was over and I still ain't find him?

"Man, where is 'dis nigga at? He got my jacks," Biggums grumbled, turning her pockets inside out lookin for a cigarette.

We was standin in fronta the club at the let-out waitin for Syco to come on, and as usual his monkey ass was nowhere in sight. I's willing to bet he was somewhere in the cut tryna sell a bag of that bush weed doused in roach spray that him and Biggums was passin off as 'dro, but for real, it was anybody's guess. You never know when it comes to Syco. Police cars started circling the block like vultures and we decided to leave before they started locking bammas up. D.C. Police ain't play that standin around shit after the party was over. Niggas out here easily resorted to violence, and besides, all us Black folks standin around might scare the outta-towners who actually thought D.C. was the same clean-cut, whitebread city they saw on TV. Biggums managed to bum a jack off somebody for the walk back to the car, only to find she ain't have a light to smoke it when we got halfway there.

"Fuck, man! Ay, Mo, you got a light on you?" she asked, patting herself down for the third time in a row like doin it was gon make a lighter magically appear.

"Nah, young," he answered, shaking his head.

Biggums rolled her eyes and asked Lakisha, then the girls walking in fronta us but they couldn't help her neither.

"Maybe dat's a sign you need d' stop smokin," Dhonni teased.

"Maybe you need d' leave me the fuck alone f' you get stole in y' mowf."

"Damn, sound like some'my havin a nicotine fit," I laughed, when suddenly, someone swiped they finger through the crease of my right thigh and my ass cheek and then,

"Hea', young, I got chu," came a voice from behind.

Biggums and I both turned around surprised at the same time to see a handsome stranger holding out a book of matches. My heart skipped a beat. He was bout six feet tall, chocolate, and built like he played sports with chinky eyes and a smirk on his D'Angelo lips like he knew he was the shit. He coulda been a pretty boy if he wanted to, but I could tell cuz was too thorough to be standing around lookin cute. Definitely my type. Youngin was rugged and sexy in a Treach kinda way, with a cocky bowlegged strut that said he was useta females falling at his feet. And got-damnit, they had ery reason to. A wife beater pulled behind his head showed off a perfect chest and the abs of life, and wide shoulders that led down to a narrow waist where he wore his shorts low enough to show the V-shaped crease at his hips. The rubber bands around his wrists hinted that he hustled for a livin, and the fresh Foamposites and baggy Iceberg jean shorts he wore hinted that whatever he sold was making him a grip. He was erything most girls wanted for them reasons alone, including me.

"Thanks, young," Biggums said, pausing to light her jack. I paused with her and watched dude go by, completely mesmerized by erything from the *Cease Fire...Don't Smoke the Brothas* shirt tied around his head down to his muscular bowlegs. Dhonni, Lakisha, and Trayonna stopped and stared with me. Even Biggums seemed to be studying him, and she wasn't one to be trippin off no dudes.

"If you'on holla at him, I will," Trayonna said, fixing her sea green gaze on youngin as he continued to walk away. "Dat nigga a bun like shit. He just *look* like he kh hit it right."

"Yeah, no buh'shit," Dhonni agreed. "Ay, Shai, you betta holla at dat boy. He bowlegged, too? You know what 'day say bout bowlegged niggas."

"Nah, what 'day say?" I asked, rolling my eyes.

"'Day be packin them donkey kongs!" Trayonna exclaimed, and slapped Dhonni five.

"Man, dat's just a old hood rat tale," Lakisha said. I was inclined to agree, but after taking one more look at the fine-ass fudgsicle of man I woulda gladly treated like a lollipop, I ain't care if he was packin or not. He had me sold off the first glance. A sexy muhfucka like that, one who probly got money? I be a gump for letting him pass me by.

"Ay, Chocolate!" I called, walkin towards cuz and his two friends. He turned around and took a couple steps to meet me with this look on his face like he just knew I was gon holla at him. My mouth went dry and my heart was pounding so hard I could hear it in my ears but I played it cool as a cucumber. I sauntered up to him like *he* was the one who shoulda been nervous and stood close enough to smell the clean sweat and natural scent on his skin before puttin a hand on my hip and blatantly checkin him out.

"So you just gon touch my butt and walk away?" I demanded, giving him an accusing look.

"Ain't no'by touch your butt, girl," youngin said all fake innocent with a naughtiness in his chinky eyes that gave him away.

"Unh-hunh, I know it was you. I ain't trippin, 'doe. You cute enough d' get away wit it." I checked him out again. "Yeah, you real cute," I added with a smile.

Youngin chuckled, tryna fight the semi-bashful grin that threatened to take over his face. He was even more appealing smiling like that. It almost made him seem huggable, like he wasn't big and bad as he looked at first.

"So what 'day call you?" he asked after a short pause, appraising me from head to toe in that way only a brotha could; licking his lips like I was a feast he couldn't wait to get into, yet such a work of art with skin the color of sunkissed sweetness and the voluptuous curves lesser women dreamed of having, that all he wanted to do was admire me.

"Suga Baby," I told him, struggling to maintain my sexy cool, then added, "But if you lucky, I might let you call me Honey."

He raised his eyebrows in interest. "Honey? Why 'day call you dat?" he asked, amused.

I looked around like I had a secret and motioned with my finger for him to come closer before leaning over and whispering in his ear,

"Cuz dat's what it taste like."

I watched youngin try to fight another smile like what I said ain't make his dick jump, but he couldn't keep a straight face for shit. He took the T-shirt off his head and tossed it over his shoulder, then ran a hand through his short plaits like he just ain't know what to do with hisself no more.

"Hunh, man," was all he could say after findin his voice again.

"Hunh, man is right. So what 'day call *you*?" I asked, expecting him to say something along the lines of Mandingo, Chocolate Thunder, or maybe even Got-Damn! But instead, he patted the Olde English lettering of the tatto on his forearm and answered all simple and sexy,

"Twon."

"Twon," I repeated, loving the way his name came off my lips like a kiss. I looked up and our eyes met, then right at that moment it hit me.

It was him!

The plaits, the hard body, the shadow of the tattoo on his arm—Twon was the one who had me ready to give it up in the club. His eyes kinda twinkled when he saw minez widen with recognition. I wondered how long he'd been playin the background and watchin me since we danced, how he managed to find me after the let-out and know that it all would lead up to this moment. He was clever. I liked that. It jive scared me a lil bit cuz it was obvious that he was stalking me…but I liked it.

"You mad cuz I's followin you?" Twon asked, practically reading my mind.

"I'm more scared 'den mad," I confessed.

"Scared? Whatchu scared uh' me for? I'on bite…Not hard."

I had a hundred things I coulda said to that but I just smiled and blushed instead. He was gettin me flustered like shit.

"Hi you find me?" I asked finally, tryin not to get lost in his dark, slanted eyes.

"It wasn't hard. You stand out," he told me, sounding so genuine that I blushed again. I ain't know what to say to such a compliment.

"You just like whatchu see," I finally managed, realizing that maybe he was talkin bout me in all my hourglass glory. I mean, I did have half my ass hangin out them shorts for the world to see.

"Yeah, you right about dat," Twon admitted, slowly lookin me up and down again. "But I like what I don't see, too."

I raised a eyebrow.

"Nah, young, I'on mean it like dat," he started to explain with a laugh. "I mean…"

"You mean what?" I smirked, thinkin to myself that he was just digging hisself in deeper the more he tried to explain.

"I'm sayin 'doe. You standin in fronta me lookin like a nigga dream come true. I'm tryna find out if what I don't see is good as what I'm seein…"

I smirked again.

"What I mean is—I wanna know the shit about chu I cain't see. Like whatchu like, hi you think…"

"How I think?" I asked. That was a new one. I could count on one hand how many niggas I met during my life that was more interested how my mind worked than what was between my knees. And none of em got me *half* as bothered as Twon did.

"Yeah, hi you think. I'm tryna get d' know you."

There was such a raw truthfulness in his voice that I knew he wasn't runnin no game. Caught me completely off guard. I was so used to being desired and using sex as communication that I ain't know no other way. I ain't think there *was* no other way. But here he was, this fine-ass stranger who aroused ery sexual nerve in my body, tellin me that he just wanted to talk to me. That he wanted to get to know me for me. Youngin had a rap so smooth it made me suspicious, but fuck it. He was cute and I was willing, so what the hell?

"Aight," I told him. "Gimme some'na write wit, 'den."

Twon got a pen from one of his friends and we exchanged pager numbers before goin our separate ways. I tried to act like I wasn't moved when I got back to my girls and they asked me a racka questions like what was we talkin bout and what did I think of him. But for real, youngin was heavy on my mind. I couldn't stop thinking about him the whole way home and it gave me a headache cuz I couldn't figure out why. Dhonni was the first one to point out the obvious as much as I denied it and tried to say it wasn't no way cuz we only talked for two minutes. But got-damnit, she was right.

Twon already had me hooked.

"Ay, you got me ona back rub? 'Day had y' boy liftin marble top desks t'day," Twon said as soon as he seen me step through the front door.

I threw my purse down on the couch and kicked off my shoes at the same time, barely listening to him as I brushed past to see if my cousin was in the den.

"Damn, 'scuse you. Gon step all on my feet and shit," Twon fussed from where he was unlacing his work boots in the livin room.

"My bad," I apologized, frantically swinging open the den door and peeking my head in. Just like I thought, Krys was nowhere in sight. That's what I get for letting her stay home this morning. She supposedly had cramps when I went to wake her up for work, so I decided to be nice and let her sleep in—you know, being all sympathetic and shit. Youngin was poseda get up with me later at the salon 'round lunch time, but when twelve o'clock rolled by, then one, then two, and three without no word from Krys, it ain't take a genius to figure out she played me. I coulda kicked myself for believing her sob story and givin her a break. The way Krys been walking 'round here rollin her eyes and mumbling under her breath at me ery since our confrontation a week ago, I shoulda known better than to be nice to her ass. Youngin took my kindness for weakness. This last lil move of hers was proof of that.

"Whatchu come up in hea' so mad about anyhow?" Twon asked, sittin down on the couch and stretching his legs out.

"Aggggghhhh!" I growled. "I'm so sicka dat girl! You see 'dis shit? See what I gotta put up wit? I'ma bust her fuckin head, young, I swear to God!" I exclaimed, goin over to the balcony door to look outside while I paced back and forth. Wasn't even no point in callin Krys' phone to see where she was at, cuz all she was gon do was forward me anyhow. All I could do was wait. And be mad.

"Why you lettin youngin get y' panties all in a bunch? Dat's my job," Twon joked.

"Do I look like I'm in'na mood for any typa panty talk?"

"Well howbout lettin me get y' panties *out of* a bunch? The boys is still at my Nanna house. I's gon take a shower and go pick em up, but since y' cousin ain't hea' eiva—"

"Exactly!" I snapped, cuttin Twon off before he could finish his offer. "Krys ain't hea' like she poseda be! Dat bitch rolled out! Gon tell me she can't come d' work cuz she got cramps, but gon sneak out when her ass poseda be in bed!"

I was pacing up a storm now, clenching my fists and shaking my head at how stupid I was for being nice. Nice wasn't in my character for a reason. Twon studied me for a second, then took one look at the hard expression on my face and chuckled. That's when I turned all my anger on him.

"What the fuck is you gigglin at?" I snapped. I ain't see why he was on joke time so hard. There wasn't nothin to laugh about.

"You cute when you mad, baby. Dat's all."

"Well, I'm glad to see you give a shit about the situation."

"I do give a shit," he told me. "I know you pissed. But you need d' chill out. It ain't dat serious."

"So what I'm poseda do, Twon? Act like nuffin wrong? Act like she ain't disrespectin me by lyin to my face? You know I'on play dat. Last bitch dat lied d' me got the shit beat outta her in fronta her own house."

"Dat's cuz yo' ass is crazy. You always tryna fight somebody."

"Well, people shouldn't be makin me dat mad, 'den!" I declared. Twon chuckled again, this time harder.

"Keep laughin at me, hea'. You gon fuck around and get y' lips busted."

"I'm tryna bust your lips, 'doe. Feel me?" my man playfully retorted with a suggestive wiggle of his eyebrows. At that, I couldn't help but smile.

"So what she snuck out? She gotta come back sometime. All her shit is hea'," he told me seriously.

"Yeah, and when she get back, she can pack it up and take it wit her to Greenbelt, too. I'm through," I said.

"So you just gon give up on her? You know her folks cain't do shit wit her. And you *did* say you'd try to rap to her before you sent her back."

"Well, I'm done wit dat shit. She ain't takin me serious. Youngin gon do what she wanna do regardless of what I tell her."

"So whatchu tell her? You talk to her yet? Do y'all even talk at all?"

"No," I admitted. Other than work or going to the grocery store, me and Krys barely hung out. She was always with her new friends, and I was always busy with my kids or tryna get some rest whenever I had free time. Besides, I still ain't know what kinda angle to come at her from. We were miles apart despite being in the same house.

"Sound like you ain't done, 'den. I'on know why you bein so stuck up about it."

"Stuck up?!"

"Whatchu call it, 'den? You'on even know her as a person. And she don't know you. Besides, how you gon give her all 'dis space to spread her wings, 'den turn around and get mad cuz she do? True, she ain't gotta be lyin to you and bein disrespectful—"

"Like now," I pointed out.

"Aight, you right. But all I'm sayin is, take some time to chill wit youngin. Say whateva it is you gotta say to her, and *then* be done wit it."

"So whatabout right now? What should I do?"

"I'on know," Twon shrugged.

"Well, I wanna punch her in'na side uh' her head," I snarled.

"Dat's one way to handle it. But she *really* ain't gon listen to you after that."

"So what should I do?" I insisted.

"I'on know. But for both y'all sake, I hope you do the right thing."

I wanted to ask him whal he meant by that, what doin the right thing would be, but he was already up and headed for the shower before I could. *Damn.* I was more than ready to say fuck Krys and send her on her way, but a part of me knew Twon made sense. Afterall, she was my cousin, and I did promise Aunt Josie that I'd do what I could to put some wisdom in her head. But how? How could I let her know in so many words that goin along with the "in" crowd wasn't always what it was cracked up to be? Youngin mighta strutted around like she knew erything but I could tell she ain't know shit from shoe polish. She had a lot to learn and I had a lot to share. Only problem was, I ain't know how to get *her* to see that.

CHAPTER ELEVEN

Aight, so I know you probly wondering what happent after that night I met Twon, right? Well I could lie and say I called him and realized he was the love of my life and we hooked up and it was all happily ever after. But the truth is, when I paged Twon the day after I got his number, we talked for all of five minutes before some bitch (who turned out to be his baby mama, Rayel) came up in the room where he was at, demanding to know who he was on the phone with. I put two and two together and figured she was his girl and they lived together, which wasn't exactly the kinda situation I wanted to get involved in. The way I useta harass and beat up them girls Dartanyan messed with, I knew I was in for a whole lotta conflict if I planned on fuckin with Twon. But as sexy as he was, I almost went for it. *Almost*. It wasn't until Rayel snatched the phone out his hand and started goin off like she just found out I was the one her best friend seen him riding around in his car the week before, that I changed my mind. Oh, hell nah! Rayel sounded crazier than me and I was not about to get my ass jumped over no nigga again. *Sheeeiiit*. That's that lil girl beef. As much as he intrigued me and made my stomach flip-flop, Twon had a lil too much drama for me, joe. I hung up the phone before Rayel could finish her tirade and threw away the Juicy Fruit wrapper with his number on it. Far as I was concerned, that was the end of that.

For days my sixth sense kept telling me I was gon see Twon again, but I dismissed my intuition as naïve hope and decided to put him outta my mind. I had too much other shit to worry about, like bailing Dartanyan's ass outta jail when he got arrested by the jump out that following Tuesday. This fool messed around and went up in the park where him and Tristan hustled right before the cops jumped out of a black Expedition with they barettas cocked, yellin for niggas to get on the ground. Tristan got away, but Dartanyan ain't even have time to toss the rocks he had stashed in his socks before them bodeens was slapping silver bracelets on his wrists. My boo was facing a mandatory five years off that shit, and since this was his second drug arrest in the past year, it was pretty much a done deal he was gon do some time. Dartanyan ain't plan on showing up at his court date in September because of it, but just to be on the safe side, he was doin that much more hustlin so me and Man-Man would be straight in case he did get locked up. Shit like that made me realize why I fell in love with Dartanyan in the first place. If nothin else, he was a man about his — a provider and a protector in ery sense of the word. He mighta cheated on me and stole the shit outta me ery once in a while, but at least he made sure me and his son never went without. Which was a lot more than I could say my own father did for my Mommy and us.

I'on know if it was seeing him be so responsible or feeling guilty that he got caught up tryna make money to take care of us, but whatever it was, I started lookin at Dartanyan in a whole different light. Maybe he ain't change as much as I thought he did. Maybe he wasn't the selfish, childish, dog-ass nigga in heat I made him out to be. I mean, the fact that he was still with me after all this time had to mean something, right? Cuz coulda rolled out back when we first started beefin and left me on my own. Instead he stayed, paid the bills, and even broke me off with cash whenever I told him I needed it. Dartanyan sure lived up to his nickname a lotta times, but he was really a aight dude when he wanted to be. And here I was so busy paying attention to his faults that I forgot to notice all the good things about him. Like the way he spent time with Man-Man without being asked, or how he basically worked two jobs and ain't complain cuz he knew he was doin what he had to do. I knew niggas who avoided they kids like the plague and was too lazy to get a job or hustle. Yet Dartanyan was doin all three. My boo was something else, wasn't he?

I actually started feeling bad for treating Dartanyan like shit. There was a racka things about him I wanted to change, like the way he could lie to my face and not feel guilty about it, but then there was things about him that I wouldna changed for the world. His sense of duty for one, and the way he could look right through me with them intense-ass eyes of his and make me weak at the knees no matter how mad I was. Damn, I loved that shit. And as much as I hated to admit it, I still loved him. I loved erything about him from the way he looked out for me even though we ain't get along, to the childish way he needed my constant attention to feel appreciated. That nigga was my heart! Was I wrong for punishing him cuz he tried to play me? Was I supposed to work with him, tell him what I wanted or something, try to mold him into the kinda man I wanted him to be? Growing up without seeing an example of what a real couple looked like, I ain't know what to do. But as a female it was in my nature to forgive, so after almost a year of hating the sight of his ass, I forgave Dartanyan and tried to forget all the shit that happened in our past.

I started being nice to Dartanyan again. Not just cuz I missed being close with him or cuz he was the father of my child and I wanted to keep our lil family together. It was mostly cuz I wanted us to go back to the way we was, and I thought if I was nice to him, I could bring the old Dartanyan back. So I took it back to the days when our relationship was good and started waking up extra early to fix him breakfast, went back to cuddling up in the bed with him at night, and finding any and ery excuse to talk to him or be near him. Dartanyan was jive confused by all the attention at first, but once he realized I was back on him for real, our small-scale cold war was over. Of course we both had secrets and separate lives that would keep a distance between us forever, but for the most part we was cool again and that's all that mattered.

Man-Man's first birthday came up on August 15th and we had a lil party for him at the house. We invited all our friends and close family over for my baby's first official BYOB (that's Bring Your Own Bud, in case you ain't know), and even though the big-ass Elmo cake was the only thing there actually for kids, Man-Man still had a ball. I watched in a purple haze as him and Zhané got elbow-deep in chocolate icing, and found myself amazed at how much my life had changed in the past year. Seemed like just yesterday when I was laid up in Greater Southeast Hospital wondering if I was really gonna hafta push something the size of a football outta me, and what would happen if the baby got stuck and decided he wanted to spend a couple extra days in there. Now here it is a whole year later and that same lil person who spent his first few months of life in my belly was growing up enough to pull away from me and explore the world outside the safety of my arms.

For the first time I started feeling like my real age was catchin up to the age I felt. It was hard to believe that in the fall, me and my girls would be startin our sophomore year at Spingarn, and come December, Dartanyan was gon be nineteen. Even harder to believe that Trayonna of all people, was almost four months pregnant. Erything was changing. Biggums retired from sellin homemade 'dro to selling rocks with Syco for this big nigga named Omar who pretty much ran shit around our way, while her other friend Mo teamed up with my brother and Pookie stealing cars for joyriding before selling the radios, the tires, and other easy-to-remove parts to this chop shop in Southwest. Lakisha decided to go against the grain and be a cheerleader with Keena and Chanel and the resta them stankin-ass 1-3 Hunniez, and Kia got bunned up with this hustler named Roe from Florida Park. She spent more time with him nowadays than Dhonni spent with the off-brand bitches she was startin to hang with since me and Dartanyan got back tight. It was kinda weird not havin my fam right there down for whateva whenever I called, but the way me and Dartanyan was bunned up again, I ain't have time to be hangin with them negroes anyhow.

Dartanyan took nine hundred dollars out the two G's we had saved up and bought us a gray box Caprice (which wasn't really *ours* cuz he ain't never let me drive the muhfucka nowhere). We was both doin what we had to do to save some more money, tryna get up to at least five G's just in case Dartanyan got caught up. Forced to look ahead to the future I faced raising a baby on my own, I wasn't really sure how I was gon make it without Dartanyan, financially or mentally. But I was planning. I had to. The boy couldn't run forever. Preparing for the worst was like second nature to me, and I thought I could handle pretty much anything that life threw my way. But when the worst came sooner than I expected and shook up my world like sand in a Etch-A-Sketch, I realized how *un*-ready I actually was.

Ma Beth had a stroke at the end of that summer in '97. Her oldest daughter Sharmaine moved in to take care of her, and no sooner than she sat her suitcases down at the door, Sharmaine was on a mission to take over her mama's house. Since the j'on would officially belong to her when and if Ma Beth died, if we stayed, me and Dartanyan would only be in the way—especially since Sharmaine wasn't lookin to have no boarders. In other words, our black asses had to go. Sharmaine started off by tryna make us feel unwelcome, doin petty shit like locking the door at the toppa the steps so we couldn't come upstairs to use the phone. Then she would come downstairs all nosy and uninvited with a racka questions bout whycome we ain't live with our parents and how long we planned on renting out the basement. Youngin was blowin the shit outta me but I held my tongue cuz I wasn't tryna get put out. Big mistake. Sharmaine musta thought shit was sweet cuz she busted up in our apartment one night like the j'on was hers and just happened to walk in on Dartanyan bagging up his yolas. Soon as she saw what was goin on, she all threatened to call the police and told us to get out, hollin' bout she ain't want no drug-dealing street trash up in *her* house. I was bout to punish her for violating our personal space like that, but I thought better of it and decided to get the fuck outta dodge till she calmed down. Good thing I did, too, cuz no sooner than I grabbed our money, the drugs, and packed a diaper bag and some clothes for me and Dartanyan, we pulled off in the Caprice right before the feds pulled up in theirs. Talk about good timing. Since Dartanyan skipped his court date the week before, if the feds woulda came in and caught him, that woulda been his ass.

We laid low for a couple days at one of the roach motels goin towards Downtown on New York Ave, tryna figure out the next move. Obviously it wasn't safe to live on L Street no more since the *Wicked Bitch of Northeast* was there. And I was not about to be fightin off thieves, fiends, and prostitutes to stay in no raggedy-ass hotel till something else came through. It was starting to look like we ain't have much of a choice, though. Dartanyan's folks was fakin on taking us in and I be damned if I was gon ask Mommy for help, so we was stuck moving from one dirty-ass hotel to another until we could find another basement to rent. Down but not defeated, me and Dartanyan went back to Ma Beth's a couple weeks later to get the resta our shit and hopefully move on with our lives. But after tearing through the duct tape blocking the basement door, we walked in on a shock that set us right back to square one.

The basement was empty.

Sharmaine had cleared all our shit out. The 32 inch TV, the stereo and the speakers, Man-Man's crib, all our clothes, and our shoes. Even erything down to the Bob Marley posters on the wall and the fake silk sheets coverin the mix-matched mattresses of our bed. Erything we stole, worked, and hustled for was gone. *Erything.* Only thing left was the lil electronic scale Dartanyan used to weigh his rocks on, which I'm sure Sharmaine left behind just to be smart. Well, you know I was ready to blow the whole city up after that shit. I tried bangin on the basement door, then went outside to kick in the front one, but Sharmaine's punk ass wouldn't come out for shit. She just stood in the picture window waving the phone like she was gon call the police again, and screaming for us to go away cuz we was disturbing Ma Beth. That's when I kirked the fuck out. I picked up one of the rocks surrounding the flowerbed in the front yard and threw it slam through the window at her ass. I'on know if the j'on hit her or what, but before I could put Man-Man down and climb over the broken shards of glass to find out, Dartanyan was pulling me by my waist back to the car.

He called me crazy but crazy wasn't the word for what I was after that. Just what the fuck was we poseda do now? We ain't have shit to our names but the clothes on our backs, the car, the drugs, and what was left of the money in our ziplock bag piggy bank. That was it. Thousands of dollars wortha our shit was gone, just like that, and to this day I still don't know if it was Sharmaine or the feds who took it. I swear, if Dartanyan ain't have that warrant out, I woulda stayed and beat Sharmaine's ass till the cops pried me offa her. Instead, I had to take it as a L and start my life all over again, miles away from the neighborhood that raised me.

I ain't bother tryna go to school them couple months we hotel hopped all over town, cuz at that point my survival was more important than my education. I got Sweet Nika and Dhonni to come with me on missions to stores where we filled up empty shoppin bags and fooled cashiers into givin us refunds, or went into dressing rooms loaded down with clothes and came out minutes later with a good three layers on under our sweats. We was goin hard, ruffin' phones, blank tapes, boxes of condoms, and basically anything sellable that wasn't nailed down. Except for bare necessities, I hustled off erything I got away with, too. I was tryna have them five G's so I'd have something to fall back on just in case worse came to worst, cuz for some reason, I had a nagging feeling in the pit of my stomach that made me wanna cling onto Dartanyan more than ever them last couple days. I could almost feel the trouble in the air, smell it comin our way like boiling chitlins in a small kitchen in the summertime (yeah, it was *that* strong). Up until the last week in October, I ignored em and tried to pretend like erything was fine, tried to tell myself that I was just stressed out from moving around so much and that's why I felt like I was goin crazy. But when I got that phone call at two-something in the mornin, I was forced to face what my intuitions been warning me about all along.

Dartanyan was in jail. He got pulled over on the way home from this crackhouse where he'd been slangin and stackin bread for the past five days. Exhausted from not gettin no sleep, but siced cuz he was sittin on a good $3,000 now, Dartanyan was breakin his neck to get home. After he stopped by Whiteboy's apartment to pick up the money he'd been stashing there (Dartanyan never kept too much bread on him at the crackhouse—ery five hundred he made, he called Whiteboy to come hold it for him), the feds pulled him over on MLK for speeding. Dartanyan's bloodshot eyes, lack of a license, and the freshly burned weed smell lingering in the Caprice was enough probable cause to make him get out while they searched the j'on. The rest is pretty much history. He was being held without bond at D.C. Jail till his court date in sixty days. In other words, I was on my own till January—or even longer if the charges stuck.

The impact of Dartanyan's words ain't really hit me till I was gettin dressed the next morning to go see him. I wasn't ready to face the reality that me and Man-Man's survival fell solely on my shoulders now. What was I poseda do? Get a job at McDonald's and get pimped for chump change? Walk the track Downtown and turn tricks for freaks? How was I poseda finish school or make money with nobody there to help me with the baby? I had a racka new problems to worry about but I ain't want Dartanyan to know I was trippin cuz I could tell he was already stressed enough when I sat down on the other side of the plexiglass cubicle in the visiting area. He ain't even hafta tell me he wasn't coming home no time soon. I could read the defeat all over his face. I cradled the phone on my shoulder and listened to him explain how in addition to gettin caught drivin without a license and drivin under the influence, the feds found the chrome plated .44 he had hidden under the driver's seat. Even though the j'on ain't have no bullets in it, they was gon give him a gun charge, and if the gun came back from the crime lab with any bodies on it, he was takin them charges, too. On toppa that, since Dartanyan already had a warrant out for his drug arrest, they was gon confiscate the $3,000 and hold the Caprice at the impound to give to auction if he got locked up. And the way shit was lookin, most likely, he was.

I got on the train home tryna think of a Plan B but I couldn't focus for shit. I couldn't believe it was over like that. The life I tried so hard to carve out for myself was done with for *at least* five years. All the scraping and sacrificing I did, leaving my family to stay with this nigga and raise our child, stealing and scheming to keep our heads above water—it was all in vain. And despite all the abuse I put up with to keep us together as a family, now Man-Man *really* ain't have no daddy.

I had to start all over again, but how? I ain't have shit. I wasn't gon be able to take care of me and Man-Man by myself, and on toppa that, I was homeless. I was too young to get on government aid by myself and too proud to ask anybody for help, especially my mother, but I couldn't afford to keep livin in hotels. I had to think of something quick or find a nice cardboard box and a corner for me and Man-Man to call home.

Desperate and outta ideas, I called up my Aunt Roz and asked if I could stay with her till I got my shit together. She sent my cousin Irshad to pick me up that same day. I stayed in Sweet Nika's room on a pile of blankets on the floor, beat down by life but thankful that at least *somebody* in this world had my back. Other than Aunt Roz pressuring me ery day bout talkin to my mother and Sweet Nika snoring like a buzz saw, I ain't have nothin to complain about the whole time I lived in Southwest. I had food to eat, a place to lay my head, and Dartanyan's auntie right around the corner to watch Man-Man whenever I was out making my paper. Aunt Roz was givin me till second semester to go back to school so I was doin erything I could to get money while I still had time. I hooked up with that nigga Omar through Biggums and and ran a couple kilo's from New York to Northeast for him on the Greyhound. I set niggas up for Syco and Mo to rob, I bought food stamps from pipeheads and re-sold em in fronta Safeway. I even ruffed a white boy for his UNICEF bucket and went around door to door in the nice neighborhoods scamming rich folks outta they pockets. I did erything short of selling my ass to keep from being broke, and when I wasn't doin that, I was on the phone or up at D.C. Jail making sure Dartanyan was aight.

His birthday was comin up on the eighteenth of December and I wanted to do it real big for him cuz his preliminary hearing was gon be the week after that. I went through the trouble of gettin him the new Jordan XIII's and a fresh Jordan shirt to match, even baked him his favorite German chocolate cake and put it all in a care package to take up there. After taking two hours gettin Man-Man dressed and squeezing into my tightest stretch jeans and a Bebe shirt, I got on the train all set to surprise my boo on his birthday and brighten up a otherwise fucked up holiday season. But when I got to the jail, the guard in charge of the visiting area told me Dartanyan was already sittin with somebody and I would hafta come back next week to see him.

I started to cause a scene cuz I was more than a lil bit pissed bout gettin all dressed up and turned away at the door, but once I realized arguing wasn't gon get me nowhere but in handcuffs, I decided to use a slicker approach. As the sayin go, money talks and bullshit runs marathons, so I dug in my bra for my stash and started questioning the guard about who was in there with Dartanyan. For a dub, he told me it was a broad. For fifty more bucks, he let me go back and see for myself. My jaw hit the ground when I peered through the doorway and saw a pretty, lightskinded girl there, all sitting across from Dartanyan with her hand up to the plexiglass partition like she was his girlfriend. I looked from the anguished tears glassing up her sea green eyes, to the uneasy expression on Dartanyan's face, to the way he was sneaking disbelieving peeks at her pregnant belly... and for a minute there I ain't wanna believe what I was seeing. But it was her. Sure as my name is Rashaiyah Deshay Williams, she was sitting there all up in my nigga's face, silently twisting a knife into my back and destroying ery ounce of love I ever had for the both of em at once.

Trayonna and Dartanyan. My best friend—my sister—was fuckin my boyfriend. I was *too* mad! I never thought neither one of em would stoop that low. Dartanyan mighta did a lotta triflin-ass shit, but fuckin my girl?! What part of the game was that? How could he kiss her and turn around and tell me he love me like ain't nothin ever happen? And Trayonna! She was a shady bitch but I ain't think she had it in her to be *that* got-damn shady. We grew up together, shared our food and clothes and shoes, knuckled up and fought for eachother. We was poseda be brown like that! I couldn't believe that two of the only people I ever held close to me, two of the only people I ever bent over backwards to please, had crossed me so bad I knew I could never forgive em.

I started causing quite a scene before the feds grabbed me up and kindly escorted my ass outta there. I was throwin cake at Trayonna and stompin Dartanyan's fresh outfit into the chocolate-covered floor, yellin threats of all kinds at they asses. Them muthafuckas! Them dirty, scandalous, two-faceded muthafuckas! It all started to make sense when I got on the train home. Shit I been overlooking for months suddenly occurred to me, like how interested Trayonna acted ery time I mentioned me and Dartanyan was having problems, or how the two of em couldn't seem to look at eachother whenever we was all in the same room together. I noticed they been like that for a while, but I ain't never think they was fuckin. I had a feeling they mighta *wanted* to, and that's why it was so much tension between em, but to actually do it? Nah, they wasn't that stupid—at least, I hoped not. I ain't wanna hafta think that the baby my play sister was carrying mighta belonged to my boyfriend, but I was seriously starting to see it was more than a possibility now. I mean, Trayonna wasn't never too clear on who the baby's daddy was, and the way her sneaky ass be goin, it wouldn't surprise me one bit if it was Dartanyan's. Shit, it wouldn't surprise me if them funky, pink panties I found under my bed that day belonged to her, too! I swear, if that baby ended up being Dartanyan's, I was gon kick his ass soon as he got outta jail. Fuck it, I was gon find a way to get his ass kicked while he was still in the j'on, and then go handle Trayonna myself!

Choking on tears and anger, I got home and told Sweet Nika, Cerrone, and erybody I knew what happened. I even called Lakisha to instigate since Trayonna wouldn't answer her phone, and by the time the sun set that same day, the whole neighborhood was talkin bout what was gon end up being the most memorable fight of the year. Seven months pregnant or not, I was gon fuck Trayonna up. Anybody who went hard enough to fuck my boyfriend *and* get pregnant by him deserved a no-fakin, sock-fulla-rocks, Northeast-style beat down. I left Man-Man with Dartanyan's aunt and called Syco to see if he could come get me. My boy came flying down the expressway some fifteen minutes later with Biggums, Dhonni, and Cerrone already in the car with him. The five of us piled up in the Delta 88 and took off for Trinidad, with Dhonni tryna convince me the whole time to chill out. She kept tellin me what I already knew bout how fucked up it would be for me to fight Trayonna in her condition. But fuck that shit! Couldn't nobody get away with doin me dirty like that! Couldn't nobody hurt me that bad and walk away without me hurting em back! It was the code I lived by, and the code I'd do time by or die by if I had to. So when we skidded onto Staples Street in fronta Trayonna's house, I was the first one out that j'on talkin noise and letting it be known that some shit was bout to go down. Erybody who was outside and ain't know what was goin on, figured it out quick after taking one look at me with my hair tied up in a bandana and my face greased up with Vaseline. Before it was all said and done, I had a crowd gathered 'round me taking bets and stretching they necks to see us scrap. It was bout to be on.

I paced in fronta Trayonna's house like a caged lion, yellin for her to come face me like a real woman. For a while nothin happened 'cept somebody peeking out the window a couple times, but eventually, the front door opened and out came Trayonna yelling for me to bring the muhfuckin drama. To my surprise, Keena, Chanel, and all them 1-3 Hunniez came out behind her to have the follow up with Lakisha of all people leading the pack. I was jive-like shocked to see such a clear line drawn in the sand, the sudden division between me and my friends becoming final, but fuck it. It was what it was and there wasn't no goin back.

I pushed past Lakisha and went at Trayonna like I had nothin to lose. Swingin my belt around like Pootie Tang off the dippas, I caught her, then Chanel with the buckle end before Keena came outta nowhere and stole me in the nose so hard my eyes started watering. Dhonni came in swinging after that and Biggums held the resta they crew back to make sure nobody tried to jump us. Next thing you know, I got the hood of Trayonna's hoodie in my hand and I'm banging the shit out her head on my knee till she fall to the ground. I got in a couple good kicks before Biggums pulled me away from stompin her out. Trayonna was balled up at my feet screaming in pain and I was inclined to spit in her face as a final fuck you, but Lakisha came outta nowhere with a heavy-ass house brick and cold cocked me one in the backa my head. That's when Biggums jumped in and started crackin bitches in the mouth like a true Jawbreaker. A couple other 1-3 Hunniez jumped in to get us away from Trayonna, and all anybody could see after that was a frenzy of nails, knuckles, and feet swingin ery-whicha-way in a all-out catfight. Braids was gettin pulled out, faces scratched up, shins bruised, and shirts ripped. Niggas was on the sidelines praying for a flash of a tiddie, but the police came before it got to that point and erybody scattered like roaches.

Of course I was the first one in handcuffs. I watched from the backseat of the cruiser I was sharing with Dhonni and Biggums as they loaded Trayonna up in a ambulance. I remember lookin out the window and seeing all the blood around Trayonna's middle, and feeling a cold chill creep up my neck as I realized I wasn't sorry at all. So-fuckin-what if she lost the baby? So what if I scarred her for life? I couldn't believe the same girl I useta play MASH with, the same girl who useta cut lines in my eyebrows and spend the night at my house, had stabbed me in the back like that. She had to pay for what she did. Trayonna violated our play sisterhood—BIG TIME—and far as I was concerned, that bitch deserved whatever I did to her ass.

The police took us all up the street to the 5ᵗʰ District P.D. and separated me, Dhonni, and Biggums from Keena, Chanel, and Lakisha, then questioned us one by one bout what happened. I pretty much kept my mouth shut cuz I wasn't tryna get myself or nobody else in any more trouble than we already was. It wasn't till they told me Lakisha blabbed out my mother's name and where she worked at that I snapped to attention. Insteada calling a social worker to come take me off they hands, the police called Mommy to come pick me up. And all I could think to myself was, *Why of all people did they hafta call that crazy bitch?* Mommy was gon do me worse than I did Trayonna once she found out I was in trouble. I mean, it wasn't like we was on good terms for her to be all that understanding bout the situation. We wasn't on good enough terms for her to even claim me as her damn child. And knowin how bad she hate police gettin involved in peoples' daily lives, I knew her gettin a call at work from D.C.'s finest was gon be far from okay.

Bloody, scratched up, and bruised like a rotting apple, I waited in a holding cell for hours before Mommy came. Erybody else got picked up and I was the only one left at the station, sittin there all blown with this homeless lady that kept talkin to herself and some shifty-eyed broad who I caught staring at my ass one too many times. I was just about to curl up in a corner and try to sleep off my headache when outta nowhere, I smelled the distantly familiar scent of Opium perfume. Mommy's perfume. That shit made me so anxious I actually started gettin heart palpitations that throbbed through the knot on the backa my head. I heard her coming down the hall to where I was, the smell of her perfume gettin stronger and stronger with each step. The familiar squick-squack of her orthopedic nurse shoes, the swish-scratch of her heavy thighs rubbing her immaculate white scrubs together, the crisp sound of her poppin her gum…I could almost see her cuz the sounds and smell of her was so clear.

I put my head in my hands and braced myself for the worst, thinkin I mighta been better off in jail knowing the shit my mother was gon do to me. Beating my ass was only the half. Hell, I'd be lucky if I still had all my teeth come tomorrow mornin. Her shoes stopped abruptly in fronta the cell and I looked up to see her staring me down harder than she ever did before, her cat eyes cutting so sharp they looked hawkish, her round, cocoa brown face drawn so tight a chisel couldna cracked her a smile. Mommy stood there glaring at me through the iron bars a lil chubbier than I remembered but just as hard and intimidating, and parted her lips to say the first words to me she'd said in over a year.

"Girl, what the fuck is wrong witchu?"

Aight. I might not be gettin ridda Krys just yet, but damn if I'ma let her keep goin the way she is. It's about to be some changes up in Forest Creek. First things first, youngin ain't goin out with her damn friends no more. Can you believe the whole Friday she skipped work came and went and her ass still ain't show up by Saturday morning? Not only did she leave without asking, not only did she stay out the whole night, but she was bout to fuck around and miss work for the second day in a row. I was so mad I ain't even have no words. Youngin was carryin it! Twon mighta talked me into letting her stay, but that ain't mean I had to take Krys' shit laying down. If she gon stay in my house, she gon hafta go by my rules. Simple as that. And as soon as she bring her raggedy ass through the door, that's just what I'ma gon tell her, too.

Meanwhile, I was pacing around the house biting my nails and waiting for some typa sign tellin me to wait or leave for work without her. I was just about to save my speech for later and get my Saturday started when I got the overpowering urge to look out the window. So I did. I peered between the vertical blinds at the balcony just in time to see Krys hop out the passenger seat of a familiar car. It was the white Crown Vic bubble. The same car that picked her up and kept her out all night on July 4th. *So that's who she was with, hunh?* I backed away and started pacing the floor in anticipation again, wondering just how in the world to handle this one. A few more minutes passed before I heard the locks rattle at the front door and in stepped Krys, braids all fuzzy, clothes wrinkled and covered in lint like she been rolling around on somebody's carpet, with her shirt inside out and smudged mascara around her eyes bout as black as the sandals she carried in her hand. The way she shuffled into the apartment with her eyes squinted shut and a look on her face like it pained her to walk, I could tell she had one helluva hangover.

"You know what time it is?" I demanded, putting both hands on my hips when I confronted her.

"Not really," Krys answered. "I ain't got no watch."

She tried to move past me towards the den, but I wasn't bout to let her off that easy. Not with no bullshit excuse like that.

"So I guess you plan on stayin home t'day, too," I sneered, back in her face again.

"Man, go 'head. You makin my ears hurt."

"I'm bout to make your face hurt if you keep playin wit me."

"Oh, God. Whatchu talkin about now?" Krys sighed.

"Who the fuck said you kn leave witout tellin no'by? I thought you was poseda be so sick."

"Damn, what is you, my muhva or some'n? I'm hea' now, ain't I?"

"So what! Look atchu!" I flipped the ends of her beat up, red braids, then pointed at her inside out shirt and bare feet. "Comin up in hea' lookin like Who-Struck-John. It's eight some'n in the mornin, girl. Where the fuck you been at all night?"

"Out wit my folks," Krys answered shortly.

"Folks, hunh? What, you forgot the nigga name already?"

"Why you always think I been wit a nigga? I coulda been wit

Iyania all night."

"Oh, so Iyania drive a white bubble now?"

"What are you talkin bout? Why you always think I'm wit a dude?"

"Cuz I know how you go."

"Whatchu mean, you know how I go? Whatchu tryna say?" Krys squawked, all on the defense.

I ain't really feel like gettin into it, but cuz with the white bubble wasn't the only knucklehead I been seeing Krys coming and going with lately. She still had her main bun from Walker Mill swingin by, and she stayed booking niggas at the mall and comin home bragging all loud on the phone to her girls bout how she was gon add em to her all-star team. It wasn't really my place to say nothin, cuz that girl was gon do what she wanted to do anyhow. But judging by the hickey on her neck and that sweaty coochie smell comin off her ass, I knew she was doin more than rappin up cuz with the Vic. I ain't wanna start preaching bout how stupid it was to be laying up with more than one nigga at a time in this day and age, but just how long was I poseda keep my mouth shut about it?

"Don't worry bout what I'm sayin. You just betta watch y'self wit all them niggas," I warned.

"All what niggas? You ack like I got twenty of em lined up."

"You do, damn near."

"Damn near? You tryna call me a rolla or some'n?" Krys screeched, her expression sharp as razor wire now.

"Look, I'on know who you think you muggin on like dat, but I ain't callin you shit," I said. "I'm just statin a fact. You need d' chill out. And you need d' learn how to sit y' ass down somewhere insteada runnin the streets all night. I'on know whatchu think you missin, but ain't nothin out 'dare but trouble. Believe me, I know."

Krys sighed, irritated, and gave me a look like she wanted to clock me one.

"Yeah, yeah. You know 'dis and you know dat. Well, whycome you'on know when to get the fuck out my face? Like some'my wanna be hearin you soon as they step in'na door and shit."

Whoa. Rewind. Was I imagining things or did Krys just say what I thought she said? I almost had to pick my jaw up off the floor cuz my mouth dropped open so wide. What's worse is how Krys leveled her eyes with minez like she dared me to challenge her. *That bold lil bitch.*

"You doin all dat woofin like you got heart, 'doe," I said, edging close with my fists balled, ready to knock her block off. And believe me, I was. "But lemme steal your ass one time, joe. Eryby gon be lookin at me like *I'm* wrong. Like you'on deserve the shit."

"Yeah, whateva, Shai. Is you done, young? I'm bout d' go lay down," Krys sighed, bored and nonintimidated.

"Is I'm done?"

It was really startin to lunch me out how hard youngin was goin. Like I had sugar water for blood and I wouldn't punish her ass. She had to be high or drunk or something. No way in the world Krys was jumpin out her square with me off the sober. She couldna been that dumb.

"You trippin. Eiva dat or you as stupid as you look right now," I said, considering whatever she got high off last night was still talkin for her. "I'on know why I bother sometimes. Let a ho be a ho, right? If dat's whatchu wanna be, then fine," I sighed, turning away to get my purse. "Lemme just gone to work before I fuck some'n up. I'll deal witchu—"

The air changed suddenly from just a lil heated to a fierce, staticky anger that stung me in the back like twenty hornets. It took me a second to figure out why. Krys had cocked back and threw one of her shoes at me so hard and so fast I ain't know what happent at first. But once I realized the fiery throb pulsing between my shoulder blades was cuzza the stiletto sandal suddenly on the floor behind me, I lost it. *No she did not just throw her fuckin shoe at me!* Bitch threw the pointy end first, at that! Fuck being cool, fuck being nice, fuck talkin, fuck erything! I whirled around and smacked Krys so hard my hand went numb, then snatched her up by her neck before she had a chance to do anything back. Next thing you know, we scuffling 'round the livin room, throwin elbows and fists, scratching at eachother's faces, pulling eachother's hair, and knocking over shit left and right. Like my man Bernie Mac would say, some furniture got moved around up in there. Seemed like it went on forever before I heard the kids' frantic yelling from the hallway, and felt Twon grab us both by the backa our necks and wedge his way between us to break it up. I was so mad it took the kids' desperate cries for me to stop lunchin before I snapped outta my rage and realized what happent.

I just fought Krys.

Now, if that ain't a sign of good intentions gone bad, I ain't know what was. It was time to stop forcing shit with that girl. There wasn't no talkin to her. Not if she was gon be fistfighting me in my own dag-gon house. Fuck no, man! Her ass had to go.

"Get out!" I cried, snatching wisps of tangled red hair away from my eyes. "Out! Fuck out my house, joe! I'm sicka seein yo' ass!"

"No problem!" Krys shouted back. "I'm sicka you tellin me what to do! Fuck you!"

"Fuck you, yol' simple-ass, scallywag, bucket-head bitch! Getcha rolla ass up out my house!"

That got Krys started again, but Twon held her by her arms and wouldn't let go. She started calling me all typesa bitches right back, all cussin and carrying on real disrespectful-like in fronta my kids. I was ready to go over there and yoke her ass up again for showing out so, but Tink was cryin and Man-Man had wrapped both arms around one of my legs. Krys wasn't worth lookin like a monster in fronta my boys. God knows I done fought in fronta them enough. So insteada goin back at Krys like I really wanted to, I calmly told her once more to pack her shit, and left it at that. I was mad it had to be this way, but fuck it. Krys wasn't my daughter. Let Aunt Josie and Uncle Travis deal with her ass.

CHAPTER TWELVE

Ain't nobody hafta say a word for me to know I was in big trouble. I could tell by the way Mommy chain smoked Virginia Slims all the way from the police station in Northeast to Wheaton, and drove staring straight ahead from behind the wheel of her new Land Cruiser like none of us was in the car with her. I had a racka questions bout why she wasn't taking me back to Southwest that night and what the hell she was doin with Man-Man strapped in the car seat beside Cerrone in the back, but I be damned if I was gon ask that psycho broad anything. The look Mommy gave me after she signed my release papers at 5-D, I knew I'd be better off if I just shut the fuck up and went along for the ride.

I stared vacantly out the passenger window as Mommy took the long way down Georgia Avenue to get home, amazed how the street got wider, cleaner, and the buildings more spread out the farther into Maryland it went. Long after we passed anything that remotely resembled the city, Mommy pulled into a townhouse development tucked up in the woods and barked something to my brother bout fixing me up a spot to sleep in. Cerrone mumbled a irritated response that Mommy chose to ignore, and stayed outside to help me with my stuff after she went in.

"I feel sorry for you," my lil brother said, taking Man-Man out the car seat that musta belonged to our baby sister. "I ain't seent Mommy 'dis mad in a minute."

"I know," I sighed. "I'on even feel like hearin her mowf, young."

Cerrone pressed Man-Man's sleeping head to his shoulder like he knew what he was doin and held his free hand out for one of my trash bags fulla whatnots. I shook my head to say I ain't need no help and pulled em both out the back by myself.

"Is I'm sleepin in your room?" I asked, watching my brother tenderly pat his nephew on the back like he been taking care of babies for years. It ain't never occur to me that since I been gone, Cerrone mighta been the one stuck playin mama to the lil ones all this time.

"Probly, till Mommy move Sparkle into Treasure room. She migh'as well. Ain't like Sparkle slept in'nat j'on anyhow."

"She still scareda the dark?" I laughed, suddenly aware it'd been over a year since I seen my lil sisters.

"You migh'as well call her 'Chicken Little'. Sparkle be scared uh' her own damn shadow sometimes."

I smiled, thinking about the family I missed, and wondered how erybody was growin up without me.

"I stay in'na basement," Cerrone told me, changing the subject. "I only got a single bed, so it ain't really no room. But chu kh have my j'on and I just sleep on'na floor."

"Good lookin out, Roney," I said, and took a look around at what I guessed was my new home. I felt outta place like shit. Coming from my side of town to the richest county in Maryland, I ain't know if I shoulda been glad to be away from all the confusion of the city or suspicious of my squeaky-clean surroundings. Where was all the people sittin on the porches? Where was the music, the smell of food, the talkin, the yelling, the scream of police sirens and ambulances that usually filled the air? Where was all the hustlers who rode around on dirt bikes with drop socks fulla whatever you needed? And what the hell was that strange rattling-chirping sound coming from behind them trees down the street?

"Crickets loud as shit, ain't 'day?" Cerrone asked, watchin my confused frown as I strained to listen to the noise.

"Is dat what dat is?"

"Yeah. Crickets, tree frogs, katydids. 'Day by dat lil pond back 'dare. Them j'ons useta keep me up all night when we first moved hea'. You jye get useta it, 'doe. C'mon."

I followed my brother inside and stumbled through the darkness to the back of the house. Cerrone flipped a switch in the hall so we could see goin downstairs and I had to do a double take at the house in the light. Tan leather and oak in the livin room, mahogany and cream in the dining room, blue and white gingham in the country-style kitchen—Mommy and Tone had that j'on lookin like something straight off a Marlo showroom floor. Houseplants and framed pictures was erywhere, even some pictures of me. It all looked so nice I had a hard time believing my family really lived there. *Lemme find out we done moved on up.* Cerrone chuckled at my amazement and told me to come on. I pushed past a hanging spider plant and followed him down into the chilly dimness of the basement, kinda eager to see what the resta the house looked like.

"I call 'dis j'on the Bat Cave," my brother informed me, and led me down a short hallway to where he slept. Unlike upstairs, the basement was just as junky and disorganized as our old room back on Holbrook Street. A unmade twin bed sat alongside a stack of milk crates that I guess was poseda be the nighstand, and was surrounded by piles of clothes and shoes on the floor. A broken fan stood in one corner, a set of mini-congo drums sat in another, and big-ass posters of Aaliyah, Foxy Brown, and Lil Kim was taped to the walls. Fliers for upcoming BYB and OP Tribe shows was thrown across the dresser along with a fifteen-inch TV that my brother had the nerve to get cable on. I sat my trash bags down by the milk crates and flopped down on Cerrone's bed. Just when I was bout to thank him again for lettin me crash in his space, Mommy's voice came booming from the toppa the steps.

"Rashaiyah, bring yo' ass up hea'!" she hollered loud enough to wake the whole house. Knowin better than to make her wait, I rolled my eyes and made my way back upstairs.

Mommy was sittin on one end of the tan leather couch with a jack in her hand and a scowl on her face that could stop a charging bull in its tracks. I sat down across from her in a overstuffed recliner and took a deep breath, tryna mentally prepare myself for what was probly gon be the fucked up end to a already fucked up day.

Didn't neither one of us say nothin for a while. We just sat there in silence, pretending to study opposite ends of the livin room like erything else was more important than makin eye contact. The invisible sea of contempt that usually lapped calmly between us seemed to silently splash and crash waves of animosity with ery second that passed. Shame it was still like that between me and my mother. A whole year apart couldn't even change the relationship we had. The distance was still there, right along with the criticism and self-righteousness that boiled beneath her heated gaze. I already knew Mommy wasn't gon hear me out or bother to ask why I was fighting in the street like a lunatic. She'd probly just come to her own conclusions like she always did and blame the whole shit on me.

"So whatchu gotta say for y'self?" Mommy asked after a while, lookin directly at me for the first time since we left the station.

"I ain't gotta say nuffin," I mumbled.

"Excuse me?" Mommy's voice went up a couple octaves. "Keep thinkin I won't knock you into next week, lil girl. Mad as I am right now, you just betta watch your mouth 'fore you wind up pickin yourself up off the floor."

I rolled my eyes. Why she always gotta be threatenin somebody? And who the fuck was she calling a lil girl?

"Whycome you ain't take me back d' Aunt Roz house?" I demanded, and gave her a quick glance. "I know you'on want me hea'."

"Yeah, you hit the nail on the head wit dat one," my mother scoffed. "I ain't exactly whatchu call excited bout havin two extra mouths to feed. But if I ain't take y'all, they's gon send you to a home."

"Whycome you ain't just let em put me in a home, 'den? You ain't have no problem leavin me somewhere before," I spat in an attempt to make her feel guilty. Too bad it ain't work.

"I hope you ain't tryna get no apology outta me—cuz I ain't sorry," Mommy snapped, rollin her eyes at me. "Ain't nobody tell you to lay up wit dat boy and have no baby. You did dat on your own accord. So what I left you in D.C.? I did dat to teach yo' ass some responsibility. If you grown enough d' make a child, you grown enough d' take care of it. Dat's what my mama told me and dat's what I'm tellin minez," she concluded with a typical, self-righteous nod of her head.

I frowned. I was all for teaching a kid a lesson, but damn. At fourteen years old, I wasn't in no position to be tryna take care of me and a child. Look at all the shit I had to go through to keep us from starving cuz I wasn't old enough to get a real job and support myself. My mother was lunchin if she thought me gettin my ass beat, running drugs, and stealing for a living was better than gettin a lil help from her.

"Man, how long I gotta stay hea'?" I asked, slouching down in the chair. I could see now we wasn't gon come to no understanding bout shit. I'd be better off back at Aunt Roz house dealing with Mommy's mean ass over the phone.

"'Till after your court date."

"Court date?" I asked, sittin up straight as a arrow. "What court date I got? I ain't do nuffin!" I declared indignantly.

"Ain't do nuffin?" Mommy huffed. "Oh, so I guess you call catchin assault and attempted manslaughter charges 'ain't doin nuffin', hunh? I guess *cuz you ain't do nuffin*, you ain't gon be on trial in thirty days, then."

What?!

"Attempted manslaughter?" I asked incredulously. Mommy had to be sicin it.

"You heard me. Trayonna went into labor after you saw to kickin her in'na stomach and shit. Girl had the baby six and a half weeks early. Surprised both of em still alive. You's a evil-ass somebody, doin dat to dat girl. Tryna kill dat baby," Mommy said, shaking her head at me like she was disgusted. Suddenly, I remembered the sight of a bloody Trayonna gettin carted off in the ambulance and I felt bad. Part of me wanted to know if the baby was aight. Part of me wished she woulda lost it altogether.

"So you ain't got nuffin to say bout dat, either, hunh?" Mommy asked.

"Nah," I answered quickly, turning my face from hers. I wanted to keep that conversation short and sweet, and her outta my business as much as possible even though she probly already knew the deal.

"So I guess you ain't gon tell me bout Dartanyan gettin locked up, either? Or you out there stealin and convincin my sister not to make you go back to school? You ain't gon nuffin to say bout dat?"

See what I mean? That bitch love playin games with me.

"Nope," I told her, and crossed my arms over my chest.

"Then I guess we about done hea'. I kh see your hardheaded ass ain't listenin to me anyhow," Mommy concluded with a sigh. She stood up to leave. "Look, it's gon be social workers and shit comin around since you done called attention to the fact that you's a minor livin away from home. I'ma get in trouble if they find out you ain't in my custody, so make sure you have your butt in'na house when they call. And stay out my got-damn way till this shit is over. I'm goin'na bed," she snapped. And with that, Mommy put out her jack and gave me one last hard stare, then went upstairs to her room.

I ain't sleep too good that night or any other night them first few weeks at Mommy's house. Didn't nothin feel right to me. The neighborhood outside was too quiet, my brother and sisters inside was too noisy, Mommy was forever finding excuses to cuss me out, and Tone was gettin on my nerves tryna be so nice all the damn time. I wanted to go back to the city so bad it made me wanna scream, but Mommy made it so I couldn't even take a shit without her wanting to know where I was goin and when I was coming back from doin it. I wasn't allowed to go outside or watch TV or use the phone, not even to talk to Sweet Nika and Dhonni when they called to tell me Dartanyan was hittin em up ery day begging for my new number. I thought I'd have a lil more freedom when it came time for me to start high school at John F. Kennedy in January, but Mommy managed to keep a eye on erything I did from her desk in the ICU corridor at Holy Cross Hospital. She worked crazy hours during the day and night so I couldn't never figure out a schedule to sneak around her rules. Sometimes I tried anyway and got beat like a dog, but after years of being her least favorite child and knuckling up with Dartanyan, I ain't really feel physical pain no more. It was being all caged in and regulated on that got to me the most.

Them social workers called and came by damn near ery day till my court date on January 12th. Of course they was tryna get all up in our business and get to the bottom of things between me and Mommy, but I wasn't for all that family therapy and mediation bullshit. I just wanted to do my time and get the fuck back to the city. I ain't know how I was gon get a steady cash flow, or if Aunt Roz would even let me move back in with her, but I knew one thing for sure—I was gettin the fuck away from my mother! I already had my bags packed the day I went to court, expecting to leave Maryland for good if I ain't get put in a detention center off them attempted manslaughter charges. But after fifteen minutes of fancy legal talk between the judge and the lawyer Tone hired for me, my heart sank with the realization that I wasn't goin no-fuckin-where. A court order put me in Mommy and Tone's custody till I turned eighteen, *and* hit me up with a racka fines to pay back the city of Washington. That shit blew me and boosted me at the same time. On one hand, I ain't hafta worry bout givin up my baby and livin in a group home for the next three years. On the other hand, all I had to my name was the two thousand some-odd dollars I managed to save up since the summer. I needed that money to get back on my feet, but fuck it. I had to do what I had to do. I forked over all I had and Tone paid off the difference. Then, just like that, I was right back to square one...*Again.*

I was down to nothin and there wasn't a damn thing I could do about it. I ain't even have enough money to get on the bus unless Tone gave me a lil something to buy lunch and I skipped a meal just to have some bills in my pockets. I was still stealing whatever I could, but it was harder to do without Kia or Dhonni by my side. I ain't have enough eyes to look for guards and cameras so I was nicked all the time, and I really couldn't get too much big shit that would sell for enough money to make it worth the risk. Being slick was especially important now that I had a juvenile record with more than some petty shoplifting charges on it. Gettin caught nowadays was gon get me more than my picture taped up at the cash register. One more slip up and my ass could be in juvi. Besides, I was finding that once I did make off with some decent stuff, the folks in my new neighborhood wasn't as open to buying stolen goods as they was back in Northeast, so I ended up having to take that long-ass trip to the city just to get my work off. Risking freedom and lugging around a bag fulla clothes and a heavy-ass baby all by myself after a couple times had me seriously thinkin about making a career change.

I needed another option. I started thinkin maybe an education was the answer. I went to school whenever I got up early enough and tried to pay attention in class, but it was hard to focus knowin I coulda been out making money insteada repeating the same ninth and tenth grade classes I failed in D.C. Besides, I felt like a sideshow at Kennedy, and I ain't like how erybody stared at me or tried to be my friend once they heard I was from the city. I started skipping school and hangin out with this cool-ass Spanish girl named Delmi who always know where the bud was at, and when I wasn't with her, I was on the train back to Trinidad with Cerrone. I mostly stayed in the house, though, just to avoid Mommy's wrath. My room was my hangout spot since I still wasn't allowed to watch TV with my brother and sisters. I had a lotta time on my hands to think about whatever popped into my head, which was usually my empty pockets or Dartanyan. Thinkin bout how I had no money vexed the shit outta me. Thinkin bout Dartanyan made my heart hurt and sent me into cryin spells that lasted for hours. To take my mind off em, I played with Man-Man or read anything I could get my hands on. Sometimes I tried to turn my hurt into creativity and wrote poems about how I felt. Other times I sat around with my bitter thoughts and plotted on different ways to kill Trayonna and that lyin-ass nigga.

I was in one of these particularly dark moods the night fate and coincidence brought me face to face with my destiny. It was the first weekend in February 1998 and I was stuck up in my room as usual. Mommy and Tone went to go see one of them Tyler Perry plays at Warner Theatre and I was jive boosted to finally have em out the house. Insteada making plans to go hang out in the city, though, I was gettin ready for a quiet night at home in fronta the big screen in the livin room. I'd just given Man-Man a bath and was gettin him all lotioned and powdered up so we could go downstairs and watch TV, when my pager started goin off. At first I thought Man-Man musta pressed one of the buttons cuz he was busy chewing on the j'on while I tried to get his diaper on, so I pried it outta his dimpled hands and glanced at it to make sure he ain't break nothin. That's when I saw the unfamiliar 202 number on the display.

"Fuck is this?" I wondered aloud, frowning. Before I could toss the j'on back in my purse, it started goin off again and the same number popped up. Partly outta curiosity, partly out annoyance that some mystery muhfucka was blowin up my shit, I scooped Man-Man up and went in Mommy's room to call whoever it was back. They picked up on the first ring.

"Some'my page Shai?" I asked cuz who answered the phone.

"Yeah…"

I waited for the resta his explanation. "Well, who the fuck is it?" I demanded gruffly when I ain't get one. I ain't never been one for them guess-who phone calls.

"Damn," youngin chuckled, undeterred. "Dat ain't hi you poseda talk to y' man."

"My man?" I rolled my eyes and bounced Man-Man on my hip. This clown sounded like he was bout to try some weak-ass rap on me and I was seriously not in the mood.

"Look, whatchu page me for?" I asked flatly.

"I fount cha number in my car," youngin started, still not put off by my abrasiveness. "I thought I lost dat j'on a long time ago. I'on know how it got 'dare, but I figga'd it must be a sign f' me d' call you up. I catch you at a bad time?" he asked, genuinely concerned.

"Nah, but..." I ain't know if I wanted to brush him off or not. Something bout his velvety smooth Quiet Storm voice drew me in. "Hi you know me?" I asked, just so I could hear him talk again.

"I met chu last summer at d' Black Hole. We was outside and I gave d' nigga you was wit some matches. 'Member you had on them real short shorts wit cuts up d' sides..."

"Cuts up the sides?" I wondered aloud. Me in booty shorts with cuts up the sides, hangin with a nigga he gave matches to? It all sounded familiar..."Whatchu look like?" I quizzed, tryna get another clue.

"Darkskin, plaits..."

I tried to remember a darkskin youngin with plaits givin one of my friends some matches outside the go-go. I searched my memory till my mind went blank, then searched it some more. Finally it came to me. I felt a surge like a jolt of electricity zap through me when I remembered the sexy, fudge-brown boy givin Biggums a book of matches on our way back to Syco's car that night. Damn! It was him! Uh...what's-his-name!

"Oh, yeeeaaaaah," I said, sittin down on Mommy and Tone's bouncy, king-sized bed. "Bowlegged youngin. What's y' name again?"

"Twon," he told me, then teased, "Oh, so *now* you remember me."

How could I forget him? I was this close to givin youngin summa that good-good the night we met. He had the supermodel body and them nice-ass lips. He liked what he saw and what he didn't see about me. He told me he wanted to get to know my mind...And he had a psycho-ass girlfriend, too.

"Yeah, you the one had dat bitch cuss me out on'na phone," I accused. A cold numbness seeped through my veins as a equally cold callousness rose up from the pit of my stomach. Twon having a girl and tryna make me think I was special was the main reason I ignored all his pages after that time we talked. If I couldn't be a nigga's number one attraction, I ain't want shit to do with him.

"Ay, my fault about dat, sweetheart," Twon apologized. "Dat wasn't even my girl, f'real...well, not technically. It's a long story, but fuck it. Youngin out d' picture now."

I rolled my eyes. Yeah, right. That sounded like some mess Dartanyan woulda said to one of his hoes after I banged her out.

"I know you probly think I'm lyin," Twon said, reading my mind. "Dat's aight if you ain't tryna believe me. I just wanted d' see wsup witchu. So wsup?"

"The sky, nigga. *Wsup* witchu callin me like we peoples?"

"To tell you the truth, young, I'on even know," Twon confessed with a sigh that said he was more baffled by his own behavior than me. "You probly gon think I'm tryna rap y' head up when I say 'dis, but...I'on know, young. I fount y' number today and I been thinkin bout you like shit ery since."

"Yeah, well, I got dat effect on niggas," I bragged, unimpressed. "The fuck dat gotta do witchu callin me now?"

I could tell I had him at a loss for words. I started to say I was sorry for making shit so awkward, but my own distrust and hostility kept me from doin it. I ain't have *no* love for niggas nowadays. Dartanyan and his bullshit had me thinkin all of em was the same, and I couldn't believe nothin that came out they mouths. Twon sounded sincere, but I couldn't let that fool me. Dartanyan useta look me slam in the eye and swear he wasn't doin me dirty—and you see what typa shit he was off.

"You makin 'dis real hard," Twon said, the smoothness in his voice gone now. He paused for a moment and I breathed a sigh of relief thinkin he was gon give up.

"I ain't no quittin-ass nigga, 'doe," he continued, doin just the opposite. "I be fluke if I ain't aks you what I called d' aks you."

Frustrated, I started bouncin Man-Man on my knee and tried to think of the meanest way to tell this bamma I ain't wanna hear shit else he had to say.

"I wanna make you smile. You gon let me?" Twon blurted out.

"Make me smile?" I repeated, frowning. It was so sporadic, such a off-the-wall thing to say, that for a minute I ain't know what the hell he was talkin bout. It was the second time Twon had ever said something odd that got my full attention.

"Dat's ain't aksin too much is it?" he wondered.

"Depend on how you plan to go about dat," I said, expecting a *bet-you-be-smiling-once-I-give-you-this-Sammy-Sausage* comment.

"Whatchu like to do, 'den? We kh do dat."

"Sleep," I told him. "And be left the fuck alone. Dat's what I like to do."

"Got-damn, sweetheart," Twon chuckled. "Dat's hi you feel? You mean as shit."

"So?"

"*So?*" he sucked his teeth and came back at me with a venomous snap. "Aight, 'den, slim. If it's like dat, 'den fuck it. Ain't no point in me wastin my time on no broad like you anyway."

"'Scuse me?" I squeaked, suddenly snatched to attention. I know this fool wasn't tryna break bad with me. "Whatchu mean a *broad like me?* Who you think you talkin to?"

"I'm talkin'na yo' angry-Black-woman ass. You hea' anyby else on'na phone?" Twon spat.

"Angry Black woman?! Who the hell is you d' be callin me names? You'on know me!"

"I ain't gotta know you. I kh hea' it in y' voice. Dat's whatchu get for fuckin wit them bammas."

"How I know you ain't a bamma?" I snickered before I could remind myself to hang up the phone. Twon was playin me like a fiddle. Once he saw that nice boy shit wasn't gettin my attention, he switched it up and started speakin a language I could understand.

"Come holla at me and you'll see," he answered simply. I blew out a half-laugh.

"Look, young, I meant what I said when I met you," Twon continued as if I wanted him to keep talkin. "I'm tryna get d' know you. I know you was beefin off the way youngin came at you on'na phone last time. But I ain't neh' f'getchu, 'doe. Like I said, I thought I lost y' number, but I fount it now so, yeah. I ain't tryna let you hang up witout promisin d' come see me at least once, young. Fuck what y' man got d' say about it."

"You makin a lotta demands, ain't chu?" I snapped, slightly amused at the way he was taking charge.

"Dat's what I do when I know what I want."

"So what is it that you want?" I asked, thinking I could get him to admit all he really wanted to do was hit it and quit it like ery other nigga I met.

"C'mon now, it ain't nothin out the way. I'on even know you like dat. I just want you in my space for a lil while, sweetheart, dat's all...I mean, I ain't gonna be mad if you lemme see for myself why 'day call you Honey, but..."

"But..."

"But dat ain't what I'm after. All I want is your time. Dat's all, I swear."

"You swear, hunh?" I smirked again. Boy, he was laying it on thick.

"Yeah, just like I swear if you let me take you out t'mar, you gon leave dat bamma-ass nigga you wit. And I swear if you start fuckin wit me, you won't be soundin mean as you do right now. I have you wakin up in'na mornin cheesin, walkin 'round the house singin and shit, girl. Bet dat."

Oh, my God. Was he for real?

"Yeah, you talk a good one," I said, fightin the twitching at the corners of my mouth.

"I know. I bet it's workin, too," came Twon's cocky reply.

I started smiling a lil bit and felt the icy numbness in my blood slowly melt away. Twon's *I'm-that-nigga* attitude and easy sense of humor was making me put my guard down. Just that fast I went from being completely uninterested to kinda curious.

"Why should I go anywhere witchu? I'on know you from a can uh' paint," I told Twon, usin one of Mommy's sayings.

"And? Whole point in me seein you is so we kh get d' know eachuhva."

I considered what he was sayin. Coulda been game. Probly was game. But at least he sounded like he meant it. And it *has* been a while since I been out with a dude, even longer since I got me some ding-ding. Cuz probly still had a girlfriend waiting in the wings somewhere, but I ain't even care no more. Twon was the first nigga I talked to since I moved out Maryland who could bend my ear for that long and match my smart mouth tit for tat. I figured it was worth a shot to go see what he was all about.

"So you gon chill wit the ol' boy or did I just jump out 'dare for nuffin?" Twon asked, the smile back in his voice again.

"We kh chill," I shrugged. Then I thought of Mommy and Tone's return later on. "Whatchu doin now?"

"Now? I'm out hea' grindin, tryna get my paper straight."

"Well, now's the only time I got to chill. So you tryna see me or what, joe?"

Twon thought a minute. Then,

"Aight," he finally said. "But like I said, I'm on'na grind. You'on mind ridin dirty wit a nigga, 'den I come pick you up. Where you at?"

"Wheaton. But I kh meet you anywhere in a hour."

You woulda thought my name was Flash Gordon the way I got off the phone with Twon and hurried around gettin ready. I ain't have shit to wear but some baggy Gap sweats and a plain T-shirt to match, but there wasn't no time to wash clothes, so I put em on with some drop socks and my black Air Force Ones and called it a day. I gave Man-Man a bottle of juice mixed with NyQuil to knock him out and begged Cerrone to make sure he kept breathing till I got back. Then I filled my purse with all the smell-goods, rubbers, and candy I thought I'd need. After smearing some country apple gloss on my lips and fluffing up my straw curl ponytail, I threatened my lil sisters to keep they mouths shut, kissed my baby good-bye, and was out the door.

Bout a hour and one long-ass train ride later, I was pacing up and down the sidewalk on Georgia Ave at Petworth Metro station in Northwest. Ery couple seconds I'd glance at my Tigger watch and think about paging Twon again, then a slow-driving car would pass by with a nigga inside breaking his neck to look at me. At first I was lookin back to see if any one of em coulda been Twon, but after a while I was muggin the shit outta bammas.

After all I went through bustin my ass to get down there and this nigga got me waitin out in the cold for fifteen minutes like a asshole? Man, I was *too* mad. I jammed my fists deeper into the pockets of my First Down bubble jacket and silently cussed myself for even wasting my time. I was just about to look for a pay phone and see if there was anything worth gettin into out Northeast, when a slow-moving box Fleetwood Caddy caught my eye. Its glossy, cranberry paint gleamed under the night lights and had ery head turning to watch the j'on glide down the Ave on gold spokes and vogues. Black tints kept us from seeing who was inside, so we all stared expectantly when the j'on came to a stop right in fronta the bench I was at. I was too pissed to crack a smile when I saw the passenger window roll down and met the very amused gaze of two slanted eyes.

"You cute when you mad," Twon said, making me forget all about being cold or angry just that fast. "Get in."

I glanced back and smirked at the hatin-ass looks all the girls waiting for the bus was throwing at me, then opened the door and sank into the cushy, berry-colored velvet of the passenger seat.

"I was startin 'na think you wasn't comin," I said after I got in, tryna cover up the fast beating of my heart. I was overwhelmed by erything at once — the tight car, the pillowy seats, the too-sexy youngin beside me. I was so boosted I ain't even care why he was late. I was just glad he came.

"I wouldn't do dat," Twon assured me, lookin in my eyes again. I felt a flush of heat on my face and knew I was blushing bright red under my honey brown. *Damn.* Twon was just as fine as I remembered him, even if he was lookin jive on the busted side. He had on one of them Eddie Bauer coats with the fur around the hood and a pair of jean shorts overtop some old, white long johns that showed the outline of his boxy knees. Faded red drop socks and unlaced Timbs clashed with his crisp black tee and neatly braided hair, but oddly enough, the look kinda worked for him. Made him seem like he wasn't caught up in appearances so long as he was comfortable. Big difference from Dartanyan, who had to be profiling just to go to the corner store.

"You jye caught a nigga off the chill mode," Twon started to explain when he caught me checkin him out. "This just some shit I threw on to go bust a couple serves. I wasn't plannin on goin nowhere when I talked d' you."

"Yeah, well, at least we on'na same page," I said, glancing down at my own outfit. Twon started lookin me over the same way he did the night we met and I felt the heat again. Eyes like his could get a girl in a lotta trouble. They had some kinda voodoo power that made you wanna do things, like lean over the armrest between us and lick the side of his neck to see if he tasted like chocolate.

"You got a pretty car," I commented, lookin away before he could see how bothered he was gettin me. I ran my fingers along the polished wood grain dashboard.

"And now I got me a pretty girl d' go wit it," Twon said, not missin a beat. I rolled my eyes like he was fulla shit and fought the twitching at the corners of my mouth again. Immediately taking a deep breath to steady myself from the dizzy, tingly feeling taking over my body, I bit my lips together and willed myself to play it cool. I had to. But I wasn't sure I'd be able to. A couple looks and a few words was all it took for me to know Twon was something special. I felt it in my bones. I knew he was gonna have an impact on me. And I knew eventually, he'd be the one to unfreeze my heart and melt me like honey butter. Only thing I *ain't* know was if I was ready to let him do it.

I called Mommy on my way to work that day and told her what happent between me and Krys. She agreed that I had ery right to send her ass home, but she also pointed out that I woulda acted the same way if somebody called me a ho to my face like that. Maybe even worse. I still thought Krys got what she deserved for throwing a fuckin shoe at me, but Mommy told me to re-think the whole situation before I sent her packing.

So I did. I thought about that shit the whole day at work, flip-flopping between passing Krys back off to her parents and givin it one last (and I do mean *last*) try at straightening her out. Times like these I wish I wasn't a Gemini. I hated the way I could see something from both sides so clearly. That shit really made it hard to stick to my guns, especially if there was a chance I mighta been wrong (for whuppin up on her the way I did). I fought with myself from the minute I hung up with Mommy till the minute I got home, when I finally decided to give Krys another chance. I had my reasons for sayin what I said, and I damn sure wasn't sorry for it, but putting her out wasn't gon solve nothin. Krys was just a dumb kid. She ain't know no better. I was poseda be schooling her, not making shit harder. Besides, she was family. It wouldna been right to turn my back on her like that.

So I went home that night with all intentions to forgive and forget the ugly scene that unfolded in my livin room just hours before. I was gon leave it alone, y'know, give us both some time to cool off and worry bout making peace tomorrow. I could hear Krys rambling on her phone through the closed den door all night, but I ain't bother to knock and say anything to her ass. I just went about relaxing and watchin after the boys as usual like she wasn't even there.

By the time I got up the next mornin, I was ready to call a truce. I took a shower, threw on some clothes, and got my mind all set to take Krys out to breakfast so we could talk about what happent. After taking down a box of cereal for the boys, I sent Man-Man to wake Krys up like I did ery other mornin when I had plans for us to do something. He came back a few seconds later, sliding across the kitchen floor in his Batman socks.

"She gone," Man-Man reported, spinning around in circles. "I think she still mad bout you beatin her butt yesterday. I be mad too, if I got munished the way she did. You was like, *Bloop, bloop! Take that bitch!*" Man-Man exclaimed, imitating my one-two combo.

"Whatchu mean, 'she gone'?" I asked, overlooking his cussin and the way he danced around the floor acting out the fight.

I scooted past Man-Man and went to the den myself. I swung open the door and looked around, noticing right away that erything Krys brought with her was gone. No dirty clothes pile in the corner. No make-up and nail polish scattered all over the bookshelf she used as a dresser. No suitcase, no fresh outfit hanging over the arm of the daybed, no shoes on the floor. All her shit was gone.

Fuck!!!!!

Lightheaded and numb as death, I rushed to the phone and dialed Krys' cell phone number with a quickness. I was surprised to see she answered on the second ring.

"Where you at?" I asked, cutting right to the chase.

"I rolled out. I'm wit my folks," she answered coolly with that same nondescript line.

"You went home?"

"Hell nah."

"'Den where you go?"

"Don't worry bout dat."

AAGGGHHHHH!!! I started pacin back and forth. Oh, my God! Aunt Josie and Uncle Travis was gon kick my ass! Krys done ran off to God-knows-where with God-knows-who and it was all my fault! I felt like I single-handedly made a really bad problem twenty times worse.

"Ay, young, you gotta come back. We gotta squash 'dis shit," I pleaded.

"What for? I thoughtchu told my rolla ass to get out your face. Ain't dat's whatchu called me? A rolla bitch?"

"Krys, go 'head, young. Don't go takin it personal. You called me out my name, too."

"So, what?" she snapped. I could almost see her muggin on me through the phone. "The point is, you said you wanted me gone. So now I'm gone."

Click.

CHAPTER THIRTEEN

I always had a cynical outlook on romance cuz ery nigga I ever called myself liking or loving turned out to be a headache with a ding-a-ling attached. I ain't believe in falling madly in love or meeting "the one" or gettin with somebody cuz it was meant to be. Being with Dartanyan made me realize all that was just a fairy tale. Love ain't mean shit to me, companionship was temporary, and as far as I was concerned, most people bunned up for money or physical reasons. All that changed after I met Twon, though. As hard as I tried to fight it, he made me feel...Well, he just made me *feel*. And it was scary. For someone who been hurt the way I had and who trained theyself to numb all matters of the heart, feeling *anything* was scary.

Me and Twon clicked. I mean, me and Dartanyan clicked when we first met but what me and Twon had was different. It wasn't a needy, clingy, desperate connection between us. It was...right. I'on know how else to explain it. Our personalities meshed together like folded hands, like two people who known eachother all they lives and at the root of it all was how much we had in common. Twon was the oldest of two sisters and a brother, so he was useta the pressure of having to be responsible when he shoulda still been on playtime. His father died in a car accident when he was ten and his mama dropped the four of em on his Nanna's doorstep a few months later, so Twon knew what it was like to have fatherless father's days and a hurtful hostility towards the woman who birthed him. He had a son he named Elijah when he was fifteen, so he knew about becoming a parent too soon and how much it changed your life before you was ready. And after a six-year relationship with his baby mama Rayel (the one who cussed me out on the phone—they was still living together at the time), Twon knew what it was to go from loving somebody to hating they guts cuz wasn't neither one of y'all ready for erything that came along with being a family.

As much as we had in common, we was opposites, and that added a lil more spice between us. Where I was unsteady and quick to react, Twon was chill and seemed to think erything through. Where I was wary of things and unsure of what to do outside of basic survival, he was a man focused on what he wanted and how to get it. He was more serious and mature than anyone I'd ever been around, yet at the same time, there was a mischievousness in his chinky eyes that showed he had a playful side, too. I liked that. I liked the way he carried it. He was different. He had direction, personality, and a good head on his shoulders. And he was oh-so-real with it. He was the perfect blend of humility and confidence, a man real sure of hisself, you know? He was quiet and he was cool but he had this arrogance to him that attracted me even more. It wasn't rude or obtrusive like some cocky niggas' ego tended to be, but Twon definitely had a way of walkin and talkin and carryin hisself that let you know he was *that nigga*. And despite my wanting to run away from it, to run away from him cuz I was terrified of gettin played again, I was blindly drawn to erything about his ass.

After that first time we chilled together, not a day went by when I ain't at least talk to Twon. I ain't wanna admit it, but I genuinely liked him. *A lot.* I was spending all my bus money to call him from the pay phones at school, and whenever I could find a babysitter for Man-Man, I was breaking down doors to go see him. Tone and Mommy finally let me off punishment after another week or so, but they wasn't too excited to hear I was out there enjoying my freedom with "some boy". I ain't care what they had to say, though. Being in Twon's presence was addictive. I was hooked on his smile, the way he laughed, the way he always smelled like bud and Jean Paul Gaultier cologne. I couldn't stop studying the details of his face, tryna read the expressions he sometimes hid behind his eyes. I lived for the conversations we had bout erything from our dreams to our favorite things to the bittersweet beauty of our Blackness. We talked about our children and the lives we led and what we wanted to make of them. He opened me up to thinkin about more than gettin what I could from folks and just gettin by. I feened for the times when we'd get so lost in eachother's words it felt like we was the only two people in the world. And I couldn't help but realize how right erything felt whenever we was together. With Twon around I ain't feel so cold or misunderstood no more, and in him I found somebody I could identify with, somebody I could talk to, and at the same time be so attracted to it was a struggle to keep my hands offa him.

He was the shit—even Dhonni, Kia, *and* Biggums told me so when I took him around Trinidad to meet my play family. Yet with all that in mind, I still ain't know what to do with him. After bout a month of talkin and spendin time together, I was still jive reluctant to be anything more than friends. Dartanyan left scars on my heart that I thought would never heal. The last thing in the world I wanted to do was jump out there and Twon end up hurting me, too. Besides, being friends kept us from being tied down to eachother—something we both agreed was one of the reasons why our past relationships ain't work out. But at the same time, there was an attraction between us that felt something like fiery bliss. Unfortunately, the way I saw it, that fire was gon burn me if I got too close.

"You cold?" Twon asked, and looked at me all wrapped up in the blanket at the foot of his bed. I tried to force my teeth to stop chattering and shook my head no even though I was shivering like a Chihuahua.

"You sure?" Twon asked again.

"I be aight," I insisted.

It was the beginning of a stormy, early spring afternoon in 1998, and me and Twon just came in from playin around outside. You would think a couple grown muhfuckas like us had more sense than to be running around in the rain, but when me and Twon got together, we was like two big-ass kids. We played video games, we played jokes on eachother, we poked, pinched, and tickled one another like we was in elementary school all over again. I guess it was our lil way of re-living the childhood days we ain't get to enjoy long enough. And a excuse to cop a feel without being obvious.

"It's quiet witout eryby hea'," I commented off-handedly about the tomb-like silence around us. For the first time in the month or so since me and Twon been hangin out, it wasn't nobody home at his house. His Nanna, who retired from selling D.C. souvenirs to the tourists Downtown, was usually home cooking and watching TV in the kitchen. But that afternoon, she went to visit a friend. Twon's sisters Antonia and Antwonette was usually on the phone or upstairs with they friends, but they went out to catch a weekend matinee. And Twon's brother Anthony, who was forever popping in on us in the basement just to be nosy, was nowhere to be found. We was completely alone.

"Yeah it is," Twon agreed uneasily. He got up to turn on the TV.

I started to ask if I could use the phone to call and make sure Cerrone got that $20 I left him for being nice enough to babysit on a Saturday, but I couldn't bring myself to talk. For some reason, talkin felt strange, almost as strange as that feeling in my stomach telling me something out the ordinary was bout to happen. I could tell Twon felt it, too, cuz he was flitting around with the same nervous energy he got whenever I hugged him too tight or he caught a glimpse of my draws peeking over the top of my jeans. Having other people around was a good way to ignore the attraction between us and pretend like I wasn't curious about him, but now, on a stormy spring afternoon, it wasn't nobody there to serve as a distraction.

"You want anything?" Twon offered, still standing by the TV.

I wrapped the blanket tighter around my damp, shivering body and decided I couldn't take being cold no more.

"Gimme some'na change into. I wanna put my clothes in'na dryer," I managed to say through tightly clenched teeth.

Twon started digging through his dresser drawers and came up seconds later with a old undershirt of Elijah's that was so small it coulda fit one of my lil sisters.

"Dat j'on kinda young, ain't it?" I asked, peeking over the black frames of my blue-lensed personality glasses for a better look.

"C'mon, man, you kh fit dat."

"Boy, if you'on gimme a bigger shirt…"

"Aight, aight. Hea'," Twon said, digging in his drawer again. He tossed me another shirt that was a few sizes bigger and squatted on his heels expectantly like he was waiting for me to put it on in fronta him.

"Out," I ordered, and pointed to the door. It was hard enough being alone and tryna control the urge to jump on him without complicating shit with a striptease.

"Oh, my bad…Aight, 'den, since you wanna be all shy about it. Like I ain't seen a girl in a T-shirt b'fore."

He shook his head and left me alone in his room. I made sure to keep a eye on the door just in case Twon decided to barge in unexpected. I twisted and maneuvered to get outta my wet clothes fast as I could. It was no surprise that the shirt he got me barely came past my hips, nor was it a surprise to see him come bustin up in the room soon as I got it on.

"Damn, nigga, don'tchu know how d' knock?" I fussed, sittin down on the edge of the bed so he couldn't see how much of my honey roasted ass was showin.

"What I'ma knock for? 'Dis my room," Twon replied. "Sike, some'my just paged me. I gotta use d' phone."

"Well, find me some shorts or some'n 'fore you do dat," I said, tryna pull the thin, T-shirt fabric down over my thighs.

"I ain't got no shorts. 'Day all in'na dirty clothes."

"Yeah, tell me anything," I mumbled. I leaned forward a little to check out his movie collection as Twon slid up on the bed behind me and got his phone off the nightstand. I pretended to be more interested in the fifty-some odd video tapes under his TV stand as I eavesdropped on his conversation. Twon was talking to his uncle that owned this moving and delivery company. He usually worked for him off and on during the week to play off the hundreds and thousands of dollars he made illegally. From what I could gather, the old dude wanted him to come help with some big move way out Waldorf. I was expecting Twon to jump at the opportunity to make a couple hundred dollars cuz he was poseda be saving up to buy a house (since living in his Nanna's basement after leaving Rayel four months ago wasn't his idea of doing good). But he surprised me by saying he wouldn't be able to work cuz he had company. I was kinda flattered that Twon put off making money to sit up in the house with me, but at the same time it made me wonder if all this was a set-up. Was his peoples gone cuz he told em he wanted some time alone with me? Did he keep me out in the rain on purpose playin keep-away with my bad hair day hat so I'd get wet and hafta change my clothes? And I know he picked out this extra medium shirt on purpose, so what else did he have up his sleeve?

"Find some'n you wanna watch?" Twon asked after he hung up the phone.

"No. All you got is them old gangsta movies. *Scarface, Casino, The Untouchables*...Damn, you got all the *Godfather's*, too...And a racka porno's.

Ugh, is dat all you watch?" I frowned, motioning toward his vast collection of XXX-rated tapes.

"Pretty much," he shrugged. "My sistas got some movies upstairs. You wanna go get one?"

"Nah. Fuck it."

I picked up the remote and started flipping through the channels.

"You comfortable like dat?" Twon asked after a while, nodding at the way I was sittin stiffly in fronta the TV.

"Yeah," I lied, even though I really wasn't. I was still cold and I desperately wanted to curl up in his warm bed, but I was not about to stretch myself out with no fuckin pants on. That's just askin for trouble.

"Hea', you want some covers?" Twon took the same blanket I had wrapped around myself earlier and spread it out over hisself on his end of the bed. I nodded and reached to grab it all for myself, but he snatched it back before I got a good grip.

"Whatchu doin, man? I'm cold too. You want some covers, you gotta come back hea' wit me," Twon said.

"Fuck it, 'den."

I crossed my arms over my chest and tried to pretend like I wasn't cold, but I was shaking like a leaf in a matter of seconds.

"Stop fakin, Shai. Get under the covers," Twon persisted, lifting up a corner and making room for me beside him. I took one look at him laying there all effortlessly sexy and knew we wouldn't be able to keep our hands to ourselves if I got any closer. Did I really wanna tempt him like that? Did I wanna tempt myself? I wasn't ready to cross that line yet, was I? Staying friends was the best way to keep from hating eachother later, wasn't it?

"Nah, young. You bout d' start some'n," I said, clearly seeing what was bout to go down.

"I am not," Twon argued. "Just cuz you got on dat lil-ass shirt and them stripey blue draws all stuck up in y' butt, do not mean dat—"

"See now," I laughed. "Why you lookin dat hard?"

"Ain't no'by lookin atchu, slim. I'm watchin TV."

"Unh-hunh," I grumbled, and gave him a *yeah, right* look that even he had to smile at.

"Aight, man, f'real. I ain't gon do nuffin to you," Twon promised. "I just want you under the covers so you kh stop shivering. You shakin 'na bed, joe."

I raised a suspicious eyebrow and climbed under the blanket with him anyway. A warm tingle of excitement went through me as a lil voice in the backa my head warned that something really was bout to go down whether I tried to fight it or not.

"Ain't dat better?" Twon asked when I got all settled in. I pulled the covers up to my chin and tried my best to keep from touching him, but my side of the bed was still cold. *Should I? Should I?* I inched a closer to the heat coming from Twon's direction and found myself instinctively snuggling up against his rock solid body before the voice in my head could tell me to stop.

"You just insist on teasin me, hunh?" Twon asked when he felt my booty in his lap.

"I'm only ova' hea' till I warm up, so don't get siced."

"Whatchu talkin bout? I ain't siced. I'm watchin TV," he insisted. Yet there was a overpowering desire between us that you could almost taste cuz it was so strong. Twon knew what I was doin, even if I ain't exactly know myself. My resistance had worn down. My fight was waning. Twon could tell that I wanted to do more than lay up against him. I wanted to reach my hand behind his head, hike my leg up, and tell him to gimme his best shot. I wanted to turn over and suck his earlobes, his lips, his tongue, and ery other protrusion on his body till his toes curled and he lay there exhausted sayin my name over and over again. I wanted to pull his hair and scratch his back, bite his neck and call him Daddy. But I needed some kinda reassurance that nothing bad would happen if I did. My body was begging to get touched and my honeycomb was crying to get fed some man meat, but my brain was begging me to stop. *You gon fuck erything up*, it warned. I seriously considered puttin my wet clothes back on for the sake of leaving our friendship intact, but once I felt Twon's curious fingertips tracing and squeezing the softness of my thighs, I couldn't convince myself to get up for shit.

"'Dis don't make no got-damn sense," Twon said, taking my unsure closeness as an invitation to keep going. He was suddenly all over me, breathing like he wanted to be all in me, with one of his hands tryna palm the roundness of my left cheek. "You got entirely too much ass, girl. Whatchu doin wit all 'dis?" he asked.

Before I could think about what kinda trouble I might be causing, I smiled, arched my back so I was that much more in his lap, and cleverly replied,

"Nah, nigga. The question is, what are *you* gon do wit all 'dis?'"

He gave me a look that said he knew exactly how to part my thighs and answer that question. The lil cautionary voice in the backa my head was goin off now, but I ignored it cuz I ain't wanna think about what it'd mean if we got together. I ain't wanna wonder if Twon would change up and start acting funny cuz he finally got what he been wanting all along. I can't say that I even cared anymore. I just wanted to get high offa him.

"You want me inside you?" Twon asked unexpectedly bold and serious, his fingers already entwined around the elastic waistband of my underwear.

"Yeah," I answered huskily.

"'Den beg me."

"What?!" I opened my eyes and looked at him like he was crazy. Twon stared back at me with the same mischievousness he had in his eyes the night we met and repeated,

"Beg me."

"I ain't beggin you shit. Who you think—"

He moved the damp part of my draws aside and slid a finger up and down my slippery crease. I eagerly moved closer to him and squirmed with impatient longing for more when I felt his fingers dip into my honeycomb. I closed my eyes dizzily, imagining bigger and better things while he wiggled em inside me. Twon hit spots I ain't even know I had and made my honey ooze out in one continuous gush, flowing like a river all over me, all over the sheets, all over his hand and down his wrist. That boy was making me so wet it was ridiculous.

"Beg me," Twon ordered again, and gave me another naughty look. Determined to be the winner of this new game between us, I shook my head no. Twon wiggled his fingers inside me harder and I grabbed his wrist to push his hand in deeper, moving with him and riding his fingers the same way I was planning on riding him. Twon stopped when he saw how excited it got me, then took his fingers out and sucked my sweetness off em one by one.

"Mmm, lemme find out. It do taste like honey," he said with a fervor in his eyes that made my legs shake. Got-damn that boy was nasty! He was turning me on like shit! I smiled at his discovery of something only

Dartanyan ever took the time to find out, then watched him lick up my thigh like he was following a trail to the source of my sweetness. Twon looked at me with the same intense wanting I felt and I couldn't seem to look away, not until he went from licking my thighs to licking my clit and my eyes unwillingly rolled back. At first, I was too shocked to move, but the more he got into it, the more I wriggled and pulled away from the powerful sensations he was sending all throughout my body.

"Where you think you goin?" Twon teased, and slid me back towards his face. "You tryna tell me d' stop?" he asked, locking his arms around my thighs so I couldn't get away even if I wanted to.

"You know I'm not," I smiled.

"'Den stop movin."

I obeyed and gripped the pillow behind my head, and let him tongue lash me till my legs shook uncontrollably. Twon came up for air minutes later and smiled at the sweat and ecstasy all over my face.

"All you gotta say is please," he told me, and wiped off a top lip covered in honey glaze. Tingling from head to toe, I shook my head weakly. I wasn't gon beg. I was gon break him before he broke me. If only he would stop rubbing his thumb on my clit and...

"Say please," Twon ordered.

...And sliding his fingers in and outta me like that and...

"Say please."

...And tickling my spot like that and...

"Say please."

...And...and...and...

"Please," I heard myself moan when he had me squirming on my heels again.

"What's dat?"

"Please," I begged again.

"Say what?"

"*PLEASE!*" I groaned, my voice cracking like I was on the verge of tears. Twon smiled victoriously and kissed up my hips, to the sensitive part of my waist, up my stomach, and licked slow, deliberate circles around my bare nipples. When he moved up to the side of my neck and lingered there on my spot, I was too gone for words. I grabbed him by the backa his head and pulled his face towards me for a deep, hungry kiss that made both of us forget all about gettin a rubber. I helped Twon tear outta his clothes and pulled his naked brown body back on toppa me. Electrified at the feel of his skin against mine, I ain't stop to think about the consequences of what was bout to happen. Neither did he. The intensity between us was too overpowering to think. All we could do was act. I wanted Twon so bad I couldn't stop moving, so bad I ain't object when I felt his tongue working over the spot on my neck again, and the smooth, slippery tip of his dick slide between my lips with no protection between us. Instead, I wound my legs around his and used the heels of my feet to push him in deeper.

"Dat's right," he smiled when he felt the fire inside me. "Now, you gon be a good girl and cum for Daddy?" Twon asked, his lips brushing against my ear and setting ery one of my nerves on end. I let another hungry kiss be my answer.

From that point on, I was a Twon junkie. I was strung out on the way he moved inside me, stretching me wider and loving me deeper than anybody before him ever could. We made love to a rhythm that was all our own: fast when I worked him, slow when I arched my back and squeezed, staccato when he worked at hittin a spot that made me lose control. He had me biting and scratching, moaning and groaning, pulling his hair and cryin out his name like it was the magic word. He gave me a feeling like nothin I ever felt before, not even with Dartanyan, who was a expert at pushin all my buttons. Twon spoiled me that day, made it so nobody but him could possibly make me feel the same way. He squeezed me, he teased me, he made me wanna scream, cry, and laugh all at once. He made me explode so hard tears rolled from my eyes, left me so high I was too weak to move or talk and all I could do was cry and hold onto him like I'd float away if I didn't. He turned me out. He made me a fiend. And after that first time, I couldn't get enough of him.

I hate people who do shit just to be smart. Krys knew we both was gon be in trouble if she left, and her black ass did it anyways. I was just waiting for Aunt Josie and Uncle Travis to call askin to speak to her, and I wasn't up for tellin em what happent. I wasn't up to lyin bout the shit, either, but what else was I poseda do? Here it is, I'm poseda be watching after the girl and she ain't even in my sight. How that look? Let her end up dead or kidnapped or fucked up alongside the road somewhere. It'd be all my fault.

I tried calling Krys a racka times, but her phone went straight to the answering machine. I tried talkin to her girl Iyania when I caught her coming out her building later that Sunday night, but she gave me the okeydoke like she ain't know where Krys was. I could tell she knew though, and that just got under my skin even more. The whole situation was really starting to blow the shit outta me. Even though it was a relief to have Krys gone and out my face for a while, it was driving me crazy not knowing if she was aight. What if she was sleeping outside somewhere? What if the nigga she was with got tired of her after a day and decided to send her on her way? I just ain't know. It was enough to make me wanna pull out all my hair. Or hers, if I could ever get a hold of her.

Man, I could see now, all this *Shai-tryna-help-the-youngin* bullshit was a big mistake. I wasn't built for regulating no hardhead teenage girl. I ain't have the patience. It was pointless. Impossible. And all this stressing and arguing was just making me go back to being the same hostile, fist-throwing lunatic I useta be. Seemed like ery ounce of maturity and mellowness I tried so hard to hold onto was goin right out the window from dealing with her ass.

So I basically had two options: either find Krys before something bad went down, or call up her parents and let em know the business. I went back to work on Tuesday and gave myself to the end of the day to do either one. First, I checked around ery store in the mall to see who all knew my cousin. Most of them bammas did, either by sight or by name, but of course ain't none of em know where she was at. Then, I decided to check barbershop around the corner where my client Shon worked. Somebody in there was bound to know something, cuz Krys spent more time in that j'on talkin to they receptionist and prancing around out front tryna be cute than she did workin with me. Soon as I got some break time, I hauled ass over there. Good thing I went when I did, too, cuz just as I was coming around the corner, a white Crown Vic bubble pulled up in the parking lot.

What the....

I recognized it as the same one that been showin up at my complex lately. It had the same chrome rims with police package searchlight, antennas, the half-mirror, and half-smoked out tints. Wasn't no question in my mind that whoever drove that j'on was the one Krys been sneakin around with, and was more than likely the one she was stayin with now. I waited at the sidewalk to see if she was gon hop out the passenger seat, wondering what kinda dumb look would be on her face once she seen me standing there to meet her. But soon as I seen my man Shon with the blue eyes get out and hit the alarm, I was the only one wearing the dummy look.

"Lemme find out," I frowned, meeting up with him right as he crossed the lot towards the shop. Little did he know, he was bout to catch one of my famous Northeast-style beat downs. I done told that nigga from the get-go that my lil cousin was jailbait. Yet, he was bold enough to be creepin with her anyways? Oh, hell nah! I was bout to lay his ass out.

"Shon!"

"Ay, wsup, Shai," Shon answered all oblivious. "Damn, you'on never come around hea'. You lookin for some'my?"

"Whatchu think?" I snapped. "Is dat your car right 'dare?"

"Yeah, I just bought dat j'on from the police auction not too long ago. Already came wit them rims and erything. That j'on wet, ain't it?" he smiled, lookin back at it like a lil boy showin off his favorite toy.

"Whateva. So you the one been pickin up my cousin, hunh? Didn't I tell yo' muhfuckin ass to leave her alone?"

"Who? Brownskin youngin dat be comin around hea'?" Shon asked, suddenly perplexed by my attitude. I never got loud with him before.

"You know who the fuck I'm tallkin bout. I toldju she was only fihteen, Shon! What, you *tryna* get fucked up?"

"Whoooaaa, young!" He threw up his hands in defense. "Pump y' brakes. I ain't messin wit dat girl. If anything, I be the one backin niggas off her cuz I know she your folks."

He sounded like he mighta been tellin the truth, but...

"Boy, I ain't dumb. Why I seen your car at my apartment twice to come pick her up? And don't tell me it musta been some'my else cuz I know dat's the same fuckin car!" I demanded.

"But it *wasn't* me!" Shon argued.

"You lyin, young! Krys done ran away and the last nigga I seen her wit was drivin your car!"

"I swear to God, young. It musta been my lil bruhva you seen. I be lettin him borrow dat j'on sometimes."

"Oh, so now you got a lil bruhva?" I asked doubtfully. "And he just happen to know my cousin? Mysterious."

"What, you think I'm makin it up?" Shon asked.

"Yes!"

"Swear d' God, I'm not. My bruhva name Javon. He stay at my muhva house in Adelphi, like five minutes from hea'. He met Krys hea' one day. I know 'day been talkin, but I ain't think they was chillin like dat."

"You lyin!" I screeched.

"Man, go 'head. Why would I lie about some'n like dat?" Shon argued, his whole body beggin for me to believe him.

"Cuz you know I'ma fuck you up if I find out you messin wit my lil cousin!"

"I ain't, 'doe. Look, I'll prove it. I'ma call dat nigga right now," he told me, pullin out his Nextel and hittin the chirp to two-way radio the boy in question. I put my hands on my hips in the same stance Mommy used when she was bout to wail on somebody and tapped my foot impatiently.

"Javon! Ay, you up?" Shon asked his brother.

"Yeah. Wsup?" a voice crackled back over the speaker.

"Where you at?"

"Home, nigga. Why?"

Shon winked at me and continued,

"Ay, you know dat girl Krys you's talkin to?"

"Yeah, what about her?" Javon asked.

"She witchu right now?"

Silence.

"Yeah," Javon finally answered. I could hear a girl's voice fussin in the background. "I mean, why? Who wanna know?" Javon asked, quickly tryna play it off.

"Nobody. I's just wonderin why I ain't seen her today. I'ma holla atchu later, young."

"Aight."

Shon put his phone away and gave me a *I-told-you-so* look. I felt stupid as shit.

"My bad," I smiled sheepishly, my hostility melting away like hot butter.

"Toldju I wasn't lyin. I think you should buy me a Icee for gettin all loud and wrong out hea'. All dat cussin wasn't even necessary, joe."

"I know, but youngin lyin, her friends been lyin…I just figured you was lyin, too. My bad, Shon," I apologized sincerely.

"You good. 'Least now you know where she is."

I nodded and breathed a heavy sigh of relief.

"Yeah, and if I know my bruhva, he got too many girls as it is. A couple uh' them j'ons is some real scunions, too. Krys gon hafta end up fightin one of em if she stay there, and for real-for real, youngin don't really look like the fightin type. She'll be back soon. Trust me," Shon assured me.

"I sure hope so," I sighed. For the sake of my already unstable sanity, I sure hoped he was right.

CHAPTER FOURTEEN

"Damn, girl. Twon must got dat croosh. I ain't seent you in bout a month," Dhonni joked with a hint of bitterness in her voice. She leaned closer to the bathroom mirror and stretched her closed eyelid flat before coloring around the outside of it with a black eyeliner pencil.

"You make it sound like I been gone for years," I said, and tore off a piece of toilet tissue to blot my frosted bronzy lipstick.

"Migh'as well be, much as you be bullshittin. It's what, Saturday now? You's poseda come down hea' how many times, young? Last Saturday, the day before dat, the Friday before dat, the Monday before dat…need I d' go on?"

"My fault I couldn't make it, young," I apologized.

"Yeah, you definitely couldn't make it wit no nigga up y' ass. Don't tell me he gotchu like dat already."

"Got me like what?"

"Whipped," Dhonni answered, and started lining the other eye. "Matter fact, you ain't even gotta answer dat, Suga Baby. I'ma just start callin you 'Cool Whip'."

"Ugh, shut up, Kiss," I laughed, and mushed Dhonni in the forehead.

"Tell me I'm wrong, 'den."

"You wrong."

Dhonni looked at me doubtfully. She knew me too well.

"Aight, fine. I'm whipped. *And what?*" I admitted with a smile.

And it was true. Twon had me on him so hard it was difficult to think about anything else. I was always at his house or ridin shotgun in the Caddy, finding ery reason I could to hear his voice and breathe his air and feel him in me, around me, beside me. It ain't matter if I had a babysitter for Man-Man or not. I ain't hesitate for a minute to drag my son along, even if it meant being on the streets at two o'clock in the mornin and exposing him to ery danger that came along with dating a hustler. I was out there acting like gettin shot, gettin robbed, or caught up with the police wasn't a possibility. Call me crazy, irresponsible, reckless, or whatever. Being with Twon gave me a high like no other, and I couldn't seem to shake the feeling long enough to see how hard I was falling for him. How in the world could I think straight when I had somebody making me feel like that?

"So y'all two a couple now?" Dhonni asked with a noticeable tinge of jealousy in her tone.

"Well...yeah...no. I'on know," I sighed.

"Whatchu mean you'on know? Y'all together all the damn time. You givin him pussy wheneva he want. You takin Man-Man around him. Y'all *betta* be goin t'geva."

"We do, jye-like," I said. Which was also true. Me and Twon was a couple in the sense that we shared ourselves, our time, and our lives together. It only made sense for us to bun up, but I guess you could say I was bullshittin bout the whole thing. I was still stressing that just-be-friends shit even though we was catching all them jealous, protective, attached feelings two people get when they don't wanna share eachother with nobody else. Twon ain't make it no secret that he wanted to lock me down. He done asked me a couple times, *"What we gonna do with ourselves?"*, which is basically a way of saying he wanna make it official. But I ain't have an answer yet. I wasn't ready for it. Twon was erything I could possibly want in a man, but I ain't wanna ruin things by putting a title on us. At the same time, I couldn't leave him alone. What me and Twon had felt like a spring afternoon—fresh, bright, colorful, vibrant, and warm but cool enough not to sweat. A big difference from the dead heat of summer I felt with Dartanyan, all stale, sticky, and uncomfortably hot with bugs constantly biting and buzzing.

"You slippin, Suga Baby. Hi you poseda get yours if you spendin all y' time wit 'dis nigga?" Dhonni asked. "He ain't even your boyfriend. I'on know why you playin him so close. There's other fish in the sea."

"I got my reasons," I told her truthfully. There coulda been a million other fish in the sea, but wasn't none of em better than the one I already had in my net.

"Like what, crazy? If he all like you say he is, why'onchu scoop dat nigga up? Migh'as well. You spend enough time together," Dhonni snickered.

"Cuz, I'on want a man right now, Kiss. Dat ain't gon do nuffin but slow me down. Besides, if he do some shit like Dartanyan did to me, I swear to God I'ma kill his ass. I ain't tryna go to jail over a nigga. I just need somebody to hit it right and leave me the fuck alone. That's what Twon do, and dat's how I'm tryna keep it. Fuck dat uh' shit," I told her.

"Yeah, I hea' you," Dhonni agreed. "Fuck em all, girl. 'Deez niggas ain't shit anyways. I ever tell you bout youngin I was messin wit after you moved?"

"Slim who drive the Range Rover?"

"Nah. Cuz wit the Lexus. Anyhow, 'dis nigga ran some game on me, girl. Had me *all typesa* gone in'na head. Had me thinkin he was all about me cuz he told me he loved me and shit. Was buyin me shit, girl, takin me out, eatin the cooty-coo, hittin it bareback—all dat bun shit, right. 'Den when I start bein like, 'wsup', wantin to make it official and shit, 'dis nigga gon turn around and talk some shit bout he *wanted* to be my man but since he was hustlin he couldn't be there for me like he should be, so we should just be friends. Come to find out, the whole time this fool was fuckin like, three uhva broads, young. Talk about game! Cuz jye played my ass, but dat's aight, 'doe. I got him back. Think I ain't slash his tires and key up dat Lex? *And* I told the feds where he be grindin at. I went straight crud on his ass, joe."

"Damn, Dhonni!"

"'*Damn, Dhonni*', nuffin. Dat's what his bitch ass get for tryna cross a Scorpio. I put myself out 'dare and dat's what he do to me? Niggas like dat be the main reason I'on even get bunned up no more. Fucka relationship. Just show me the money! Speakin uh' which, is Twon at least givin you dat?" Dhonni frowned.

"Sometimes."

"Whatchu mean, 'sometimes'? I know you ain't wastin y' time wit no scrub nigga, young. Not my pimpin partner in crime. Don't tell me you goin out like dat!"

"Nah, man. He got money," I frowned back. Twon still worked with his uncle frequently throughout the week driving trucks and delivering furniture into peoples into new homes and offices. Plus, he got his hustle on 24/7, so having money wasn't never an issue.

"Well, if he got money, he need d' come up off it. Why you fuckin wit a stingy nigga anyways?" Dhonni sneered.

"He got money. I ain't tryna get him for it, though," was my meek reply.

"Why not? Break em all, girl! Fuck being nice. Don't you remember *anything* Kia taught us? You betta ack like you know and get dat nigga for something, cuz shit ain't gon be sweet foreva. Is you hearing me, joe?"

"I hea' you but like I said…I'on know, young, I just…"

I wanted to share with Dhonni how I felt and how Twon made me feel, but I knew she'd never understand. She was still thinkin like I used to. We was taught to get as much as we could out a nigga before he could use us, then move on without a second thought. Anything otherwise was absurd. If you wasn't with a dude cuz you got knocked up, or cuz you pimpin the nigga, or cuz you finally decide he's worth givin up the game for, there was no point dealing with him. I was stuck in a world of in-betweens with Twon, but Dhonni probly wasn't tryna hear all that. And I ain't particularly feel the need to explain myself.

"Look, I'on wanna talk about it no more," I told my best friend firmly.

"Fine, 'den. Don't. I'm just tryna figure out why the fuck you been carryin me all this time for some nigga you'on even go with," Dhonni snapped, the bitterness back in her voice again.

"Who said I been carryin you? Girl, ain't no'by been carryin you."

"I cain't tell. You'on even call me no more. And you damn sure don't know how d' call no'by back," Dhonni pouted.

"You sicin it."

"No, I'm not, eiva. When the last time me and you really talked before t'night?"

I stopped to think cuz I knew it couldna been more than two weeks since I had a real conversation with Dhonni. Okay, maybe three. But it ain't been a whole month, has it?…Or has it?

"Fuck it, I'm hea' now," I said, and gave Dhonni the most confident, assuring smile I could muster up. "We gon do like we do any uh' Saturday and hit the Icebox and have fun and take pictures and it's gon feel like I wasn't neh' even gone."

"You mean it 'dis time, Shai? You ain't gon bullshit again is you?"

"Yeah, I mean it, you big-ass baby. I'm hea', ain't I?" I teased, and grabbed my play sister up in a hug. Dhonni started fussing for me to get off her, but she was steady huggin me back the whole time. It was one of them tender, sisterly moments that felt extra all warm and fuzzy cuz we ain't had one in a while.

"So what I been missin 'round hea', since you claim I been gone for a month and shit?" I asked after starting back on my make-up again.

"Well," Dhonni kissed at her reflection and decided she needed more chocolate lip liner. "You know Kia havin anuh' baby, right? She moved in wit dat nigga Roe now. He got them livin in 'dis nice-ass apartment out near Brookland station, girl. Dat j'on laid out like a muhfuckin palace. Big screen TV's, big-ass liquor cabinet, marble countertops, real silver forks and shit—*girrrrl*, you won't believe it till you see it."

"Damn. What he do, sell real estate or some'n?" I joked.

"Nah, he got hisself a lil barbershop out Florida Park. You know how dat go: cut hair in the front, cut yak in'na back. Got the sweet-ass hustle, man."

"Lucky bitch," I chuckled, knowin how siced my play mother probly was to find somebody who could make thousands in a day.

"Hunh, man," Dhonni agreed.

"So whateva happent d' Tejuan?"

"Tejuan? Hell if I know. Kia stopped talkin to his ass a while ago."

"Why?" I asked.

"I'on know. Don't no'by ever stay t'geva wit they first baby fahva," Dhonni explained as if it shoulda been common knowledge. She changed the subject. "Anyways, Lakisha moved to Mar'land—not dat anyby care. Trayonna still walkin 'round hea' showin off dat baby like she ain't did shit wrong. Oh, and Pookie and Cerrone finally started dat go-go band."

"Yeah, Roney told me," I said. Our brothers had been talkin about putting together a go-go band since we was kids, but neither one of em had the focus or the drive to actually do it until now.

"I'm glad them fools finally found something to do other than steal cars," I commented.

"Well, him and Pookie still stealin cars," Dhonni informed me. "But not as much 'day used to. After Mo got locked up, 'day chilled out on dat shit a lot. You know he at Oak Hill till he turn eighteen, right?"

"Yeah, Roney told me bout dat, too. Damn, I'm glad 'day ain't get caught wit dat fool."

"You know," Dhonni agreed with a relieved sigh.

Mo caught a bad deal a few months back when him, my brother, and Pookie tried to pull off this heist on Rhode Island Ave. They broke into some old people's house and snatched up erything they could before peeling off in the stolen bucket they came in. The three of em got all of half a block away before the car cut off right in the middle of the street. Cerrone and Pookie bailed out and made a clean getaway before the old folks let they German Shepherd loose. Mo, on the other hand, wasn't so lucky. That dog tore into his ass before he had a chance to get both feet out the car, and left him holding the full rap *and* enough gashes from head to toe to need eighteen stitches. A bamma-ass nigga woulda snitched but Mo kept it treal. He zipped his lips and took the fall for all three of em.

"Yeah, but, 'day be practicin at Foots house," Dhonni continued, filling me in on the rest. "Sound good, too. Pookie do the rappin, Cerrone on the congos, and 'day got Foots on'na lead and shit—you know how his voice jye stand out."

"Yeah, it do. So who sing? I wanna be the singer," I said.

"Well, you shote. 'Day already got Biggums."

"Biggums?! Go 'head, young! I ain't know she kh sing."

"Yeah, she kh hold a note...By the way, you know she turnt dike, right?" Dhonni asked suddenly. She raised her eyebrows as if she was waiting for the shock to register.

"Whatchu mean, 'turnt dike'?" I frowned. "She been like that long as I known her."

"True. Biggums always been jye-like on the manly side, but she a straight *nigga* now, young," Dhonni told me. "Ery since she hooked up wit Omar and started gettin dat money, she been on some uh' shit. This bitch be taping down her tiddies and erything now, out 'dare wit Syco bookin bitches, bunnin bitches—all typa shit. Done cut her hair off in a fade, too."

"Nuh-unh! All dat pretty-ass hair?!" I exclaimed.

"Yeah, girl. Biggums be out hea' nowadays lookin like she probly take a piss standin up. Wait till you see her ass at the Groovers show t'night."

The heavy grumble of a car with no muffler followed by the goose-like honk of a horn sounded right outside the building and interrupted our conversation. Dhonni ran to go open the livin room window and yelled for whoever opened one of the squeaky car doors to come upstairs.

"Dat's our ride," Dhonni called back to me, sweeping the fronta her long, burgundy crochet braids into a rubber band.

"Aight. Who drivin anyways?" I asked as she left the window to go open the door. I thought I heard her holla something bout her baby was takin us when my pager started to vibrate. I took it from where I had it clipped on my jeans pocket to see who it was, and almost immediately, my heart started pounding harder than a drum. *831-00-831*. It was the code Twon used when he wanted to see me.

"Damn," I sighed, sticking the tip of my thumb in my mouth outta sheer confusion. I wanted to drop erything and call to tell him I was on my way, but the stubborn part of me was sayin ignore him and go be with my girl for a change. I ain't want Dhonni to think I was really putting Twon over her on my list of importance. But then again, Dhonni ain't have that butta love, and besides, I ain't seen Twon all day. What to do, what to do?

"C'mon, Shai, you ready?" Dhonni called again.

"Uhhhh...Yeah."

I clipped my pager back on my hip and checked my make-up one last time in the mirror before making my way towards the livin room where Dhonni was chatting loudly with somebody. I was all set to tell her bout how I was putting off my Pooh Bear so I could chill with her crazy ass, when I looked past her and stopped short in shock at the end of the hall.

There, sitting on the tweed couch with her feet propped up on Miz Darlene's coffee table like she owned the joint, in a pair of booty shorts despite the cold outside, and sporting a weave so long and silky straight that the only person she was fooling was herself—was Baby.

"What the..." I looked from her to Dhonni with my eyebrows raised, waiting for one of em to explain what the hell was really goin on, but they was so busy talking and laughing like good ol' pals that they ain't even notice me standing there.

Ugh, man. Of all the people Dhonni coulda been hangin with since I moved away, she picked Baby. The same Baby whose grandmother wouldn't let her come off the porch when we was little, the same Baby who we useta throw rocks at on the walk home from school, the same Baby who Dhonni wanted to beat up for crashing my brother's going-away party two years ago. This was who we was poseda be partyin with? The girl my brother and his friends nicknamed Doorknob cuz erybody who grabbed her got a turn? The one who Cerrone told me got G'd by half the Spingarn football team (includin the towel boy) and came to school the next day braggin bout the shit? Dhonni musta lost her got-damn mind if she think I'ma go anywhere in public with that rolla broad. Just being *seen* with a bitch like Baby could fuck up your reputation.

"Dhonni," I snapped impatiently. "Kh'I talk to you for a second?"

"Yeah, aight. Baby, you 'member Shai, right?"

"Who? Oh, I ain't know no'by else was comin wit us," Baby commented snottily, lookin over at me for the first time since she got there. "I'on know if we got room f' her. It's already four of us down in'na car."

I grit on her and started to let her ass know wasn't nobody pressed to be goin nowhere with her or the likes of anybody she rolled with, but Dhonni grabbed my arm, whirled me around, and started marching me down the hall towards the bathroom before I could give Baby a piece of my mind.

"Dat's who we goin wit?" I demanded when we was halfway outta earshot, yanking my arm free and giving Dhonni a disgusted frown.

"Yeah, her friend Tamika the only one got a car," Dhonni started to explain. "And her folks know the one uh' the niggas in'na band, so 'day gon get us in free. Why you trippin?"

"Whatchu mean, *why I'm trippin?* I'on like dat bitch."

"Damn, Shai, you'on even know the girl. She ain't as bad as we useta think she was," Dhonni tried to convince me. "'Sides, she be havin the hook-up d' get in all the parties: Back, Junk, Essence, Norfeass—whateva. She always got a way d' get in free *and* get on stage."

"Dat's cuz she a damn groupie. She probly givin all them niggas dome," I smirked.

"Go 'head, young. Baby cool as shit."

"She kh be cool all she want. I ain't goin nowhere wit dat ho. Andju best d' tell her talk to me like she got some sense, cuz I will straight pull her card bout dat football team shit."

"Aww, c'mon, man, you believe dat shit?" Dhonni laughed. I crossed my arms over my chest and gave her a look.

"Hold up, you really think she did that shit?" Dhonni asked again as if the thought never crossed her mind before.

"I wouldn't put it past her," I sneered. "Look, y'all go 'head since it ain't no room for me no how. Twon just paged me, so I'ma go Uptown—"

"You gon what?" Dhonni squeaked, her bemused smile completely gone now. She looked at me to see if I was serious and saw the determination in my eyes. I wasn't goin with her if Baby was coming.

"I cain't believe you, man!" Dhonni exclaimed when she realized I was really gonna change our plans.

"You cain't believe me? Shawdy, I cain't believe you," I retorted. "You the one all buddy-buddy wit Miss Wide Open Spaces out 'dare."

"Whateva, Shai! Hi you gon come down hea' like you too good d' be wit muhfuckas from y' own neighborhood? What, you a certified Mo County bitch now? You all high seditty and shit since you live in the gotdamn suburbs?"

"It ain't got shit d' do wit dat. I just rather be around Twon 'steada some—"

"See, and dat's anuh' thing!" Dhonni snapped, cutting me off and glaring at me with a sudden ferocity that caught me by surprise. "You fakin on me f' dat nigga again, young! *Again!* I swear d' fuckin God, ery since dat nigga came along, you been ackin brand new like shit!"

I took a step away from her and cocked my head back like I usually did before I started cussin a muhfucka up one side and down the other. Dhonni was really starting to blow me with this new hostility she took on ery time I mentioned Twon's name. It was almost as if she was jealous that I spent time with him, like I was being a bad friend for having a life outside of her.

"Whatchu mean *I'm* ackin brand new? You the one ackin new, runnin around wit Baby stank ass," I retorted. "Now all of a sudden y'all peoples and shit. When dat happen?"

"When you moved away and forgot who the fuck your real friends was," Dhonni spat, and turned around so fast that the angry wind from her crochet braids slapped me in the face.

"What's dat poseda mean?" I demanded, following after her back into the livin room.

"F'get it, Shai. Gone Uptown, 'den. I just holla atchu later," Dhonni snapped, and motioned for Baby to come on. I watched her gather up her keys and go out the door without a second glance back, each step she took putting more and more of a distance between us.

I woke up to a sunny Sunday morning, but it might as well been raining, gloomy as I felt. A whole week later and Krys was still gone, stuck up under Javon far as I knew. If it wasn't for Shon, I wouldna even known that much since Krys still ain't call to say cat, dog, or kiss my ass since she left. Aunt Josie and Uncle Travis ain't hit me up lookin for her yet, but my nerves was shot just the same. I was tired of worrying bout that girl, tired of not sleeping, and tired of wondering if the strange feeling in my stomach was cuz something happent to her or cuz something else was bothering me.

See, Krys wasn't the only thing heavy on my mind that morning. It was August 12, exactly one year to the day when my brother got killt. I knew it would come around sooner or later, but nothing could prepare me for the way I'd feel when it actually happened. Cerrone's death left me with a aching, empty hurt that I tried to drown out with weed and work and focusing on my kids and Twon. Usually I did a pretty good job of numbing the pain, and keeping myself distracted so I wouldn't think about it. But now, a year later, I couldn't get the boy outta my head.

Cerrone. My lil brother. My main man. He was the only person in my life I could always count on to be there. The only one who ain't hesitate to stand up for me or stick by me. He was my right arm. My best friend. The most irreplaceable person in my life. I missed him more than words could say. I ached for him more than the two J's and three shots of Remy I took to the head that mornin could cover up. I ain't know how I was gon make it through a entire day feeling like this. How long would I be able to sit around wondering what he'd be like, what he'd look like, and what he'd be doin with hisself now if he was alive.

I coulda stayed in bed and slept till tomorrow so I wouldn't hafta face my misery. I coulda talked to Twon or called Mommy and cried on they shoulders till it ain't hurt no more. But I didn't. I dealt with it the same way I always dealt with shit. By my-got-damn-self. I grabbed a fresh pack of Backwoods and the half ounce of 'dro Biggums sold me a couple days ago, then took what was left of the liquor and sat in my usual spot on the balcony so I could get fried. The way I saw it, gettin fucked up was the only way I could cope with the pain.

Twon and the kids pretty much stayed outta my way, and except for the phone calls from Mommy and a couple muhfuckas I grew up with, nobody bothered me. I was all ready to piss the resta the day away drinkin and smokin myself to oblivion, when who of all people but Redz called me. Ery since our lil lunch date bout a month ago, I ain't really said much to him. I was still curious bout my father and jive eager to hang out with him again, but we was both busy with work and all so I guess we just ain't get around to making time yet. It was odd that he chose to call me that day, though. I flipped my phone open with a curious smirk, wondering what it was that he wanted.

"Yeah?" I asked, skipping the whole *hey-hi-you-doin* thing. At a little after three in the afternoon, I was already too twisted for formalities.

"Hey, Baby Redz."

"Hey."

Redz cleared his throat.

"I was just callin to see hi you holdin up."

"Whatchu mean?" I asked. It ain't occur to me he was talking about Cerrone's anniversary. I ain't think he remembered.

"Well, y'know, t'day is the day Cerrone uh…Ain't all dat shit happen a year ago t'day?" Redz said.

"Yeah," I answered soberly.

"I was uh…thinkin bout goin down the gravesite. Go dust it off and leave him some flowers or some'n. Wanna know if you tryna come wit me."

"Come witchu?"

It was more than a lil bit ironic that Redz was more willing to visit Cerrone on the day he died rather than seeing him on one of his birthdays when he was alive.

"Aight," I agreed before the liquor made me say something smart. I ain't really plan on visiting my brother's gravesite cuz it'd bring back too many memories, but somehow, goin with Redz ain't seem like such a bad idea. In a way, his invitation allowed the three of us to spend time together as a family. *Finally.*

"I cain't drive. I'm too drunk," I told my father, slightly slurring my words.

"It's aight. I'on mind drivin. Where you live at?" Redz asked.

I gave Redz directions to my apartment and waited on pins and needles for him to come through. It ain't occur to me till then that I'd be introducing him to Twon and my kids. The meeting I never thought would happen was actually gon happen. I tried to imagine how strange it'd be to show Man-Man and Tink they blood granddaddy, and how weird it'd be when Twon shook hands with a nigga who known me since I was born but ain't *know me-know me* half as good as he did. All I pictured was awkward hello's and curious stares when Redz strolled up in my place all cool like he lived there. That's exactly what happent, too, when I opened the door for him bout a hour later and invited him to sit down. Awkward hello's and curious stares.

"Y'all, 'dis my fahva. Redz," I announced, motioning towards the male version of myself standing in the middle of the livin room floor. Tink was the only one to speak at first. Man-Man just looked Redz over like he was tryna size him up, while Twon, jittery as any son-in-law would be, went towards him wordlessly and offered his palm. I smiled in somewhat relief when him and Redz slapped eachother a handshake and chuckled a easy greeting. I'on know why I cared if they liked eachother or not, but I was glad to see em smiling that *he-seem-cool* smile men give eachother when they first impression is good.

I went around the room telling Redz erybody's names, then offered him a seat in fronta the TV. No sooner than he sat down, Man-Man broke his suspicious stare and climbed on the couch beside him.

"You got a dolla?" Man-Man asked with his lil hand out like he expected Redz to put something in it right away.

"Boy, you don't ask people for money like dat! Get out his face!" I scolded.

"I want a dolla, too," Tink piped up, already tryna climb in Redz' lap.

I could tell my father was more amused than perturbed cuz he bubbled over with another easy chuckle and started digging in his pockets.

"Redz, you ain't gotta do dat," I apologized, embarrassed. "I'on know why they ackin like I'on feed em. Don't give em shit. Get down, y'all two!"

"Nah, nah. It's aight. What else is a old man good for?" Redz smiled, giving both of em five dollars apiece. The boys bounced around excitedly after that, rambling on and on bout how they was gon spend the money.

"Don't blow it all in one place," Redz advised.

"Now what do you say?" I prodded. They was already halfway down the hall tryna get they shoes on so they could go hunt down the ice cream truck.

"Thanks, Redz!" Man-Man called over his shoulder.

"Yeah, thanks!" Tink added.

"I'm sorry if 'day was rude," I told my father. "You know how boys are. I'on know what I'ma do when 'day get older. Them two is gon put me in'na nuthouse by the time I'm thirty. Have me down St. Elizabeth's wrapped in cold sheets and shit."

Redz gave another smile that seemed to marvel at the bold personalities my kids had. Maybe they reminded him of me and Cerrone when we was that age. Maybe of some other kids he had. Either way, Redz ain't say. He seemed to have a lot to say to Twon, though. They made small talk about this and that, mostly concerning what part of the city they was from. Both of em being from Uptown, they know a lot of the same people. I woulda let them go on all day cuz I liked how easily they took to eachother but I was eager to get movin. When I started pointing to the low level of brown in my Remy bottle, they said they good-byes and me and Redz was on our way.

We hopped in his ride, a black '95 El Dorado, that was just as slick with its black on black interior as my father was with his diamond studded earrings and Gucci short set. I smiled to myself cuz the more time I spent around Redz, the more I saw how we was alike. Wasn't neither one of us anything close to rich, but we sure knew how to twerk a dollar to make it seem that way.

Redz stopped at the liquor store to play the numbers and cop us another bottle, then got some flowers off Spanish cuz selling em at a red light on Bladensburg Road. Soon as we came up on Mt. Olivet cemetery and crossed the borders into Trinidad, I felt my stomach drop to my knees and my eyes well up with tears. I had such mixed feelings bout being back around the way. I mean, I wouldn't trade growing up in my 'hood for the world. Erything I seen and went through out there made me the person I am today. But on the other hand, all I could remember was how them same streets I did my rough and tumbling on served as the concrete cushion to my brother's dead body. I wanted to be there and I wanted to forget it. I loved it and I hated it all at once.

Me and Redz spread out a blanket and sat in fronta Cerrone's headstone. First thing we did was tap the bottle and pour out a sip for my brother. After a long, silent look around and a couple swigs of liquor, I was numb enough to forget my conflicted feelings.

"Know what Roney always said?" I asked Redz, clearing away some weeds that had sprouted up around the marble slab bearing his name. "Said he was born out hea' and he wanted to die out hea'. Ain't that some ironic shit?"

"I'm sure he ain't think he was gon die young," my father replied.

"I know he didn't. We was poseda get old t'geva. Buy houses side by side and raise our kids t'geva...Now, I'on even like bein in'na city no more," I sighed. "And Roney ain't get to live long enough to have no—"

I stopped talkin cuz I was gettin all choked up.

"He gone but he still hea' in spirit. I kh see a lotta what I remember of him in your boys," Redz told me, rubbin my back.

"Bad as them two is, you just might be right," I smiled through the escaped tears rollin down my cheeks.

"Yeah, they's something else. I kh see you got em in check, 'doe."

"Damn right I do. I ain't raisin no knuckleheads. Them two gon lissen to me if it's the last thing I do. And when 'day get bigger than me and start thinkin 'day kh punk me, I'ma just have Twon bodyslam 'day ass when 'day get outta line."

"Yeah," Redz kinda smiled. "I kh see Twon stickin around dat long and bein a cool-ass pops. He ain't as young as restless as I was at dat age. Slim real settled witchu."

"You sayin dat like you like him," I kinda smiled back.

"Aww, he aight for a young huckabuck. He make a good impression, knowmsayin?"

Again, I was tickled that my father dug the love of my life. Call it an instinctive need for daddy's approval.

"You know all dat after talkin to him for a couple minutes?" I asked, tryna shrug off the compliment.

"Baby Redz, I been around a long-ass time. Done came across all types. I know what I see."

"Yeah, Roney said the same thing after Twon got his shit t'geva," I smiled again.

Silence for a while.

"I miss him, young. I really do," I told Redz, downing another desperate gulp of Remy and thinkin hard about my brother.

"I know…I'll never forgive myself for not bein there for him…Not knowin him."

Silence again. This time it was Redz fightin tears.

"You woulda liked Cerrone," I assured my father after a while. "He was one of a kind. Some'my you kh never forget."

"Oh, yeah?"

I nodded in agreement and went about tellin Redz all the things he never knew about my brother. Bout his temperament, his irresistible charm, his silliness, and his adult-like seriousness when the situation called for it. I even told him bout some of the crazy things we did growin up, the jokes we played on eachother, the way we always banded together when Mommy tried to play us against eachother. Just some things I thought he should know. I had Redz crackin up one minute, then shaking his head all somber the next. Had myself cryin and laughin at the memories, too. I ain't mean to open up so much to Redz, but I did (thanks to the liquor), and it put us a lot closer together. Made me realize how dumb it was to hold a grudge against him for being gone all these years. Hell, if I could forgive Twon for half the bullshit he done put me through, I could certainly forgive my own father. Especially since he was givin such a honest effort to make it right with me.

Finally, when the liquor started to get low and my words no longer came without a flood of tears followin em, we got quiet. Just sat there and tried to make the best of such a sad, tranquil summer afternoon.

"We all leave 'dis world eventually," Redz said suddenly, pouring out another sip for my brother. "Be hea' one day, then gone the next. Cain't afford to waste no time."

"Yeah, you right about dat," I agreed, thinkin of all the people I known in my life who done already passed on into the next one. Then, of those who was still here but already starting to fade out.

"I wasted a lotta time. Wit all y'all…But I'ma see to it I'on waste no more. I'ma be there any way I can from now on," Redz promised. "I got a lotta years to make up for."

And with that, we toasted the bottle once more, then poured out the rest for Cerrone.

CHAPTER FIFTEEN

I ain't fully know the meaning of what happened the night I found out Dhonni was friends with Baby, but whatever it was, it definitely wasn't good. Our argument that night wasn't like the other lil tiffs we had over the years where we fought over dumb shit like who's butt was bigger or who was jockin who's style. It was way deeper than that. The way Dhonni made it seem, I abandoned her and our friendship by moving away and finding another person I fucked with as tough as I fucked with her. On one hand, I felt guilty for finding a new home, a new happiness, and not sharing it with my girl. On the other hand, I was mad at her for being mad at me for them same reasons. Just cuz our lives changed a lil bit didn't mean I ain't want Dhonni as my best friend no more. Youngin was my ace boon coon. My play sister. I'd do anything for her. But here she was catching feelings cuz I ain't spend as much time with her as I used to.

Damn, young. Was she really beefin off that shit?

I got my answer two days later when Dartanyan called me at Mommy's house. Lemme say that again. *Dartanyan* called me at *Mommy's* house. In the four months since I last seen him, Dartanyan managed to get in contact with me. Not cuz he dialed 411 and got my number. Not cuz he finally convinced Sweet Nika to give up the digits. It was cuzza Dhonni. Dartanyan told me he called Dhonni to get word about me and Man-Man like he been doin since we stopped talkin, and that heffa had the nerve to tell him I said I wanted him to call me and gave him my number. After all I went through avoiding that dumb bastard and tryna forget him, Dhonni got on some bamma shit and made it so I *had* to deal with him again. The petty bitch!

I was so fucked up with Dhonni I ain't know what to do other than stop speaking to her for real. Thanks to her, Dartanyan was calling me two and three times a day now, sometimes even more. After about a week,

Mommy threatened me to talk to the boy or she was gon put a block on the phone and make me pay a dub for ery call he made so far. I ain't particularly wanna talk to Dartanyan, but I be damned if I was gon pay to *not* talk to his ass, either. I guess it was high time I holla'd at him anyways. I mean, I still ain't confront him about the baby, but I knew. I just knew. Dhonni told me a long time ago that Trayonna's lil girl had Dartanyan's bright eyes, and the fact that her name was Traytanya Calhoun said a lot, too. I ain't wanna hear Dartanyan try to justify what he did or make me feel sorry for him. I was sicka his lies. But I did wanna know why he did it. I wanted to see what kinda excuse he could come up with for fuckin one of my so-called play sisters. So I finally decided to answer his collect call one day and told him to put me on his list. It was time to go up there and get to the bottom of things.

D.C. jail looked a lot different since the last time I was up there. The walls seemed closer, grimier, and fulla broken dreams, desperate men, and regret. There was a grayness to its institutionalized walls that I never noticed before, a grayness that made the faces of the men it held prisoner sag with some kinda incurable melancholy. At the same time, there was niggas in the j'on who who seemed too comfortable, even a lil excited to be there, like jail was one big summer camp that would mold them into the men they thought they should be. I found it ironic how Dartanyan, somebody who couldn't stand being told what to do, ended up in a place like this, where strangers dictated when he got to eat, sleep, or go for a walk. I knew as well as I knew him, that the longer he stayed in jail, the tortured grayness and false righteousness of it all was gon slowly but surely wear down his fiery, unafraid spirit.

I spotted Dartanyan at the end of a long row of telephones facing sad-eyed girlfriends, baby mamas, and relatives. In the time we been apart, Dartanyan was lookin different, too. Older. Meaner. He had frizzy sideburns and a lil goatee fuzz now, and stress around his bright eyes that made him look like he was constantly squinting. His hair was twisted up in a mess of haphazard plaits I could tell he did hisself, and he had a permanent crease between his eyebrows from frowning so much. He was nineteen but he coulda easily passed for twenty-five. Jail was robbing him of his boyish good looks.

When he saw me his eyes kinda lit up for a second, then they got sheepish like he suddenly remembered why I came up there in the first place. He bit his lips together like he was tryin not to smile. I guess he wanted to see how I was gon carry it. The sight of him disgusted me and pulled on my heart at the same time, and I found myself blinking away confused tears as I sat down across from him and picked up the phone.

"Wsup witchu," Dartanyan said, lookin me hard in the face after I got settled in.

"Wsup," I answered. I paused. There was so much to say. "Hi you been?" I asked finally.

"Maintainin. You know how it is. Howboutchu? You doin aight?"

"Yeah, I'm good," I told him.

"Ain't no'by been fuckin witchu, have 'day?" he asked as if he could personally do something bout it if they was.

"Nah, erything straight."

"Good...How's Man?"

250

"He good. Gettin big," I sighed.

"Send me a picture or some'n, shawdy. I wanna see him."

"I will."

Dartanyan glanced down at his hands.

"You look good," he told me after a while, chewing nervously on his bottom lip. "Bet them niggas out 'dare won't leave you alone, hunh?"

I tried to shrug it off but he knew me too well. I was too attractive to be alone and miserable, too hungry for affection to be without a man.

"So what, you gotchu a lil boyfriend or some'n now?" Dartanyan asked knowingly.

"I'm talkin'na some'my," I told him, shrugging my shoulders once more.

"You must be doin more 'den talkin, phat as you gettin."

"Whatchu talkin bout? I look the same."

"No you don't," he disagreed, then took a slower look at me. "Look like you pregnant, young."

"Pregnant?" I frowned. Wasn't no way in the world I could be pregnant. Me and Twon used condoms like it was goin outta style. It was safe sex or no sex with us, and there wasn't a time when we ain't strap up...Well, except for the one time at his house on that rainy day...

"I ain't pregnant," I said, rolling my eyes to the ceiling. "Don't be tryna curse me, man."

"I ain't cursin you. I just know the last time I seent you gettin all thick like dat, you was pregnant."

I paused and thought about how tight my clothes been lately and how I been telling myself it's cuz I shrunk em in the dryer, but I ain't want Dartanyan to think I had a reason to worry bout being pregnant, so I laughed off his comment and tried to start up the conversation again.

"Anyways—" I began.

"Anyways, nuffin. What's 'dis nigga name, young?" Dartanyan asked, cutting me off.

"What nigga?"

"Slim you fuckin wit."

"Why?" I frowned. I wasn't ready to tell him bout Twon yet. I ain't think it was none of his business. Far as I was concerned, my doings ain't been no concern of Dartanyan's since I found out about him and Trayonna.

"Whatchu mean 'why'? I got a right d' know who gettin my honey while I'm in hea'. So what's his name?" Dartanyan demanded again.

"Nunya."

"Nunya? Aight 'den, since you wanna be cute. Betchu probly fuckin one uh' them Mar'land niggas, hunh? Or some ol' bitch-made, bamma-ass Uptown nigga. One uh' them soft-actin muhfuckas. Dat's your type, ain't it?"

"Whateva, Dartanyan," I sighed, and rolled my eyes.

"Yeah, whateva. I figga'd you wasn't gon wait f' me. Dat's aight, 'doe, cuz once I get out..."

Dartanyan's voice trailed off. In his dim eyes were the promises a man makes to hisself when he got nothin but time to think about what got him behind bars. Seeing Dartanyan like that made me tear up again. I was useta the old Dartanyan, all fulla confidence and swagger with a fuck-erybody attitude that made you wanna be down with his cause and say fuck erybody, too. But now...

"I'm glad you came d' see me," Dartanyan said suddenly, changing the subject. "I'on be gettin a lotta visits."

"Y' muhva don't be comin up hea'?" I asked. He gave me a look like I shoulda known better.

"C'mon now, you know my muhva don't fuck wit me like dat. My niggas be comin through d' put money on my books and shit, but dat's basically it."

For some reason I ain't think Dartanyan was gettin as few visitors as he was claiming. He was probly just tryna make me feel bad for not coming to see him myself.

"So your girl don't be comin up hea'?" I asked, turning his comment around to make him feel guilty instead.

"My girl who? I ain't seent you in bout six months now."

"It's only been four, and you know damn well I ain't talkin bout me, dummy." I thought again of Trayonna being there the last time I came and remembered the bitter, hateful taste it left in my mouth to see em together.

"I'm talkin bout y' girl Trayonna," I said pointedly, and Dartanyan looked away.

"What's all 'dis girlfriend shit you poppin, young?" he objected, squintin harder so I couldn't read the expression in his eyes. "You know you the only one dat's my girl."

"You's a lie," I accused. "Guess next thing you gon tell me is dat baby Trayonna carryin around ain't yours."

Dartanyan started biting on his bottom lip again.

"Why you startin 'dis shit wit me already, man?" he asked irritably, the guilt plain as red paint all over his face. The phone started trembling in his hand and I could tell Dartanyan was shaking his knee like he do when he nervous.

"So it's yours, hunh?" I asked, talking over the tightness in my throat.

"You really wanna know the answer to dat?" Dartanyan asked.

"Nigga, I already know the answer. Damn baby look like you and got the nerve d' be named after you. Of course it's yours," I spat.

"'Den why you aksin me all 'deez dumb-ass questions?"

"Cuz I wanna hea' the truth out your mowf. Kh you at least do dat? Tell the fuckin truth for once in y' life?" I asked sarcastically.

He looked away again and was silent for a while.

"Aight, 'den, man," Dartanyan finally said, his voice barely above a whisper. "Fuck it. The baby minez. Youngin got the blood test d' prove it."

I just stared in a dumbfounded silence. Now that the truth was out there, I ain't know what to say.

"Youngin be comin up hea' sometimes wit the baby and shit, but dat ain't my girl or nuffin. You my girl," Dartanyan said, and flashed me one of his big-eyed I'm-sorry looks. "Look, Shai...I know I fucked up, but Trayonna, man, she..."

He sighed and put his hands up to his face. As bad as I wanted to cuss him out, I was gon try to be an adult about the shit and wait for him to explain.

"I ain't got no good excuse for what happent, joe. Youngin started throwin the pussy at me when we was goin through our lil shit or whateva, so —"

"So dat make it aight?" I snapped, cutting him off.

"I ain't sayin dat make it aight. I'm just lettin you know why I smashed the broad."

"So why didju?" I demanded, old feelings rushing back to the surface.

"Look, young, your girl been on me from the jump. Ery time I turn around, she's sayin some slick shit, tryna rap *me* up. 'Ooh, Cruddy, you so sexy', and 'I'm tryna see if that thang like Shai be sayin it is'. Bitch was pagin me *69-00* and erything, joe. But I backed off, knowmsayin? She was fuckin wit my man Black and I was fuckin witchu so..."

He paused and let out another heavy sigh.

"I'on know, young. She came at me one day off the late night when I was down Sowfeass. Youngin just left Black house and she was mad at him bout some'n, so me and her just started talkin and shit. I was already off the Paul Masson, so when she started touchin on me and shit...Man, you know how I get off the drinks, 'specially if some'my kissin on my ears...Anyhow, next thing you know..."

"You fucked my best friend," I spat, finishing his sentence.

"If dat's hi you wanna look at it," Dartanyan grimaced like he was mad I ain't let the story unravel his way.

"Whatchu mean *if dat's hi I wanna look at it?* Dat's what the fuck you did, didn't chu?" I could see he was still up to his same old tricks, all tryna sugar-coat the truth and twist it so he wasn't in the wrong.

"Man, look. It was just some one time, one minute shit. Ain't like I was strokin the j'on like I was doin you. I just got my nut and sent dat bitch on her way."

I cut my eyes. I couldn't believe the stuff that came out Dartanyan's mouth sometimes. What kinda fool he take me for? I still remembered the awkward silences when the three of us was around eachother and how funny Dartanyan would act when Trayonna said something to him in fronta me. I knew the shit between them was deeper than what he was tellin me. Dartanyan *had* to be tappin that ass on a regular basis. Why else would she be comin up here visiting him like she was his girl?

"You gon sit 'dare and lie d' me like dat?" I asked, fightin back tears. "You gon say some dumb shit like dat, 'den tell me I'm your girl like it's all good?"

"Shai, young, I swear dat was the only time—"

"Bitch comin up hea' bringin you shit and bringin y'all baby up hea' so you kh see her, but *I'm* still your girl? Go 'head wit dat shit, Crud. Trayonna your girl now, not me."

"C'mon, man. Dat ho ain't my girl."

"'Den why she be up hea' so much?"

"I'on know. But I ain't gon tell her no if she wanna come see me and bring me some jacks or some'n, young. Ain't like *you* was doin it for me."

"Was you expectin me to after the shit you did?" I asked, astonished.

"Yeah. After all dat shit I did for you when we was t'geva, you owe me, slim," Dartanyan stated matter-of-factly.

"What?!" That fool was *really* trippin now. "Nigga, please. The only reason I got kicked outta my house and needed you for anything was cuz I was havin your fuckin baby! You wouldna been no typa real man if you *ain't* take care uh' me. I'on owe you shit!"

"The fuck you don't!"

"The fuck I do!" I yelled, completely appalled now. "You know what, Dartanyan? To hell witchu. My nerves too bad f' this shit. I ain't gon sit hea' and let you try d' make me feel guilty for some foul-ass shit you done did. Unt-unh," I said, getting up to leave.

"Wait, man, damn!" Dartanyan interjected. He held up his hands to try and make me stay. "Look, I'on wanna argue witchu, young...I'm wrong, I know it. It's done, so get ova' it already."

"*Get ova' it?* Got-damn, Dartanyan! You call dat an apology?"

"Man, whateva. I did apologize. You already know I'm sorry," he huffed, and leaned back like he had nothing else to say on the matter.

"Yeah, you sorry aight. You bout the sorriest muhfucka I know," I retorted. That's when Dartanyan's bright eyes blazed.

"Oh, so now I'm a sorry muhfucka? After I take care uh' you and break my back f' you, get my ass locked up for you and dat's what the fuck you call me?" he asked angrily. "You gon come in hea' bringin up old shit 'den talk to me like I ain't shit? Whataboutchu out 'dare freakin? Ain't like I was the only one fuckin around. Oh, but you quick d' forget dat, hunh? All you 'member is the shit I did!"

For a second I actually started to feel bad. Then I realized he was twisting the situation around to look like I was wrong, like I was the one who cheated first and broke our bond, like *I* was the one who had a baby with one of *his* peoples.

"I ain't playin 'deez games witchu no more, Dartanyan!" I snapped. "You the one had a baby by my best—"

"Nah, fuck dat! You ack like you some muhfuckin princess and shit. Whataboutchu, Rashaiyah? You goin out 'dare partyin wit niggas, goin to the movies and Kings Dominion, havin hundred-dollar dinners at Hogates and shit. You out 'dare sneakin around, takin niggas money, probly givin up dat top piece for all I know—"

"Fuck you, Dartanyan!" I screamed, and punched the Plexiglas barrier separating us. My eyes clouded blindly with tears at the memory of our love dyin. My heart hurt with the burning truth of his accusations. "Don't try d' make 'dis about me! You the reason erything got fucked up! You started dat shit, and I put up wit it! So what if I had a nigga on the side? I ain't neh' do my dirt in fronta you! I ain't disrespect you by bringin no niggas in'na house! I ain't have no baby by y' bruhva! Dat's how *you* was goin, witcha dirty ass! So fuck *you!*" I yelled, my throat raw and my entire body trembling in anger.

I wiped away my liquefied pain before it could run down my cheeks and tried to calm down, ignoring the curiously entertained stares of erybody around me. Dartanyan put his head in his hands and it seemed as if he was tryna calm hisself down, too. It was a while before either one of us spoke again.

"My bad, young," Dartanyan started softly. "What I did was fucked up. I know dat. But I swear d' God I'ma make it up d' you, Shai," he promised, his eyes all wide and pleading. "Swear d' God. Just wait till I get out. Don't get bunned up wit no'by, man. And don't be havin dat fluke-ass nigga you wit 'round my muhfuckin son, man, f'real...The courts all backed up now, but soon's I get my trial, I'ma find a way d' get out 'dis j'on. And I'ma get back on and me and you gon get us a place, and raise up Man-Man like we said we's gon do. 'Member dat shit, Honey? 'Member we said we was gon stay t'geva forever? Hunh?"

Tormented tears escaped the corners of my eyes.

"We gon have a rack more kids and get us a big-ass house..."

I stopped listening. It was all bullshit.

"...I mean, it Shai. Don't give up on me, sweetheart. I needju right now. Don't no'by love me like you do."

I started cryin so hard my whole body shook. He was right. I still loved him, even if it wasn't as completely as I did before. Dartanyan's name still occupied a soft spot in my heart that nobody, not even Twon, could make me erase. He was my first love, the father of my child. Why shouldn't I forgive him? Why shouldn't I take him back and give him a second chance? Maybe if I came up and saw him more often, started sending him cupcakes and cookies and pictures I could make erything okay again. Maybe if I wrote him letters and told him how I felt I could make him love me the right way. I could change him into the man I wanted him to be, so by the time he got out he'd be erything I needed. Dartanyan definitely had it in him. He had enough Mr. Wonderful potential to fill a football field. All I had to do was bring it outta him, right?

I thought about the endless possibilities me and Dartanyan had. Then I thought about Twon. Twon who told me I was his dream come true. Twon who never lied to me, who never hit me or threatened me or made me feel like shit. Twon who never verbally said he loved me but showed me all the time in his actions, in his eyes. Twon who made me feel special and giddy and who did his best to please me any way he could. I thought about him, then I thought about Dartanyan and I saw the truth for what it was. Dartanyan ain't love me. Yeah, he needed me and he wanted me, he was infatuated with me and secure with me, but he ain't *love* me. He ain't know how to. He was too selfish to love anybody but hisself. He ain't light up my life or make me so happy I got dizzy with joy. He ain't inspire me or excite me. He made me tired. He dragged me down. He made me hafta second guess erything he said cuz I couldn't tell what was a lie and what was the truth. Why did I need that? Why was I gon stop fuckin with Twon to go back to *that?*

"I love you, Shai. You hea' me?" Dartanyan said, holding his hand up to the glass. "Swear d' God I love you, young. I promise I'ma make it up d' you. You believe me, right?"

I studied Dartanyan for what seemed like the last time. The creamy smoothness of his reddish brown skin, the way his lips moved when he talked, the something about him that was so needy and incomplete. I saw the desperation in his eyes, the same big, bright eyes that could make any girl forget her name, and finally came to realize that nothin I could do was gon make him change. Dartanyan was gon be Dartanyan just like the sun was gon be the sun and that's all there was to it. All this time I'd been making the mistake of loving him for what he *could be*, not for what he *was*. And at the tender age of fifteen, I finally learned what ery woman comes to understand at some point in her life: you can't change a man. It's something he gotta do on his own when he ready, and for real, I ain't have time to wait.

"Bye, Dartanyan," I said, and hung up the phone. I was up on my feet and outta there before he could say another word.

Someone was at the door. I heard it from all the way back in my room, under the covers, with Twon's loud-ass snoring damn-near vibrating the paint off the walls. I knew I wasn't trippin, though. There was a faint scratching against the door jamb, a muffled voice in the hall, then the bold rattle of somebody tryna turn the doorknob.

"Baby, wake up," I said, shaking Twon by the shoulder. He was so dead to the world that his breathing ain't even change. "Wake up," I repeated, shaking him again with a lil more force.

It was almost as if I wasn't there. *Damn, that nigga sleep hard.* I practically gotta be screamin bloody murder for him to even turn over.

"Antwon! Some'my at the door!" I said in a hushed whisper right over his ear. Twon's eyelids fluttered a little and he grunted, but he was still knocked out.

"Antwon! Get the door!"

At that point, I knew talking and shaking was useless. At two-something in the mornin, nothin short of a four alarm fire was gon wake his ass up. Not unless I grabbed him by the goodies and stirred him with some slow, wet kisses. Or poked him along the ribs under his arms where he was ticklish.

"Stop, man," Twon grumbled when he felt me jamming my finger repeatedly in his side. He waved a heavy hand in my direction and scooted away a little.

"Some'my tryna break in," I told him before he dozed off again. "You hea' me? Some'my at the door tryna break in!"

He sat up suddenly, groggy but fully alert.

"At the front door?" Twon asked, reaching between the mattresses to get the Desert Eagle hidden on his side of the bed. He stumbled across the floor and went digging in the closet for a full clip to slide in it. We was both nervous as hell, but steady.

"What uh' door we got? Hurry up, young. I hear em fuckin with the knob again," I warned.

Twon took off for the livin room and I hopped outta bed and down the hall after him. The closer we got to the door, the more distinct the sounds was. I went to look off the balcony and see if there was a strange car at the curb or anything, but I ain't see shit except a Diamond taxicab waiting by the curb. Cautiously, Twon peered through the peephole and asked who was there. All he got was more mumbling in response.

"You see some'my?" I asked.

He shook his head no and started to undo the locks. Seconds later, the dim hall light spilled into our apartment. Then, the crouched figure leaning against the door came spilling in right along with it.

"The fuck? Young, dat's Krys!" Twon exclaimed, uncocking his pistol and tucking it into the back of his waistband.

I stared from across the room in amazement as my lil cousin came stumbling into the house, her arms stretched out in fronta her like she was tryna find something to grab onto. Youngin was a hot mess. Hair all over her head like a bird's nest with her button-up shirtdress half coming off and her flip-flops sliding around under her feet. Twon kept asking what was goin on, but Krys' words ran together in some typa unrecognizable gibberish. Something was definitely wrong.

It was then that I saw the blood tricklin down her legs and the bright red stain it left on the pale pink fabric at the seat of her dress.

"She bleedin, young!" I cried, my heart poundin loud and hard. "Oh, my God, Krys, what happent?!"

She mumbled more gibberish followed by a lotta crying and talking too slurred to understand. All I could think about was how her condition was all my fault. I shoulda never let her stay gone so long. Shoulda never left her out there to dry. Now she was all fucked up, probly done got raped or some shit, and it was all my fault for lettin her run wild. Fuck, man!!! FUCK, FUCK, FUCK, FUCK, FUCK!!!!!

"You aight, Krys? Talk to me. What happent?" I asked, tryin my best not to panic. I grabbed her other arm and helped Twon drag her down the hall to the bathroom where I immediately started running some warm bath water. I had to do something to clear the blood away and find out where it was comin from.

"Krys, you aight?" Twon questioned her, helping me peel off her shoes and clothes. It wasn't till then I noticed that she was missing her panties. "Who did this to you?" I asked. "Some'my rape you? Dat boy rape you?"

Again, I couldn't understand her answer. I searched Krys' face to see if there was any evidence of shock that a rape tended to leave, but I ain't see any. I could see that she was on drugs, though. Some typa shit I ain't never did. Whatever it was left her with a vacant, keyed-up expression like what'd happen if you hit a dippa and snorted coke at the same time. Scared the fuck outta me.

"Krys! Krys!"

Her eyes rolled in the backa her head and her head lulled from side to side like she was tryna bring em back down. A clammy sweat trickled from her brow to her neck and made her shiver even though she was burning hot in my arms. I was so terrified I ain't know what else to do but pray.

"God! Please don't let this girl die on me!" I cried at the air above our heads. "F'real, God! Don't let her fuckin die on me!"

"I'ma call a ambulance," Twon said, dashing off to get the phone.

"Hurry up, man! I'on know what's wrong wit her!"

I got Krys to sit in the tepid water and tried to wipe her off, my hands shaking so much I could barely hold the washcloth I was using. I couldn't believe what I was seeing. Couldn't believe things got this outta hand. Shit just seem to go from bad to worse with me and this girl. First we fight like cats and dogs, then she run away on me, and now this. How the fuck was I poseda deal with this?!

CHAPTER SIXTEEN

"Thought I heard some'my out hea'. Whatchu doin up 'dis late?"

Cerrone slid open the screen door separating the livin room and where I was sittin on the deck steps, interrupting the jumble of thoughts clamoring through my head. I squinted at my watch through the dim light coming from our neighbor's back yard and saw it was goin on two o'clock, which musta meant I been sittin out in the dark in the same spot for a good hour. By all means, I shoulda been in bed sleeping off the rest of a perfectly good Sunday like erybody else, but tonight was one of them nights I just couldn't sleep. I had too much shit on my mind.

"Whatchu want, man?" I grumbled, relighting the half of a bob I sparked earlier.

"I'm tryna get deuce on that j'on, if you sharing. I'll match you," Cerrone offered, and held up a skinny J of his own. I shrugged an answer as my brother squeezed his narrow behind on the step beside me.

"Whatchu doin out hea' anyway?" Cerrone asked, adjusting his cut-up jean shorts and the swim trunks he wore under em. He spit-shined a mark off his Hi-Tek water shoes, then glanced over at me curiously like he was waiting for an answer.

"Mindin my business," came my curt reply. I wasn't in the mood to talk to him or anybody else for that matter. Not since Dartanyan's words came back to haunt me this mornin when I went to the clinic to find out why my period spotted last month only to skip this month, and got a answer I wasn't quite ready for.

"Ugh, young. Whatchu gettin smart wit me for?" my lil brother asked, putting a bony arm around my shoulder and pulling me into a choke hold. I was so tired of thinking, so tired of worrying, that I ain't even have the energy to wrestle my way out of it. Cerrone let go once he saw I wasn't fightin back, and used the rough tips of his fingers to turn my face towards him.

"What's wrong?" he asked seriously, lookin into my eyes with a quizzical, cat-like stare. My brother knew me well enough to know that if I was passing up a chance to punch him in the chest, something definitely wasn't right. The worry in his freckled face matched the worry I had knotted at the bottom of my stomach, and for a second there, I wanted to tell Cerrone what was goin on. I wanted to spill my guts and let him know how much I was stressin bout money and findin another place to live, and what would happen between me and Twon once I let the cat out the bag. Just how much would my life change once I admitted that for the second time in my fifteen years, I was bout to bring another life into this world?

"Damn, young, you aight?" Cerrone asked. Before I could toughen up and tell him I was fine, a lone tear of frustration escaped the corner of my eye.

"Shai, young, f'real. You break up wit cuz or some'n? You bout d' cry?...Damn, man. Hea'."

Cerrone pulled off the old Rugid Wear T-shirt he was wearing so I could wipe my face and put his arm back around me. He pulled me close again, only this time it was to be supportive, and asked once more what was bothering me so bad I had to sit outside fightin tears and staring at the moonless, night sky. So I told him.

"I'm pregnant," I said in a pinched voice barely loud enough to hear.

"Pregnant?"

"Yeah. Pregnant."

As in I'm bout to get real fat and be real moody and hungry for the next few months. Having a baby wasn't nothin new, nothin I was scared of or ain't know how to handle. Shit, I done been pregnant before. Only difference was, the first time around I had a boyfriend willing to take care of me and the baby on the way. This time, all I had was a friend with boyfriend potential that was liable to run for the hills once I broke the news to him.

"You tell cuz yet?" Cerrone asked, probly thinkin me and Twon argued bout the shit and that's what had me so upset.

I shook my head no and the same knot I felt before balled up in my stomach like greasy, old carryout food. Me and Twon ain't even known eachother a year and here I was bout to complicate shit with a baby, a baby I had no way to take care of if he decided he ain't wanna be bothered.

And even if Twon did stick around, how much could he really do? He already had a child, and Rayel was forever hittin him up for rent money and daycare money and *give-it-to-me-or-I-take-you-to-court* money. A lotta what he made out on the block went to her ass, and believe me, that shit got under my skin like a mug. I was tempted to just save myself the drama and down a castor oil concoction to flush out this kid before it got too late, but ery time I looked at Man-Man and remembered how he brightened up my darkest days, I felt guilty for even entertaining the thought.

"So whatchu gon do?" Cerrone asked gently. "You gon keep it or you gon..."

"Whatchu think?" I snapped before he could get the rest out. Of course I was gon keep the baby. The question was how would Twon react once I told him? Being friends with benefits was one thing. Popping up pregnant was another. Twon was a pretty responsible-minded dude, but this kinda pressure had the potential to make any nigga flip the script. And here I was thinkin the worst thing that could happen was changing our friendship by becoming a couple. Havin a baby now wasn't gon do nothin but make shit a hundred times more complicated, and I honestly ain't know how erything was gonna be once I let erything out in the open.

"So when you gon tell him?" Cerrone asked quietly.

"I'on know. I'on really wanna tell him at all. He might..."

"Might what?" Cerrone's brow furrowed into a frown that was both concerned and hostile at the thought of what I was implying. "You think slim gon carry you?" he pressed.

I shrugged again, and it seemed to make him even more upset. Suddenly, all of Cerrone's lil-brother protectiveness kicked in at once, just like it did them times he jumped between me and Mommy to keep the peace, or when he punished this boy at our school a couple weeks ago for slamming me into a locker cuz I wasn't tryna give him no rap.

"If dat's how he goin, I'ma hafta get in his shit," Cerrone vowed, cracking his knuckles like he was ready to rumble right then and there. "Ain't no'by carryin my sista, young. Fuck no. Dat nigga ack new, you let me know, young, f'real."

I pictured Twon's bad reaction to the news and tried to imagine ol' skinny bone Cerrone goin after him. Wasn't no doubt in my mind that my lil brother was bout it, but I ain't see him handling Twon unless he planned on shootin. I mean, Twon wasn't no killer or nothin, but I knew a thoroughbred when I saw one. I could see Cerrone now tryna approach that nigga and goin out like cuz on *Menace II Society* who got stomped to the ground for tryna be a hero.

"He ain't gon gimme no problems," I said as if I was sure, even though I really wasn't. Twon just might carry me, but the last thing I needed on my conscience was Cerrone gettin into some crazy shit on my behalf.

"'Den whatchu worried about?"

"Mommy," I answered simply, knowin her reaction would be the next most important. Me and Mommy still ain't get along for shit, so I knew soon as I let on that I was pregnant again, she was gon be the first one packing my bags and coming up with a million and one reasons why I had to go. As many times as she caught Cerrone with weed and had to bargain with the police to get him outta trouble with the law, I knew she was gon have a helluva time findin it in her heart to forgive me. She always been the hardest on me. Why? Maybe cuz I'm the oldest. Maybe cuz I look too much like my daddy. Maybe cuz I'm erything she useta be and she thought her tough love would put me on the right track. Hell if I could figure it out. What I did know is I wasn't hardly in no position to be gettin kicked out on the street again.

"Don't worry bout Mommy, young. I got her," Cerrone told me after a while, lookin me in the face all serious. There was something in his voice that actually made me wanna believe I could stop stressin, but then I remembered what happent the last time I was in this situation and knew I'd be up shit's creek without a paddle if I ain't prepare for the worst.

"Whatchu mean, '*don't worry bout Mommy*'? You know how she is."

Cerrone shook his head stubbornly and persisted,

"Yeah, I hea' you. But don't worry bout Mommy," he repeated, taking the J from me. "If dat's whatchu trippin off, 'den stop. I ain't lettin her kick you out again—I'on care *how* mad she is. She just gon hafta get over it 'dis time."

I smiled a lil bit, relieved even if I ain't really see how Cerrone was so sure he could convince Mommy to let me stay when he couldn't do it before. Besides, Cerrone wasn't in no position to be making demands bout who got to stay in the house and who didn't. The only reason he was still livin at home was a miracle in itself. Tone done already let him know if he ain't stop skipping his midnight curfew and hiding out in the city for days at a time, he might as well get his shit and leave.

"I'll take care uh' Mommy. You just make sure dat nigga Twon ack right," my lil brother advised, holding the J out to pass back to me. Then he thought better of it. "Matter fact, I'ma take care uh' this, too. You'on need it. You got a baby d' think about."

A baby to think about...
Cerrone's words echoed in my head that night long after I went to bed and tried to force myself to sleep. I had a baby to think about. In other words, I could kiss what was left of my youth good-bye. Even though I only had myself to blame, I was mad at the whole world for gettin in the same predicament that messed me up the last time. Now, insteada hoping to graduate high school with my class and fantasizing bout how vicious my prom dress was gon be, I had to figure out how the hell to feed and take care of two kids. I needed Twon's help. Wasn't no other way around it. Wasn't no other way around gettin bunned up, either. The damage was already done, and damn if I was gonna have that nigga's baby on my own.

Insteada wasting time and wondering how the shit was gon turn out, I went Uptown the next day to give Twon the news and see what he was gon say. Wasn't no point in beatin 'round the bush, so when I found him at the abandoned house where him and his boys ran shop, I took him 'round back in the alley and told him straight up—I'm pregnant, so what we gon do about it. Twon just kinda looked at me at first like he was tryna look through me, and ain't say nothin for a while. His silence was making me more nervous than I'da been if he started yellin or some shit. I mean, I wasn't expecting him to start cheesin and jumpin for joy or nothin, but I wasn't expecting such a blank response, either.

"You sure?" Twon asked after a while, letting out a deep, troubled breath.

"Yeah, I'm sure."

"You went to the doctor and erything?"

"Yeah."

"And you pregnant f'real?"

"Yeah."

He got quiet again.

"So whatchu wanna do?" he asked, his eyes full of a thinly veiled hope that I'd ask him for money to get ridda it.

"I'ma keep it," I sighed uneasily. I looked at Twon to see what he was gonna say, but all I got was more silence followed by a irritated shrug.

"Well?" I pressed.

"Well, what? Don't matter what the fuck I say. You done already made up y' mind," he finally grumbled, and spat at the ground.

Twon started to walk away as if there was nothin else to say on the matter, leaving me with just as much assurance as I had before I came. Was he gon stand by me or what? Was we beefin now? Did he need some time to think about it? When I tried to grab his arm and turn him back around, Twon yanked away and scowled at me so hard I coulda sworn he was gon steal me.

That's when shit got ugly.

"How the fuck you get pregnant? I strapped up ery time, young," Twon snapped, looking at me doubtfully.

"Yeah, ery time 'cept that one time. And don't try to act like dat was all my fault cuz you knew what coulda happened just like I knew. So now dat it's happened and I'm keepin it, whatchu gotta say about it?"

"What I gotta say?!" he spat. "Look, I fucks witchu and all, but I ain't tryna have anuh' kid. I got a hard enough time takin care of the one I got. Fuck I need wit anuh' one?...I'on even see how dat j'on minez, f'real."

"Twon, don't play," I frowned. He knew damn well I carried the shit outta ery nigga who even *looked* like he wanted to talk to me, so I obviously wasn't dealing with anybody else. Besides, I wasn't ready for another kid no more than he was, but Twon was steady actin like it was my fault. Like he ain't take off his clothes and go half on this baby, too. That nigga was pacing up and down the alley shaking his head and erything, still refusing to believe I was going against what he obviously thought was the best solution.

"Man, shawdy, look. I'ma give you five hunned right now and you go do whatchu gotta do bout dat shit," Twon said, pausing to shoot me a serious look.

"Whatchu mean, *do what I gotta do?*"

"I mean I ain't tryna have no baby right now, so you do whatchu gotta do, young. *Dat's* what I mean."

I couldn't believe my ears. He wanted me to have an abortion.

"And if I don't?" I demanded, pissed off at what he was implying with his hostile glaring and pacing.

"'Den don't expect a whole lot outta me, young. I got enough shit on my plate. I'm takin care of my Nanna bills, I'm takin care of my baby muhva bills, payin for my son, savin up for 'dis house, payin my bills, lookin out for my bruhva and sistas...I ain't got shit left for you, slim. I ain't got *shit* left."

Was he serious?

"Well?" he asked.

"Well, what? I'm keepin the baby, Twon," I repeated, firmly this time.

"Dat's on you, 'den. You heard what the fuck I said. Don't expect shit outta me. *Not a muhfuckin thing.* I can't do it," Twon grumbled, and started to stroll off like that was the end of the conversation.

He was really gonna leave me high and dry! After all that talking, all that buddy-buddy shit, all them so-called precious moments and time invested—this is how he acts when I need him the most?! I was so hurt and mad I ain't know what to do. Twon's words stung like a heavy-handed Dartanyan slap that instinctively made me wanna hurt him back, so before he got too far away, I kicked off one of my China doll slippers and went on his ass till I broke the damn buckle off. Twon was my erything, my all, the nigga who made the sun rise and set for me. I shared my mind, body, and soul with him. How could he think I'd even consider givin somebody else what I was givin him? How could he tell me he wasn't gonna have my back in a situation that he was partly responsible for? He just brushed me off like I wasn't shit. Carried me like I was no different than the resta them scandalous-ass, money hungry hood rats he usually got involved with, which really hurt my feelings cuz I thought he thought more of me. What a time to find out the truth. Twon hurt me so deep I couldn't breathe, and the whole way home I sat on the train with teary eyes and a hollow pain in my chest that reminded me I knew all too well what a broken heart felt like.

Twon called me later on that night, I guess to apologize, but I couldn't even part my lips to speak to that man. I ain't wanna hear what he had to say, or wanna know how he felt about the situation. I wasn't ready to see how me being pregnant snatched him out the spring we had together and dropped him into a bitter cold winter. I wasn't ready to understand why he wanted to run away from me cuz I created another responsibility for him to take care of. How instead of being his solace, now I was just another person in his life with they hand out asking for something from him. I ain't have shit to say to that nigga. In a matter of minutes, he broke my heart and made me think he never really cared about me in the first place. It was too much for me to handle at once.

Needless to say, we wasn't too cool after that. Me and Twon went from being together all the time and talking on the phone four-five times a day, to barely speakin and not seein eachother at all. Hurt and angry beyond words, I wrote him outta my heart, put him outta my mind, and built my defenses back up with cinder blocks and bricks that I vowed would never get broke down again. In a way, I did it to protect my already fragile emotions. And I also did it in hopes to make Twon miss me so much he'd come back to me on his hands and knees beggin for forgiveness. It ain't quite work out like that, though, cuz Twon pulled away from me, too. He was always busy now. Whole days and nights he spent drivin trucks and hustlin, and sometimes, whole weeks would go by without a phone call from him. I took his absence to mean he ain't care about me no more, which jabbed at my heart even harder than it did when he ain't bother to call and wish me a happy sweet sixteen on my birthday that year.

It was a tough time for the old girl. I struggled all alone with the constant misery of morning sickness that wouldn't quit and the looming fear of Mommy findin out I was pregnant before I came up with a backup plan. I nursed myself through heartburn and heartbreak, sometimes in such pain from one or the other that I couldn't sleep at night. Even with my brother always there to offer a ear or a shoulder to lean on, I grappled with a biting sadness and a stark loneliness from not having Twon by my side. I missed him more than I cared to admit, and a lotta times I think it woulda done me some good just to talk to him. But he was always busy. And whenever I finally did get a chance to talk to him, he was always moody and hostile. Even worse, Twon made a point to let me know what an inconvenience I was droppin on him by being pregnant. His lack of support hurt at first, but eventually, it began to inspire me. My stomach wasn't even poking out good before I decided to stop feeling bad for myself. If Twon wasn't gon be no help, I had to make my own way for me and the baby.

I made plans to drop outta school before fall came again so I'd have time for a full-time job with a hustle I could twerk on the side. Workin the cash register at a retail store woulda been perfect, but none of em was dumb enough to hire me after they seen my juvenile record. So I started lookin around at the fast-food places, and ended up gettin a job at the Wendy's down the street from my house. Flippin burgers and cleaning bathrooms wasn't exactly my dream job, but I couldn't afford to be picky. I'd hafta put up with doin grunge work for a few months, at least till I could save up enough money to move out and be about my business. Cuz as much as Cerrone tried to convince me otherwise, I was sure Mommy was gon kick me out soon as I started showing.

For real-for real, I ain't even think it was gon take her that long to do it. Mommy acted like she was tryna trick me into telling the truth whenever she asked why I stopped hangin tough with Twon. I claimed it was just cuz we ain't get along no more. I thought she'da been glad I quit being his groupie, but that only made her suspicious cuz she knew how into eachother we was. She knew it had to be something big, so she kept pressin me till one day, she took a good look at my swollen nose and my swollen feet and asked if we broke up cuz he found out I was pregnant. I coulda lied, but I knew all she'd hafta do was pull up my shirt and expose the dark line goin up the middle of my rounding stomach to see the truth for herself. Besides, Cerrone was standin there when she cornered me in the kitchen and I knew he'd have my back if she started swingin. So I told the truth. And Mommy got to hemmin and hawin and cussin so loud that erybody in the house came runnin to see what the fuck was goin on. If it wasn't for Tone holding her back and Cerrone pleading for her to stop, Mommy probly woulda knocked my ass all the way to Kingdom Come that day.

I pretty much knew how the resta the scene was gon play out, so I started to go upstairs and pack my shit. I ain't know where I was gon go or how I was gon get there, but knew I had to get the hell up outta that house before Mommy got loose again. That's when Tone stopped me and let Mommy know long as he was still payin the bills and his name was signed on the line as one of my legal guardians, I wasn't goin *no-muthafuckin-where.*

For days, she fought him tooth and nail, usin her same ol' excuses bout me being a bad example for my sisters and being grown enough to take care of the child I was grown enough to make. But with Tone ridin for me and Cerrone using his pull as Mommy's favorite to convince her how messed up it was to abandon me in my condition, she pretty much gave it up.

Mommy agreed to let me stay, but I only had till the baby was born to find my own place. I called Twon to let him know just how real it was gettin, and told him if he ain't at least help me get an apartment, I was gon go to court and put his ass on papers like Rayel did once she found out through his sister that he was havin another baby. I ain't wanna hafta do it cuz I hated the idea of gettin the government involved in something we coulda really handled ourselves, but around that time, Twon wasn't givin me the time of day—much less anything for our child. He acted like it was gon break him to put me up somewhere till I could pay my own way. Shit, he did it for Rayel's stankin ass. That nigga was *still* paying her rent off the strength that she was taking care of his son, but he acted like I was crazy for expecting him to do the same for me. I tried ery approach I could to reason with him and make him feel bad for not helping me out, but the more I pressed him, the more he accused me of tryna get him for money he ain't have, and the more I started to see gettin help from his ass was gon be bout as easy as gettin blood from a turnip.

The irony of it all made my head spin. I ain't never ask Twon for something I ain't need. *Never.* Yet he was makin it look like I was tryna play him the same way I played other niggas without a second thought. Ain't that some shit? I broke ery rule my play mother raised me with just cuz I fucked with Twon that tough, and now it was blowin up right in my face. All the times I coulda lied to him and faked pregnancies for abortion money, used Man-Man to get sympathy money, or made up wild stories bout needing a couple hundred dollars for court or one of my friends' bail—I didn't. Now I ain't have shit to show for it. I coulda kicked myself for being so nice to that bamma. Something told me I shoulda took Dhonni's advice and pimped his ass in the first place. Maybe then I wouldn't hafta choose between being homeless or sleeping on somebody's cold, wooden floor again.

When I got to be about eight months, I was so heavy and miserable I had to stop goin to work. I managed to save up most the money I made at Wendy's but I could tell it wasn't gon last me very long. Not with the way Man-Man was growing and all the stuff I was gon hafta pay for once the new baby came—and that's not even including rent. I was still scrambling around tryna find a place to live but I wasn't coming up with much. Apartments was expensive and I couldn't find nobody renting out a basement for the right price. Even when I did, they wasn't willing to take in a sixteen year-old girl with a racka issues and two kids, let alone allow me to sign a lease cuz I was still underage. I thought about applying for Social Services and ridin that j'on out till I could get me a decent job, but with the money Mommy and Tone made, wasn't no way in the world I could qualify unless they emancipated me and I tried to get it on my own. Which of course, was impossible cuz my court case from that Trayonna bullshit had me stuck in they custody till I turned eighteen.

I ain't know what the fuck to do. I needed money and I needed help, and I ain't have nobody backing me up 'cept my lil brother and maybe Tone. Muhfuckas I woulda normally been able to turn to wasn't nowhere in sight. Twon was still carryin it, Sweet Nika was too busy being a normal teenager to be bothered with my problems, and I ain't talked to Dhonni since the night I found out she was friends with Baby. Other than Biggums offering to gimme a lil something to get on my feet, Kia was the only one of my homies making any real effort to look out for me. She was gon ask her man Roe if I could stay in the apartment where he kept his stash, but I wasn't really sure if I was tryna be livin nowhere I had to worry bout gettin robbed or killt over some dope that wasn't even minez. It was starting to look like I ain't have much of a choice, though. In a matter of weeks, I was gon be out on the street with two kids and all of nine hundred some-odd dollars to my name. Talk about being stressed! Man, I was so tired and mentally unstable, that by the time December came around, I ain't even have the strength to have the damn baby at all.

If I coulda prolonged that shit I would have, but nature called me two days before Christmas and I managed to squeeze out lil Keyjuan DeVaughn Johnson after nine hours that left me feeling completely dead and hollow inside. I'on remember a whole lot more of what happent that night, except looking down at the chinky-eyed boy who reminded me of the relationship I sacrificed and the home I was bout to lose, and wondering what would happen if I decided to leave him right there at the hospital. I knew I was poseda be happy I had another healthy, handsome son, but all I felt was a deep sense of dread that made me wanna push him away. I ain't want no more babies, especially this one. Tink cost me erything I had before he even breathed his first breath. Why should I take care of him? He was a leech, a greedy-ass leech that sucked ery ounce of energy and happiness out my life, out my body, and lay there cryin in my arms with his tiny mouth open, begging to suck some more. The nurses kept encouraging me to feed him but I acted like I ain't hear em. I ain't care if Tink starved or not. Erything from the way he looked to the way he breathed and the way his frail, clinging hands reached for me got on my nerves. His hungry wails hurt my ears like nails on a chalkboard and made tears run down my cheeks uncontrollably. I turned my back when they laid him in the crib beside me cuz the mere sight of my own child filled me with a lingering sadness I couldn't explain.

The doctor in charge of delivery told me I had postpartum depression and gave me a shitload of drugs to cope. I don't remember half the pills I popped except the oxycodeine-type shit that put me in the *Twilight Zone*. I was real comfortable there, more than in real life. Them two days I spent in the hospital was a jumble of paperwork, bright lights, and people talkin at me non-stop. Ery now and then, I tried to shake myself out the daze that came over me, but the will to push on was gettin harder and harder to hold on to. I ain't know where I was gon go or what was gon happen to me and my kids once I got up outta that bed. I ain't know how I was gon get all my stuff from Mommy's house or if Twon's evil ass got the message she left for him after I went into labor. I ain't care, either. The only thing I could do to deal with my problems was pop pills and sleep, and hope that whenever I decided to wake up, my nightmare would finally be over.

So I slept, and I slept, and I sank deeper into the gloomy abyss of dark thoughts and feelings that sucked me in so far I thought I'd never come out. I had crazy dreams bout overcast skies with the sound of cryin babies in the background. I thought I saw Twon in them dreams sometimes, standing over me and looking painfully into my eyes like he could feel erything I was goin through. I thought I imagined myself ridin shotgun in his Caddy, zigzagging through rush hour traffic on Georgia Ave with Man-Man and Tink in the backseat. Thought I was hallucinating when I woke up one mornin and wondered why I was in his bed, wearing one of his shirts. *Could it be? Was I lunchin?* Sleep became a fuzzy mix of Twon and darkness, all disjointed and thrown together like one long, tortured dream that ain't make no sense no matter how hard I tried to separate it from reality. Voices sounded like echoes, time ain't seem to pass at all, and movement felt heavy and delayed like it did when I was in the deepest of sleep. I couldn't tell if the times I caught myself stumbling to and from the bathroom was real, or if I imagined standing frozen and staring blankly at Tink while he cried and cried till he turned red all over. Even after I'd been deprived of my pills, I was a fuckin zombie. I ain't talk, I barely ate, and when I wasn't knocked out, I sat for hours on end staring at the wood paneling of the room I was in, rockin back and forth like doin it was gon move me farther away from my problems.

Ain't nobody know what to do with my ass so they just left me alone. Someone came downstairs to make me eat and change my clothes ery so often, and some old lady sat by the bedside ery day like clockwork to read from her Bible and pray for me, but other than that, I ain't notice shit else. I was a mess, plain and simple. Part of me knew it, too, but the part of me that was sicka dealing with it all wouldn't let me do nothing about it. So I stayed like that for weeks, seeing things but not seeing em, sleeping, staring, and rockin myself into oblivion. I hated my life. I hated the people in it. And I really ain't give a shit if I died. What was the point of livin anymore? Nobody wanted me around. Erybody who ever said they loved me threw me away like trash. I was alone in this world. All alone. And the more time I spent sulking about it, the harder it was to cope with.

I was sixteen years old and I wanted to die. I could feel myself slippin, fast and outta control like a airplane caught in a tailspin. My mind fought itself constantly, stuck between choosing the relief of death or facing the mess I made outta my life. *Rest in peace or live and struggle?* I just couldn't decide. I started to let go of my spirit cuz holding on was making me crazy, and all I really wanted to do was quiet the commotion in my head. I'da done anything to silence them voices tellin me I wasn't gonna make it. Anything to shut em up and relieve me from the pain I was feeling. But for some reason, I kept visualizing the tears Man-Man would cry when he realized his mommy was dead, and the guilt Tink would carry the resta his life knowin he was one of the main reasons I let myself go. I couldn't mess them boys' head up like that. It wouldn't be fair.

I wanted to give up. I really, really did. But I couldn't. I was close enough to feel my toes hangin over the edge of sanity, but I couldn't jump. Underneath it all, I knew letting myself die woulda been stupid and selfish. It was impractical, not to mention irresponsible. Knowing that and wondering who would take care of my boys after I was gone was the only thing that shook me back to reality.

My own practicality kicked in at the last minute and saved us all. Gradually, I started coming out the depressed funk that held me prisoner in my own mind for over two weeks. I knew I could take care of me and my kids. I wasn't no stranger to gettin money by any means necessary. And so what if Mommy and Twon ain't want me? So what if Dhonni ain't wanna be my friend no more? Fuck em! My kids was the most important people in my life and I owed it to em to be there and raise em right. I couldn't leave em behind and expect somebody else to bring em up the way I would. I couldn't expect somebody else to kiss they boo-boo's and teach em not to cry or whine like sissies when they ain't get they way. I couldn't expect somebody else to give em the honest truth about erything. I had to do it myself. Just like with anything else, I had do it myself.

It took a while but I finally broke the chains that wound theyself so tightly around my mind, and woke up one day feeling like somebody snapped they fingers and I could see clear again. Suddenly, I wanted to take a steaming hot bubble bath and find out where my sons was, and eat a big bowl of something that would sit heavy on my stomach. I was starving! And funky. I needed to stretch and run and talk again, I needed to laugh and smell rain and see colors other than black, gray and red. Feeling odd and outta place like I just came out a coma, I untangled myself from the sheets covering me and made my way towards an open door where the dim glow of TV light flickered bright colors against the wood panel walls. I wasn't sure where I was since it occurred to me I ain't have a home no more, so I tiptoed cautiously into the open space of what looked like somebody's basement. Through the flashing lights I could see a person sitting on the couch right in fronta me, and my first reaction was to back away when they got up and started in my direction. I balled up my fists and readied for a fight when I realized they was gettin closer, my eyes struggling to focus on the shadowy, approaching figure. Wide shoulders and the outline of bowed legs was the first thing I remember seeing after my eyes adjusted to the blue-white light. My knees weakened at the sight of em and my heart began to beat with the erratic flutter of butterfly wings. I knew that silhouette. But why was he there? How? Was I still dreaming? Could it be?

He was in fronta me now, stopped at a arms length to peer into my eyes and find out if I was up for real or just sleepwalkin again. I grabbed the wall behind me for support cuz I couldn't believe what I was seeing. Apparently, neither could he. We stared into eachother's faces with equalled amazement, him not believing I was awake, and me not believing it was him who been takin care of me all this time. I wanted to beat him till he was bruised and lumpy for putting me through hell. Yet the softness in his eyes and the apology I read all over his face sedated me.

Twon saw me struggling to stand and offered a hand I immediately shied away from. He was like a distantly familiar stranger. The same something reminding me he took care of me when I needed him the most was the same something doubting I could really trust him again. I was conflicted as shit. Entranced by his eyes, I found myself too scared to come closer for fear that he'd hurt me again, yet too scared to move away for fear of losing him. So we stayed like that, staring at eachother from a safe distance separated by a gulf of unsaid words and much-needed apologies. Waking up to see my kids — I was sure I wanted to do that. But facing Twon? Well, *that*, I wasn't so sure about.

I hate hospitals. I try to avoid em cuz the last couple times I been in one, it was under some pretty bad circumstances. The birth of my second child. The death of my brother. And now this: pacing up and down the still, white, antiseptic-scented hallways waiting to hear what was wrong with Krys.

When the paramedics came, they checked her vitals and told me from what they could see, she was gon be okay. They did, however, hafta bring her here to make sure she was stable and test her blood to find out exactly what kinda drug she was on. I was curious as hell to find out. Twon stayed home with the boys and I hopped in the backa the ambulance with my cousin. Goin to the hospital was the last thing I wanted to do, but I wasn't gon be fool enough to leave her side again. My conscience wouldn't let me.

I paced up and down the same hall outside the emergency room for what seemed like hours. In the thirty long minutes since we got there, I bit all my nails off and shredded the Kleenex I used to wipe my worried tears into teeny bits of confetti. Nervous wasn't the word. I was bout to go crazy. I ain't know whether I should call Aunt Josie and Uncle Travis to tell em what happent, or shut the fuck up and wait for the doctors to gimme the whole scoop before I went and worried anybody else. I ain't know what to do. So I paced. And I paced. And I paced some more till finally, the head of ER called my name and waved me over.

"Your cousin's gonna be fine," the very tall, very distinguished, and slightly disheveled Physician Assistant assured me, after flipping around some pages on his clipboard.

"Tell me what's wrong."

"She was drugged. The MDMA could have been ingested voluntarily, but the Rohypnol we found was definitely given to her unknowingly. It's rarely taken willingly."

"Ro-hyp-what? What the hell is that?" I asked.

"I'm sorry. We found traces of Ecstasy and a date rape drug they call 'roofies'. Anyway, she had a pretty bad reaction to it—dehydration and such. But we're in the process of detoxing her now so she'll be on her feet in no time."

I nodded, still anxious.

"Whatabout all the blood?" I asked.

"She came on her period earlier today. Because of her state, we figured it'd be best to run a rape kit on her. There's evidence of some sexual intercourse, but nothing seems to be wrong with her," the P.A. assured me.

I nodded again and let out a sigh of relief. What happened to Krys was fucked up alright. I mean, *real* fucked up. But it wasn't hardly as bad as I thought it was. Thank God.

"She talkin yet?" I asked.

"No. She's asleep. She'll come to in a hour or so."

"Good. Cuz I'ma kick her ass."

The P.A. gave a sympathetic chuckle that said he understood. Then, just as suddenly, he was stonefaced and serious.

"Miss Williams, I think it'd be appropriate at this time to notify her parents of the situation," he said, checking his clipboard again. "Is there any way you can contact them? Or give me their information so I can contact them?"

"Um..."

I thought about it. Krys was already in deep shit with me. But her parents was probly gon ship her off to boot camp once they got wind of this. Again, I felt like it was partly my fault. If I never beat up on her like I did, Krys wouldna never ran away and got into this mess in the first place. I was just as much at fault as her, wasn't I? So Aunt Josie and Uncle Travis was gon be just as pissed at me, wasn't they? I couldn't go out like that. I couldn't disappoint them. I was poseda be returning they child in newer, better condition than before. Not all detoxed and ran through like she was. Damn. What to do, what to do?

"'Day on vacation," I lied before I had a chance to think about it. "Off on some cruise to the Bahamas. I'on know which one and they ain't got no cell phones. She in my custody till 'day get back, though."

The P.A. eyed me suspiciously.

"Was she in your custody at the time of the incident?" he asked.

"Um...Not exactly."

"May I ask why?"

"Cuz, um..." I had to think quick. Lie without really lying. "We, uh...we had a argument and she stormed out. Dat's the God-honest truth. I ain't know she was gon be takin E-pills and doin all that extra stuff, 'doe."

Ol' boy gave me another suspicious look.

"And just how old are you, Miss Williams?" he questioned.

"Nineteen goin on thirty. I'm legal, man."

I could tell he ain't wanna believe me, but one of the doctors holla'd for him to run over and check something in the emergency room and he started fidgeting all uneasily like he wanted to press me out but he had to leave.

"You're sure you're capable of watching her, Miss Williams?" he asked, crossing his arms sternly over his chest.

"Yes, sir. I'ma take care of her. She ain't leavin my sight till her folks get back."

"Promise?"

"I put dat on erything."

"Well," the P.A. sighed, throwin up his hands. "Fill out the paperwork I left at the front desk and y'all are free to go. You can find your cousin in room 229, right down that hall."

"Bet."

I turned and went in the direction of the desk.

"Uh, Miss Williams," the P.A. called at my back.

I whirled around to face him again.

"Please be more careful next time. Things could've been a lot worse."

"Yeah, doc. I gotchu."

"Good night, Miss Williams."

"'Night. And thank you. Thanks a lot."

CHAPTER SEVENTEEN

"Honey, I'm home!"

I recognized the raspy voice calling for me out in the livin room but I still ain't get up to meet its owner. Man-Man, on the other hand, slid off the mattress like a slinky and took off runnin so fast he almost knocked over Tink playin with his building blocks in the middle of the floor.

"Tackle! Tackle! Tackle!" he called in his chipmunk voice. I could already picture him wrapping hisself around the man's legs and tryna pull him down.

"Wsup, Smoke," I holla'd, continuing to lazily flip through the *XXL* magazine at my elbow.

"Wsup witcha," he answered before appearing in my bedroom doorway with Man-Man trailing excitedly behind him. I stopped reading for a second to offer my cheek for a kiss, then gave Smoke the usual half-interested glance so he wouldn't think I was ignoring him. My twice-a-week roommate looked like he always did—ashy black and fresh from head to toe in a glitter glue designed T-shirt, jean vest, and hat from the City Life shop with long plaits hanging down to his shoulders and a rolled-up J tucked behind his ear. Smoke had sleepy eyes and a weeded out expression on his face that constantly got him harassed by the feds off the late night. His vapid look suggested he was always smacked and probly kinda stupid, but cuz was actually sharper than a lotta youngins I knew. I guess to be Roe's right hand man, he had to be pretty smart.

Maybe I should explain how me and Smoke got to be roomies and what it had to do with Kia's boyfriend Roe. Well, ery since I snapped out my nervous breakdown-slash-postpartum depression, I been staying at Roe's stash house on Pomeroy Road in Southeast. After fumbling around in the darkness for two weeks and some change at Twon's house, I decided to strike out on my own. I mean, I owed Twon and his family my life for taking care of me and both my kids when my own mother ain't so much as call to see if I was alive. But shit wasn't the same between the two of us no more and I ain't see the point in stickin around longer than I needed to. I still had love for Twon and I missed being close with him, but I ain't trust him no more. For the week or so I spent at his house tryna get back into the swing of things, we spent ery day awkwardly tap-dancing around eachother, him tryna explain hisself, and me keepin myself too busy to have any real conversation or contact with him. I knew he was sorry; he said it a lot. But all I could remember was the way he treated me when I was pregnant with his child and what it did to me tryna handle all that shit on my own. I ain't know what to make of Twon's coldness in the past or the way he stared in my face after I got better like he was searching for the right time to suggest we get together for real. So before he could trick me into putting my guard down again, I called Kia and decided to take her man up on his offer.

Livin in a stash house in Southeast was just as unnerving as I thought it'd be. Growin up in Trinidad jive prepared me to deal with the constant gunfights and threats of danger, but it still took a lotta gettin used to. Southeast was different than my side of town because of its rich Black history. There were schools named after Black people, rows and rows of Black owned and operated stores, and neighborhoods that had been historically Black since the city was planned out by Benjamin Banneker (who also happened to be a Black man). There was a sense of pride in certain areas, a sense of Afrocentricity...and a sense of danger in others. For all its good, Southeast had a notoriously bad side, too. It was home to some of the most treacherous streets in the city. Streets that produced all typesa criminals and psycho's and Dartanyans. You know, kids who were missing Daddy or Mommy and the love, direction, and focus it took to become functioning members of society. Crack hit hard out there back in the day. As a result, there were shattered families, shattered communities, and block after block of deteriorating streets overlooked and overrun with crime and brutal cops.

Seemed like ery time I turned around somebody was gettin shot, locked up, or jacked for they cars, they cash, or the shit in they house. Police was deep as shit out that j'on but it ain't help a damn thing. Niggas on the Southside bucked at the feds, too. As a outsider, I was a target, but

I carried it like a bitch with a pistol in her purse, so nobody really fucked with me. For the nine months I stayed there, I played it low key. I was cool, but not too friendly, and I stayed the fuck outta other people's business.

Anyhow, about Smoke. He was jive-like the guardian of the stash house. Main man came through a couple times a week to run dope and money back and forth for Roe, then stayed the night to play it off so muhfuckas in the neighborhood wouldn't figure out what the apartment was actually being used for. I wasn't really trippin offa Smoke at first cuz at twenty-seven, I thought he was entirely too old for me to be hollin at. But the more lonely nights I spent feenin for the old days with Twon, the more Smoke started to appeal to me. Shit, why not? He was decent-lookin, he had bread, and he was always willing to rough-and-tumble with my boys like they was his own. Plus, ery week or so, he slid a few hundred dollars my way just because. Old head or not, I had to be crazy to turn that down. *Sheeeiiit*, Kia ain't school no dummy. Sometimes it ain't all about being in love with a nigga. Sometimes you gotta put feelings aside and bun up for convenience. I mean, Smoke was a aight dude and all, but he ain't exactly make the earth move for me. That ain't stop me from enjoying his company, though. Or spending his money.

I hated playin a role, but pimpin was pimpin and I had to do what I had to do. Smoke kept me laced and made sure me and my kids never went hungry or homeless. Between the money I got from him and the money Roe gave me for cuttin his dope cookies into crumbs ery once in a while, I *stayed* caked up. I ain't even hafta pay bills cuz the two of them took care of the rent, paid for the cable, the utilities, and the phone. All I had to do was buy food and pampers and pay for the boys' visits to the clinic. That was it! I had money to blow, boy. Enough to cut up $100 bills and glue em on the tips of my acrylic nails Lil Kim style. Enough to cut my hair short and dye it Charli Baltimore red and go get it done at the first sign of a drooping curl. The ol' girl never had it so good! I coulda went crazy in the malls all with the dough I had stacked up, but after treating myself to the flyest shit Georgetown and Pentagon City had to offer, and buyin me and Man-Man matching M&M Nascar jackets, I bought me a lil bucket to get around in and saved the rest.

I was livin good and gettin by, but after nearly a year of sitting on my ass doin nothin, I got bored as shit. I started stealing make-up and paper and dumb shit like that just to keep myself occupied. Damn near ery day I was goin back to Trinidad to see what was what, but a racka old people moved out and new people moved in, so I found myself feeling oddly outta place in my own damn neighborhood. I usually ended up sitting in on my brother's band practices or kicked back on Biggums' porch blowin big J's, watching people and watching life pass by. Sometimes I saw Trayonna walkin past with a lil girl who looked so much like Dartanyan, I had to grit my teeth to keep from cryin. Other times I saw Dhonni walkin around with Baby or fallin out some nigga's car at dawn's first light, all drunk and stumbling like she been gettin tossed up the whole night. I kicked it with Syco sometimes, but he made me uncomfortable cuz he had gotten into the bad habit of hittin them woo bobs, and he had a weird, unstable look in his eyes that was worse than his usual evil glare. Then, there was the times I kicked it with Foots and realized how much of a loser I musta been to have a friend who was bout to graduate high school with honors and a scholarship to Morgan State, where my dumb ass ain't even make it through tenth grade yet. Erybody I known since childhood was changing, either moving forwards or backwards into the patterns that would become the resta they lives. And what was I doin with minez? Here it is bout to be the millennium and all I had to show for it was two kids, some clothes, and a '86 Buick Regal that cut off when I tried to gun it past sixty. Nothin else belonged to me. I was gettin too comfortable livin life slow and taking other people's handouts. Most broads woulda been glad for the opportunity, but that *get-it-on-your-own* mentality Mommy instilled in me started gnawing at my conscience. I couldn't keep depending on muhfuckas like I was. I had to do something with myself.

Amid the Y2K scare and whole lotta 'dro, I brought in the year 2000 with a bottle of Nectar Imperial and a promise to myself to get it together. Living in Roe's stash house with Smoke was cool for now, but I wanted my own place somewhere I ain't hafta worry bout my kids catching strays or falling under the wrong influence when they got old enough to chill outside. I ain't want em to hafta struggle like me, or be hardheaded like Cerrone and throw dirt on the good life Mommy tried so hard to give us by moving out to Maryland. My goal was to get my GED and find a job, then take the money I had saved up and get me a lil place around Kia so we could raise Zhané, Man-Man, Tink, and her new baby boy Tavares side-by-side. I'd already bought the books to take the GED test in March and was skimming through the classified ads ery day tryna find someplace affordable to live. But just like any other time when I made plans to do some shit, life threw me a curveball that shut my whole operation down.

Trouble got a way of findin you in Southeast. I'on know who did it, or how long they been watching us. But all I know is, I went out one day to find some new snowboots for Man-Man, and on the way back home, Smoke paged me and told me to stay out for a while longer cuz something wasn't looking right back at the apartment. I killed some time by taking the boys to McDonald's for dinner, but after we ate, it was dark and the boys was tired, so I made my way back to Southeast to go in the house.

I heard the sirens soon as I turned on Benning Road, but I ain't think nothin of it cuz we heard them j'ons jive-like ery day. It wasn't till I saw the bodeens seven cars deep outside my building, that I got a sinking feeling in my stomach something was up. I parked and went runnin to the front door where police tape and a racka gruff-lookin D.C. cops blocked anybody from gettin in or out. This young girl Jarena who lived on the floor below me was bouncin her daughter on her hip and arguing with one of em till he pointed a stiff finger in her face and told her to get lost. I pushed through the crowd of confused and amused neighbors to get to her and asked what the fuck was goin on.

"Some'my kicked in y'all door," she told me, switching her chubby infant from one hip to the other. "Blasted y' man right 'dare in fronta the TV."

"What? 'Day shot him?" I asked, squeezing my sons close to me so I wouldn't freak out if I heard any more bad news. "Is he aight? He alive?" I asked with baited breath.

Jarena shook her scarved head.

"Nah, young. The ambalambs just took him outta hea' a lil while ago. Cuz was DOA."

"Fuck, man," I whimpered, suddenly feeling like somebody knocked the wind outta me. Smoke was dead. But why?

"Ay, the police said whoever shot y' man went through and tore up y'all closets lookin for some'n. Ain't even go through the resta the house. Why is dat, 'doe? Whatchall had up in'nere? Dat was y'all stash spot? I knew y'all was up to some'n..."

Jarena kept asking questions but all I could hear was the sirens and the icy February wind whistlin past my ears. Suddenly, I felt the temperature drop and my whole body started shaking uncontrollably. *What the fuck to do now?* It'd probly been foolish to tell the feds I lived there just for the sake of gettin my stuff and the four and a half G's I had left in the apartment. The way Jarena made it sound, whoever did this probly already got all the dope and the money we had anyways. It was too big a risk to go see what was left. The pigs probly knew this whole shit involved drugs and all they had to do was find the scales, the baggies, and all the resta the paraphernalia scattered throughout the house to make a case that would land me in jail if I went up there claiming shit. Fuck no, I couldn't go back there. But where *would* I go?

I turned away before Jarena could ask anything else and trudged down the street to the nearest pay phone. I'on know why I decided to call him first insteada calling Roe, but I just ain't know what else to do. I had to talk to somebody who could make sense of what happened and help me figure out what to do next. Two minutes barely passed before the pay phone was ringing me back.

"Wsup? What's goin on?" Twon asked, tryna mask the worry in his voice. I paged him with my code and *911* (something I rarely ever did), and I could tell he hoped I wasn't calling to tell him something happened to me or the boys.

"'Day shot Smoke," I blurted out. "He dead. Feds won't let no'by in'na apartment. My money gone...'Day gon know it was dope up in'nere. My fingerprints is erywhere—"

"Where you at?" he asked, cuttin me off.

"Up the block from my apartment. I—"

"I'm on my way."

Good ol' Twon always saves the day. He came swerving down I-295 fifteen minutes later, lookin bout as stressed out as I felt. I climbed in the passenger seat and spilled out the story bit by bit, peppering ery detail with escaped tears and choked sobs bout what happened to Smoke, the dope, and erything I owned. Twon let me ramble on and on till I ran outta breath, then rolled up a fat one, put the radio on 102.3's *Magic After Dark*, and drove around his neighborhood on autopilot till the weed kicked in and the kids fell asleep in the backseat.

"First of all, you gotta go back and get y' shit," Twon told me. "Trust me, whoeva robbed y'all ain't take your important papers or half dat uh' shit. Sound like all they came for was the coke and the money."

I nodded. Twon was definitely right about that cuz when I went back later that night to clear out me and my kids' clothes and stuff, wasn't nothing gone but Roe's precious stash.

"Second of all," Twon continued, and pressed two hundred some-odd dollars in the palm of my hand. "I know it ain't shit, but take it for now. You gon need some more bread, so sell your car."

"How I'ma get around, 'den?"

"Hop y' ass on'na bus like you useta do. That car gon cost you more than you got to work wit right now, so you migh'as well get ridda it."

I nodded and he continued,

"Gettin around is the least uh' your worries. You need a place to stay. I'on know if you got somewhere to go or not, but you kh go stay at Nanna house. Or you kh come stay wit me. I got my own j'on on 14th and Columbia."

I nodded again, figuring his Nanna's house was probly the safer place to go. I still ain't trust Twon, or myself around him, especially during times like these when I was so nervous and vulnerable. The way Twon could always see clearly for me when my own mind was blurry made me wanna hug him around his neck and call him my hero. But I couldn't do no bamma-ass shit like that. I had to be strong. Place or no place, money or no money, I wasn't never gon let myself be putty in Twon's hands again. It'd been ages since we did anything more than hug good-bye, yet I could still remember the comfort of his arms and the way he left aftershocks goin off inside me for days after we got together. Nobody I talked to after him could measure up to his appeal, or his intelligence and his powerful cool. And from what Twon's sister Antonia told me, all the girls he had since me was more like something to do rather than somebody to be with. Erybody thought we should get back together—even Cerrone forgave him once he saw how active Twon was in both my sons' lives. But Twon stomped on the last lil bit of love my heart had left and I never really got over that shit. That's the main reason I been keeping our contact limited to brief phone calls and visits to his Nanna's house for the kids over the past year.

I took a few days to regroup before talkin to Kia and Roe at Smoke's funeral. There wasn't no word on the street bout who hit us, even though Roe knew in his heart it was this crew out the South (Southside) he been having turf issues with for the past few months. In any case, he had to shut down shop till he could re-up and get back on track after the heat died down—and who knew how long that was gon take. Roe was already being investigated by the FBI for conspiracy, and the murder just made his whole operation that much hotter.

Before it was all said and done, Roe ended up catching a 25-to-life less than a year later, after retaliating Smoke's death. Some greedy, hatin-ass nigga from his own crew snitched that Roe was the ringleader of the murder and the nigga holdin the weight just cuz Roe wouldn't move him up to Smoke's old position and put him higher on the payroll. Kia took the money Roe left behind and skipped town not too much later. Nobody seen or heard from her after that.

Yeah, but basically, Roe ain't have no money to be giving me at the time, no matter how bad I needed it. I took Twon's advice and sold the Regal for a G before gettin the idea to call my brother and see if he wanted to get a place together.

Cerrone needed somewhere to go anyhow. The tension between him and Tone had finally bubbled over the boiling point. Plain and simple, the two of em ain't get along, but that was only cuz Cerrone always had a problem with authority, especially authority coming from a older Black man. I guess he figured since we grew up with no daddy, he was above havin some nigga tell him what to do. And since he been man of the house all the years before Tone came along, he figured he could still make his own rules. Obviously, Tone ain't see it that way. Cerrone rolled out after they last argument and had been spending the past few days camping out on Miz Darlene's couch. My brother was the perfect roommate since he was my favorite sibling anyway and I already knew his habits. Besides, he was making cake playing at parties with his go-go band and working a job at Modell's in Hechinger Mall. *And* he still knew how to pull a jack move whenever he was in a bind. Coming up with rent money wouldn't be no problem.

I ran the idea past him and we ended up finding ourselves a three bedroom right there in the 'hood we grew up in. The landlord was this creepy old, white dude who owned a couple buildings around the way.

According to Biggums' man Omar, he supported his nasty coke habit by doin deals under the table and turning his head when somebody used one of his apartments as a crackhouse. Neither me or Cerrone was old enough to sign a lease, but after three hundred bones down and a gram of Omar's finest snow, ol' boy gave us the keys and told us he expected $650 on the first of ery month. It was easy as that.

Now, all I needed was a steady cash flow. The only thing I knew how to do other than stealing and cutting dope was braiding hair, thanks to growing up with two lil sisters, two play sisters, and having a play mother who was a kitchen beautician. I got me a job at this braid shop up the street from the apartment to make ends meet. At first I was only sweeping up hair and filling in for girls who came in late. After a matter of weeks, though, my supervisor noticed how good I was and offered me a booth to rent. Think I ain't hop up on that? The work was monotonous and my fingers stayed cramped, but braiding hair was more steady than anything else I had going. I made me some fliers and handed em out to ery bad weave, broke-off ponytail sporting broad I passed by. I even used my good looks and smooth talk to charm niggas into coming there and paying me salon prices to do they cornrows. By the time it was all said and done, I had a small clientele and I was pulling enough walk-ins to make me a good eight-nine hundred dollars a month. It wasn't a lot, but hey, the rent was paid, my kids was fed, and I still got to treat myself to a new outfit ery once in a while.

My eighteenth birthday was comin up and I decided it was high time I started doin some grown woman shit, like opening a bank account and maybe even signing up for some cosmetology classes so I could be official. I finally took and passed my GED test, then started lookin up tuition costs and financial aid at Dudley's Beauty College. Mommy musta got wind of my plans from Cerrone, cuz one day, she called to leave me a number for her hairstylist Trisha, and told me to holla at her if I was serious bout being a beautician. I ain't know Trisha's ass from a can of paint, but I called her up anyway. It was a decision I'd never regret. If I stuck with her, Trisha said, I could be a for real-for real beautician in a month! I wouldn't have to waste no money on tuition or buying them plastic heads to practice on, neither. I'd be shadowing her as an apprentice at her shop by Mommy's house, working on real people and making real money when she passed her clients my way. Depending on how long it took me to learn the basics of chemicals, color, cutting, and heat, I'd be ready for the state board in no time. Talk about siced!

I was jive suspicious of Mommy's nice gesture, but I made plans to work with Trisha anyhow. I cut my hours down to three days a week at the braid shop, then got a hook-up thru Biggums on a QP of bud and started selling it on the side to make up the difference. Between my job, my hustle, and the tips I was making working under Trisha, I was doin aight. Goin way out Mo County ery Tuesday, Thursday, and Saturday was killin me, but I was determined to have myself a career by the time the next new year rolled around. So what if I ran myself ragged in the process? The payoff was definitely gon be worth it.

I worked so much I barely had time to eat or speak to my kids, let alone speak to Twon or any other dudes. All I did was work, come home, hit a J, sell some bags, and go straight to sleep. Before I knew it, August was halfway over and I realized I almost missed the whole summer. Kia kept urging me to party with her at the Zulu Cave, but I wasn't up for that shit. I ain't even wanna go to the Ritz with my girl Delmi from Mo County, even though we knew the bouncers and they let us in free. I just wanted to chill. You know, sit back and spend time with my kids like I shoulda been doin anyhow. Cerrone told me I was turning into a old lady and invited me to a Parasuco Party his band was playin at for this new nigga name Mike around the way. I wasn't too excited bout being cramped in somebody's dark, musty-ass rowhouse basement on a Friday night, but once he told me there'd be free drinks and Miz Darlene already volunteered to watch the boys for me, I figured what the hell. It'd been a while since the last time I seent my brother play anyways.

"Damn, young. I hope them jeans don't never go outta style."

Me and Biggums was posted up against her box Lincoln in fronta the rowhouse where the party just let out, people watching and taking swigs of Hennessy from the fifth Cerrone handed off to us earlier. Dozens of eager, sweaty bodies spilled out into the mid-August night under a cloud of house party steam, each of em holding our attention in some kinda way. Since Mike was new, a lotta the people he invited was from his old neighborhood further out Northeast. I was busy peeping out the sea of new faces for a nigga with a freak look in his eyes and a confident, big dick walk to put a end to my six month dry spell. Biggums, on the other hand, was watching all the broads strutting past in they tight, Parasuco stretch jeans, checkin for tongue rings and readin faces to find a girl who liked girls. We really shoulda been inside helping the resta the band pack up equipment and shit, but the two of us was too twisted to be much help to anybody.

"What jeans? 'Sucos?" I asked after another hefty swallow of rusty water.

"Yeah. Them j'ons be fittin youngins right. Even make skinny broads look phat. Make you wanna peel em off 'day ass like banana skins."

"Damn, not banana skins," I chuckled.

"Man…You just don't understand," she sighed with a satisfied shake of her head as a girl bout my size jiggled past in some bleached, cut-up jeans.

A few more minutes passed before Biggums got into hustle mode and reached through the window of her car to stuff a CD in the stereo deck. Bone Thugs' *Exstacy* song came crackling to life through her speakers and she turned it up loud enough for erybody on the block to hear.

"I got them E-pills for whoeva tryna roll!" she announced to erybody walkin by. "Who want dat sleazy? One for fifty, two for senny-five! Buy em now 'fore you hit the mo-teezy!"

Poppin exstacy was still jive taboo to most Black people in 2000, but all it took was a couple rap songs to have muhfuckas curious. Personally, I preferred my drugs green and leafy, but I been tempted to roll a couple times cuz I heard about how good it make you feel. I just ain't have the balls to take something rumored to have coke, heroin, and God-knows-what-else in it. The only people I knew who did was crazy white kids that went to them rave parties, freak hoes, and people who'd try anything as long as it got em high.

"Lemme get two uh' them j'ons," a girl said from the sidewalk behind us.

I turned around slowly to face the familiar voice and found Dhonni staring back at me with Baby faithfully by her side. The two of them looked like they just came from Unifest in they Sergio Valente miniskirts, backless shirts, and cowboy hats with flat, strappy sandals wrapped up they legs. They stood out like neon lights compared to the resta the girls who came to the party in wife beaters, Nikes, and regular ol' Parasuco jeans to get in free.

I wanted to ask her if she lost her got-damn mind, but something told me not to bother. Just like Trayonna and Lakisha got on some bamma shit and became total strangers, Dhonni hooked up with Baby and changed into a whole 'nother person. I heard about her out there goin off the Bacardi and gettin G'd out by some niggas 'round 18th and D. Rumor had it she was stripping at this club called Macombo Lounge all the way Uptown, too, even though she was barely old enough to work there. I ain't wanna believe none of it was true, but the way I saw her acting at the party that night, I knew muhfuckas couldna been lying. Her and Baby was up in there backin it up on niggas, all shakin, droppin, and poppin they ass like they was tryna be the next Sunshine and Juicy. I had to step back when I seen my girl in the middle of the floor on a handstand with half her booty hangin out and a racka niggas standing around staring and touching on her all nasty. Seein Dhonni go like that left me feeling real disturbed. It was hard to believe the freak bitch waving her cookies around for all to see was the same pretty, Hershey brown girl I useta call my play-sister.

I turned my head and pretended to readjust my shoestring headband just so I wouldn't hafta look at her ass. I ain't like seein Dhonni no more, much less talkin to her. She spoke whenever she felt like it during them rare times we crossed paths in the neighborhood. Usually, we just made small talk about my kids and the niggas she was pimpin, or how she was gon come see me at the shop to get her pixie braids done. It was all for show, though. Years gone by and miles of misunderstanding still kept us from really being friends again.

"I hope you got some money t'day," Biggums grumbled, reaching down to take a couple pills out the plastic baggie hidden in her Marvin the Martian socks. "Your credit bout bad wit me, bitch. You still owe me for dat last one."

"C'mon, Biggums. We go way back like car seats! Hi you gon carry me like dat?"

"I'ma getchu 'dis one last time, Kiss. Your girl gon hafta pay, 'doe," Biggums said, passing Dhonni two pills and nodding at Baby.

"Dat's fucked up," Baby fussed. "But it ain't no thang, mo. Hea'. I gih' you the whole senny-five right now."

Baby flipped Biggums a stack of one dollar bills, then her and Dhonni slinked off just as quick as they came up.

"Dat's *your* friend," Biggums said, watching em cross the street and hop in the backseat of some youngin's shiny, blue Caprice bubble. "Kiss so wide open now you kh drive a tractor trailer up in her ass. Dat ho Baby even worse. *And* I heard she burnin. I know two niggas said Baby left em pissin lava, joe. Nasty bitch. Dat's why muhfuckas be callin her 'The Clapper' now."

"'The Clapper'? Like the light switch j'on?" I laughed.

"*Just like* the light switch j'on," Biggums confirmed with a double clap of her hands.

After they finally finished loading the equipment into cars to take back to Foots' house, Syco, Pookie, Cerrone, and Foots came 'round front to meet us and do a lil parking lot pimpin before we crashed in our respective homes for the night. Since it was a neighborhood house party, bammas was still hangin out in the street undisturbed by police, drinkin they drinks and smokin they smokables. I went to go post up with Cerrone against his '74 Thunderbird so we could polish off the resta the bottle me and Biggums was sippin on.

"Hea', crush dat j'on, young. I'm bout ready d' go," Cerrone told me after a while of sitting and talkin to passerbys. He flipped off his bell-shaped Chinese straw hat and passed me the last sip of Hennessy. I gulped it like a champ even though I was so fulla liquor I thought it was gon come up through my nose.

"Wsup wit a J for the road?" my lil brother asked, givin me one of his big, freckled smiles.

"I got one d' sell."

"Sell?"

"You muhfuckin right, nigga. 'Dis shit some grizza. It ain't free. I give you a dub for ten since you family, 'doe," I offered.

"Dat's hard," he complained, diggin in the pockets of his Warner Bros. jean vest for some money.

"Times is hard, my brotha."

Cerrone hopped off his seat on the trunk hood, I guess to check his glove box for a roll-up, and almost slammed face-first into this big, brownskin girl passing alongside his car. Drunk, horny, and a lil too bold, he purposely fell into her double-D tiddies and pretended like he needed to hold onto her so he wouldn't fall down.

"Damn, my bad, sweetheart. You aight?" he asked, gently grabbing her by the arms and acting like he was tryna steady her.

"Yeah, I'm aight. Is *you* aight?" she replied with a shy smile.

"Of course I am. You see 'dis S on my chest?" he asked, pointing to the Superman logo on his jean vest. "Super Nigga always land on his feet. I'm like a cat, young. A big-ass tiger. You tryna make me roar?"

Oh, God. I rolled my eyes to the sky and stifled a giggle even though I wanted to crack up laughing. Lemme find out my lil brother think he got a rap.

"Make you roar?" the girl laughed.

"You heard me. Witcha cute ass. Mnh, you got a belly, too? Dat shit is sexy," Cerrone said, running the back of his finger down her round, pudgy stomach. My lil brother always had a thing for chubby broads, I guess cuz he was so bony and he needed something to hold on to. He pinched the fat on one of the girl's elbows and smiled. I could tell it was boosting her to be the object of such a handsome boy's affection.

"Ay, don'tchu play congas in'na band?" she asked, blushing a lil bit.

"Yeah. Why, you tryna be my groupie t'night?"

"Nah, I got a boyf—"

"Nay-Nay! Fuck is you doin, young?"

I got a bad feeling when I seent the angry dude comin our way with an overly aggressive frown on his face. He had the same insecure hostility about him that most abusive men had, like he was the type to smack the teeth out a bitch mouth and tell her it was her fault for making him mad enough to do it.

"Deon! I-I-I was lookin f' you—"

"Fuck is 'dis?" dude snapped, cutting the girl off and sizing up my brother all at once. Obviously, he wasn't from around here. Youngins 'round the way ain't get buck like that with Cerrone. They knew better than to disrespect a young veteran.

"Ay, my fault, cuz. Dat's you?" my brother asked, holding his hands up to show he wasn't tryna step on dude's toes.

"Yeah, dat's me," he spat. "Bitch, bring y' muhfuckin ass on. Fuck is you talkin to 'dis clown-ass nigga for?"

Youngin grabbed girly all rough by the same arm Cerrone tenderly pinched a few seconds ago, and yanked her in the direction of his car down the block. Something bout that and the way he called my brother a name musta rubbed him the wrong way, cuz the next thing you know, Cerrone was turnin all red in the face and clenching his jaw like he do when he mad.

"Fuck dat ol' bamma-ass nigga, joe. Gon jump bad wit me cuz he know I take his girl," my brother sneered loud enough for the dude to hear. Youngin spun around and started coming back our way.

Aww, shit.

"What?! Nigga, whatchu say?!" dude demanded.

By now, erybody in the street was lookin. Biggums, Syco and Foots came rushing over from where they was posted two cars down to see what was goin on. I got up off the trunk to have Cerrone's back in case slim started lunchin.

"Is 'dare a problem?" Syco asked, his chest all stuck out like he was ready to start swingin. Pookie walked up taking off his gray Looney Toons hoodie like he was preparing to do the same thing.

"It ain't nuffin," I intervened before shit got too outta hand. "Cuz trippin, but erything cool. It's cool."

"Bitch, ain't shit cool," youngin snickered. That's when I whirled around and grit on him, ready to fight my-damn-self.

"Nigga, don't be callin my sista out her name," Cerrone grumbled, steppin forward like he was bout to pounce on dude. Biggums and Foots grabbed him before he did and held his skinny ass back.

"Fuck you and dat bitch. *And* them weak-ass niggas you rollin wit," cuz jeered.

"Man, who the fuck is 'dis bamma? Anyby know 'dis sucka-ass nigga right hea'?" I asked aloud, lookin around to see if one of his friends was gon come simmer his hostile ass down. Nobody moved, though.

"Fuck you need d' know who I am for? Why'onchu mind y' muhfuckin business, bitch."

"Look, cuz, I ain't gon be too many more uh' your bitches," I warned, punching my palm with my fist. He mighta had his girl shook but I wasn't scared to wreck no dude.

"Fuck 'dis nigga, joe. I'm bout d' slump his ass," Cerrone said.

"Chill out man," Foots intervened, being the voice of reason. Biggums got a better hold on my brother as if to say the same thing.

"Nah, don't chill out," the dude kept instigating. "You bold enough d' push up on my girl *and* talk like you gon shoot a nigga, 'den do some'n, cuz. Fuck all dat bamma shit."

"Fuck all the bamma shit? Nigga, fuck you! You know where you at?" Cerrone asked, motioning around at erybody from our neighborhood who was creeping to the forefront to throw down.

"Man, fuck your neighborhood. Weak-ass Norfeass niggas. I'm from the Sowfside, shawdy. Y'all muhfuckas ain't scarin me! Fuck you and eryby out hea', you piss yellow bitch!" cuz declared.

Cerrone tried to pull his way loose, but Biggums told him to chill out and held onto him even tighter. Pookie, Foots, and a racka other niggas we grew up with inched in closer, though, just in case.

"Chill out, Rone. Cuz just tryna show off for his girl," Biggums pointed out.

I knew she was right. Cerrone knew she was right. But if my brother was anything like me, he was fightin the urge to save face or squash it. Cuz was basically calling him out. Cerrone couldn't back down. He'd be lookin fluke as shit if he walked away. Smart, but fluke nonetheless.

"Man, get the fuck outta hea'," Cerrone sneered angrily at youngin, deciding to be the bigger man and let him go with a warning. "If I see you when I come back from hittin 'dis J, I'ma show you how a piss yellow nigga go."

Normally, that move woulda ended all beef if the niggas involved both had good sense. But after cuz spat at the ground in response to his challenge, it was obvious Cerrone was the only one thinkin right. Youngin *wanted* to beef. And my brother was only making it worse by trying not to sound weak while backing down.

"You seein me now," slim said, coming closer, still testin nuts. "I'm right in fronta y' face now, cuz. So wsup?"

"What?"

Now, Biggums ain't no small girl, and Cerrone was taller than he was heavy, but he shook her off with a sudden strength that even she couldn't match, and went at slim before anybody could stop him. Next thing you know, Cerrone done crossed the five feet of space separating em and smacked cuz slam in the face. Smacked the shit out him like he was a bitch, with a open hand and erything. It was the most emasculating thing I ever seen. Embarrassed, youngin reeled back once he felt the blood trickling out his nose and stole my brother so hard his head snapped. While Cerrone swung blindly tryna get at the right angle to sleep him with one blow, dude reached under his shirt and pulled something dark and shiny from his waistband.

"He got a hammer!" somebody screamed. I watched in slow motion as cuz aimed his piece at my brother and erybody took off runnin.

Syco and Biggums started reaching for they shit but it was too late. The firecracker pop of gunshots slashed the night air like lightening bolts, and my first instinct was to duck behind one of the cars along the street with Pookie so I wouldn't get hit. But once I seent my brother's body jerk backwards and fall to the ground in a twisted heap, I stood there frozen in shock. My eyes had to be playin tricks on me. I refused to believe I was seeing Cerrone's thin body writhing on the pavement with blood-soaked holes all in his Superman vest. I ain't believe my eyes was seeing Foots on the ground beside him, holding his side and lookin at the bright red blood on his hands with genuine horror written all over his face. I wasn't seein Syco and Biggums retreating behind Cerrone's old Thunderbird, dumpin ery bullet they had into that dude till he went down. I wasn't seein none of that shit. It was a movie. A bad dream. The result of too much Hennessy. It couldna been real. *It wasn't real. It wasn't real. It wasn't real...*

Krys been tiptoe'n around me for two days now. Ery since we got home from the hospital, she been holed up in the den like I put her on punishment or something. I'on know why. I ain't said shit to her bout what happent the other day or anything else, for that matter. I ain't really have no words for her yet. I kept flippin from upset to relieved to furious so much that I ain't know what feeling to run with when I talked to her. So I didn't. I kept my mouth shut and let her walk around on eggshells, waiting in anticipation for me to kirk on her. Sometimes I thought it'd just be easier to go in there and squeeze her neck till her fuckin head popped off. But then I got to thinkin bout the last time we fought and had to remind myself violence ain't solve shit between us. It only made things worse.

So I played it cool. Krys went outta her way to avoid me, and looked at me all apprehensive when we did happen to cross paths. I coulda went on youngin a racka times already, but I just let her guilty conscience work her over cuz it seemed to me she was doin a good job of beating herself up. Like I said, Krys wouldn't come out that den for shit. She wouldn't talk to her lil friends or try to go nowhere or do anything. I could tell by the way she moped around lookin all sad and embarrassed that she was mad at herself, too. Good enough for her ass. After all the shit she put me through, I hope she give herself a damn ulcer.

Aight, that was mean, but y'all know where I'm coming from. Here it is, barely three weeks of summer left and Krys done spent most of it gettin on my fuckin nerves. We was nowhere near being cool yet. And I was no closer to the root of her personality change than I was when she first came over. I ain't know what I could say to scare her ass straight, but I knew if I didn't, she'd be completely outta control sooner than later.Her last episode was proof of that. I was left thinkin she'd end up gone in the head if she kept goin out there learning things the hard way. Which is why I had to come up with something ASAP.

If there's one thing I know, it's that you can't save somebody who don't wanna be saved. You can't make people see shit they don't wanna see, and you can't force em to listen if you sayin something they don't wanna hear. That's how it was with Krys. I couldn't even begin to find an angle to get through to that girl cuz to her, erything she was doin, no matter how much it worried her folks or how much she had to compromise her real self to fit in, was fine. It woulda been one thing if she'd genuinely changed into this characer she thought she should be. I'da recognized that, too. But as far as I could see, Krys was tryin the shit out the same way someone tried on a pair of shoes. She walked around wearin this persona, this pimpalicious, big chiefin', tough girl act like some six-inch pumps, not knowin how much damge she could do if she stumbled. The life she was tryna live had no stumblin room, not if you plan on livin long. At the very least, I wanted her to understand that.

I could tell she was starting to realize it, too. Krys was different now. Not quite as docile as she was when we was younger, but far from that fake, made-for-MTV broad she been lately. Babygirl musta realized just how close she came to dying by tryna be somebody else. I'm sure it ain't ery day she take a bad combo of pills and find herself smacked out her mind, fucked, left on a doorstep, and laid up in the hospital with a IV in her arm. She was probly kicking herself for trusting the muhfucka who ended up doin her dirty. Matter fact, I knew she was. Krys' ashamed silence said it all. The whole ordeal rocked the lil world she built for herself and forced her to come crashing back to reality.

Ironic, isn't it? Damn near the whole summer go by with our petty beefin back and forth, and the one thing that wakes Krys the fuck up happens because I let her go. I mean, Aunt Josie and Uncle Travis wouldna put up with no two-week disappearance. But because I did, Krys went through what's probly been the most traumatic experience of her life. She learned a hard lesson and I felt bad about throwing my hands up to let her do it. But I'm glad I did. And I'm glad she made it through okay. Maybe now, she'd understand the stuff her parents been tryna tell her bout the company she kept and things they led her to do. Maybe now she saw how one decision really could affect the resta her life. Maybe now she knew all me and her folks been tryna do this whole time is protect her from the cruelty in the life she was so pressed to be a part of. Maybe now she'd listen when somebody tried to talk some sense into her ass...

"Ay, Krys, c'mere!" I called, craning my neck to the side at her passing figure walkin across the livin room. I was in my usual spot on the balcony, tryna cool out after a long day's work. It was the Saturday after my brother's anniversary all I wanted to do was get a buzz on and enjoy the resta my weekend in peace. I knew I couldn't do it with me and Krys still not speaking, though.

Krys slid open the balcony door and peered at me through the fly screen. "You call me?" she asked, her eyebrows raised in surprise.

"Yeah. Come sit wit me," I said.

I saw the hesitation all over her face, but Krys came out and sat in the chair beside me anyhow. Neither one of us said anything for a while. Krys just sat and watched in silence as I went about rollin up a J. She was probly wonderin why I called her out there when I was obviously bout to smoke. Especially since I made it clear at the beginning of the summer that I wasn't ever gon smoke with her. Truth is, I wanted to have a real heart-to-heart with my cousin but I knew she wasn't gon open up all that easy. So

I planned on usin the weed as truth serum. I know, I know—after all she been through, I was wrong for tryna drug her up to make her talk. But at this point, I was willing to do whatever it took to make youngin relax. If I gotta get Krys high to get her comfortable with me, then it's high time we put one in the air for the cause.

"Hi you feelin?" I finally asked, turning to look at her.

Krys shielded her eyes from the blazing orange of the evening sun and shrugged.

"Better, I guess."

"Good...So you wanna tell me what happent dat night?"

"When? Dat night I came hea'?"

"Dat would be the night I'm talkin bout."

"No," she said firmly, pursing her lips together.

I just smirked and sealed up the J. See what I mean? Slim was forcing me to use force. I let her think I was gon leave it alone and sparked up, then took a couple pulls and held the weed out to her. Krys looked at me like I had to be kidding.

"Hea', nigga. You wanna hit 'dis or not?" I asked, jerkin the J in her direction again.

"You sure?"

"Yeah, I'm sure. You still smoke, don't chu?"

"Yeah, but—"

"But nuffin. Hea', you gon take 'dis shit or you gon let it burn up?"

I could tell Krys was suspicious, but she took the weed anyway and another long silence passed between us. We just sat there quietly watchin the sun set behind the trees and listened to the youngins in the neighborhood causing they usual ruckus in the street. After a few short drags between the both of us, I could feel the THC start to kick in. Krys was already mellowing out, too, with her eyelids half shut and her head leaned back like her neck was suddenly too weak to hold it up. I knew what that meant.

"You smacked, ain't you?" I asked with a laugh.

"Definitely is."

Good. I let another silence pass.

"So..." I started before either one of our minds could drift off any further. "When the last time you talked to y' parents?"

"Yesterday. Why?"

"'Day know you was in'na hospital?" I asked.

"Nah, I ain't tell em."

"So I guess you ain't tell em you was runnin the streets for two weeks, either, hunh?"

"Nope."

"Well, kh you at least tell *me* where you was?"

"You already know I's wit Jovan," Krys sighed, rollin her eyes to the sky. "I was 'dare when Shon called him aksin about me."

"So Jovan the one got you high and left you in fronta my house like dat?" I asked, even though I knew he wasn't. I went lookin for Shon the day after Krys came home to see if I was gon hafta put a hot one in his brother, and found out she only stayed with Jovan the first days of the two weeks she was missing. Nobody knew where she spent the resta the time.

"Nah, Jovan ain't do it. Dat was some'my else. 'Dis uh' nigga I know," Krys answered vaguely.

"I hope you'on consider dat uh' nigga a friend, 'den. Cuz friends don't do shit like dat to people," I told her.

"I know, Shai. Believe me, I'on fuck wit cuz no more."

"Good. So who 'dis nigga anyways?"

After another pull and a short stretch of quiet, Kyrs sighed and began, slowly and real hesitantly, to tell me the story of how she left Jovan's house the day one of his girlfriends came up there with three broads tryna start some drama. Apparently, one of the lil heffas seen Krys coming and going with Jovan and let his girl know. Soon as Jovan's grandma called the police and sent em on they way, Krys dipped. She ended up staying with her boy from Palmer Park after that, but he shared a house with six other people, including a small-ass room with his younger brother. Krys ain't like the fact that they ain't never have no privacy, so she called up one of her girls from back home and crashed at her place till youngin's moms started looking at her like she wanted her gone. Krys hung around there till she finally wore out her welcome four days later, when she called up this guy Jay she met at the mall.

He said he had his own place and she was welcome to stay long as she wanted. Nevermind the fact Krys known him less than a week and had no clue about him or his background. He coulda been a rapist, wife beater, child molester, or whatever. Krys dumb ass just rolled with him, ended up ridin with cuz way out the Southside to supposedly get something from his man's house where all the shit went down. No sooner than they got there, Krys got the feeling something was funny. It had a lot to do with the four other dudes and two girls up in the j'on actin all giddy and hyped up like they just hit the lotto or something. When she saw Jay get comfortable in the livin room insteada gettin whatever he had to get and leaving, Krys got the urge to duck out. But she didn't. She stayed. She kicked off her shoes and drank the whole cup of orange juice Jay brought out to her a lil while later. Then she watched TV till she started feeling light-headed. Then tried to run to the bathroom cuz outta nowhere, she suddenly felt the urgent need to throw up, but soon realized she ain't have the strength to stand. She tried to ask Jay what he put in her drink, but realized her voice wouldn't work. She thought of screaming for help, but ended up crying silent tears cuz it suddenly occurred to her that she got set up.

To make a long story short, Jay and his friends was planning on G'in my lil cousin out. They slipped some pills in Krys' orange juice hoping it'd get her all loosey-goosey like it did the other girls, but instead it made her sick. Once Krys got to dry heaving like she was bout to throw up, Jay took her to the bathroom where he tried to run up in her shit while she was bent over the toilet. That's when he noticed she was on her period and got mad. The bamma pushed Krys around for a while, then threw her out in the street to find her own way home. Mind you, it was going on midnight and she was in one of many rat trap neighborhoods in the twisted maze of Southeast. Krys ain't know where she was or where to go, and if anybody more crudball than her boy Jay woulda found her, she probly woulda suffered some more. Thankfully, though, a Diamond Cab driver saw Krys teetering at a bus stop and picked her up. It took a lotta patience to figure out her murmuring, but soon as the cabbie found out she needed to get to Forest Creek, he brought her to the complex and left her near the rental office. She staggered around till she got to my doorstep. By then, she was exhausted and out of it. If Twon ain't open the door when he did, we probly woulda found her in a heap on the hallway floor the next morning. And who knows, by then it coulda been too late.

It scared the fuck outta me to know how naive Krys was. I was literally shaking all over by the time she finished. Not only could she have got raped that night, but she coulda died if that cab driver ain't bring her here. I was speechless. Dumbfounded. Sitting there in shocked disbelief cuz just that easy, my lil cousin coulda been dead and it woulda been partly my fault.

I ain't hafta tell Krys how stupid it was to go off alone with somebody she barely knew. Babygirl understood that crystal fuckin clear. I wanted to get at Jay with Twon's gun, but in all the confusion, Krys forgot her phone at the j'on in Southeast. It was the only place she had his number, and she ain't know where he lived, or if Jay was even his real name. It bothered the hell outta me to know cuz was gettin away scott-free with what he did to her. Bothered me even more to know my cousin wasn't street smart as she liked to think she was. I really had to stop biting my tongue with that girl. It was time to let her know some things.

"Krys whatchu gon do when you get outta high school?" I asked, ashing the J and leaning deeper into my chair.

She thought a minute. Frowned. Shrugged.

"I'on know. Probly go to college. Dat's what my parents want me to do. I think it's a big waste uh' money, 'doe. My best friend bruhva graduated from Hampton two years ago and he still cain't find no job in his major. Nigga workin at Up Against the Wall and shit," Krys smirked.

"Well, dat's him. Don't mean it'll happen to you...What's your best subject in school?"

"I hate school...But I guess if I gotta choose, I say I like chemistry. I'm aight in math, too," my lil cousin told me with sort of a smile.

"What?! You like science and math? I *wish* I understood dat shit. Only math I know is how to add, subtract, multiply, and divide. I cain't fuck wit all that *a-plus-b-equals-twenty* shit. Don't make sense to me."

"It ain't dat hard."

"To you, maybe. You got any idea what all you kh do wit dat, 'doe? Be an accountant, a engineer—all typesa shit. And if you good in chemistry, you kh be a doctor or some'n. Be workin at NIH by the time you graduate college. Up 'dare curing diseases and makin medicines and shit. Dat's where the long money at," I told her enthusiastically. I was serious, too. If I had any typa school smarts, I'd be doin just that myself.

"I'on wanna stay in school dat long. Doctors gotta be goin for like eight-nine-ten years and shit. Besides, I kh make long money uh' ways. Fucka school. I'on see why you pressin the issue anyhow. *You* ain't go to college and it look like you doin aight f' yourself."

I paused to relight the J and handed it off to Krys after a couple puffs. I know it was kinda strange hearing me of all people tryna convince somebody to go to school, but Krys ain't come from the same background as me. I ain't want her to throw away years of private school and tutoring and erything else her parents did for her to end up like me: workin like a dog five days a week and having to watch ery penny.

"*Looks* and *is* is two diff'rent things. I might be doin aight, but we ain't no more than a couple checks away from losin erything." I was sicing it a little cuz me and Twon was doin more than aight. We had a nice chunk of change put away for hard times. But I was tryna make a point.

"Well, whateva," Krys shrugged. "I still don't like school."

"'Den what's your Plan B for when you graduate in two years?"

"I got some ideas," Krys answered just as vague.

"Like what?"

"Like…um…I'on really know no more. I jye-like wanna be a video girl," my cousin confided.

"A video ho? I'on think 'day make a lotta money. Dat's a lotta competition, too."

"It's a good way to get out there with modeling, though. I was thinkin bout that, too."

"Then go do modeling school and get with a agency. I ain't knockin video ho's or nothin, but you ain't guaranteed no modeling career with that shit. Just a bikini and a background with some bamma-ass rapper."

"I know. Well, I kh always be a stripper," Krys suggested. For a second, I thought she was playin, but her face was serious as shit. That's when I took my weed back cuz youngin was lunchin a lil bit too hard.

"You musta lost y' fuckin marbles," I finally said when the shock wore off. "You know how much shit you gotta put up wit d' be a dancer? You gotta have elephant skin to deal wit that shit. Niggas disrespectin you, broads tryna turn you out, pimps tryna rap you up, club owners be all coked out tryna get you d' sell ass and shit. Girl, you ain't ready for the strip game."

"That's whatchu think. Shit, I'm ready for anything where I kh make a G a night."

"Sweetheart, we are not in Atlanta. You ain't makin a G a night out hea' unless you sellin ass on the side. *Trust me.* Besides, strippin is like sellin dope. Dat money is good, but it ain't steady. Sometimes you make six hunned a night, sometimes you barely break one hunned. All depends on where you at and what you willin to do for dat dollar."

"Well, I'ma be out 'dare breakin pockets without goin. You see 'dis ass?" Krys asked with a conceited smile as she patted herself on the rear.

"Whatabout it? You think you the only one out hea' wit a phat ass? Better yet, whatchu gon do when dat p-h-a-t turn into f-a-t and ain't no'by tryna pay you to see it no more? 'Den what?"

She shrugged, probly never thinkin bout the possibility of gettin old and flabby.

"I'on know. Start a business wit the money I saved, I guess."

"What kinda business? How you gon run it if all you been doin is strippin? You gon take some business classes or some'n? Is you sellin clothes, bean pies, openin a salon? Fuck is you gon do?"

"I...I'on know. I'on know what kinda business I want," Krys admitted.

"You don't know? Damn, Krys, what be on your mind these days?"

"Whatchu mean, 'what be on my mind'?"

"I'on know about chu no more, man," I fussed, gettin down to the nitty-gritty. "You poseda be a good girl. Now you runnin 'round wit rapists, talkin bout you wanna make a livin swingin 'round a pole and shit?"

"Why eryby be sayin it like dat?" Krys grimaced.

"Sayin what?"

"Good girl this, good girl that. I'on see the point uh' bein a good girl if eryby just gon beat me up about it," my cousin grumbled.

In her eyes was the tortured conscience of someone who had it good coming up. Krys ain't never had to want for nothin, never had to struggle or work hard for shit a day in her life. I already knew there were certain people who'd give her a hard time because of that. And instead of being glad for what she had, she tried to relate to them certain people and be more like them. For what? To fit a stereotype of what Black people were supposed to be like? Man, I useta see it all the time when I lived out Mo County: youngins thinkin they missin something by growin up in the suburbs, so they try to come out and play with youngins like me who's busy tryna find a way *out* the chaos. Krys was no different. I was willing to bet someone made her feel bad for being a bookworm and talkin proper and shit, just like me and my brother useta do. Years and years of hearin the same thing can make anyone wanna switch it up. So there Krys went, switchin and changin into a "realer" Krys until she ended up at this point. I wasn't really mad at her rebelliousness; we all gotta rebel to find out who we really is. I was mad at her recklessness. She was dangerously naiive.

"Krys, I'm only gon tell you this once," I started, ready to break down for her what she was too immature to see. "Fuck what uh' people got to say. Fuck tryna change to impress em. Them same muhfuckas you out hea' stuntin for ain't gon be shit after high school. Once you graduate and move on witcha life, you ain't even gon be thinkin bout em. I promise you."

I paused to throw the roach over the side of the balcony and continued, "And it ain't nuffin wrong wit bein who you are, Krys. The worst thing you kh do is try to be some'my else. Look where dat got you."

Krys nodded. The hazed-out, pensive look on her face let me know what I said was starting to sink in. So I kept on with it.

"And stop trustin 'deez dirty-ass niggas, man. Niggas do not love you, and as much as you think you usin them, they the ones usin you. Don't sell y'self short. Niggas don't respect you if 'day know you only fuckin em to get money. You know why? Cuz dat's prostitution. No matter which way you cut it, if you gotta give up some ass to get something back, 'den you trickin. Plain and simple as dat."

I paused again. Thought of all the dudes I pinballed between when I was tryna get over the hurt and anger of my relationship with Dartanyan. Thought of how dirty I felt sometimes knowin I used my body as a bargaining chip before I got a lil older and wiser and stingier with it. Then, I thought of friends of mine who voluntarily sold theyselves and ended up worse off than they were before they got the money and things they wanted. I turned to look Krys slam in the eye when I told her,

"Pimpin ain't all it's cracked up to be, either, babygirl. Cuz when it's all said and done, whateva you got from them niggas ain't nothin compared to what you gave them. Remember dat."

She nodded again. And I went on.

"Besides, we live in a different day and age," I told Krys. "It ain't cool to be jumpin from one nigga to the next. Muhfuckas is out hea' dyin from dat shit. The majority of people is ignorant or dishonest, so they'll give you whateva disease 'day got and not think twice about it. You see how dat boy Jay tried to do you, right?"

"Yeah, but I ain't even know—"

"Fuck dat, Krys. Don't never put y'self in a situation where a muhfucka kh catch you slippin like dat. You ain't know dat nigga. Besides, if he did dat d' you, he probly done it d' some'my else. You'on know what typa person he is. What if he was out there raping prostitutes and shit? He could be burnin. Or what if he was in jail fuckin dudes? Lotta niggas be doin that shit deez days and you'd never know by lookin at em. 'Den 'day come out here and pass dat sauce around to any dumb-ass broad who won't make em strap up. You tryna go out like dat?"

"No!...But Jay wasn't—"

"Hi you know, Krys? You ain't even know his real name. You cain't trust no'by wit your health, girl. *No-fuckin-body*. Not even your lil some'n-like-a-boyfriend, cuz you never really know what a nigga's comin to the relationship with or what he out 'dare doin on the side. Just be smart, Krys. Watch y'self. Life ain't no game. Sometimes you'on get a second chance or a free pass, knowmsayin?"

Krys nodded again, this time her face serious as mine. Erything I said might just dissolve from her memory by tomorrow morning, but at least I said it. At least I tried. I had Krys thinkin and that's all that really mattered.

CHAPTER EIGHTEEN

Ery since my daddy dipped out on us, I trained myself to deal with hurt. I was useta being disappointed, overlooked, betrayed, and shortchanged. I was useta broken promises and rejection, broken hearts, deception, and distrust. But none of that shit, alone or combined, could help me deal with the pain of losing my brother. Watching Cerrone die that night fucked my whole world up. It cut me so deep and left me so empty, I felt the sorrow stab me in the heart with ery breath I breathed. It was hard. Real hard. For years I'd replay the scene over in my mind and blame myself for not dragging Cerrone away before he said the words that sealed his fate. For years, I'd wonder what woulda happent if I gave him one of my Backwoods so he wouldna never ran into that big tiddie girl in the first place. I'd have dreams bout wrestling the gun out that dude's hand before he got a chance to shoot it, bout jumping in fronta Cerrone and taking the bullets. But most of all, I'd keep seeing the terrified look on my lil brother's face as he choked on his own blood and realized he was bout to die.

Cerrone took a piece of me with him the night I kneeled at his side and watched the light fade from his eyes like sunshine being overtook by storm clouds in the sky. I tried not to go to pieces when the paramedics came some fifteen minutes later and put that white sheet over his body. I even held myself together when the coroner came and stated the obvious after desperately checking for a pulse. It wasn't till Mommy broke through the crowd all disheveled and distraught in her crisp, white work scrubs, that I let myself break down and cry. The devastated look on her face let me know what I witnessed wasn't merely a bad dream. The boy who gave me sloppy, wet kisses on the cheek just to annoy me was dead. The one who always had my back and gave me a helping hand when I couldn't help myself was dead. Mommy's only son, her favorite child, her pride and joy had ceased to exist. It was a loss that hit both of us like a ton of bricks.

Damn shame it took my brother's death to make my own mother cling to me and thank God I was still alive. Damn shame Cerrone had to die before me and Mommy started seeing eye to eye.

Quick and easy like they did it a racka times ery night, the coroner's folks zipped my brother up in a body bag and drove him to the morgue. Mommy and I started towards her truck so we could follow after them, but we ain't even make it off the street that still ran red with rivers of Cerrone's blood before the grief kicked in. We held eachother and sobbed hysterically, both of us connected by a pain that felt like swallowing a handfulla knives. Cerrone was both our favorite for whatever reasons, and often times the only thing in this world that kept the two of us from losing contact completely. He was the icebreaker, the peacemaker, the one who could crack a joke or tickle you silly and make you forget about whatever was on your mind. And now he was gone. Gone into the dead nothing that was just as still and black as his last view of the night sky. All for what? Some broad? His pride? Respect?

I was sick of it. Sicka the tough talk that bruised egos and led to drastic actions fueled by emotion. Sicka the city life and the mentality that being cut-throat and go-hard was the only way to prove yourself. Sicka the defensiveness and the hostility and the way we all walked around with chips on our shoulders, daring eachother to knock em off. I'd seen enough youngins die over bullshit. Seen enough tough muhfuckas cry unashamed in public cuz they done lost they closest friend. Seen enough mamas cry from they souls cuz they done lost they child. My mind was cluttered with scenes of violence and sadness that played over and over again like a broken slideshow. And I was just plain sick of it.

I went with Mommy to be her support while she filled out Cerrone's final paperwork at the hospital. I held her up and wiped her tears like any good daughter would, offering whatever comfort she needed as she struggled through the most harrowing moment of her life. That night it ain't matter if I had a grudge against her for treating me like a redheaded stepchild all these years. It ain't matter if we rarely ever talked. We was coming from the same deep pit of hurt that night. Mommy spoke in disjointed spurts, telling me time after time how she only wanted the best for us and how hard she worked to do right by us. The more she talked, the more I wondered how tragedy could change the way a person been acting for years in a matter of minutes. For the first time ever, I saw something other than contempt in my mother's eyes when she spoke to me. I saw her heartache and distress. Her humanness. I saw the unconditional love she had for my brother, for all of us — even me. I saw her for the person she was, as my mother who cared about all of us equally even though she might not have always showed it.

When Tone came to the hospital later on that night to see what he could do, I left out that j'on feeling like I stepped into another world. I left messages at both my jobs to let em know I wasn't gon be in for a while, then went back around the way to collect my kids from Miz Darlene. I wanted to go somewhere far away, maybe out to Maryland's eastern shore to walk some deserted stretch of beach. Anything to get away from Trinidad and all the memories from the night before. I changed out of my blood-soaked clothes and hopped in Cerrone's bullet-laced Thunderbird with what was left of my last QP, tryna convince myself I was strong enough to put up a front that I was fine. But I ain't even make it down Florida Ave before I was blinded by tears again. I couldn't hold myself together. I wasn't strong enough at all. I pulled over at the nearest pay phone and dialed the first number that came to mind.

"Hello?" a groggy voice answered after five rings.

"Twon, it's me."

"Shai?"

He sounded surprised that I was calling him at six-something in the mornin. And worried. I started to feel bad for always calling him when I had a problem.

"What's goin on, young?" Twon asked. I could hear a broad's voice in the background asking if something was wrong, but he hushed her sharply and focused back on me.

"Oh, I ain't know you had comp'ny," I said, fightin the jealousy that added to the hurt I was already feeling.

"Fuck dat. Ain't nuffin. What's goin on?" he repeated.

"I need you d' watch the kids for me. I gotta go somewhere."

"Right now? Where you goin?"

"Kh you do dat for me?" I asked, my voice cracking. Suddenly, a wave of anguish hit me and I started dripping tears and snot onto the phone's receiver uncontrollably.

"I ain't doin shit till you tell me what's goin on," Twon said.

I tried to tell him but I couldn't stop cryin. I just couldn't stop fuckin cryin.

"I'on wanna talk about it," I sobbed when I was finally able to catch my breath. "I'ma meet you out fronta your buildin. Five minutes."

Then I hung up.

I actually waited bout ten minutes cuz I had a feeling Twon was gon need some time to kick his lil bedwarmer to the curb before I got there. Sure enough, no sooner than I walked up to his building with Man-Man and Tink in tow, he was coming down the steps in some pajama shorts and nothin else with a very angry-looking chick right behind him. Me and her exchanged evil looks before she brushed past tryna finish putting on her shoes and fixing her hair. As fucked up as I was, I coulda banged her ass out right there on the sidewalk, but I was too numb to fight. I just wanted to drop my sons off and go be alone for a while.

"You gon tell me what's wrong now?" Twon asked, lifting Tink's sleeping body from my arms.

"Not in fronta the kids. I need d' go ride around for a lil while. Clear my head," I said.

"Well, when you comin back?"

"When it don't hurt no more."

"When what don't hurt no more? Whatchu talkin bout? Ay, where you goin at?" Twon asked all confused.

I shrugged a answer and started walkin back to the car. I ended up ridin around for three whole days and nights before I was able to stop cryin. No insurance, bad tags, no license, no food—I ain't have shit but some bud and money for gas. I went all over the city, from Haines Point where me and Cerrone watched the planes take off with our father, to Union Station where we stole from the stores and robbed outta-towners for they jewelry and wallets, and in and out our old neighborhood to visit the playgrounds and schools and alleys where we did most our growin up. I went erywhere that reminded me of him. Ery place we ever did something together. Part of me hoped to see Cerrone there, sitting on a bench or leaned up against a lamppost hitting a jack or aiming a rubber band to pop me in the forehead. But when all I saw was emptiness that reminded me just how gone he was, I'd start crying all over again. My lil brother was dead.

It was hard to maintain, but I managed to pull my wits together in time to go to Cerrone's funeral. Erybody and they mama was there. Erybody we knew from the old neighborhood showed up, including a racka old friends, ex-buns, and youngins we grew up with. Kia, Roe, Dhonni, Trayonna, Pookie, Foots, Baby, Precious...even Syco and Biggums came through despite the fact they was on the run for shootin at the dude who killt my brother. My mother's side of the family crowded the front of the church with Twon and his immediate family not too far away. I was surprised to see a lotta people from my father's side there, too, cuz ain't none of them muhfuckas had a whole lot to say to me and Cerrone since we was kids. You can imagine my shock when I saw my father up in there with them muhfuckas fronting like he was all broke up. I kirked out when I recognized his freckled face among the mourners. I was so mad it took my brother's death for him to finally come around that I could barely speak through all the tears and anger I was choking on. That sorry son-of-a-bitch! It took three grown men to pull me away from where I stood at the pulpit cussin his ass out. How dare he show face at a time like this! Did he really think payin his last respects would make up for years of ignoring his own flesh and blood?!

I calmed down after a few minutes in the church basement where, like at any Black funeral, there was already tables of soul food buffet set up for the reception. After the service and procession to Mount Olivet cemetery, I watched in a daze as they lowered my lil brother into the ground for good, while eryone else rushed back to the church to eat and go on talkin and mingling like we was at a fuckin wedding or something. I was too upset to think about food, but Tone wouldn't let me excuse myself, so I sat at the table with him, my sisters and my cryin-ass mama and stared at my hands the whole time. Erybody was quick to come by and offer they condolences, but nothin they said made me feel any better. They apologies wasn't gon bring my lil brother back. Neither was they prayers or they sympathy. And when I heard that the nigga who shot Cerrone had the nerve to still be livin after taking five bullets, I almost lost my got-damn mind. I was fucked up with erything by then. Fucked up with people. Fucked up with God. Fucked up with it all. I shouldna had so much darkness in my heart at such a young age. And my brother shouldna been dead. Not over some girl he ain't know. It just wasn't fair.

I ain't think I'd ever smile again. My heart was too heavy. I felt the same black abyss that welcomed me after I had Tink, calling to me again. Ery minute I spent in the apartment we shared, I saw shadows of Cerrone out the corner of my eye. I heard his voice in runnin water. I saw his smile in the sunset. My brother's memory haunted my thoughts, my dreams, and ery room in our apartment. Being there after a week without him got to be too much for me. I couldn't stay in that j'on no more. I packed up what I could fit in his car and did what I did any other time something hurt me. I ran away from it.

Goin to live with Mommy was outta the question. I couldn't face Cerrone's memory there, either. Twon been telling me since the funeral that I could lay low with him if I got tired of being in that apartment all alone. He knew me better than I knew myself cuz he also offered to put me up in my own place till I could pay for it on my own (just in case I was still runnin from him, too). I ain't see the point in wasting no money when he had a extra room for me and the kids to crash in. Besides, after losing his coke connect to a police raid and having a close call with the feds hisself, Twon put hustlin to the side for a while to work with his uncle full time. And since I quit the braid shop, it was more of a practical thing for us to move in together—at least till I got some Section 8 vouchers for my own space.

Livin in such close quarters with Twon wasn't easy. Part of me wanted to keep rejecting whatever comfort he offered. Another part of me wanted to crawl in that big bed of his and spill my guts bout erything—how fucked up I was without my brother and how fucked up I been without him. I wanted to talk to Twon so bad I couldn't concentrate on anything else, but I kept it bottled in. All my sadness, all my uneasiness—I stored it away in the same well where all my broken dreams and unfallen tears lay. It was what I did and how I coped. It was the way I got by till that day Twon got fed up with me moping around and watchin him from afar, and finally forced me to open up.

"How long you gon do 'dis shit?" he asked, standin between me and the balcony where I was goin to down yet another pint of Tanqueray. I been drinkin heavily and smokin like a chimney for a good month since my brother died. I had to be zooted just to get through the day.

"Do what?" I asked back.

"'Dis sleepwalkin shit you doin. Your eyes is open but your mind somewhere else," he said.

"Whatchu talkin bout? I'm woke."

I might not have been a zombie like I was the last time I was depressed, but anybody could see I was a shell of my former self.

"I'm woke," I repeated, and gave Twon a paper thin smile. He wasn't convinced, though.

"Look...I been tryna give you time to get through 'dis shit on your own cuz I know how you is, but you need some help. You slippin."

"Slippin? Nigga, I ain't *slippin* nowhere but out the door to drink 'dis muhfuckin Tanqueray," I sneered, tryna push past him. I knew he was telling the truth but I wasn't ready to hear it yet.

"Would you stop? C'mere." Twon tried to pull me back, but I wasn't having it.

"Get off me!" I yelled, yanking out of his grip and turning to face him in a fit of misdirected anger. "*Now* you wanna be up my ass! Mysterious how you ain't play me 'dis close when I was carryin your fuckin baby!" I exclaimed, furious at the first thing I could think to get mad at him for.

"I apologized for dat," Twon said calmly. "You know I wasn't ready for no more kids."

"So what? You think I was, you asshole? Get the fuck out my way!" I snapped. Twon ain't move, though.

"Damn, I gotta be all dat, 'doe? What, you gon hold dat shit against me forever?" Twon asked, stepping closer so I couldn't get past without touching him.

"Yes," I spat.

"You stupid, 'den."

"Stupid? Muhfu—"

"I was 'dare for you *ery* time you needed me after Keyjuan was born," Twon cut me off, hotly jabbing his finger in my chest. "Name one time I ain't do for you after dat shit. Name one time!"

I tried to think of a good example but I couldn't. Twon more than made up for the way he acted when I was pregnant. He baby-sat, he came out the pockets without me asking, and he spent time with Man-Man like he was his own. He made a point to get to know my family since he was a part of it now, too. He even opened up his home to me and all my problems. Twon did erything he was poseda do as a father and a man, but I was still mad at him cuz it was easier than confronting the loss of my brother.

"Dat's only cuz you was guilty!" I accused Twon anyway.

"Guilty? You know how many niggas make a babies and roll out forever? Or how many niggas got so many kids 'day cain't keep track of 'day names, 'day birthdays, or who 'day muhva is? Same niggas who buy 'dayselves gators and diamonds and don't give 'day baby mama shit? So what's guilty? Fucka guilty. Only reason I still fuck witchu is cuz I realized what I'd be losin if I left you like dat," Twon ranted. "I done said I was sorry, young. I'm sorry and I was wrong, aight? If I ain't love you, I wouldn't be able to admit dat."

I almost fell out at the sound of that shit. In all the time that we'd been together, after all the staring into eachother's eyes and falling asleep in eachother's arms, not once did the L-word ever come up. It was something that was more feelable than speakable between us. But now that he said it, I ain't know what to do.

"What?" I snapped, all flabbergasted. I couldn't believe my ears.

"I said...You heard what I said, young. I...I love you," Twon repeated nervously with somewhat of a sigh. I looked in his eyes to see if he was just talkin out the side of his neck to make me feel better, but I could tell he wasn't. There was a scared truth all over his face, like he was just as reluctant to put his heart out there as I was. Shocked the shit outta me, boy. Made me wanna hug him up and break down all my defenses and tell him the same thing, then thank him for being there and putting up with my mentally unstable ass. Made me wanna cry tears of joy cuz he finally said the three words we both been holding on the tips of our tongues since we first hooked up. But I couldn't. Call me stupid, or scared, or whatever, but I couldn't risk more heartbreak. I was hurting too bad already.

"What the fuck do love gotta do wit anything?" I asked after a long stretch of silence with a cold, purposely unfeeling glare that Twon responded to with a pained frown. I could almost see his heart drop down to his socks, and no sooner than I realized I really hurt him, I regretted saying the shit. Twon blinked at me, dumbfounded for a second, before he shook his head and took a step back like *he* was tryna get away from *me* now.

"Dat's hi you feel?" he asked softly, lookin down at his feet where his ego musta lay.

"Yeah, dat's how I feel," I told him, even though I really didn't. I loved Twon. And I needed him more than words could express. I needed him in my life to fill up my empty spaces and be one of the inspirations for me to keep on livin. I knew I was being foolish by turning him away, but I was feeling so fucked up that I had to make him feel it, too. Misery loves company.

"I'm leavin in'na mornin," I said suddenly, pushing him out the way so I could go outside. The drama queen in me wanted Twon to stop me, to object, but he ain't make no moves. Not until I was halfway out onto the balcony, did he grab me by one of my jeans pockets and start pulling me back towards him. I wanted to fight my way free just for the sake of goin against the grain, but I ain't have no more fight left in me. It was gone. And once again, Twon was there to pick up the pieces and save me from my own weakness. I hated myself for needing him like that, but the Teflon tower of my very being was starting to bend. Who better to set me straight than the only man I hated and loved the most? Who better to be there for me than the one man who told me he loved me and meant it from the bottom of his heart? I couldn't resist no more. Wasn't no way. Limp, weak, confused, and flat out emotionally drained, I succumbed to his pull and melted into the hug that would ultimately catch me before I fell for good.

"You ain't goin nowhere," Twon whispered into the top of my hair. "I'on care whatchu say. You ain't leavin me."

"I wasn't really tryna go anyway," I whispered back into his shoulder, letting my tortured tears escape onto his shirt. That's when Twon hugged me tighter, the way you would hug somebody you loved. Like you wanted to become a part of them, like if you could help it, you would never let go of them. It was all I needed to stop holding back.

From that day on, I was a totally different person. Twon helped me get through my grief and established what would become the official beginning of our relationship. He was there for me constantly and he loved me unselfishly. That in itself was more than anybody had ever did for me.

It wasn't no overnight transformation, but I got better. Eventually. I woke up ery day thinking bout my brother, but I still managed to finish my lessons with Trisha and pass the state board on my first try in October. I coulda applied for a job at any shop a lil closer to home, but I stayed on with Trisha cuz if it wasn't for her, I'd probly still be out there cutting dope and shoplifting. To celebrate, Twon took me to Atlantic City and treated me to a five star hotel room, two nights in a row of steak and shrimp dinners, and more nuts than I could count on both hands and feet. Because of all the shit that happent over the past year, I wasn't busting at the seams with joy or nothin, but I was happier than I been in a long time, and more content in my relationship with Twon than I could ever remember.

Tink's approaching birthday reminded me it had been almost two whole years since me and Twon fell apart. Now look at us. Tragedy, distance, and true understanding of what it meant to love somebody all played they part in bringing us back together. It was a feeling like finding the match to a sock that been lost behind the dryer for months. Relief and a sense of completion was the best way to describe it. Twon kept hinting that he was gon hafta marry me if I kept cooking him barbecue wings that fell off the bone and wetting him up with my honey two-three times a day. I ain't think he was serious, though. Not until Christmas rolled around and he surprised me with the keys to my gold '76 Monte Carlo and a white gold engagement ring. I liked to fell out the damn chair when he got on one knee at Christmas dinner at his Nanna's house and proposed to me. I couldn't hold back my tears or excitement when he put that one karat rock on my finger and let it be known in fronta his whole family that he wanted to be with me forever.

Boy, life was something else. It was one big circle of delight, disaster, and a whole racka crazy shit in between. At eighteen, I felt like I done did fifty years of livin. I came a long way from playing double dutch and dragging my lil sisters around with me to my friends' houses. Long way from Cerrone and Pookie beaming water balloons at our heads and karate chopping us in the backa our necks. Long way from stealing erything I could get my hot little hands on and arguing with my mother just because.

Shit, you might could say me and Mommy was actually cool now. She changed a lot after she got through the worst of her grieving. We was even speaking over the phone at least once a week. It ain't like we was having no two-hour long sistagirl conversations or nothin, but for me and Mommy, asking eachother how our day been was big progress. It was awkward at first but losing Cerrone really did change the way we got along. An odd comfort settled between us, a comfort that finally allowed me to confront her about why she was so hard on me all these years. Mommy ain't really have a good reason for being such a bitch, but I lumped up her explanation as tough love. As the oldest of her brood, my mother expected a lot outta me. Ery time I made a mistake or went against her rules and set a bad example for the younger ones, she held it against me. I guess she figured doing things her way would turn me around. And even though it was extreme, when she put me out on my ass with a baby in each arm to worry about, she was just tryna teach me a lesson bout responsibility. Mommy's biggest wish was for me to have a better life than hers. She wanted me to go to college, travel the world and strive for more without being strapped down by a buncha needy kids like she was. And when I made it clear I wasn't gon do that, she put me out the nest to go build one of my own. She called it making me sleep in the bed I made.

I preferred to call it child neglect, but whatever. I guess she kinda made sense.

We never really got into why she favored my brother more and how that shit affected me. Mommy shortchanged me on a lotta love and understanding in the past, and I definitely fell short of a lotta her expectations, but even she had to admit I turned out aight to have had such a tumultuous upbringing. I traded thieving and runnin the streets for a calmer life. I stopped hating Twon, I stopped hating my mother, and even though he was still in my heart ery waking minute of the day, I stopped thinking so hard about Cerrone. I started seeing past fast money and material things. I was through with begging, scheming, and pulling some quick shit in order to feed my kids. It wasn't bout gettin high all day and hanging out with my friends no more. I had to focus on building a career and a marriage and raising up two bad-ass boys in a era where morals and compassion was things of the past. Feeling inspired to share my newfound wisdom, I started going around Mommy's ery weekend to keep a eye on my sisters and make sure they wasn't gettin into none of the shit I did at they age. And I tried to read to my sons and teach em something new ery day so they'd grow up to be better than both they fathers. It was a time of healing, growing, and tying up loose ends. A time to look forward and remind myself that long as I stayed focused and remembered all that I learned, erything was gon be aight.

I got inside Krys' head that day we got smoked out on the balcony. I coulda left it at that, with just our lil talk or whatever. But I had her open now. And there was a lot more I wanted Krys to know. I had literally a week of summer left with my cousin and there was still a million things I wanted to show her. She ain't think college was worth it, but I knew some people who could assure her it was. She thought strippin was easy money but I knew girls who could give her the uncensored truth about what it really took to make a dollar. I wanted her to see the end results of that life she thought was better than the one she had. And I knew just how to do it.

Georgia Avenue Day was the last Saturday in August and I was excited as shit to hit the city and see my people take over the strip. Erybody who lived anywhere remotely close to Georgia Ave was gon be there. I'm talkin from Mo County to Uptown to down 'round my cousin Sweet Nika's neighborhood in Southwest. Damn near erybody I knew was gon show face and I couldn't wait! It was the perfect opportunity to see folks I ain't seen in years, and introduce Krys to all the offbeat characters in my life. Pookie, Syco, Biggums—they was all blowin up my phone that mornin askin me when I was comin down. I was anxious to holla at all my long lost play family, and even more anxious for they crazy asses to meet my lil cousin. The lives we lived so far spawned enough wisdom to fill a book. Hopefully my friends could give Krys some perspective. Or at least help me show her that the street life was something to get *out of*, not *into*.

I wanted to be comfortable and cute, so I put on this gray Shooter's skirt set made outta extra soft sweatpants material and slid into my cleanest pair of Princesses. Krys tried to joan and say I was a bamma for still rockin Reeboks, but fuck it. Nothin else matched and I knew I'd look silly wearing hi-top Keds with the laces wrapped around my ankles like she had. After a hour of primping and making sure we looked good as good could get, me and Krys hit the liquor store and picked up a couple friends to come along for the ride. Krys hooked up with Iyania and I ran out Trinity College to scoop up Delmi. After a quick run through the car wash, we finally rolled out to the city.

Perfect summer weather and a feel goodness in the air set a vibe that brought back memories of outdoor festivals past. Between the Caribbean Festival, Unifest, Stone Soul Picnic, the Black Family Reunion, and Howard Homecoming, Georgia Avenue Day was my favorite outdoor event in D.C. It was a place where you was guaranteed to see the young and not-so-young came out to show off. All you seen was shiny cars, fresh gear, and characters of all kinds spittin they "A" game to the opposite sex. Anybody could expect to catch a rap on Georgia Avenue Day. Unfortunately, you could also expect some typa violence to go down by nightfall. It ain't been a Georgia Avenue Day since '96 for that very reason. It's rare for my people to get together without beefin. I'on know, we just got this code that say we gotta go hard at all times. Even if you a cool muhfucka, there's always someone out there ready to test you and bring out your dark side. It was a way of thinkin that caused a lotta good clubs and events to get shut down over the years. It was almost expected for somebody to get bucked at before sunset, but I was determined to have me some fun anyhow.

Traffic was thick from Twon's old neighborhood on down, so soon as I found a good spot around Kenyon Street, I parked my car on the Ave and opted to walk through the rush hour-like gridlock.

"Glad I wore flat shoes," Krys complained as we made our way a few blocks down towards Howard University. Erybody who was anybody would be posted up down there at the McDonald's that served as the unofficial 7th Street landmark, so of course we was pressed to get there.

"F'real," Iyania agreed. "I'm bout to ride out wit one uh' them in a minute," she continued as a line of youngins on Ninja bikes in ery color of the rainbow zoomed up the Avenue along the center line.

"They fast as a mug. I'ma laugh if yo' ass fall off," I joked.

Biggums chirped me on my Nextel a couple minutes later and told me to meet her on Hobart Street, where she was waiting with Syco and Pookie at her cousin's house. It was just like old times when we finally made it there. I was so glad to see erybody that I couldn't stop smiling. It wasn't till then that it became painfully obvious how long I been away and how much I missed the people I grew up with. Besides Syco, Pookie, and Biggums, there was a couple other youngins from Trinidad with em, some that was friends with my brother. It felt great to see erybody, even if all of us wasn't there to enjoy it.

We stayed at Biggums' cousin's house for a long while, just sippin, smokin, jokin, and reminiscing on good times. When that got boring, we relocated to the steps at Banneker rec center to get a better view of the scene, and kept eachother in stitches joanin on ery busted-ass car or person that went by. Aside from that, ery five minutes, it seemed like somebody I knew was walkin past or ridin by in the traffic and stopping to say wsup. I was never more happy to be in the city, never more glad to see old friends, never more elated to be with the only folks I held closer to me than most the muhfuckas I shared bloodlines with. I never thought I'd miss being a kid, or that I'd long for the days when shootin the shit on somebody's front porch was my idea of fun. Never thought I'd regret fallin outta touch with the many acquaintances who filled in the gaps when my main homies wasn't there. It kinda sucks how life changes so fast you never get to appreciate the good times while they're goin on. I missed my old neighborhood and erybody I grew up with. Went without sayin that I missed my brother the most. Damn, I wish Cerrone was still here. I wish I could rewind time and take ery day slow enough to treasure each minute with him and erybody else we had fun with.

Thinkin bout all that and aching for the past made me feel even more for Krys. She was at the prime of her young life, at the age where most of her peers ain't have no bills or babies or bullshit to deal with. She shoulda been enjoying them days while they lasted. I knew from experience that that kinda freedom don't last too long. Once you're grown, you're grown. You never get to feel anything so true and pure, so fresh, exciting, or new as you do when you young. I wanted Krys to understand that. I wanted her to be the carefree kid I never got to be, to have all the fun and take advantage of all the opportunities I never had. So in between hearing stories that took me and my friends down Memory Lane, I tried to throw in a lesson or two. Delmi told tell her bout college and all the doors that would open once she got her CPA. And I had to remind Krys of my struggle from being so young with two kids. Biggums and I both went on and on bout all the bammas we grew up with who was dead or in jail from gettin too deep in the streets. And just listening to Syco slurring and gettin stuck was enough to convince her drugs could fuck your whole shit up. I knew we all helped give my cousin some insight on what I been tryna tell her all along. And I was sure hearing it from a stranger would help it stick in her brain. There was one more person I still wanted her to talk to, though.

I pulled out my phone and hit Dhonni up for what had to be the tenth time all day. We was poseda hook up and put one in the air for the occasion, but I needed her around to be the icing on Krys' cake while all that talking was fresh in her mind. Me and Dhonni done been through a lotta shit over the years, but aside from it all, youngin was still my girl. Couldn't nothin change that for good. It's a long story as to how we got to be cool again, but for now, I was more concerned with finding her than dwelling on that shit.

"Damn, slim, kh'I get dat back?" I fussed after yet another hungry dude grabbed a handfulla my ass as we tried to squeeze by. We was all headed to Banneker field where BYB was gon be doing an outdoor show. In true D.C. nigga fashion, bammas was taking advantage of the crowd and grabbin ery nice ass that passed. I was so useta bold moves like that, I couldn't even get mad no more. Home wouldn't be home if I wasn't gettin groped by a stranger in public.

"'Dis shit is startin to blow me," Krys complained, cuttin through the same buncha dudes I just did. If this had been earlier in the summer, she probly woulda been glad to get harassed. But now, the disturbed look on her face screamed that she ain't wanna be touched at all. I guess after what happent to her a couple weeks ago, what was just friendly flirting probly felt like a serious violation.

"Oh, my God, Shai! Hurry up! You know I got a skirt on!" Delmi fussed, pulling her long, wavy ponytail outta some hawkin-ass nigga's hand.

"Wsup, Butt-Butt! I like your hair," cuz called after her.

"Damn! Muhfuckas ack like 'day just got outta jail and shit," Iyania laughed. "Is it always like 'dis?"

I ain't answer her cuz I was too busy laughing at the dude in fronta me hollin out "skeeza" and gettin ery girl with a "eesha"-sounding name to turn around and look back at him. Slim and his friends was gettin a real kick outta making them girls answer his insult like that. It reminded me of some shit Pookie and my brother would do.

"Is we all t'geva?" I asked, checking briefly to make sure my cousin and all my friends was still with me. We practically had to hold hands to keep from gettin separated.

"Right behind you, dog pound!" Biggums called. "Hurrup, 'doe! 'Day hittin my song!"

We pushed through all the people to go "Shake Them Haters Off". It was like trudging through silly putty tryna make our way to the crowded high school football field where the go-go was all the way live. We was just about to be at the stage when the sudden rapid fire pop of a semi-automatic weapon broke up the party mood. Just like that, erybody went from socializing and walking around all friendly-like, to runnin like the feds jumped out. It looked like a got-damn stampede, the way erybody took off in one direction at the same time. Muhfuckas was running blindly and trampling anyone who ain't move quick enough. It all happened so fast I barely knew what was goin on. My instincts told me to get the fuck out the way, though.

"What happent?" Krys asked after I snatched her and Iyania behind a brick wall across the street. In all the confusion, we got separated from the resta our crew.

"You ain't hea' them gunshots?" I screeched.

"Dat's what dat was?"

"Yeah, fool. Whatchu think it was?"

"I'on know."

Krys' voice trembled so much when she answered me that I had to look at her to make sure she wasn't crying.

"You scared?" I asked, already knowin that she was. It was obvious the way her eyes suddenly got all big and worried.

"*Sheeeiiit*, I done been in worse shoot-outs 'den dat," I told her. "Been plenty uh' times I ain't think my black ass was gon walk away. Dat wasn't nuffin 'doe, Babygirl. It wasn't even all dat close to us. You be aight. . .Ay, you hea' me?"

Krys snapped outta her shocked stupor and watched with the resta us as another wave of panic overtook the crowd and erybody took off running again.

"Damn, young! Why Black people cain't never get t'geva witout shootin?" Iyania fussed.

"Dat's just how it be out hea'," I answered with a shrug. I wasn't the least bit shocked. The worst had happened, just like I thought it would. Krys, on the other hand, looked like she was bout to pee her pants.

"Ay, Krys, you aight?" I asked my cousin again.

She still ain't say nuffin. I started to press her more, but my phone rang. It was Dhonni. Since it was obvious another Georgia Avenue Day was gon be cut short, we decided to hook up back around the old neighborhood. The afterparty was gon be in fronta our building on Holbrook Street. I two-way Biggums and them to let em know the plans, then gathered up the girls.

"C'mon, y'all, we bout d' dip," I told Krys and Iyania. "Bodeens bout d' be thick as shit flies out hea'. It's time d' go."

"To where?" Delmi asked.

"My folks house in Norfeass. C'mon…Ay, Krys. Krys!"

My lil cousin stood uneasily and looked around all nervous like she was expecting more gunshots to pop off. I guess that shit rattled her nerves more than I thought at first. Babygirl was really scared, and for real-for real, a part of me was glad for it. After all she seen and heard today, I knew Krys was more aware of reality than she ever been. She'd understand just how real life could get after she talked to Dhonni, too. My girl was gon put the cherry on top. The shit I wanted Dhonni to tell Krys was probly gon blow her mind clear outta this world. I knew cuz when she told me, it blew the hell outta minez.

"C'mon, Krys," I said, shaking my head and motioning for her and Iyania to follow me. "I got some'my I want you d' meet."

CHAPTER NINETEEN

When the year 2001 rolled around, me and Twon was ready to move. Between child support payments to Rayel, his grandma's bills and our bills, Twon wasn't ready to jump out there and buy a house yet. His pockets wasn't quite right for all that, especially since his coke connect got busted. On toppa that, he got arrested twice for loitering (luckily, he was clean both times) and he wasn't feelin his alley set-up no more. With all of us depending on him, he knew it'd be selfish to risk taking over somebody else's block. Ridin dirty was risky, too, since the cops knew his face and had an idea of what he was all about. His instincts managed to keep him a free man all these years, so he listened to them and decided to chill for a while. Unless we was really in a bind and his legitimate job couldn't cover it, Twon decided to keep his hands clean. I was especially thankful for that cuz the last thing I needed was another baby father behind bars if worst came to worst again.

As a result, money was a lot slower, but we made do. I finally got a housing voucher that had us paying next to nothing for a two bedrrom apartment. We found a decent lil spot in Forestville that, although it was 'hood, had enough safety of the suburbs appeal to satisfy me. Forest Creek wasn't exactly Mayberry or nothin, but at least niggas out there ain't shoot up shit in broad daylight like they did in D.C. Just like when I moved out Wheaton, I felt strange in Maryland's quiet spaciousness. But I was through with ducking bullets and constantly looking over my shoulder. Cerrone woulda called me soft for wanting to hide out in "the country" as he called it, but it was his death and Smoke's death and countless other homicides that inspired me to raise my sons in a less hectic place than the Dirty Diamond City.

Trisha got me a hook-up to work at the hair salon in P.G. Plaza so I could be a lil closer to home. It was around this time when Aunt Josie called me with Krys' drama, and feeling inspired to help a young wildchild out, I agreed to let her stay with me for the summer. It was also around this time when I got the most unexpected phone call of my life.

"*Hun-nay!* Telephone!" Twon called from the kitchen. I finished tucking Man-Man into bed and jogged for the cordless in our bedroom.

"Yeah, wsup?" I asked breathlessly, cradling the phone between my neck and shoulder.

"Suga Baby! Wsup witchu, girl?"

"Who 'dis?" I frowned. It been a long time since anybody called me by my Suga Sweet Huneyz nickname. Biggums was my only friend from the old crew I had left, and she just called me Shai.

"It's me, nut. You done forgot my voice already?" the girl asked with a familiar giggle. I'on know who this broad was, but she sounded a lot like...

"Kiss? Is dat you?"

"The one and only," Dhonni answered. "Wsup, girl? Hi you been?"

"Chillin. Cain't complain. Wsup witchu, 'doe? Hi you get my number?"

"Miz Brenda gave it to me. I hope you don't mind."

"Nah, it's cool," I told her, even though I wondered why in Bob's name Dhonni went outta her way like that to holla at me. I hope she wasn't calling to tell me somebody else done died.

"I know you probly wonderin why I'm callin you," Dhonni said, knowin me all too well. I let my confused silence answer her. "Well...I was just tryna catch up witchu, see hi you doin. So wsup? What's happ'nin?"

"Same ol' shit," I answered suspiciously.

"Yeah? Well, whatchu doin t'night? Kh you come out and chill?" Dhonni asked in a suddenly serious tone of voice. I let another confused silence pass. I wasn't sure what that girl was up to. Was she tryna set me up and rob me or beat my ass or something? I just ain't know. Dhonni been coming from left field for a couple years now.

"I really need d' talk to you," she told me, still gravely serious. I started to say hell no cuz I wasn't bout to willingly walk into nobody's trap, but something in her voice was pulling me. She sounded like the old Dhonni beggin to confide in me like she useta when we was kids. We may have been on non-speaking terms now, but the tightness of our friendship in the past wouldn't let me say no.

"Aight," I agreed. "You wanna meet me somewhere or is I'm pickin you up?"

"I ain't drivin, joe. Come meet me at my muhva house."

"Aight," I agreed again, uneasily. "I'll call you when I'm outside."

I ain't know what Dhonni had planned, but if she tried any slick shit, I had a switchblade tucked away in one of my socks for her ass. I put on some chill clothes I'd be able to run or fight in and made my way down to the city. Soon as I passed the cemetery where my brother was buried and entered the unmarked outskirts of Trinidad, I started to feel like a soldier coming home after a long war. I couldn't tell you the last time I been back around the way. I ain't have no reason to go. Except for Pookie and Miz Darlene, there wasn't really nobody I was all that pressed to see. Biggums moved to Potomac Gardens with this girl she met around there, and after Foots healed from the gunshot wound that clipped his right side, he went off to Morgan State in B-More and ain't been back since. Syco was still around, and just as strange as ever, but I ain't kick it with him hard as I useta cuz he been turning into something like a junkie ery since my brother died. That nigga went from woo-bobs to dippas and unstable-looking to zombie status. There was still a few muhfuckas I liked to see ery once in a while, but for the most part, I stayed outta Trinidad. It was fulla too many memories.

I pulled up in fronta my old building and called Dhonni to let her know I was outside. She came downstairs dressed fresh to death as usual in a short, black dress, crazy legs stockings, and flat boots with a long, black Coogi sweater duster to match. She hopped in the car after circling it twice and sicin how nice it was, then we exchanged awkward greetings. I ain't know where to go and she ain't have no suggestions, so we just rode around the way, opting to sight-see and make small talk till one of us got hungry or bored and decided to go back in the house. We rapped for a long time bout my kids and the old crew and all the fun we useta have when we was younger. We talked about how much the 'hood was changing now that the ol' lumpy head, bowtie-wearing Mayor was expanding Downtown and gentrifying a ton of white folks to the inner city — even on the fringes of Trinidad. We talked about erything 'cept why we stopped speaking and what sparked us chillin now. Erything I thought about Dhonni tryna set me up went right out the window. Years apart had changed both of us, but Dhonni was basically the same ol' Dhonni, just as loud and spirited and smart-mouthded as ever. I knew her well enough to know she had good intentions, but the whole time we talked, I could tell she was holding something back.

"So, wsup, Kiss? Whatchu wanted d' see me for? We ain't hung out in I'on-know-how-long," I said when I couldn't take the mystery no more.

"Ha, I know, right?" Dhonni smiled wryly. "Yeah, you got wit Twon and I started chillin wit Baby and shit ain't been the same since. You still wit Twon, ain'tchu? I see dat ring on y' finger and shit."

"Yeah, we still together. We gettin married next year," I beamed. Just the sound of his name and knowin how happy I been since we put the bullshit aside made me giddy as a kid on a sugar high.

"Dat's good to hear. You know I'on chill wit Baby no more, right?" Dhonni said.

"Nah, but dat's good to hear, too. I'on like the way you act when you wit her," I said bluntly.

"I'on like it eiva," Dhonni sighed. "Dat bitch is out 'dare, young... Lemme shut up, 'doe, cuz I was right out 'dare wit her."

Dhonni looked like she wanted to tell me something important for a second, but she changed the subject instead.

"You still smoke, right?" she asked.

"All muhfuckin day, homie. Why, you got dat?"

"Yeah. You gotsta blow 'dis blueberry wit me."

"If it's anything like dat watermelon 'day be havin out Sowfeass, you betta roll up, nigga," I laughed, and elbowed her playfully in the arm. I flipped through the CD book behind my seat and put in some smoke and ride music for us to get high to. After a half a J and being serenaded by Devin the Dude, me and Dhonni was in the zone.

"Dat shit taste good, young. *And* it's some grizza," I commented, licking the sweet, fruity taste from the flavored marijuana off my lips.

"I kh tell, the way you was coughin. Dat's dat fire, joe. My boy stay wit some green. *And* I gets it for free."

"You still big pimpin, hunh, man?" I chuckled. She musta been doing something cuz ery since that dumb cowboy of a President cheated his way into office, it's been a weed drought like shit. Wasn't nobody I knew tryna come up off no decent bags for free, and if they was, it was some bush.

"You know the ol' girl still be rappin niggas up," Dhonni smiled. "But

I done chilled out a lot, 'doe. I'on even be gettin at niggas like dat no more. I'm tired uh' playin dat role," she sighed with a faraway look on her face. She started to say more on it but decided to roll up another J instead.

"Ay, 'member when we was little?" Dhonni asked after a while, reachin for her Nascar lighter. "And Pookie and Cerrone would spray us wit them water guns all the time?"

"Yeah," I smiled sadly.

"And Cerrone would fill up them water balloons and sneak up on us..." her voice trailed off. "Then *whap!* We standin 'dare lookin all wet and stupid."

"'Day useta make me *too* mad wit dat shit."

"'Member dat time we got smacked and went to the playground and was makin dat song on the slidin board? It was dat day Foots and youngin name Leon got in a fight cuz Leon said Foots was so short he had d' buy all his clothes at Baby Gap."

"Yeah. Dat's when 'day started talkin bout makin the go-go band," I chuckled with tears in my eyes.

"I miss dat nigga," Dhonni said, gettin all teary-eyed, too. "Even when me and you wasn't cool, Cerrone would come to the house and we just chill together, young. Be sittin outside joanin on people. Gettin smacked and watch cartoons and shit. Dat was my boy. He was like my bruhva f'real."

I bit my lips together and nodded, forcing myself to swallow the lump in my throat. I was still getting useta the idea of Cerrone being gone.

"Shai, I'm sorry I wasn't 'dare for you like I shoulda been when he died," Dhonni said suddenly, then paused. "I'on know. I was on some uhva shit. Tell the truth, 'doe, I ain't been the same since Cerrone got shot. We ain't hea' long enough to be trippin off some dumb shit, y'know? One day you hea', next day you six feet under."

We both got quiet again.

"Whatchu think happen when you die?" Dhonni asked finally. "You ever think about dat shit?"

"Yeah," I admitted. I thought about it a lot ever since I was ten and this older boy I useta like got shot and killed by the police for running when they tried to arrest him. I liked to think he was a ghost, looking down on me and following me around like a guardian angel or some shit.

But after a while of pretending I felt his presence and realizing I really wasn't feeling nothin, I came to the conclusion that once you're dead, you're dead. Ain't no Heaven, ain't no Hell, ain't no Purgatory, limbo, or any of the resta that made-up afterlife shit. Death ain't nothin but being sleep without dreaming. It's like one big void in time and consciousness that you ain't even aware of, just like the blank before you was born.

"I think about it a lot," Dhonni told me. She took another pull off the J and turned to look me in the face. "I'ma die one day," she said in all seriousness, her weed-chinky eyes full to the brim with tears. I got kinda uncomfortable cuz I ain't know where the fuck she was coming from with all this emotion.

"We all gon die," I shrugged. "Ain't shit. Just make the most uh' your life while you live it."

"I ain't got dat much life to live," she sighed again. I got the feeling Dhonni wanted to tell me something but, once more, she was quiet.

"Whatchu talkin bout, Dhonni?" I prodded. A long stretch of silence passed with Dhonni sniffling and wiping her eyes like she was crying.

"Man…I just fount out some shit," she told me, and paused again. "Went to the doctor a couple days ago to see why I kept gettin 'deez real bad yeast infections, right…I'm thinkin it's the soap I use or some shit. Some'n slight like dat."

Dhonni got quiet again.

"So what 'day say?" I asked. She was drivin me crazy with all this suspense.

"I got the sauce, young," Dhonni sputtered, wiping away more tears.

All of a sudden my ears was ringin and my heart was poundin so loud I could hear it. I thought for a second that maybe I ain't hear her right. She couldna said she had the sauce.

"You say you got a dog?" I asked, turning down the music.

"Nah, I said I got the sauce. HIV."

Oh, my fuckin God. I looked at the J we been sharing and wondered if her spit was gonna infect me, too. I looked over her plump thighs and chubby cheeks, tryna see if she lost any weight. Then, down at her hands and the exposed skin on her neck to see if she had any big, ugly lesions. But I ain't see nothin unusual. Dhonni looked as healthy as she always did, maybe even a couple pounds healthier since the last time I seent her.

"Don't look at me like dat. I ain't sick yet," she told me, watching me scrutinize her with my eyes.

I tried to act normal after that, but I couldn't help but to feel kinda funny. I listened as Dhonni told me how chillin with Baby went from partyin and fun to strippin and trickin. I listened to her tell me bout all the dudes they met and manipulated with they bodies to get money from em. How gettin drunk and ran through started to feel less and less wrong the more she did it. How E-pills got her loose and made her feel incredible no matter how many unidentified dicks been in her over the course of one night. How her thirst for money and material things pushed her to sliding down the pole at different strip clubs where she hooked up after-hours for private parties and did any kind of sexual favor that filled her pockets with money, yet had a way of making her feel empty after it was all over. I listened to her tell me bout her constant trips to the clinic to clear up some burn or itch the night before had left her with. How she woke up in the middle of the night sometimes on toppa wet sheets covered in cold sweats that she knew meant the worst of the worst had happened to her. I watched her wipe away frustrated tears as she recalled where she went wrong, and how she realized too late that there was more to life than dressing good and riding in some nigga's big, fancy car. Then I held her as she wept in agony knowing there was no way she could get outta the death sentence her own foolishness had locked her into. AIDS ain't have no cure and it ain't seem to be one in sight, and if you couldn't afford the medications, then you was short. Getting diagnosed with HIV in those days meant that within five to ten years, your ass was grass — no questions, no exceptions.

Dhonni cried her eyes out that night and I cried right along with her. Not only cuz I knew how close I was to being in her shoes, or how sorry I felt knowin all the sickness and pill cocktails she'd hafta put up with from now on. Not cuz I knew she was gon spend the best years of her life waiting to die. I cried cuz I realized this cruel saga we called life had done it again. It created roads and situations where somebody else I loved ended up dead at the end.

If I ever go to another Labor Day cookout, it'll be none too soon. Mommy was blowin the shit outta me, calling my phone ery five minutes to remind me bout some other stupid thing for the barbecue she was throwing at her new house in Largo today. *Don't forget to bring the hamburger rolls, chop up the potatoes small enough for her potato salad and put paprika on toppa the deviled eggs.* Do this, do that. Get this, get that. Nag, nag, nag! That woman was gettin on my nerves so bad I couldn't even think straight.

"Got-damnit, Ma!" I exclaimed as the cordless phone rang in my lap again. I was willing to bet it was her calling again even though I just hung up with her less than two minutes ago. I picked up without checking the Caller ID first and let out a big, frustrated sigh.

"Yeah?" I asked into the receiver.

"You have a collect call from…"

Damn, as if I wasn't vexed enough. Dartanyan was the last person in the world I felt like talking to right then. All he gon do is say something smart and blow me that much more.

"Whatchu want?" I asked after accepting the charges and his line clicked in.

"Hello to you, too. Fuck wrong witchu?" Dartanyan snapped back.

"Nuffin, man. My muhva stressin me out over this damn cookout she havin, so…I just ain't in the mood for no shit right now, aight."

"Well, I wasn't eiva till you came at me like dat," Dartanyan replied after a short while, his voice somewhat hurt. I started to feel bad for a second cuz I really ain't have no reason to go on him the way I did.

"Aight, aight. My bad. Wsup? You wanna talk to Man-Man?" I asked.

"You tryna get ridda me already? What, I cain't talk to you? *Dat nigga* got a problem wit me talkin to my baby muhva or some'n?"

"He ain't got shit to do wit shit," I replied, wondering just how long Dartanyan was gon hate on the fact that I was with Twon and ten times happier than I ever was with his ass.

"I cain't tell. Fuck, you ack like you'on love me no more ery since *dat nigga* came in'na picture."

"Didn't I say I wasn't in no mood for no shit right now, Dartanyan? Say whatchu gotta say or go back to beatin your meat, or whateva the fuck it is you do to kill time out 'dare."

Dartanyan was silent for a while. I felt bad again, cuz where he was locked up at, jerkin off and playin cards probly was the only things he did when them slavers ain't have him cleaning up roads, landscaping and digging ditches out there in the desert. I guess I should mention Dartanyan ain't in D.C. jail no more. Ain't been there for almost a year now. Like a lotta youngins around here who got caught up in the system off some fed charges, Dartanyan got shipped off to a private prison. Ery since Lorton shut down, D.C. niggas been getting shipped all over the country to serve they time, and Dartanyan wasn't no exception. Why they sent him to the Arizona Detention Center insteada Clarksburg or Jessup, I'll never know. I guess it had a lot to do with the way he was out D.C. Jail wreckin bammas and kirkin on C.O.'s ery time somebody so much as looked at him wrong. Dartanyan ain't start doing that shit till I stopped visiting him and had Tink, and I know it's cuz he having a hard time dealing with me not being in his corner no more.

"Dartanyan?" I asked into the muffled silence on the other end of the receiver.

"I'm still hea'," he mumbled.

"Whatchu want, man? I'm on my way out the door in a couple minutes."

"Fuck it now, young. I was just tryna see hi you was doin, but since you got a attitude, neh'mind dat shit. Where my boy at?"

I took the phone away from my ear and listened down the hall to see if Twon was still getting Man-Man and Tink dressed. From the sounds of it, the three of em was still digging around in the boys' messy closet looking for the two pairs of American flag Chucks I wanted em to wear.

"He puttin some clothes on. You wanna wait or call him back?"

"Uhhh…"

"Sometime today, Dartanyan. Whatchu wanna do?" I snapped, thinking of all the food I still had to drag downstairs and pack up in Twon's car. I ain't have time to be bojanglin with this fool.

"I'on care, man. Do whatchu gotta do," Dartanyan sulked with a desperate sigh.

I couldn't see his face, but I could almost imagine the regret written all over it. I could hear it in his voice. He ain't hafta say shit for me to know Dartanayn regretted falling into the same trap a lotta niggas did, where he got caught up in a game with no long-term reward. He was lucky enough to still have his life, unlike my man Smoke, but he ended up losing his freedom in the process. If it wasn't for the drug game, me and my kids probly woulda went without a lot more than we did, so I can't knock it completely. I still hate the shit, though. I done seen people on the giving and receiving end of drugs get they lives all fucked up with they families tore apart by addiction, death, and prison. I bet Baby and Precious wouldna turned out so fucked up in the head if they mama ain't get strung out on that shit and do what she did to em. I bet Smoke woulda found something else to do with his life if he still had it. And I bet Dartanyan woulda eventually saved up some money and opened that T-shirt shop he always wanted. Instead they all caught a bad deal, Dartanyan's situation being the worst in my eyes. Damn shame that after all the shit our ancestors went through tryna get outta chains, him and about a million other niggas found a way to put theyselves back in em less than ten generations after slavery.

"Hold up for a minute. I'ma get Man," I offered, then yelled for my oldest boy to come talk to his father.

Man-Man bounced out to where I was in the kitchen wearing one Chuck on his foot and the other on his hand. He took the phone with his free hand and turned his back to me.

"Wsup, Pops?" he said all serious into the mouthpiece. I chuckled a lil bit at how much Man-Man was already starting to inherit Dartanyan's mannish attitude. My baby was barely five, but you woulda swore he was four times that, the way he carried it. I thought about how all the crazy shit I had him going through as a baby was probly to blame for that, and felt a lil guilty for forcing him to grow up faster than he needed to. He got it honestly, though.

"Put that uh' shoe on when you done," I ordered before strolling off to give em some privacy.

I grabbed the two baking sheets of deviled eggs I spent all morning making and took em downstairs to put in the car. Krys was out on the front stoop with Iyania and a racka other lil youngins from the neighborhood, I guess sayin her good-byes and exchanging numbers to keep in contact later.

I started to get on her for sittin around when it was obvious I could use some help, but I decided not to trip. I done enough yelling at that damn girl.

After a whole summer of being a pain in my ass, Krys was finally going home today. As much as slim made me wanna smack her with a brick, I gotta admit, I was gon jive miss her a lil bit. I liked having somebody else to boss around and ride to work with me in the mornings. She was pretty cool to smoke with, too. We did a lot more beefin than getting along, but I think it all worked out for the best. I had a feeling she learned something other than how to fight and roll a tight J after staying with me, too. Krys' attitude changed drastically, but then again, she was still young and dumb and it'd probly be a matter of time before she picked up her old habits again. I thought about inviting youngin to come visit ery summer so I could keep her ass in check, but I was still kinda hesitant. I wasn't really sure if I wanted to be bothered just yet. After all the stunts Krys pulled these past couple months, one summer at my house was enough.

I side-stepped her and the crowd on my steps and made a couple more trips to the car with arms fulla food. By the time I had erything packed up like a game of Tetris in Twon's trunk, the boys was dressed and ready to roll. More than ready to go stuff ourselfs stupid, the five of us piled up in the Impala and zipped up the Beltway to Mommy's cookout in Largo.

The first thing I thought of when I seen my mama's new house on the hill was all them mansions the celebrities be havin on MTV *Cribs*. Mommy's j'on wasn't quite that big, but it was just as fancy, with floor-to-ceiling windows and crystal chandeliers, six bedrooms, a big-ass sunroom, and a loft in the master bedroom. There was even a jacuzzi in all the bathrooms, marble floors and countertops, and a full bar in the basement with bar stools and a mirrored wall and erything. I ain't never seen something so nice. It was exactly the typa place me and Twon was saving to move into. And the best part about it was Mommy's new neighborhood was one of the up-and-coming majority Black developments in P.G. County. It filled me with a sense of pride to see my family rubbin elbows with the seditty folk. My lil sisters just ain't know how spoiled rotten they was. They'd be able to go to the best schools and join the best academic and athletic programs in the county. They'd be able to get in the best colleges and have six-figure careers by the time they hit they twenties. Plus, all three of em had they own rooms and enough other rooms in the house to escape to when that wasn't far enough. They'd never hafta worry bout being smothered or distracted like I was growin up. There was even a rec center right down the street where they could hang out with them goody-goody kids and do goody-goody things like play tennis and field hockey insteada chillin in alleys and smoking weed like I did with my friends coming up. It was fuckin great.

"Why ain'tchu build this j'on when I was still livin witchu?" I complained, dragging a huge pan fulla chopped potatoes into Mommy's enormous kitchen so she could add the mayo and mustard. She was in there with both my aunts and a racka Tone's family.

"Whatchu come in hea' fussin bout, girl? Didju even speak to erybody?" Mommy asked from where she stood over the stove stirring around a pot of boiled ribs to barbecue on the grill.

"Hey, Aunt Roz. Hey, Aunt Josie. Hey, eryby…Ma, lemme get one uh' them bedrooms upstairs. I need me a hideout from them kids," I pleaded. Erybody who heard me started laughing but I was dead serious.

"Rashaiyah, I know you ain't complainin bout two kids. Did I have anywhere to go raising y'all monsters?" Mommy joked.

"C'mon, Ma. I'll pay rent. Wash dishes. Scrub windows—I know you ain't gon feel like cleanin them big-ass windows."

"If you don't set them damn potatoes down and get out my face. Go downstairs and speak to your uncles an'nem. It's some'my who wanna see you down there, too."

"Who?" I asked, just as Man-Man and Tink came running up all excited and outta breath.

"Grandpa hea'!" Man-Man squealed, jumping up and down in fronta me.

"I wanted to tell her," Tink fussed. "Mommy, I was gon tell you first. Grandpa hea'!"

"And he gave us five dollas each!" Man-Man exclaimed, waving his money in fronta me.

"Look!" Tink piped up, waving his. I raised a eyebrow cuz they only had one livin grandpa I knew of and he couldna been the one they was talkin bout. What in the world would he be doin here?

"Grandpa who?" I asked.

"Grandpa Redz," my boys responded at the same time as if I shoulda known.

"Redz is hea'?" I squeaked, turning back to my mother.

"What, I cain't invite y' fahva to my cookout? I needed some'my to bring the ice."

"You invited him for real?"

"Yes, Rashaiyah. Is dat okay witchu?"

It was fine with me. I ain't have no problem with that man no more. I was just surprised that he actually came around. I ain't think him and Mommy smoothed shit out and got on good enough terms to be at cookouts together and shit. And what about Tone? Did Redz and Tone get along? Furthermore, why Redz monkey ass ain't tell me he was gon be here today? I musta had a helluva look on my face cuz Redz bust out laughing soon as I made it to the bottom of the steps and spotted him at the card table out back with Tone and my uncles Travis, Ray-Ray, Willie, and Boo.

"Ay, Rashaiyah!" Uncle Travis called. "Wsup, shawdy?"

"Nuffin much. Wsup witchall? How eryby doin?"

"Be doin good once this black son-bitch stop cheatin," my great Uncle Willie grumbled, noddin at Uncle Ray-Ray. "Gon play hearts when we playin diamonds, then break out the hearts again. Ain't no'by dumb, boy."

"Y'all playin spades?" I asked.

"You know it. And Willie, I'on 'preciate you accusin me of such things," Uncle Ray-Ray started. "If anybody cheatin, it's you, old man...Hey, turn that stereo up, boy. Dat's my jam!"

That song *Rock Creek Park* by the Blackbyrds got about twenty times louder after one of Tone's nephews put the volume on full blast. Leave it up to my family to make so much damn noise in such a nice neighborhood.

"Aww, yeah. Had me some good times offa this song back in'na day," Uncle Ray-Ray bragged, dancing in his chair and taking a swig of Seagram's.

I just stood back with a smile and listened to em all rambling and carryin on like Redz came to family gatherings ery year. They was all playin it so Cooter Brown you'da never known this was the first time Redz done showed face at a cookout in thirteen years. Redz looked up and gave me a smile that said, just like he promised, he was making a point to be around from now on. I smiled back at him, glad he was being true to his word. Even if he up and disappeared a month from now, at least he made it this far.

"Hey, Rashaiyah?"

It was Aunt Josie, coming towards me with this eager look on her face. She tiptoed it across the lawn to where I was standing and motioned for me to follow her.

"So what's the verdict?" my aunt asked when we got far enough away from the house so nobody could hear us.

"For Krys?"

"Yeah? You talk to her? She act up too bad witchu?"

"Nah," I chuckled, thinking of the tension and the fight, then Krys' two-week disappearance and her E-pill incident. "Nuffin I couldn't handle. We talked. I took her around, showed her some things. She know more now than she did when she left y'all, but what she do wit dat is a diff'rent story."

"Yeah," Aunt Josie sighed. She gave me a conflicted smile. "I hope you'on mind me and Travis not callin to check on her," she started after a while. "I thought I'd just leave y'all to y'allselves. You ain't need us breathin down your neck askin for updates ery five seconds. Plus we needed a lil time to ourselves, *if you know what I mean.*"

"Dat's fine. I ain't mind," I chucked understandingly. Shit, I'd give anything to get ridda my kids for the summer and spend uninterrupted quality time with Twon ery day.

"Good. So how much I owe you?" Aunt Josie asked, pulling her checkbook out her purse.

"Whoa, whoa. Whatchu mean?"

"I know that girl was eatin you outta house and home. I'ma give you some extra money for your trouble."

"But you already gave me money."

"Well, take some more," Aunt Josie insisted.

Now, the old Shai woulda threw my hand out quick-fast and told her just how much to break me off with. But, somehow, it felt like I'd be taking advantage if I did that—even though Aunt Josie offered. I ain't wanna dig in her pockets. I ain't do her no service that needed to be paid for. Shit, Krys was family. I wouldna been no typa real family if I ain't take her in and look out for her at such a influential time in her life. The way I saw it, I was just doing what was right.

"Please, Aunt Josie, you'on owe me nuffin. I had her workin at my job wit me. Trust me, Krys paid for erything she ate up in there," I said.

"You sure?"

"I'm positive."

"Thanks again, Shai. You really ain't hafta do this."

Aunt Josie pulled me into one of them warm hugs of hers I always loved getting and I sincerely returned the squeeze. She was such a sweet lil lady. I'on know how her and Mommy grew up in the same house and turned out to be total opposites. I probly woulda been a completely diff'rent person if my mother was as warm and open as Aunt Josie, but that's neither here nor there. I just hope Krys appreciate what she got, cuz a mama as caring and forgiving and understanding as Aunt Josie ain't something erybody get blessed with. Let alone a father like Uncle Travis who been in his child's life from day one. Damn, I hope that simple-ass girl get her shit together. Krys got it entirely too good at home to be acting like she don't.

"No problem, Aunt Josie. Anytime you need me, just let me know," I promised.

"Believe me, I will."

Aunt Josie went back towards the house and I went back towards the card table to see if Twon joined the party yet. He was pulling up a chair beside Redz, both of em sipping beers and adding they two cents bout ery move in the spades game. I decided to leave em alone to do they grown man thing, and went to look for my sons instead. They was busy jumping on the trampoline Mommy set up in the side yard for all the kids. Since one of Tone's relatives was over there to supervise, I left them alone, too. I ain't feel like being around no buncha screaming brats anyhow. Krys was over by the buffet tables near the grill where Cousin Peanut was cooking the hell out some barbecue wings, talking to our cousin Irshad. I started to make a beeline for her so we could rap some more cuz we never did get to talk after Georgia Avenue day, but my cousin Sweet Nika came outta nowhere and pulled me to the side.

"I heard you was playin 'Captain Save Em' this summer," she teased, talking about me and Krys. "What, you a mentor now?"

"You damn right I am," I answered.

"Well, you go right ahead. You better 'den me cuz if Aunt Josie woulda aksed me to do dat shit, I'da said hell-to-the-nah. I ain't the one. I'da had to wring that girl's neck, young."

I just shook my head cuz as tight as me and Sweet Nika was when we was younger, we was like night and day now. While I went from running the streets to having babies and working full-time jobs, Sweet Nika lived a sweet, carefree college life. She went to Virginia State damn-near year round and was always telling me stories bout the parties she went to and the boys she met on campus and the things she did with her Alpha Kappa Alpha sorority sisters. It was enough to make me green with envy cuz a part of me wished I could be as fun and fancy free as she was, but we followed different paths to adulthood and mine ended up being just fine.

"Dat's why she ain't aks you. Wasn't you at summer school anyways?" I said.

"Yeah, girl. Studyin, partyin, and gettin drunk as shit," Sweet Nika told me in a you-shoulda-been-there kinda way. That jealousy in me tinged again cuz I spent my whole summer working and being blown, but I shook it off real quick.

"I hope you ain't fail nuffin," I told my cousin.

"Girl, please. I'm always on point. I got all A's and B's…Ay, is Krys still a bamma? She still be stutterin and shit?" Sweet Nika asked with a snide snicker, nodding at the formerly dorky object of our childhood ridicule.

"Nah, young," I chuckled. "Krys be doin some bamma shit, but youngin aight. She turned out d' be pretty cool."

"Damn, lemme find out you defendin Krys the Cross-eyed Lion. Hell must be freezin over."

"Aww, go 'head, young."

Krys stepped off from Irshad and started towards the food table to fix herself up a plate. I excused myself from Sweet Nika and jogged over to catch her before she could.

"Ay, come holla at me right quick," I said, jerking my head at a bike path not too far away.

"Why? Where we goin? You tryna kill me in'na woods or some'n?" Krys joked.

"Yeah, dat's it. C'mon, take a walk wit me."

Krys and I dipped off and made our way down the path like we knew where the fuck we was going. Neither one of us had a clue, but it ain't really matter. It was a nice day for walking and talking, and I kinda figured now would be the best time to have a lil one-on-one before she left.

"So wsup, lil cuz? You ready d' go home?" I asked after a long stretch of silence between us.

"I guess so. Wish I kh get just one more week uh' summer, 'doe. I'on wanna go back d' school for shit."

"I hea' dat. I cain't believe it's time f' you to leave already. It's gon be weird not havin you around no more. I ain't gon have no'by to fuss at now."

"Yeah, I'm sure you gon miss dat," Krys smirked.

"Not as much as you gon miss me, hunh?"

"If you say so…"

"F'getchu, 'den, Krys," I laughed. "Ain't no'by thinkin bout you anyway."

"Sike, I'ma miss you," my cousin admitted after a short stretch of silence.

"Well, you know where I'm at now. Holla at me sometime."

"I will. I'ma probly be chillin wit Iyania an'nem ery once in a while, so I'll just see you then."

"You betta see me more 'den dat, girl," I said. "I gotta keep a eye on you."

"Why you gotta keep a eye on me?"

"Cuz I might hafta go on yo' ass if you start actin up again."

Krys smiled.

"Man, I ain't gon be doin all dat crazy shit I did before. Fuck dat," she promised. "I mean, I'ma still have my fun but…you jye gave me a lot d' think about."

"Oh, yeah?"

"Yeah," Krys nodded seriously. "Like the shit dat happent wit y' bruhva, young. I ain't know it went down like dat. And the shit Biggums told me happent to Roe and dat dude Smoke is crazy, too."

"Ain't it, doe? I'm just glad I'm still hea'."

"Yeah…Ay, can I ask you some'n, doe?"

"What?"

"What happent to your friend Syco? I mean, why he talk like dat? Is he burnt out or some'n?"

"Oh, yeah," I shrugged. "My man useta hit a lotta dippas back in'na day. Dat shit jye fried his brain. But don't get it twisted—if you smoke enough weed and you kh end up the same way," I preached.

"So why you still smoke?"

"Cuz I'm grown. And I can. And I still take care of my responsibilities, dat's why...But neh'mind what I do. We poseda be talkin bout you and whatchu gon do witcha self now. So you gon stay in school or you gon drop out and do shit the hard way?" I asked.

"Young, I hate school. But I gotta go, right? Fuck else I'ma do?" Krys sighed.

"I thoughtchu was gon be a stripper so bad."

"Stripper? Fuck no, young. Not after the shit your girl Dhonni told me dat night...I still cain't believe she got the sauce, young. She only nineteen. Dat shit ain't fair."

"Life ain't fair," I reminded Krys. "Shit happens all the time. You gotta watch y'self these days. I'm sure you know dat now if you ain't know it before."

"Oh, I'm sure. 'Specially after dat night I had to go to the hospital... By the way, you ain't gon tell my parents, is you?" Krys asked, worried. I cracked another smile.

"I should, but I ain't. You just don't do nuffin dat stupid again. You came out real lucky dat night, you know dat, right?"

"Yeah, I know. It jye scare me to thinka what coulda happent if...All I know is ain't nuffin like dat ever happenin again. *Ever.*"

"Good girl," I beamed.

Well, from the sounds of it, Krys had some typa sense in her head. She just might be aight without me there looking over her shoulder all day. On the other hand, she might get tired of being a good girl again and go right back to where she was. I had my fingers crossed that she wouldn't, though. Had em crossed good and tight that she'd stay outta trouble from now on.

"I guess we betta be gettin back," Krys said suddenly, rubbing her grumbling tummy. "I'm hongry as shit now."

"Me, too. Let's go. I race you."

"Race me?"

"Yeah, nigga," I chuckled, feeling playful. "You scared or some'n? Think I'ma beat you? C'mon. I bet I smoke you, young."

"Talkin all dat shit. C'mon, 'den. I'm bout d' roast yo' ass."

"Dat's whatcha mowf say."

"Dat's what my mowf know."

"Yeah, aight. You ready, young?…On y' mark…get set…"

I took off running before sayin go, and Krys took off tryna catch up with me. She tripped the backa my feet to slow me down and I tried to trip her back, which of course, was extra funny cuz we was both acting like lil kids. By the time we got close to the house, we was both scuffed up and dirty from the knee down. I ain't mind, though. Ain't too often a old girl like me gets a chance to be silly with her favorite cousin.

GLOSSARY

In case you don't know what the hell I'm talkin bout...

A

a buck: a hundred (a buck fifty is a hundred fifty)
ace boon coon: really good friend, main apple scrapple
ack: act
actin new/brand new: acting like you're too good; acting totally different than usual
ain'tchall: ain't y'all (aren't you all); didn't y'all (didn't you all)
ain'tchu: ain't you (aren't you); didn't you
aks: ask
andju: and you
an'nem: and them
anuh'/anuhva: another
anyby: anybody
ash: to tap the ashes off whatever you're smoking

B

babysittin/sittin on: holdin the smokeables too long
backa: back of
ball/ballin: play basketball; drive fast; to be rich; a hundred dollars
bamma: someone who can't dress; someone who acts stupid; something or someone that ain't cool
bareback: having sex with no protection
beast: the best, tight
beefin: conflicting, fighting
b'fore: before
big: a lot
black: a Black and Mild cigar
blazin/blaze: to smoke weed
blown: too upset for words/at a loss for words; your high got brought down
B-More: Baltimore, Maryland
boat: weed dipped in embalming fluid, black weed, wet weed, dat ill
bob: a joint, J, rolled up weed
bodeens: police, them boys, the feds, one time, five-O

bogard: to cut in front of somebody, to try and take something before somebody else can get it

bojanglin: lying, faking, bullshittin, wasting time

boost: to make someone's day, to make someone happy; something that makes your high go higher; a bonus

box/bubble: kind of Caprice, Crown Victoria, Impala, Lincoln, Buick, Oldsmobile, Mercury, and Monte Carlo cars (a box has boxy edges and a bubble has round edges)

bread: money

break bad: to get an attitude with someone

bruhva: brother

buck at: to jump at someone like you're gonna hit them

bucket: old beat-up car

bun: a cute boy or girl; your boyfriend or girlfriend; to make someone your boyfriend or girlfriend

bush: bullshit weed, weed that don't get you high

buh'shit: bullshit

C

Caddy/ 'Lac: Cadillac

cake: money

catch one: get beat up, catch an ass-whuppin

carry: diss (disrespect), embarrass; act/do things a certain way

'cept: except

cheesin/cheese: smiling; smile

chour/cha: your

chu: you

church: to talk a lot on the phone (like how preachers be pontificating in church)

Classics: Reebok Classics

c'mere: come here

crank: music that makes you wanna dance, music that you feel; to turn your music up loud

croosh: (crucial) something that's really good or really hard to do

comp'ny: company

cruddy: dirty, grimy, mean, inconsiderate, purposely hurtful

cut: somebody/something that's bullshit; somebody with really defined muscles; sex

cuttin up: acting up, being bad

D

d': the; to

daps: a pound (fist-to-fist handshake)

'day: they

'dayself: themselves

dead: what you call a party/event that wasn't tight or didn't happen after it was supposed to; when something is over
deep: when there's a lot of people somewhere; something or someone that makes you think deeply
'deez: these
didn'tchu: didn't you
dip: leave, be out, ball out
dipper/dippa: a cigarette dipped in embalming fluid, sherm
'doe: though
dog pound/dog nuts: good friend, someone you fucks wit real tough
dome/top: head
don'tchall: don't y'all (don't you all)
draws: underwear
'dro: hydroponic weed
dunkey/donkey: big butt

E

ear hustlin: eavesdroppin, listenin in on somebody's conversation, bein nosy
earl/call Earl: throw up, vomit
Eddie: an Eddie Bauer coat (the kind with the fur around the hood)
ery: every
eryby: everybody
erything: everything
e-pill: a pill of the drug Ecstasy

F

fahva: father
fakin: bullshittin; acting like you wanna fight then backing down; acting like you're interested in someone but you really aren't and they know; acting like you're gonna do something then you don't
feenin: fiending, wanting something really bad
f'get: forget
f'getchu: forget you; also a nice way of sayin "fuck you"
fih'teen: fifteen
flickded: messed up, jacked up, to' up from the flo' up
fluke: bullshit, when something gets siced and it's really not tight; a punk
flunk/flunky: to boss someone around; someone who'll do whatever you say
fount: found
f'real: for real
fried: high; burnt out
fronta: front of
f'sho (for sure): yes, alright
fry: to joan on someone to a ridiculous point

G

G: a thousand dollars
G'd (gangbanged): havin sex with more than one person
get your man: being your best at something; partying real hard; sex
go hard: not caring about the consequences, doing whatever you feel; hardcore
go-go: a kind of music originated in D.C.; a club/party where go-go is played
got: surprised, caught off guard, shocked; unbelievable
got hands: can fight
gotchu: got you
got your heart: when someone is scared to fight you
green/grizza/bud/smoke/fire: weed
grip: a lot of something
grit: to look someone up and down like you disgusted with them and you wanna fight them

H

head: other than the obvious it means that someone is a pothead or a crackhead or a cokehead; a person
heffa: (heifer) something you call a female you don't like
hi: how
hold the sauce: wait a minute, hold up, slow down
hollin/holla'd: (hollering/hollered) to talk to somebody; tryin to hook up with someone
hot: dangerous, something/someone that will get you caught up with the police; fast in the ass
hunned: hundred

I

I'on: I don't
in'na: in the
in'nat: in that
in'nem: in them
in'nere: in there
in'nis: in this
it's how you wanna carry: it's up to you
it's whatever: I don't care; whatever happens happens

J

J: a joint, a bob, rolled up weed
j'on (joint): thing, place, whatever you're talking about
jack: cigarette (usually Newports); jack shit (as in "I ain't gotta do jack!")

jye(jive)/jye-like (jive like)/slam: kind of; emphasizes a point or a thing
joan: to make fun of, to talk about something to get laughs
jump out there/put out there: to cross the line that separates talking and fighting; to put your business out

K

kh: can, could
kirk: go crazy, go off
knowmsayin: know what I'm sayin?

L

L: loss (to accept something as a loss)
letchall: let y'all
like dat: tight, nice, official
lovah: lover
lunchbox: someone who's silly or crazy
lunchin: trippin; acting silly; going off for no reason; high

M

maintain: sober enough to act normal; doing okay even though you've been stressed out
match: to put up the same amount of weed that another person has and smoke together
migh'as well: might as well
moankey: monkey
Mo County: Montgomery County
mo-teezy: motel
mowf: mouth
mug: short for muhfucka; to stare hard at someone like you wanna fight them
muhva: mother
munish/punish: to beat somebody up; to eat something up
mushed: when you push somebody in the face or head
must/don't think it's sweet: to think someone's a punk or that they won't fight

N

'na: the
'nat: that
neck/neckbone: when someone says something loud and wrong or stupid, you karate chop or slide your fingers real hard across the back of their neck (that shit hurt!!!!)

neh': never
neiva: neither
nicked up: paranoid, jumpy
no'by: nobody
'nother: another
Norfeass: Northeast, DC
Norfwess: Northwest, DC
nuffin: nothing

O

off the nut: way of saying something is crazy or silly
off the top (t-o-p)/off the break: from the beginning, a way of letting someone know something before you get into it; to do something without saying anything first
official: tight, proper/propa, nice, the best
one'a: one of
on E: (on empty) something bad or ugly or bammafied
on dicks: sweatin somebody, bein pressed to be like or be around someone
on'na: on the
out there: crazy; being hot; something far away

P

peeps/peoples/fam/family/folks/youngins: your friends or family
pimp: to use somebody, to get money out of somebody, to make you work hard and you get little or nothing in return
phone bonin: talkin to your bun on the phone
pockets: money (money in the pockets); the tight part of a go-go song
poseda: supposed to be
plaits: individuals (single braids)
pressed: to be too concerned with someone or something; to sweat someone or something
Princesses: Reebok hi-top or low-top freestyles
profilin (profiling): looking good, dressed to catch attention
pull: to hit (smoke) something; to book someone/get their number
punished/banged out/crushed: to beat someone up real bad, finish something (crush)

R

racka: (a rack of) a whole lot of
rap: game, how you talk to the opposite sex
rep/repped/reppin: represent/represented/representing—as in representing where you're from or who you're with; reputation
re-up: to re-supply on your drugs

ridda: rid of
rock: crank, pump; something tight/official; to wear
roll: to leave; to take an e-pill
roller/rolla: freak, ho
roll ups: Blunts, Optimos (Ops), Backwoods (woods) or anything else that you roll weed in
rows: cornrows
ruff: to steal/cuff something; steal somebody and catch them off guard

S

sauce: somebody's business; another way of sayin "shit"
seent: seen
sehnteen: seventeen
senny: seventy
Sergios/Sucos: Sergio Valente stretch jeans; Parasuco stretch jeans
sho'nuff: sure enough
shote: (short) outta luck, too bad for you, you're gonna have a problem
sice: to make something seem really tight/good; to do something for someone that boosts them; to add something to something; to instigate; excited, eager
sike: just kidding; yeah right
skrill/bread: money
sleazy: Ecstasy pills
sleep on: to not take someone seriously, to not take someone as a threat
slum/slummin: bad, boring
smacked: high
smoke down: smoke a lot of weed
some'n: something
some'na: something to
Southside/The South/Sowfeass: Southeast, DC
Sowfwess: Southwest, DC
steal/stole: to punch somebody
straight: okay, fine, word that means you agree with something; sober enough to maintain
studdin: (ain't studdin) not trippin off of someone or something, not letting someone or something get to you
stuck: zoned out; confused
supa: super
swellin/wellin: lying, exaggerating
swole face/tight face/face: to be embarrassed

T

t'geva: together
the buttas/yak/yolas: crack
the sauce: HIV/AIDS
t'mar: tomorrow

t'night: tonight
toppa: top of
trash: something/someone that's bamma or some shit
treal: the realest of the real
twerkin': a way of moving one's hips; sex
typa: type of

U

uh'/uhva: other
Uptown/Up Top: Northwest, DC

W

water: embalming fluid, sherm
way'ment: wait a minute
weak: wack, stupid, bamma, not tight, unofficial
we'on: we don't
why'on: why don't
why'onchu: why don't you
wet: tight, official, the best of something
wife beater: sleeveless mens' undershirt
wit: with
witchall: with y'all (with you all)
witchu: with you
witout: without
woo-bob: weed mixed with coke/crack
wolfin: in need of a shave, haircut, or cornrows
wreckin: fighting

Y

y': your
yay: cocaine
youngins: boys or girls (depending on who's saying it); kids; young Black people
you'on: you don't

HOW U PRONOUNCE THAT?

Character Names

Cerrone	*Sir ♦ own*
Dartanyan	*Dar ♦ tan ♦ yen*
Dhonica	*Don ♦ ick ♦ uh*
Dhonni	*Don ♦ nee*
Irshad	*Err ♦ shawd*
Iyania	*Ee ♦ yon ♦ nee ♦ yuh*
Karrysta	*Kuh ♦ riss ♦ tuh*
Kebian	*Key ♦ bee ♦ inn*
Kia	*Key ♦ uh*
Nika	*Nee ♦ kuh*
Rashaiyah	*Ruh ♦ shy ♦ uh*
Roe	*Row*
Staria	*Star ♦ ee ♦ yuh*
Trayonna	*Tray ♦ on ♦ uh*
Traytanya	*Tray ♦ tan ♦ yuh*
Tristan	*Triss ♦ tawn*

www.ingramcontent.com/pod-product-compliance
Lightning Source LLC
Chambersburg PA
CBHW051445260626
47162CB00001B/257

```
*  9 7 8 0 9 7 7 7 9 7 8 0 6  *
```